Russian Love Stories

Middlebury Studies in Russian Language and Literature

Thomas R. Beyer, Jr.
General Editor

Vol. 31

PETER LANG
New York • Washington, D.C./Baltimore • Bern
Frankfurt am Main • Berlin • Brussels • Vienna • Oxford

Russian Love Stories

An Anthology of Contemporary Prose

Edited by
NADYA L. PETERSON

PETER LANG
New York • Washington, D.C./Baltimore • Bern
Frankfurt am Main • Berlin • Brussels • Vienna • Oxford

Library of Congress Cataloging-in-Publication Data

Russian love stories: an anthology of contemporary
prose / edited by Nadya L. Peterson.
p. cm. — (Middlebury studies in Russian language and literature; v. 31)
Includes bibliographical references.
1. Love stories, Russian—Translations into English. 2. Short stories,
Russian—Translations into English. 3. Russian fiction—20th century—
Translations into English. 4. Russian fiction—21st century—
Translations into English. I. Peterson, Nadezhda L.
PG3286.R893 891.73'0850805—dc22 2009018150
ISBN 978-1-4331-0717-7
ISSN 0888-8752

Bibliographic information published by **Die Deutsche Bibliothek**.
Die Deutsche Bibliothek lists this publication in the "Deutsche
Nationalbibliografie"; detailed bibliographic data is available
on the Internet at http://dnb.ddb.de/.

Cover image:
The Kiss by Vladimir Lubarov, 1996. Private collection.
By permission of the artist.

The paper in this book meets the guidelines for permanence and durability
of the Committee on Production Guidelines for Book Longevity
of the Council of Library Resources.

29 Broadway, 18th floor, New York, NY 10006
www.peterlang.com

Printed in Germany

FOR HENZLY WITH LOVE

Table of Contents

Acknowledgements

This book could not have appeared without the generous assistance from the Hunter College Russian and Slavic Division's Felia Holzman Fund and the sponsorship of the Department of Classical and Oriental Studies at Hunter College. The 2004–2005 Fulbright Research grant, PSC–CUNY grant and the support of the International Research Exchange Board allowed me to collect the material for the anthology and to meet some of the authors featured here. Sylvia Maizell, with her impressive experience as an interpreter of Russian language and culture, was instrumental in getting the project off the ground. Emma Eklof offered invaluable editorial and creative insights, while Elizabeth Beaujour provided important suggestions about the book's major theme. Tom Beyer, the editor of the Middlebury Russian Language and Literature Series, gave me hope when it was most needed and steered the project along.

I am profoundly grateful to the authors for agreeing to include their stories in this anthology, as well as to the translators whose dedication and love of the craft makes projects such as this possible. I thank the following publishers and/or copyright holders for granting me permission to include the stories in the anthology:

"Happy" by Liudmila Ulitskaya, © Lidumila Ulitskaya 1993, translated by Nadya L. Peterson. © Nadya L. Peterson. Published in Russian in Bednye, zlye, liubimye (Moscow: Eksmo, 2004). By permission of the author.

"Earth Mother" by Boris Khazanov, translated by Sylvia Maizel. © Sylvia Maizell. Published in Russian in Gorod i sny (Moscow: Vagrius, 2001). By permission of the author.

"Liubka" by Dina Rubina, © Dina Rubina 1987, translated by Nadya L. Peterson. © Nadya L. Peterson. Published in Russian in Na Verkhnei Maslovke (Moscow: Eksmo, 2004). By permission of the author.

"Brother's Keeper" by Vladimir Makanin, translated by Byron Lindsey. © Byron Lindsey. Published in Words Without Borders [www.wordswithoutborders.org], September 2008. By permission of Words Without Borders, an online magazine for international literature hosted by Bard College and supported by the National Endowment for the Arts.

"Three Loves of Masha Peredreeva" by Galina Shcherbakova, translated by Rachel Osorio. Published in Present Imperfect: Stories by Russian Women (Westview Press, 1996). By permission of the author.

"Teardrops on the Flowers" by Evgeny Kharitonov, translated by Arch Tate. Published in Glas: New Russian Writing (No. 4, 1993). By permission of the publisher.

"Individualist's Notebook" by Yurii Mamleev. Published in The Penguin Book of New Russian Writing (Penguin, 1995). By permission of the author.

"The Dead Hour" by Nina Sadur, translated by Matvei Yankelevich. Published in Russian in Vechnaia merzlota (Moscow: Zebrae, 2004). By permission of the author.

"Mid–game" by Victor Pelevin, translated by Andrew Bromfield, from THE BLUE LANTERN AND OTHER STORIES, copyright ©1994 by Victor Pelevin. Translation copyright © by Andrew Bromfield. Reprinted by permission of New Directions Publishing Corp.

"Prime Passed" by Galina Shcherbakova, translated by Nadya L. Peterson. © Nadya L. Peterson. Published in Russian in Lovestorii (Moscow: Vagrius, 2004). By permission of the author.

"Babel in Paris" by Evgeny Shklovsky, translated by Byron Lindsey. © Byron Lindsey. Published in Russian in Ta strana (Moscow: Novoe literaturnoe obozrenie, 2000).

By permission of the author.

"Two Days in the Life of Zhenia D." by Elena Muliarova. Translated by Nadya L. Peterson. © Nadya L. Peterson. Published in Russian in Vremia rozhat' (Moscow: Zebra–E, Eksmo, 2001). By permission of the author.

"The Kiss" by Vladimir Lubarov, 1996. Private collection. By permission of the artist.

My thanks also go to Gleb Kuznetsov for his expertise in manuscript preparation and willingness to help at a moment's notice, to Veronika Rodrigues for being my faithful reader and adviser, and to my students for inspiring me in my work. Finally, I am forever indebted to Volodya Gopman for his friendship and for introducing me to the work of the incomparable Vladimir Lubarov.

Introduction

While the selections in this anthology offer a broad range of narrative styles, philosophical agendas, and points of view, they are all about love. The modern idea of love was unknown to Old Russian Literature, and the transformation of the very notion of love from the love of God to the love between a man and a woman is a direct result of the westernization of Russia–"the window to Europe" forcefully opened by Peter the Great three centuries ago.

If the eighteenth century is responsible for legitimizing the idea of secular love in Russian literature, the theme finds its fullest articulation in the following century. In Eugene Onegin, Alexander Pushkin's groundbreaking novel in verse, the nineteenth century's Romantic notions of love are shown to be illusory when confronted with the complexities of authentic relationships between people. Pushkin's Tatyana, who in the end refuses to succumb to love recognized too late, becomes a stock character in the works of subsequent generations of Russian writers. Even Leo Tolstoy's view of ideal love is a variation on Pushkin's theme. In Tolstoy the eroticized body is constantly battling the strictures imposed on it by moral sense. And perfect love, as a union between a rational man and a virginal wife whose life is dedicated completely to the family and children, ultimately appears as fragile as a love ruled solely by physical impulses.

In spite of Fyodor Dostoyevsky's reverence for Pushkin, his descriptions of love as inseparable from suffering, and of sacrificial love bringing people closer to God, have much more in common with the frenetic Romanticism of Nikolai Gogol than with the Classical harmoniousness of Pushkin. In Anton Chekhov the Pushkinian and the Gogolian coexist to create a world suspended in a balance of irresolution. Chekhovian love is uncertain, painful, and rooted in human solitude. Comic and tragic in turn, it is often presented as a fantasy highlighting the essential emptiness of the lives of Chekhov's characters.

In the twentieth century scores of Soviet writers appropriated Pushkin's strong woman character, as well as his tale of a sacrifice for the sake of a higher purpose, to suit the notions of utility, didacticism, and gender equality of socialist realist literature. As a model for emulation, or subversion, the legacy of Russian and Soviet literature allows little reprieve from the tyranny of its influence for today's writers. Descriptions of life as it should be, new Soviet men and women, heroic deeds on the road to the perfect Communist future were the binding standards of Soviet literature and are a legacy which current Russian writers address in their own works. Virtually cut off from the rest of the world's culture for most of the previous century during the Soviet period, contemporary Russian literature is still essentially self–referential.

To be sure, a Proustian forbidden love, universally condemned and painstakingly recorded for a more forgiving posterity, is evoked in Yevgeny Kharitonov's narrative about his character's homosexuality, included in the anthology. Yet the belligerent tone of the story and its overall sense of a willful if painful opposition to the notions of propriety is Dostoyevskian through and through. Similarly, Galina Shcherbakova's recurring character of the predatory female is a startling mutation of Dostoyevsky's "insulted and injured" women characters.

Nina Sadur's work, with its aura of fantastic eroticism and allusions to folklore, has Marquezian overtones. The writer's exploration of deviant sexual practices, however, has much more to do with a defiant reversal of Soviet certitudes than with Gabriel Garcia Marquez's magic realism, while the notion of tortured resentment coloring the lives of her couples is the result of the writer's appropriation of Chekhov and Lermontov. Ironic approach to loving in old age, familiar to the readers of John Updike or admirers of Robert Altman's films, is palpably felt in Vladimir Makanin's recent prose. Yet in the story chosen for the collection, the writer's main focus is on the inevitable miscommunication that occurs between the old and the young, as well as on the love that is offered with no hope of return.

Clearly, parallels between the narratives collected here and those of modern Western literature, cinema, or television are largely superficial. It is Chekhovian illusory love, Dostoevskian tortured passions, Gogolian demonic obsessions, or Pushkin's morally validating love that guide contemporary authors in their exploration of the theme. And it is Soviet literature and its take on loving in the age of revolutionary change, followed by that of imposed conformity, that the writers probe, appropriate, or challenge. Thus, Boris Khazanov's portrayal of an incestuous affair between a boy and his schoolmate's mother brings to mind Isaac Babel's nostalgic view of young love in his Odessa stories, Yevgeny Shklovsky's story is yet another evocative tribute to Babel's exuberant women, Elena Muliarova's tale about today's young lovers is indebted as much to the trendy television series Sex and the City as to the Soviet "youth prose" of the 1960s, while Victor Pelevin, Galina Shcherbakova, Liudmila Ulitskaya, and Yurii Mamleev shape the fates of their characters to reflect, almost allegorically, the inexorable decline of their own society.

All of the authors in the anthology were born in the Soviet period, each has been molded by a particular set of shared practices and beliefs, and all offer a distinctive perspective on their experience. The writing, evenly divided between that of men and women writers, those who work in Russia or abroad, is anchored in the period from the middle of the last century to the present, offering the reader an insider's view of Soviet and post–Soviet life. Yet the writer's position–sometimes from within that time, sometimes from a perspective of a backward glance at the past–is emphatically that of an outsider. Some of the writers in this anthology, such as Makanin, Pelevin, or Sadur have now gained wide recognition with readers both at home and abroad. Others, like Dina Rubina, Ulitskaya, Mamleev, or Shcherbakova, who enjoy great popularity in Russia, are known only to a few connoisseurs of contemporary Russian literature in the West. Yet none can be accurately labeled mainstream, since in their narratives the entrenched orthodoxy of the Soviet experience is always challenged by the marginality of topics, genres, narrative styles, personal biographies, and, most important, of the writers' distinctive take on the reality described.

With the exception of Muliarova and Shklovsky, the authors in the anthology embarked on their writing careers in the late 1960s when, in the wake of Stalin's death, Soviet literature was revitalized and invigorated. The loss of traditional Russian values, anticipation of ecological catastrophe, fears of nuclear obliteration became the prominent literary themes of the subsequent decades. Quite a few writers, Pelevin and Makanin among them, interested themselves in the grotesque and the fantastic and relied on popular genres, such as mystery and science fiction, in their works.

Many of the participants in this anthology have been known for their experiments in style and structure, as well as for their apolitical yet socially subversive stance. In the late Soviet period Mamleev, Pelevin, Sadur or Makanin, for example, deconstruct the mythologies of the Soviet state by means of the distortion of traditional norms of writing and by a focus on taboo subjects. Impotence, incest, masturbation, homosexuality, prostitution, transvestism explored by these writers had been proscribed by the official Soviet literature. Equally alien to Soviet models of writing was the authors' postmodernist stress on the power of language, its artifice and manipulative strategies. For them, subversion of established norms has been a gesture of non–conformity designed to challenge preconceived notions of social and human behavior. Other writers in the anthology, such as Muliarova, for example, write today in a style devoid of the density and deliberate ambiguity of meaning associated with postmodernism. Rubina, Shcherbakova, Ulitskaya, as well as Khazanov shun the literary games of many post–Soviet writings and offer plainly realistic accounts of human foibles and obsessions.

Love and time are intertwined here in a curious fashion. Many kinds of love are depicted in these stories. Whether it is familial love or love between strangers, carnal or platonic, real or imagined, these writers insist on making it central in the lives of their characters. A keen curiosity about the intricate and unpredictable paths of loving and a strong belief in the power of love unites them all.

Nadya L. Peterson
New York City, 2009

Happy

Liudmila Ulitskaya

Bertha and Mathias would visit their son every Sunday. Bertha made sandwiches, poured tea into a thermos, carefully tied a bit of paper string around a sweeper made of twigs, grabbed a jar just in case and packed it all into an old bag patched up by Mathias. Mathias handed her a coat, or a raincoat, or a jacket, and they went to the market to buy flowers. Then they would wait at the tram stop for the infrequent tram.

With time Mathias became shorter and looked more and more like a cabinet made of red wood; you could guess he had been a redhead by his dark pink face and brown sunspots on his arms. At one point it seems Bertha was of the same height but now she towered over him. Unlike her husband, she became less unattractive with time. The big, downy moustache, which spoilt her looks when Bertha was young, was thicker now but less noticeable on her old face.

The long and bumpy tram ride would, depending on the season, be either hot or cold, but always oppressive. They sat as if made of stone and were always offered seats by other riders. Even when they were first married, however, they were offered seats.

The road led unswervingly to a brick fence and then down under an arc where it left them on a tidy and somber path. On both sides of the path–amidst greenery, or snow, or chilly fog–they were met by old acquaintances: Isaac Bentsionovitch Halperin, with little, bright blue eyes, cheeks the color of raspberries and sunsets, and a blue bald spot; his wife Faina Lvovna, a calculating woman with a tight mouth and shaking hands; Ivan Mitrofanovich Semerko, a colonel in the Corp of Engineers, broad shouldered, like the epic hero Ilya Muromets, a wonderful guitar player, singer and so young, poor soul; then Boren'ka Mednikov, two years and two months of age, together with his fading grandparents; the rather unpleasant Kraft family–tall, clumsy and white fleshed, ostentatiously showing off the elongated Gothic engraving of their names; and wonderfully friendly old Rabinovitches with rhyming names–Khaia Rafailovna and Khaim Gabriilovich–always embracing, both with light grey hair, almost festive, who took flight one day and left everybody perplexed...

Around the corner the path narrowed and brought them straight to their son. Vovochka Levi, seven years and four months old, met them with a smile that had been chosen for this occasion many years before, the smile that pushed his lip up, baring a strip of small square teeth with a gap where one tooth had fallen out. All other expressions of this broad sweet face, in retaliation for not being chosen, slipped away without notice and disappeared, leaving this one and only smile out of innumerable multitudes of possible facial expressions.

Bertha would untie the parcel, take out the sweeper, and fold the newspaper in which it had been wrapped, while Mathias used it to brush the dust (or snow) from a simple green bench. Afterward Bertha spread the newspaper on the bench and sat down. They rested for a while and then tidied up this house–skillfully, without haste, but efficiently, like good proprietors.

Bertha placed a paper napkin on a small rectangular table, poured tea into slippery plastic cups, and arranged a stack of identical fresh sandwiches. This was their weakly family meal and, after many years, constituted the very heart of the ritual that began with wrapping the sweeper and concluded in twisting the top on the empty thermos.

Profound silence filled with shared memories was unbroken by any chance word; other times and years were set aside for words. After this mass they were off, leaving in their wake the smell of freshly washed floors and aired rooms.

At home Mathias drank his Sunday vodka at dinner.

He filled Bertha's father's silver Passover goblet three times, and Bertha, unable to respond in any other way, thrice sighed a big cow–like sigh. Then she took the dishes to the kitchen, washed them thoroughly with soap and ammonia, and dried them with a clean towel. Afterwards they climbed into their high marriage bed.

"Oh, you old man," whispered Bertha lowering big eyelids over her small eyes.

"It's all right, it's all right," he mumbled, turning his unresponsive wife to him strongly and heavily with his left arm.

They dreamt their ordinary Sunday dreams, lunch time dreams, in which they saw the happiest eight years the three of them had lived together. It began with that vivid, life changing day when she, exhausted by dark thoughts and without saying anything to her husband, went to see an oncologist about her swollen breasts and other problems. The old woman doctor, her girlfriend's sister, examined her for a long time, squeezed her nipples and, after asking several shameless medical questions, said:

"You're pregnant, Bertha, and pretty far gone."

Bertha lowered herself into a chair and, without putting her bra back on, cried, wrinkling her old face as she did. Large tears swiftly coursed down her cheeks, slowed down on her moustache and, now cold, fell on her big white chest with its black perky nipples.

When she told him about it, Mathias looked at her in surprise. He had known for a while, because his first wife had given birth to four girls; the dust of their bodies, however, had long scattered over the pale fields of Poland. He understood her silence in his own way and, to tell the truth, never imagined that she couldn't have known.

"I'm forty seven and you'll be sixty soon."

He shrugged his shoulders and said kindly:

"Well, what it means is that we, old fools, will be parents in our feeble age."

They took a long time choosing a name for their little boy and called him "yingl," which means "boy" in Yiddish, until he was two months old.

"It would be more proper to name him Isaac," said Mathias.

"No, these days they don't name children that. Let him be Jacob, in honor of my late father."

"We could call him Jehuda, he's a redhead."

"Don't be foolish. The child is very beautiful, it's true, but you wouldn't name him Solomon, would you."

They named him Vladimir. To them he was Vovochka, reserved like Mathias and gentle like Bertha.

When he was five, his Father began teaching him what he himself was taught at that age. Over the course of three days the little boy learned the crooked, similarly shaped, ant–like letters and after a week started on a book that his Father read from right to left all his life. In a month he could easily read Russian books as well. Bertha would go to the kitchen and do the dishes with a vengeance.

"Oh, what a boy! What a boy!"

She admired him, but at times a cold draft, like the one that escapes from a sealed window frame in winter and pricks a bare hot arm like a needle, would brush her heart.

She washed her dishes, expertly whipped the cream that never whipped for other housewives, baked pastries and made pâtés. She became slightly unhinged about culinary recipes and completely forgot the poor, runny cream of wheat in the bottom of aluminum bowls, or about thin green soup that she had cooked out of new nettles collected in the back of the dilapidated two–story house where there lived at first forty eight and, at the end of the war, eighty eternally hungry, sick and dirty children. She forgot the blue, tender and bristly heads of young boys, their naked, exposed, defenseless ears, or thin clavicles and blue veins on the necks of little girls. Her intense love for all of these children in general focused now on Vovochka like a sharp beam.

Every day of her life she savored the closeness of the little red–haired plump boy, often touching him with her hands to prove to herself that he was hers. She washed him, he yelled, and she admired his disproportionally large feet and the sacred little triangle above.

When he became older she watched him play with the same admiration; his games looked like real, and boring, work–for hours he would weave small rugs out of multicolored strips, cleverly connecting them together. Mathias, a Warsaw tailor of Parisian pedigree worked in an exclusive atelier and brought little pieces of material for his son. He helped him cut the pieces into ribbons…

Deep down in her heart Bertha was embarrassed about her excessive love, considering it even a bit sinful. Not inclined toward self–analysis, she did not bring her feelings to the threshold of verbal identification but lived in avoidance of such introspection.

Mathias came home after work, had his dinner and settled on the couch. Vovochka snuggled next to him like a little pie made out of leftover dough next to a large one. They read and talked together, while Bertha superstitiously went on washing her sparkling dishes…

In her dream she entered the past easily, as if it were a neighboring room, and moved in it as easily, happily breathing the same air as her son. Her husband, Mathias, with his Stalinesque moustache, was silently present as an important part of the setting. These dreams were like an addictively charming performance seen many times over for a very long time, always ending a quarter of an hour before Bertha brought little Vovochka home from the courtyard on her outstretched arms–pale, with a fresh scratch on his cheek, the result of the morning labors over an airplane model that arrived on the heels of his interest in the cleverly woven little rugs. The collar of a striped shirt was unbuttoned and on his neck, completely open and lengthened because of the head thrown far back, not one little vein was beating.

Everything happened in an instant, like a crudely drawn cartoon–a big red and blue ball suddenly rolled out into the middle of the road, a boy ran after it like a shot out of a sling, then came the screeching of the brakes from one of the very few cars that passed there on Sunday. Having had time to cross the road in front of the truck, the ball continued its lazy roll and then lost all interest in movement. But the little boy, with his arms spread, stayed on his back in final immobility; still perfectly healthy, with fresh unspilled blood that had not yet stopped its motion to the tips of his fingers, but already irrevocably dead.

Mathias was standing next to the little wall mirror with shaving cream on his cheeks, his chin high and, moving the right hand with a heavy razor aside, was trying to reach a tough spot on his neck.

...Shortly after six the old ones woke up. Bertha slid her thin gray feet into fur slippers and went to put the kettle on. They sat at a round table covered with a tablecloth as hard as plywood. A little dessert dish out of the china cabinet filled with homemade honey cakes sat proudly in the middle. For fifteen years a small jacket made by Mathias out of his own coat stayed draped on a child's chair in the corner. The left shoulder facing the window was bleached by the sun, but it wasn't noticeable under the lights.

"Well, your turn to deal now," said Bertha and stretched to get her glasses. Mathias began to deal.

Translated by Nadya L. Peterson

Earth Mother

Boris Khazanov

"I," said the storyteller, taking a sip from a fine porcelain cup, "have welcomed the idea of our gatherings and listened with pleasure to the ladies, who spoke before me, but now it's my turn and I feel somewhat apprehensive.

"You see, it all has to do with something in the very distant past. I feel compelled to be open, utterly open–as they say, you can't back out once you've begun–but at the same time the subject is such that it may be altogether impossible to talk about it in proper literary language which we're still attached to here, far from Russia. It's a dark, forbidden theme.

"Besides, I must not only remember and tell everything as it was, but also return to my former self, to that boy who remains there and continues to live his own life. You know how easy it is to get lost in the past and how hard almost impossible it is not to drag in the present together with all the rubbish, all the accumulated pain of life. We plod along hugging memory close, but memory fools us and we end up coloring the past.

"We all have agreed to tell each other the story of our first love. One may ask what's so special about such an experience, something that's almost inevitable in everyone's life, almost always fleeting, because, isn't it true, it cannot, it should not last. Yet, why is it that no other event pierces so deeply, becomes part of our soul forever as the memory of a first passion. I'm not talking about that early time of infatuation with every passing skirt, every girlish silhouette, and an expectant time when everything around–books, movies, conversations, gossip–whispers 'You, what about you? And when will it be your turn?' I'm talking about enchantment, about a sudden electric charge. About something incomprehensible, that comes from nowhere, secret and degrading, yet at the same time lifting you above your peers, above everything around you. Someone once remarked that girls do not know childhood. I can't venture to judge if that's so (by the way, all such pronouncements are made by men), but the upheaval a boy goes through, that fatal encounter like a train collision between the ideal and the real, I mean the reality of sex, is practically unknown to a girl. She somehow naturally gets used to her body, and, unlike a boy, delights in its changes. In a certain sense, she's already known everything before, not because she's read about it in books or heard it from friends, but because the knowledge existed in her body before it finally reached consciousness. What for a boy becomes a painful burden–the hands he can't seem to settle, the body he's ashamed of–for a girl is natural and desired, and without any effort, as if it were all perfectly obvious, with a confidence unknown to boys, she enters womanhood when the time comes. Or maybe I'm mistaken.

"What's even more important is that girls become social creatures more easily and sooner. Oh, I know how much has been said on this subject. Yet you'll never determine where the influence of upbringing, habit and prejudice ends and nature asserts itself. You'll say man is a social animal and that by puberty he's already completely socialized. But these very conventions, imposed by society, are so potent it's difficult not to suspect they're in some conspiracy with the endocrine glands. Why is it that the girls' skill in jumping rope, which it seemed they never tired of, only provoked contempt on the part of the boys, and pastimes like stamp collecting and chess which consumed us, didn't interest the girls in the least? Could it be that the zeal for collecting and single combat was a male adventure from which girls were excluded? For my part, I'm inclined to think that the girls' indifference to these passions had to do with that very same deep connection to real life: the magic of postage stamps, the war of little wooden figures seemed to them an empty pursuit. This all represented childhood, a childhood they had outgrown, whereas the boys still wallowed in it.

"I don't sleep well at night or I have disconnected dreams. In my sleep I realize I'm dreaming. I see myself as a boy and at the same time realize that I'm an adult, that I'm growing old. But it's as if this awareness somehow is not mine. In sleep, strange as it may seem, I experience true reality, because my 'I' loses all control over it. It can't be helped. Imagine that in front of you is not a pudgy, flabby, balding man who has long since squandered, as they say now, his 50 kopecks, but rather such a creature between two eras, childhood and youth, or rather between the ages of fourteen and fifteen. This takes place–now what year was it again? Oh, well, it's not important.

"It all started and ended with chess and stamps, but more on that a bit later; for now we're still in that idyllic kingdom, at that age, when the two camps would prefer to keep their distance: the girls, who were no longer girls and the boys, whether they realized it or not, who wanted to remain children. The chess battles protected us from the encroachment of reality; the sheltered garden of stamps was our refuge, where we sat it out, trying to put off the inevitable.

"We liked to spend all our free time in the courtyard. As you remember, Moscow in those years was a grid of narrow, crooked lanes, of yards with through passages, where it was possible, by making your way between firewalls, taking off from one gate ledge to another, to find yourself suddenly on a neighboring street that emits hostility. You had to keep an eye out. There someone could come at you from a corner, could come flying from behind, there some snot–nosed bastard with pen knives could greet an intruder. There the chauvinism of the courtyards raged. There they would search you in dark entranceways. It was not this Moscow, rife with treachery, but our alley and yard, protected by gates, that was our homeland. The yard was like other yards, gloomy and chilly, with fire escapes, with laundry hanging on clotheslines tied to drainpipes, communal apartment windows gazing down from three sides. All the tenants knew one another, they all fought with one another, all lived a common life. A fourth brick wall served as a firewall and propped up against it was a shed of wooden planks for the snow–melter. From time to time junkmen, aging beggars, fiery–eyed fortunetellers would drop into the courtyard. A blind guitarist would raise his face towards the windows and from the little vents they would throw to him coins wrapped in paper; in the mornings you could hear the knife grinder's song. Over the winter a mountain of snow, carted from the alley, would rise in the courtyard. In the summer the sun glanced off the brick firewall and the window shutters on the upper floor banged furiously; we rushed around the yard as if possessed, turning somersaults on the cross–beams of the firemen's ladders. In the yard we played with fantiki, those little wrappers folded in squares, and exchanged stamps.

"There was a certain Yura Kishchuk, nicknamed Pike, an unpleasant character from the building next door. One day he showed up in the courtyard holding under his arm a large, lacquered box fastened with a hook.

"Two hosts lined up opposite each other on a yellow–brown checkered chess board, two rows of infantrymen unable to retreat, behind them the royal pair, generals and mounted guard, flanked by attacking turrets. The sound of the battle horn like a car horn proclaimed the battlefield. The first to advance across two squares was a soldier in a round helmet coming face to face with a black mercenary. The cavalry charged out at a gallop, outdistancing the foot soldiers. From behind this living wall of soldiers the queen came flying in her chariot.

"Our fans surrounded us. We sat on the roof of the wooden shed, the only place the sun reached. It glinted in the windows and lit the tall carved figures on the green cloth linings. Compared to the old, chipped and broken–off chess pieces which consumed us for days on end, Kishchuk's freshly lacquered chess pieces radiated an unfamiliar prosperity. You might say they were an emblem of class superiority, something we all sensed vaguely.

"It was here that I discovered how the size of the board affects the skill of the player: I began to lose catastrophically. These traitorous pieces from another world masked a kind of meanness; they played into the hand of their owner; it was as if they let you know you were not worthy to engage them. Chess pieces can live a life of their own–a subject of fantastic stories that is borrowed from reality. A series of more or less forced exchanges partly set my affairs straight. I managed, to the accompaniment of the spirited snorting and impatient cries of the onlookers, to make it to the end of the game.

"As you know, the king is the most defenseless piece, but when there's no more army, the king himself draws his sword. The king entered the last hopeless battle. They were already celebrating victory on the other side of the board. Several times, with evident malicious pleasure, they proposed we surrender. Suddenly, oh, happiness. 'Stalemate!' I cried.

The storyteller smiled.

"Keeping in mind that the present company too was at one time girls, I'll explain that stalemate is a situation where you can't make a move without endangering the king, and once you can't make a move, then your opponent can't either: stalemate is a forced draw. And so, imagine that, you think you have it sewed up–and suddenly it's a draw. Pike, irritated, claimed that I cheated. He started to show how the pieces had been standing and now I had to expose him as a cheat. 'No, it was a stalemate!' 'It wasn't a stalemate! The king was here.' 'No, here!' It was impossible to prove anything, as he was already gathering up his chess pieces. We jumped off the little shed. He stood there, clasping the chessboard, and we gave each other a shove in the chest. The other guys were on my side. He took off.

"Blinded by hatred, I ran up against a wet sheet and got tangled up in the clothes line which gave my enemy the chance to clear out of the yard. I sprang out from under the gates. Pike bolted home. He ran up to the main entrance and we flew up the stairs. I overtook him on the third floor landing. He wasn't able to slam the door shut.

"Allow me to interrupt myself," said the storyteller, staring into his cup. "I'll tell you about a certain dream. The further all this recedes, the more difficult it is, you see, to separate the memory of one's past from memories of dreams. I enter someone's apartment; before me is a large entrance hall. Not a soul. Suddenly an unknown woman comes out to meet me and asks what I need. The light from the room behind her is blinding. I can't make out her face. And although I have urgent business with her, I am unable to utter a word. Sounds come tearing out of my throat like the wheezing of someone being strangled, and I wake up.

"As I've already mentioned, this Yura Kishchuk lived in the neighborhood but his apartment didn't look like ours or for that matter like any other apartment in our building. Our place was packed with tenants. We, that is I, my younger sister, my parents, and a certain relative who arrived from a remote region and whom I remember vaguely dwelled in one room which somehow accommodated a dining table, wardrobe, bed, sofa and even an upright on which my sister was learning to play. Although to all appearances Kishchuk also lived in a communal apartment, it seemed completely uninhabited and besides that there was something like an apartment within an apartment. We would all drop in on each other; Yura never invited anyone, so it's only now that the whole story has come out. He dashed through the entrance hall and disappeared in the corridor with me right behind him; I yanked open the door and found myself in a room which seemed to me luxurious. An assortment of mirrors, wardrobes, armchairs, a chandelier hanging from the ceiling. There was no one there. I stopped, breathing heavily, not knowing what to do. Then the curtains parted and a woman emerged in a housecoat, belted carelessly, her fair hair all matted. Obviously this was Pike's mother. Strange as it seems, I don't remember anything more–about what I was asked and what I answered. Actually, that's not true. She led me up to a mirror and told me to comb my hair. Then she added, 'Well, now that's more like it. Now you can go.' And I left.

"After this, if one keeps to a chronology–although it's not the best form of narration, in any case, not obligatory–after this, probably two or three weeks went by. Everything was already awash in spring. There was just a short time left before exams (we called them 'ordeals'), and then vacation, which I hoped to spend in town because I hated the pioneer camp into which my parents intended to install me. Two or three weeks had gone by since my intrusion and one day I saw Yura Kishchuk's mother on our side street. She was wearing a bright spring dress, high–heels, with a thin overcoat over her arm, fair–haired and in a circle of light. No, it wasn't Cupid who tweaked me with his arrow, it was as if one of the young bandits who swarmed around the neighborhood had stretched back his catapult and a stone hit me on the bridge of the nose. I stopped, paralyzed with fear. A psychoanalyst would probably find a reason for this fear. I just don't know whether I'd be convinced by his explanation. In any case, there weren't any grounds for this feeling, unless you consider the discovery, which struck me like thunder: for the first time in my life I realized that a woman can be beautiful, blindingly beautiful. She came nearer and asked me about something. I wasn't able to answer. She touched my cheek with her palm and we parted.

"Beauty instills fear, because it makes excessive demands of everything around it. Beauty debases, it destroys what surrounds it. Beauty intimidates and stirs up confusion, because by its very existence it reduces everything that once had meaning. Why it exists is a mystery. It would seem that nature arranged things in such a way that beauty must stimulate desire in the male. But in fact beauty surrounds a woman like a ring charged with a current of high–voltage: if you touch it, you die.

"It probably won't be out of place to say a few words on how well–informed I was in these matters. I already knew, just like all the kids of my age knew, what a man and a woman surrender to in private. As with all kids, this was formal knowledge. For example, I never could see in my little sister, whom I couldn't stand, a creature who might be of interest from a certain particular point of view. It simply never entered my head. Although our family lived in one room, my parents shielded the children. I neither saw nor heard anything. Their private life didn't interest me. I didn't sense any mystery here. Oh, my papa always irritated, my mama always worried. Conversations about prices, standing in line, the neighbors. My sister eagerly participated in trifling domestic affairs, whereas not only did I feel totally indifferent this world, but also I let it show readily. I didn't like to stay at home. I think our cruel way of life, contrary to the usual notions, not only didn't encourage promiscuity but rather was a condition of a repressive morality. I never even saw my parents kiss. Our dreary circumstances forbade embracing and kissing, forbade girls to flirt with men, and reestablished with a certain surprising ardor the mythology of the noble upper and the carnal lower; this rigid mythology simply outlawed the lower half of the body. Morality was on the track of sex, the hidden enemy, and drove it into hiding, just as border guards in the old films shadowed a saboteur. Like gas in a container, sexuality was compressed into thousands of atmospheres, and one day the vessel had to explode.

"Did I myself have the sense I was becoming a man? No doubt. There were mysterious dreams, painful awakenings. But these physical changes that come with puberty are of little interest, don't you agree. I'm talking about something else, about how first love, romantic, idealistic, denies these stirrings of the body which are so frightening. Without success, obviously.

"Don't expect any revelations from me. It's all been said before. Yet each person must begin all over again. You see, this is the point: anyone who thinks the boy's discovery–one could compare it with a loss of faith in God if we weren't living in an atheistic society–anyone who thinks the exposure of the secret of sex is that very boundary beyond which childhood ends–is mistaken. One can keep in mind all the words and know, more or less, what they mean, and remain a child. The real downfall, the end of childhood, comes when the earth dissolves under your feet, when a black chasm opens. When you find out for yourself that love is not content with adoration and with horror you become convinced that being in love turns into humiliation for both, because it leads inevitably to physical closeness, that love is doomed to end up in sex.

"I had the strange thought of making peace with Pike. Now I knew where he lived, on what floor, in what apartment, and I set out for his place more agitated than one would expect in such situations. Back then, even well–appointed houses often didn't have elevators. I went by the stairs, one flight after another, the higher I climbed, the more reluctantly, and when, at last, I found myself in front of the door with the right number and the cardboard placard my courage completely failed me. Barely able to ring the bell, I slipped downstairs. Hiding on the landing between flights, I heard how the door opened, and slammed shut. Once again, as if I were being dragged by a rope, I climbed the steps and once again read: Kishchuk–ring once and extended my finger toward the small button. The bell rang behind the door, but this time no one hastened to open it. I rang again and again, pressing hard on the button. Finally I heard some shuffling. A gloomy old woman peeked out from behind the door.

"She plied me with questions–who do you want and what for–and suddenly something happened that had been in my dream: Pike's mother came out into the corridor. This time she didn't seem to be such a dazzling beauty, perhaps because, just as that time when I burst into their place, she was dressed carelessly, and I felt relieved. In some vague way she reminded me of Yura. Once again I found myself on the threshold of a bright room with a chandelier and mirrors, with curtains drawn apart, behind which was another room, and the sun was shining in the windows.

"'Yura's not here,' she said, as if cooing, in her deep, chest voice; it seemed that Pike had gone off to his grandmother's or some other place. 'Why are you standing there, come in. It's just that I forgot,' she added, 'your name.'

"When someone holds out his palm to you as an equal that means he's offering to overcome the distance of age, sex and social position, but as soon as he gives his name and patronymic, all barriers are raised again. It was customary to call women teachers by their first name and patronymic. And once again, the difference between an adolescent and a grown woman, between an awkward, uninvited guest and a bemused hostess paralyzes you and takes away the gift of speech. I entered, or rather, dragged myself behind her, behind her voice, her light hair, her lazy, mincing steps. I felt she was inviting me out of politeness. Out of politeness people ask absolutely uninteresting questions. 'What do your parents do and how are your grades?' She knew that Pike and I were in the same classes.

"But you obviously expected me to describe what she looked like in more detail. I'll try, although maybe you shouldn't trust my description; after all, I was seeing rather an image I myself created, not a woman who existed in actual fact.

"To say she was of medium height or rather not tall, around the same height as I, somewhat plump, with sloping shoulders, is to say nothing at all. Although memory is quite capable of reproducing her specific features, they add nothing to her image that exists all in an instant. Her image is what she is. This woman, Olga Varfolomeevna–that's what they called her, although I myself, it seems, never called her that–appeared before me as a whole. Men, and boys even more so, tend to see women as a whole, at least when they first get acquainted. Of course, I have not forgotten her appearance; on the contrary, I remember her in the most trivial ways, but at the same time my memory, or better, all my being, resists such analysis. I cannot describe her as do novelists their heroines; I remember everything, but can't find suitable words. I see her face in a cloud of light hair, I see the expression of her eyes, but it's difficult to say, for example, what color they were. Grey–blue? Green? This time she wasn't wearing high heels but downy house slippers without backs, and I remember her slender heels when she walked in front of me into the room behind the curtains, yellowish–pink heels, which told me she wasn't wearing stockings. In a pale rose flannel dressing gown resembling a bathrobe, she was girded by a thin belt which made her form charmingly clumsy and defined her low–slung hips.

"When I came the next time, it was Olga Vafolomeevna who opened the front door. Again Yura had disappeared somewhere, but this time it didn't surprise me. I somehow felt I wouldn't find him. I was holding a book she had given me. She was astonished: 'You really read it that quickly? Did you like it?' In the large room was a carved bookcase. 'Take whatever you like,' she said. I went closer and began to look through the glass at the printed bindings; these were pre–Revolutionary editions. In a minute, I thought, she will say, you can go now, and I will go. She will say go, and I will go. I sat, clasping two extremely interesting books, which I have read since then. Olga Varfolomeevna settled herself opposite me, crossing her legs. She was still in the same flannel dressing gown and had drawn up the skirt. I noticed this movement. I even seemed to glimpse her round knee. A slipper dangled from her foot.

"She showed me her family album. We sat next to each other. 'And this one,' she said, 'is my husband and I in Simeiz. Yura wasn't born yet. He was still in the planning stage. And you, of course, also didn't exist. Were you ever in the Crimea? In this one we've already moved to Moscow. Before that we lived in the Urals.' Some of the photos showed her husband in a soldier's shirt with a belt and shoulder strap, with a decoration in a buttonhole. She–in a fantastic hairdo, with lips darkened from lipstick and he, this time in a tie, their heads pressed together. A little girl with ridiculous bows in her hair who again reminded me of Pike was also she. 'And this one,' she said thoughtfully, peering at some completely unfamiliar faces, and suddenly burst out laughing, 'My god, where's this from?' A photo in an oval frame showed a man in a top hat, monocle, and bowtie, his chin propped up on the knob of a cane. 'He was an admirer,' she said, 'an artist.' I asked what had become of him. 'He disappeared!' she replied, then added, 'He didn't go anywhere, just got married, then divorced, how should I know. Well, that's how it is,' she said, slamming shut the album, 'and now another admirer has appeared!'

"I couldn't come up with an answer and didn't quite understand whom she had in mind; to be more exact, I didn't understand whether she was joking or not. I expected her to say any minute, 'Well, it's time to say goodbye, we've sat a while, now go along,' something like that. 'Or maybe I'm wrong,' she said, looking at me sideways. 'No,' she answered herself and nodded slightly. 'No, I'm not wrong. Young man,' she said softly, 'do you know how old I am?'

"I met her several times on the street. She would walk by without noticing me and I guessed she didn't want to see me anymore. Then once, unexpectedly, she entered the yard and stopped, obviously searching for her son. 'Do you happen to know,' she asked distractedly without looking at me. 'Do you happen to know … I can't find the right place …' 'Today they have six classes,' I said, 'plus a class gathering.' 'Is that so?' she replied quickly. 'Good heavens.' She threw up her hands. 'I completely forgot about it. You can imagine what I've been thinking. There are troublemakers around. Well, thanks.' I felt she wanted to say something, and was waiting for me to speak first; but I kept silent. She seemed to look down at me, like a teacher reprimanding a student. 'Why don't you drop over?' It was as if her question meant she was inviting me to visit her, not Yura.

"It can happen that a certain thought, maybe not even a thought but something more fleeting, like a pin prick, twinges and disappears yet leaves a trace, and this trace of a thought, like a pricked spot, lingers on. That's the way it was with us.

"'Were you angry with me?' she asked when I followed her into the large room, one filled with anticipation. It was the next day. Spots of light quivering on the parquet floor, encroaching darkness, like a whirlpool, an oval mirror–there were many mirrors in this apartment–and in it, leaning against one another, books in golden bindings, and the lace curtains swaying. Voices rose from the cool bluish mist of our alley. There the life of the old block went on. May was just beginning, the wash drying in the courtyards, the kids sitting on the roof of the shed housing the snow–melter, and the girls jumping rope. But here she was living in opulent seclusion, the sounds of the street barely reaching her ears. Just to be sure I asked, 'How about…' 'At his grandmother's,' she replied tersely.

"We didn't talk anymore about books or photographs. We were silent. She got up and went to the mirror. I saw her from the back and saw her face in the curve of the shining glass. But her large eyes which had darkened were not looking at me, her eyes were devouring the void. 'What on earth are we doing,' she muttered, as if delirious. 'As God is my witness, I didn't want this. Oh, how I didn't want this.' The sun spots on the floor dimmed. Probably, beyond the windows, low lying clouds were drifting over the city.

"I cannot go into details. You sense we had approached a forbidden, obstructed place. One can assume that when we first got acquainted, Olga Varfolomeevna allowed herself to start up a little game with me. The silent adoration of a young boy can be no less flattering than the attentions of a grown man. But now it was no longer a game.

"Yes, we had approached a terrain encircled by barbed wire, surrounded by defensive armor, all to instill holy terror. The obscene is the underside of the deeply intimate. What is sacred becomes profane once it is uttered. And it will always be so, despite the attempts to exorcise the demon and all sorts of sexual revolutions. We lack the language to express what we would like to express; we have many languages and they are all wanting. One can speak about sex only in the language of myth, but the curse of our century, our education, of, perhaps, our entire civilization, is in the fact that we interpret myth only as allegory.

"She kept standing in front of the mirror, kept looking at herself and at me, and I watched her lips move. 'It's fate,' she muttered. 'Do you believe in fate?' People usually think a young lout is tormented by curiosity. Nothing of the sort. I experienced only fear and confusion. It was no longer the teacher and the guilty student, the grown woman and the child, before whom something he was not yet supposed to know opened up for the first time. Everything that had defended and supported me as if on braces, my parents, school, the courtyard, the games, the crayfish shell of life–the childhood which I strained to leave and with which it was so terrible to part–everything flew away, dissolved, and I remained alone as if kicked out beyond the gates of a comfortable prison, face to face with her and what she called fate. We were alone, we were a man and a woman, no one else.

"She–I say she, because we had lost our names. She lingered, pulling at the tie of her robe, and her face, gray like mercury, with its huge eyes and lips slightly parted, observed me from the mirror. Because it was slightly inclined, I saw practically all of her, and she seemed to look at me distrustfully. Maybe she expected I would come to my senses and run away. Her fingers were fidgeting with something, opened it wide apart, and I saw her dark red nipples, outlined with circles, her belly, and a shadowy fold that resembled the letter epsilon. Oh, I know what you're thinking–a mature woman was tempting a young boy. But you can just as well say I was her unintentional temptation. Actually it was something else, something that turned us into somnambulists, that deprived both of us of will, or more precisely, that filled us with an indomitable will. All of this–

there, by the mirror–lasted an instant; she closed her robe. Her face took on a determined expression; she went up to me and quickly kissed me, as if I were about to have a dangerous operation. I plodded along behind her into the next room and there, it turns out, was yet another room. The stillness gave off a stupefying scent; she sat on the edge of an unusually wide bed that took up all the space and I stood in front of her like a recruit; she unbuttoned and removed my clothes. And it was on this bed, just imagine, that something shameful and amusing happened to me. You'll laugh, but I lost consciousness.

"Yes, I fainted, if you can say that about a person who is prone anyway; I fainted, but not from some physical trauma–it seems to me I didn't feel anything at all– but from agitation, which was perhaps associated with the smell of perfume. When I came to, my temples felt cold; she was wiping me with cologne. Her light, perfumed hair tickled me and I moved away. 'Are you alive?' she asked. 'Don't worry, it happens.' She got up, and drew back slightly the curtains of the large window. She had nothing on. I tried not to look at her. 'What happens?' I asked dully. Never in my life had I experienced such humiliation.

"'Practice makes perfect!' she said. To cap my shame she carefully wiped off–on me and on herself–the sticky, unpleasant something that had flowed out of me. She caressed and comforted me, like a little child. She lay down beside me. I turned away from her almost with hatred. My eyes filled with tears. Suddenly it struck me, as if I had only now noticed, that we were lying under a sheet, that outside the window was the sky, white as cotton wadding, and that in the apartment was a kind of ominous silence. A terrible thought stuck to my lips: what about Pike? What if ...? What would we do then? But it was as if she hadn't even considered this. It was as if we had become invisible. And, you know, it actually was in store for me, as in the famous Wells' novel, to become invisible–until someone saw traces in the snow.

"'What are we going to do?' she asked distractedly, anticipating my question. 'We're not going to do anything. Right now we'll get up and drink tea. But you have to look away. We'll drink some tea and you'll go. It's time for your homework.' I shot back angrily, 'They're not giving any more assignments.' 'Oh, yes,' said Olga Varfolomeevna, 'I completely forgot; but you have to prepare for exams.' We remained lying there, covered up to our chins. 'And I keep I thinking all the time,' she went on, 'do you understand what we're doing here? You're a minor and I... Just go home and we'll forget about what happened, okay? We went too far and nothing good will come of it. Do you understand me? You never came here and there was nothing between us. And you don't know me at all. Okay? That's it. Now turn away. I have to get dressed.' I was silent and she was silent.

"Then she asked: 'Is that what he's called? Don't get upset, Yura will be here tomorrow. He's at his grandmother's. She loves him dearly.' 'And you?' I asked. 'What about me?' 'Do you love him too?' She shrugged her shoulders. 'I'm his mother. Is it possible your mama doesn't love you?' With a wry smile she added: 'You're not jealous, are you? Don't worry, this is completely different. The truth is I love only you. It's terrible, it's horrible,' she said, laughing, 'yet I love only you. But now this doesn't mean anything anymore.' 'And I love you too,' I said. She smiled, 'I know. I knew it at once.' I felt better somehow and wanted to ask, 'How about....?' but stopped short. I didn't know what to call this man. 'Are you thinking of my husband?' she asked. 'He's coming later, at dawn. And he'll sleep until one in the afternoon. It's going to rain,' she went on. 'This morning was so clear, without a cloud. No, this isn't love. It only seems that way to you. It's an infatuation. Boys are often taken with older women. It will pass. But still I really love you. Does this seem strange?'

"She kissed me. 'If you want,' she said cautiously, 'we can try once more. Only this will be the last time, do you hear?' She caressed me deliberately, slowly. 'And we'll part. Move closer, that's it. Don't rush. We still have lots of time. It's raining now; see how dark it's become... Only don't rush. Slowly. My only one.'

The storyteller looked around at the audience.

"And, just imagine, everything somehow turned out well. It probably surprises you that I recall all the words, all...the details, so confidently. It surprises you because: thought and memory disappear in those moments, something like a drowning man's lungs flood with water. I think one can go even further and compare our bed to a ship at sea. Outside the window everything flashed and rumbled and a heavy rain pounded the glass.

"Whether because it was for the second time, or owing to my lover's remarkable sensitivity, our connection took place simply and naturally, except for the final moments of complete madness, so that now it's difficult for me to decide, and at that time all the more impossible to understand, whether she was satisfied with me or whether all her efforts were concentrated on making me feel like a man. A certain fragment by Novalis, if I'm not mistaken, describes an assignation as at once a physical descent along the steps of sensuality to the point of orgasm and an ascent along the ladder of the soul, to ecstasy.

"Gradually I calmed down; everything had changed; I began to orient myself in what was for me a new world, a world of tenderness and rapture. I began to feel the subtleties in a wind of hair fanning me, and white, soft hands enveloping and embracing me. I saw what was before me without concealment, with ingenuous openness, but it demanded a new perspective. Now I understood everything differently; I was discovering this body as a child discovers a picture book, or as someone who tries to make sense of a text in a strange, as yet incomprehensible and delightful language. It seems she was not put off by my curiosity; she found it amusing and with a supercilious smile allowed me study her, confident in herself, as a goddess. I was astonished by the slenderness of her waist and her broad, round hips. I wanted to embrace them, to bury my head in them and... I cannot hide from you the completely wild thought that glimmered beyond the reach of reason–that this split shell could have brought me into the world too. It's possible this thought is not so absurd after all. In a certain sense that's what had happened. She gently sent me on my way and from that day on we began to meet.

"Sometimes I was let in by the sinister old woman who, perhaps, harbored no evil intentions; in any case, she didn't ask any more questions, just turned and shuffled off silently into her cubbyhole and I would forget about her at once. I almost ran down the corridor, opened the door wide without knocking and we rushed toward each other with such impatience that sometimes our lovemaking happened right there on the floor in the first room. And no one knew of these meetings, except the gloomily secretive granny–who she was, a nanny, a relative or simply a neighbor, I don't know. Once, when I was running down the stairs, skipping a step and whistling loudly, I ran right into Pike. He was coming toward me and somehow strangely narrowed his eyes, or so it seemed. We didn't say a word and I jumped from the landing. I immediately forgot about this meeting and it's possible it really had no meaning. Nothing had meaning any more.

"The school year ended. My parents didn't suspect anything and for them it was a complete surprise when, returning home after my first test, in a white full–dress shirt with a turned–down collar and freshly ironed pioneer tie, I announced I had flunked. The re–examination was set for the fall. My mother burst into tears and my sister stared at me with round eyes. My father said nothing, only curtained himself off with his thick eyebrows, which he did at every new blow of fate. But a miracle took place. I didn't have a clue as to what actually happened, besides, what did I care about the details? School interested me like last year's snow. Olga Varfolomeevna came to my aid, feeling, as she confessed, guilty; it turned that my beloved had 'certain connections,' pressure was put on someone, almost certainly the director himself, and my situation changed instantly. They allowed me to re–take the test right away, at the end of the examination period, and somehow I got rid of this burden. Another truly dire misfortune, about which I'll tell you now, hit both of us like a bolt from the blue.

"Of course it had to happen sooner or later. The traces of an invisible man, the imprint of bare soles running through the snow! If you had seen the Wells film that was showing in Moscow in those years, you should remember this scene. But even before that something began to change in Olga Varfolomeevna. She became irritable, fidgety, kept losing things, and found fault with me at every opportunity. I was to blame because I stayed away so long, to blame because I came too early. Because of me she arrived late somewhere, spilled something on her new dress, because of me–this I readily believe–she didn't get along with her mysterious husband. In a word, I was the cause of everything going wrong. I had brought unhappiness into her peaceful home. 'It's hardly peaceful,' I would object. 'Don't you dare talk like that,' she would shout back. 'You don't understand anything.' She surrendered herself to me feverishly, she who was so sensible, moaned and urged me on, and this feverishness communicated itself to me, and finally, when out of exhaustion we kept away from each other, I thought I wouldn't show up any more. It seemed to me that our meetings no longer brought her any joy.

"Once she suggested we ride out to a dacha. 'To your dacha?' 'No, to another place.' I asked whether something had happened, whether anyone had seen us. 'Nothing's happened. We'll walk a bit and have a breath of fresh air. The next day you'll go back.' 'And you?' I asked. 'You'll go back and I'll stay.'

"I realized it was useless to keep asking her questions; I told them at home that the school had organized an overnight hike, which sounded unlikely, since classes were over already, but I couldn't come up with anything better; my mother prepared sandwiches for me and I struggled to squeeze an old tarpaulin backpack onto my shoulders. Olga was waiting near the ticket booth of the Belorus station. We got off at the Perkhushkovo stop and walked for a long while through woods and fields. At that time these were places of breathtaking beauty. The dacha stood at the edge of a development, an unprepossessing, wretched little house, perhaps meant for the help. Not a soul around. The area, about which I, of course, knew nothing, was a kind of closed zone.

"We sat for a long time late at night on the steps of the porch. The next day we got up late and set off for the station. It was already close to noon. The train approached and she embraced me. I stood in the door of the railroad car. She kept looking around. We didn't know what to say to each other as we parted. The stationmaster's whistle sounded and she rushed toward me. We sat by the window in the half empty car and just then a woman came in, an elderly gypsy, barefoot, dried–out like an apricot pit, in a frayed, silk shawl that kept slipping from her coarse, oily hair; she sat down next to Olga Varfolomeevna. Out came some cards followed by an offer to tell her fortune. 'You should tell his fortune,' Olga objected. The old woman wiped her gap–toothed mouth with her palm and asked: 'And who's he to you?' 'My son' 'Oh, you're lying, missie. You're not telling the truth. He's not your son. Don't worry,' said the gypsy, lowering her voice, 'no one will hear us.' 'What's there to be afraid of?' Olga Varfolomeevna asked. 'You probably know yourself. O–oh, I see, I see right through the both of you.' 'Get the hell out of here,' said Olga Varfolomeevna. 'Why so nasty? Better I tell you something. He'll leave you. You see how young he is. But you're old. I know a charm.

When I cast my spell he'll stick with you forever. You'll bind him tighter than all the chains.' 'Beat it, witch!' Olga shouted, crying from rage. We both ran out of the car. It was some sort of way station. We looked around, not knowing which way to turn.

"But I wanted to tell you about a more important event. I said it was like a bolt from the blue. It happened in our old courtyard. After the war, that is the World War which at that time was not yet called the First, Germany lost all its colonies–Southwest Africa, the Cameroons, Togo and all the rest, and as the philatelic rumor goes, the last colonial stamps were issued in dark frames. But it wasn't a rumor or a legend: I can say with pride that I was the only one in the class and in the yard who owned this series. Stamp collecting was the great adventure of our childhood. To this day it's still a mystery to me, how, living in a closed country, we found ways to get hold of postage stamps of far away, exotic countries and islands which weren't even mentioned in the geography book. Not all the kids were able to leave for the holidays. Pike was in town. He brought his collection into the yard. One could look at his album forever with its hard, embossed binding, thick, ruled pages, and coats of arms of principalities and kingdoms that were long gone. A magnificent pre–Revolutionary album, slightly frayed, probably requisitioned from someone who disappeared without a trace in those times. It goes without saying that our drawing pads, bought in the stationery store, couldn't compare with it in the least.

"Pike proposed a swap. He had had his eye on my colonies for a long time. What was offered wasn't bad at all: the Vatican with little golden keys and a tiara and some other things thrown in. It began with the usual bargaining. He raised his offer, I dug in my heels; I really didn't feel like trading at all. It began peacefully, but ended not with the usual argument, as would happen with chess, but much worse. 'Well, all right,' he said with ominous composure. 'If you don't want to–you don't want to. Just let me take a another look'

"'What's there to look at,' I said. 'Come on,' Pike drawled. And, without waiting for permission, he pulled my stamps out of their pocket with the tip of his finger– we used to glue long pockets out of transparent paper to the album pages. He placed the stamps on his palm. 'They're beautiful,' he said. 'Put them back,' I said, anxiously. He just laughed and emptied the stamps into his album. 'You snake!' I shouted. 'Huh?' He screwed up his eyes. 'Pike,' I said, 'just give them back, okay.' 'What did you call me?' 'Give me back the stamps.' 'No, repeat it.' 'Repeat what?' 'What you just said. Say you're sorry!' He looked at me savagely. 'What's there to apologize for,' I said disdainfully. 'He gets his hands on my stamps and I'm supposed to apologize.'

"He looked around and, although we were standing almost on top of each other, he beckoned with his finger. 'If you,' he began in a conspiratorial tone, 'open your trap, you scumbag, you stinkpot, you know what I'll do with you?' He paused. 'I'll tell my father everything, you get it?' 'So what are you going to say?' I asked, dumbstruck. 'You know,' he answered. 'I don't know anything.' 'Do you know who my dad is?' 'Yeah, I know.' 'So apologize to me. Say: Pike, I'm sorry.' I muttered something. 'I'm sorry, I'll never do it again.' 'I'll never do it again,' I said. 'Pioneer's word of honor.' I gave my pioneer's word of honor. 'Great!' said Pike. 'I'm tough, but fair. I'll give you Spain with a king and a Roman pope for your colonies.' 'That's all?' I asked. 'So, it's not enough? You little sneak. Okay,' he said, 'I'll throw in a Uruguayan. Just so you know I'm fair.'

"I don't think Pike knew anything, perhaps just suspected something. A week or so passed and he didn't appear–he evidently had gone off to the dacha or wherever they took him for the summer, which made me happy and not happy. It could mean that she and I would be separated for three months. Suddenly one day I caught sight of Olga Varfolomeevna. She was standing between the doors of a gateway; the sun was striking her back. I was unable to distinguish her face and saw only her dark figure and the fiery nimbus of her hair. It seemed she was beckoning to me. I jumped out of the yard into the narrow street. She wasn't there. It was a vision that had beckoned to me. After a few minutes I saw her again; she was walking on the opposite side, and again I was struck by the beauty of her hips, her narrow, sloping shoulders, the beauty of her walk, and the light dress of exotic colors fluttering about her legs. She was striding with broad, even steps toward Kharitonevsky street, unhurriedly, without looking around, carrying a little hand bag under her arm. She went off to the right and we drew even near the school built on the site of a church which I still remember; they say Pushkin was married there. And although it wasn't true, still everyone knew that Pushkin was married in this church.

"She didn't notice me, didn't turn her head or quicken her step, and said, 'Go ahead, I'll catch up with you.' I crossed the streetcar tracks and went through the turnstile onto the boulevard. Perhaps these places are memorable for you too. I remember them as if it was yesterday. The area around 'Chistye prudy' was then much cleaner and in any case more spacious. The lushly green trees, the lawns with yellow and lilac flowers, the sandy ring along which a camel walked on Sundays, the carousels, and ice–cream venders. She bought me a round ice cream, the biggest one for 80 kopecks, sandwiched between two waffles on which was stamped the name Olga.

"'I want to tell you something,' she said, addressing me in a way that was special to her. Since then no one has called me by this name and so it has remained our secret. 'I must tell you something ...' 'Me too,' I replied quickly. And right away I regretted that I had let something slip: why did I have to tell her. 'What do you mean 'too?'' she asked. 'Don't be afraid,' I said, 'it's nothing. He's just making a fool of me.' 'Why don't we sit down?' said Olga Varfolomeevna, and we sat down next to each other on a bench. 'Who's making a fool of you?' 'No, first you tell me.' 'You tell me, then I'll tell you.' 'He knows, 'I said. 'Who?' 'Pike. He didn't say it straight out, just hinted. I had to tell about the incident with the dark colonies. It's nothing,' I added. 'He's just trying to bully me. He really doesn't know anything.' 'You think so?' she asked thoughtfully. She looked at me and said, 'You've got yourself all dirty. You can't be so sloppy.' She unclasped her tiny pocketbook and wiped off the drops of ice cream on my shirt with her perfumed handkerchief. Then she wiped my cheeks as if I was a little boy; I moved away in disgust. 'What did he say to you?' she asked. 'Try to remember.' I replied that Pike didn't talk about anything directly, an extra proof he didn't know what was going on. He just threatened me that if I opened my maw, he'd tell his dad everything. 'You know what,' I said, 'let's go away somewhere. Let's go away, far away, where no one will find us. Let's take off to the Urals, or Siberia, or someplace else,' I said, all fired up. Olga Varfolomeevna listened to me carefully and nodded with a serious look. 'I've thought it all out,' I went on, 'the main thing is not to say a word to anyone. You'll take only what you really need. We'll meet at the train station. I'll not say anything to my parents either.' 'But they'll think that something happened to you. They'll be terribly worried,' she objected. 'We'll write to them from the road. Or send a telegram. I'll write it myself. I'll tell them not to look for me.' 'And where will you get the money for the ticket?' 'You'll give it to me. As a loan,' I said. 'Then, when we arrive, I'll give it back' 'You'll give it back…okay.' She kept nodding her head. 'You're foolish,' she said. 'Where on earth will we go? They'll find us everywhere.' I looked at her and realized she hadn't taken one word I said seriously. 'You don't love me, or you wouldn't have said that. I'm just a toy for you. You've had your fun and you're out. You're laughing at me, you were always laughing at me.'

"I clenched my teeth. I felt like strangling her. She smiled bitterly. 'I,' she asked, 'don't love you?' For a while she fixed her eyes on something in the distance. 'You don't even know, you can't imagine,' she muttered, 'what you mean to me. I gave everything to you. I have nothing left. Nothing, except you. All the rest has turned into smoke, into a phantom. You don't have the right to judge this.'

"Now I saw she had become really angry too, frowning and pursing her lips. 'What can you know,' she said, 'what can you know about this altogether, you puppy?'

"She couldn't have come up with a worse insult. We sat and looked in different directions. In a little while I would have gotten up and left. She would never have seen me again. 'So, that's what he said. You're certain that's what it was — I'll tell your father?' I shrugged my shoulders. 'Do you know where my husband works?' 'Sure I know. He's with the secret police.' 'Who said that?' she asked in amazement. 'My dad,' I replied. Of course, I didn't know he meant somebody high up. 'Tell your dad,' she snapped, 'that he should hold his tongue.' She fell silent, then added, 'It seems you don't quite understand what this is about. Do you know what he can do to you? To you, your parents, your sister. And of course to me … If you were older, I could tell you some things…' I wheezed. Again she was reproaching me with my age. 'Don't be angry,' she said softly and called me once more by that name which together with her, has slipped away forever. She took my hand. 'Let me congratulate you. You've now become a real man.' 'Really?' I said, surprised. 'Yes. I've been meaning to tell you. You became a father.' 'What do you mean?' I asked. She shrugged. 'It's very simple. I'm pregnant.'

"Somehow it didn't sink in right away what she was talking about and I objected rather foolishly, 'What do I have to do with this?' She answered, smiling slightly, 'It would be great if you didn't have anything to do with this. But look, I haven't slept with my husband for a long time. He comes home at dawn and collapses like a dead man. It's his job. You're my husband!' said Olga Varfolomeevna and burst out laughing.

The storyteller continued:

"My son is wandering around somewhere. The years have wiped out the difference in age, and was it really so great? Now we're almost contemporaries. My offspring is living somewhere with the name Kishchuk, my blood–or maybe it's a daughter. Probably Olga Varfolomeevna took measures so that her spouse didn't become suspicious. Women always find a way out. So neither my daughter, if it is a daughter, nor the official father suspect my existence. Providing, of course, he survived and didn't fall, which is completely possible, into a trap of his own making.

"I suppose Yura followed in his father's footsteps. Most likely he has a high rank now. And if he were really so clever, he probably realized that I was his stepfather. But it could have turned out differently. You remember what times they were. The rats had begun to sink their teeth into each another. And if a husband was arrested, they had to send the wife to a camp. As for the children, maybe it was to my son's or daughter's advantage to take on a stranger's paternity right away. Is Olga Varfolomeevna still alive, I wonder? She kept out of sight. I didn't know what to do with myself. At the risk of setting off a terrible scandal, I flatly refused to go to pioneer camp. I hung around the empty yard and basked in the sun on the roof which I could reach by the fireman's ladder. I kept thinking of Olga. I didn't know if she was in the city. I couldn't bear it and set out for her place. I remember so well how I climbed the stairs, not knowing what I would say to her and to Pike, if he happened to be home. The neighbor opened the door. It was on a latch. Usually I was let in without a word. This time the old woman asked, 'Who do you want?' 'Yura,' I said. 'There's no Yura here,' she replied and was about to shut the door. 'I'm looking for the Kishchuks,' I said. 'There's no Kishchuks here. They went away.' 'To the dacha?' I asked. 'They're gone for good. And there's no point in your parking yourself here.' 'Wait a minute,' I burst out. 'What do you mean "for good"? What's this "for good"? Where did they go?' 'How should I know?' she answered. 'They gave them a new apartment. Now go away. You've got no more business here.'

"I remembered suddenly that I should have asked where this apartment was. I ran up the stairs and, without hope, kept ringing. The old woman came again. 'How should I know,' she said and slammed the door.

"So... she had run away in the grip of fear. I stood in the stairwell in an empty reverie. She had run away, that was clear. She had not stopped loving me, but fear turned out to be stronger than love, stronger than everything that bound us, that gave meaning to our lives. By comparison nothing else had any importance. Seduction of a minor or whatever they call it. Stupid, senseless words. A triumphant exposure. So what of it? I'd stake my life in any court that there was absolutely no seduction. But there was fear. A husband–a werewolf–here and not here, who wears civilian clothes in some photos and in others a Red army belt and a medal in a buttonhole, unremarkable and omnipotent. A new apartment, well, that's probably true. They all had a right to separate apartments in private houses. Maybe he already had two medals by now. The apartment isn't the problem but the fact that people are governed by fear, that much I understood. The one who instills fear has the power. You don't even have to show this power. Not once did I see her husband; he didn't interest me. Maybe he really didn't know anything; probably not. The main thing is that the power of fear existed everywhere; it's just that I didn't know about it.

"I walked down the staircase, step by step and came out of the entrance. It was a glorious day. I felt that everything on earth disgusted me. She had disappeared. She had abandoned me as one kicks off in flight a shoe that gets in the way. I decided to think everything over coolly. It took me a few days. I don't remember if I told you that on both sides of the gate were two dark passageways that led into the yard. Through one of them you could get down into the basement. You had to descend a short, narrow staircase and go through a door, behind which, in a tiny dark corner, was a broken ceramic toilet seat over which hung a message scribbled by the janitor for the tenants. I remember one sentence: There are no lackeys looking after you. It was obvious that indeed there weren't any more lackeys; everything was stuffed with garbage. Further along was a dark corridor and beyond that the former boiler–room which fell into disuse when the house was connected to central heating. The corridor and the room in which a piece of cable hung from the ceiling were the place of secret adventures of our lost childhood. Waiting until it got dark, I went down into the catacombs with a pocket flashlight. From the underground room it was possible to get to a manhole in a corner of the yard. I didn't begin to investigate this second corridor, and that led to the failure of my enterprise.

"Everything was prepared: a box that was rickety but suited to my purposes, rope and soap. I was skilled in making a sailor's knot. I tied the rope to the piece of cable and wound it around the insulator for security. A note lay in my pocket; I made use of certain expressions I had found in books. Of course there wasn't even the slightest mention of Olga. I had anticipated everything except one circumstance. I forgot that the basement served now and then as a flophouse for drifters. The janitor was waging a war against them with variable success. This time a beggar had settled himself in the corridor leading to the pothole. He was an elderly, refined man. I would meet him now and them on our street. He extracted me from the noose.

"Somewhere I copied out a sentence from an Egyptian papyrus. 'Those whose names are pronounced are still alive.' It's true: a name possesses magic power. To lose a name is the same as to die. I cannot reveal to you the name Olga Varfolomeevna called me. This name has remained there, in Russia, just as I myself, at heart, have remained there, and the person you've been listening to–is another man."

In response were heard enthusiastic cries: an exceptional cake had been brought in and attentions turned to tea.

Translated by Sylvia Maizell

Liubka

Dina Rubina

Liubka's legs were smooth, provocative, and seemingly powerful, even though a tattooed "They're tired" shone blue on each of her feet along the toes. Just look at her–sunken cheeks, bony shoulders, stomach as if frozen to the back, but those legs–weird–Psyche's couldn't hold a candle to them!

"Get dressed, please," said Irina Mikhailovna and, watching the shivering girl fumble hurriedly with the straps of her tank top, became thoughtful.

The heartrending tattoo did not unsettle Irina Mikhailovna. She had worked in the factory's infirmary for two years, had seen all kinds of things in that time, and understood that a person's childhood and youth do not always unfold on trim lawns. Liubka behaved modestly, looked decent, and curved her toes shyly during the exam.

While she was getting dressed, awkwardly twisting the sleeves of her flimsy green sweater this way and that, Irina Mikhailovna waited, then called her into the hall.

"Listen, Liuba...," she said, looking into the girl's face. "You can't imagine what hard work it is being a metal skinner. In a month you won't recognize your hands. They'll be completely covered with welts and burns."

Liubka watchfully held her tongue, trying to figure out what the hell else the caring doctor wanted from her.

"Won't you work as a nanny for me? I have a child, eight months old. There's no one to help out. My situation's pretty difficult...And I'll pay you sixty rubles."

The doctor looked like a well–bred girl from an educated family. Plain, freckled. It wasn't that her nose was so large, but it stuck out as if to say: It's me; it's me you see first. And the entire face fashioned to reach out to another human being with enormous attention. Soft, full lips, sad, apologetic eyes. The letters "I.M.Z." were cozily embroidered in blue silk on the pocket of the whitest of coats.

So, lady doctor... You want a nanny, maybe, why not.

Liubka wrinkled her forehead like an accordion and said:

"I'll think it over. Get your address down."

Two or three little streets of two–story houses around the market square, a post office, five shops in shacks cobbled together with plain boards, and a couple of dozen barracks—this little town had glued itself to the metallurgical plant and was its direct outcome. The small infirmary where Irina Mikhailovna was placed after graduation also belonged to the plant.

It was September of 1951, and harsh stifling winds scoured each little side street with flying sand.

Actually, had she submitted the certificate of pregnancy in time, she could have been placed more advantageously after graduation. But her mother–and she was a decisive and commanding person–said to her careless daughter: "How can you not understand, Irina? Right now the provinces are our only salvation. It's OK. Grab your belly and let's go."

By that time it had been two years since a grey, silk suited, faceless man in the window at the prison office informed them that her father had been transferred to another camp with no rights to correspondence. Parcels were not accepted. Her mother had long been fired from the hospital where she headed the department of neurology, and they had been living on Irina's stipend. Therefore, Irina's future salary seemed to be their only reliance for survival.

So, they "grabbed her belly" and arrived at the "site of placement." They were given a room in a brick house–a decent enough space of about a dozen square meters in an apartment with one neighbor; and the kitchen was large. There was even a bathroom with a heater. What else would you want! Everything was just fine, fine. Irina Mikhailovna worked for three months and then went on maternity leave. Sonechka was born in that very same infirmary. But why and how, and whose child she was–that was nobody's business. A strictly private matter.

Most important, nothing was frightening with her mother around. She knew how to do everything–to turn a coat, to bargain at the market, make a borscht out of nothing, sew diapers from a torn duvet cover–perhaps that's why she graduated at one time from the Sorbonne. In short, Irina Mikhailovna had grown up fully convinced that her tough mother would not let her down.

But her mother did let her down. She died just like that. One moment she was standing in front of a window with a five–month old Sonechka in her arms, then suddenly said calmly: "I'm not feeling so well, Irina, why don't you get me some water," had time to lower the child into the carriage, and—her mother was never sick–fell flat on her back.

When, spilling the water, Irina Mikhailovna ran back from the kitchen with a glass in her hand, her mother was lying on the floor and no longer breathing. For a long time the qualified physician Irina Mikhailovna crawled around her mother like a bear cub around its dead mother, filling the apartment with her howling, attempting artificial respiration, and not understanding why her mother did not have a pulse or any other sign of life.

So that's how it was... After the funeral at a sandy, half–empty cemetery (Mama, where is the Sorbonne, where is my father, where do I look for you now?) –after the funeral, Irina Mikhailovna, numb with grief, had to make a decision about Sonechka. True, the factory offered daycare, but the hell with the daycare. Nobody with a heart would send a child there.

Then her neighbor Kondakova offered her services. She worked as a telephone operator at the post office, was on duty every two days, and was ready to babysit. It was not cheap, because only fools babysit for nothing. But there was no other way. When Kondakova worked, Irina Mikhailovna brought Sonechka to the infirmary, and she crawled around the interns' room all by herself, getting into corners and innocently leaving puddles in her wake.

Yes, she had to make a decision about Sonechka. And beside that, Irina Mikhailovna didn't have a moment to do anything around the house. She cooked cereal for Sonechka after work, but there was no time left to think about herself. She washed a thing or two but there was no strength to tidy up. The house became neglected, dust balls gathered under the wardrobe. Mama, mama...

In short, someone was needed at home. And where in this hick town could you find someone?

Year after year the factory swallowed, ground, digested hundreds of inmates from a nearby camp, Japanese POWs, and, of course, civilian workers.

Liubka was a civilian.

She showed up that evening in the same faded sweater–no suitcase, no bundles. She exuded proud homelessness. Leaning her shoulder against the wall in the corridor, she said:

"Today I won't come close to the child. I'll sleep here in the hallway. Just throw down any old blanket on the floor for me."

Surprised, Irina Mikhailovna obeyed. As became clear later, Liubka could distribute the intonation in a phrase in a way that made any questions or clarifications superfluous. She also made a light, dismissive gesture with her hand, as if implying that words were not needed.

Next morning, on Sunday, Liubka got up early, asked for kerosene, and, locking herself in the bathroom, washed for about three hours.

"Getting rid of the lice, is she," gloated Kondakova.

Nanny's income was slipping out of her hands, and Kondakova was extremely miffed about it. She was standing by her kerosene stove, energetically stirring boiled fruit, waiting for events to unfold. Kondakova was a middle–aged bride–in–waiting, with round eyes the color of milky fog, plucked eye brows that looked like bared chicken butt, on which every morning she drew, moistening a brown pencil with her saliva, two sharp, short little arcs wide apart.

Finally Liubka emerged, naked and steaming, asked for clean clothes, and, while Irina Mikhailovna rummaged around trying to find something suitable in her scant wardrobe, Liubka, wrapped tight in a towel, played casually with Sonechka in the kitchen. Kondakova, pretending to be stirring the boiled fruit, kept glancing at Liubka's bare legs of marble beauty, trying to decipher the tattoo. Since it was hard to do, Kondakova screwed up her eyes and lowered her head to the floor. When, dying of curiosity, she twisted herself into a pretzel, Liubka suddenly raised her leg and stuck her foot in Kondakova's face.

"Here, squinty–eyed, read it," she said in a threatening voice, her lip curling. Kondakova grabbed her saucepan and whisked herself away into her room where she hid until the evening.

Liubka, in the meantime, attired in a wrinkled plaid dress made at one time by the best Tashkent seamstress for a prom, took a while puttering around the stove, energetically turning her decrepit sweater in the fire stove with a poker.

"You know what, doctor," said Liubka, narrowing her eyes affectionately in the dancing flames of the fire, "Don't give me my money. Put it away somewhere…so I don't know where it is."

She quickly took upon herself all of the household chores. She scrubbed, did the laundry, boiled, cooked, looked after the little one–losing herself in her work. The simple folk have a phrase for it: "work your tail off." Irina Mikhailovna worried, tried to restrain her—no way! Simply, when Irina Mikhailovna came back home from the infirmary, the house was tidy, dinner ready and wrapped in her mother's old shawl, the child fed and quieted. Just in two or three days Irina Mikhailovna's life acquired an aura of warm and nurturing domesticity, as if her mother had come back, and this feeling caused her heart to whimper faintly at night.

About two weeks later, with Liubka's passport in hand, she went to the local police station to register a housekeeper.

Major Stepan Semenych looked inside the passport, leaned back abruptly, and did not even say anything at first, just kept shaking Liubka's open passport in front of Irina Mikhailovna.

"Irina Mikhailovna! What are you doing?" The major finally shouted. "She is a gang leader, you know, recently got out after serving her time!"

And he threw the passport on the table.

"And what if she robs you clean?" Irina Mikhailovna sat down, looked at the major, turned Liubka's rather ordinary looking passport in her hands, and thought about her mother. Mama, a strong person, always said: "To hell with conventions!" In a girlish gesture Irina Mikhailovna straightened her skirt over her knees, delicately pushed Liubka's passport toward the major with her finger and said guiltily: "If she robs me, I'll come to you".

On her way home she was torturing herself thinking how to behave around Liubka. Should I say cheerfully: everything's OK, Liuba, I trust you? Ugh, how phony! The main thing is not to show how scary it is to fall asleep in the same room with a gang leader.

Irina Mikhailovna took her coat off in the hall, snuck up to her door on tiptoe and opened it a little. Someone was singing in the room, quietly, mournfully. Liubka was sitting in the dark, with her back to the door, rhythmically rocking the baby carriage. A narrow beam of light from the hall slashed her between the shoulder blades and fell to her feet. The carriage creaked and crackled–the basket had been woven out of willow twigs by a Japanese POW, Taketori, whom Irina Mikhailovna had nursed after a case of peritonitis. In a misty, throaty voice Liubka softly spun a strange lullaby, adjusting its rhythm to the creaking and crackling:

A stranger pro–o–o–mised
Cloth for my mo–om–my.
He's a ch–ea–ea–t, your mommy'll weeeep,
Now sleep, my baby, sleeeep.

Irina Mikhailovna closed the door and, still on tiptoe for some reason, went into the kitchen. There at her table sat Kondakova, gloomily washing down a lump of yellow Uzbek sugar with tea from a bowl.

"She's squeezed me out of my own kitchen!" she complained to Irina Mikhailovna, sucking her tea in a long and noisy slurp. "Fries and bakes all day long, like for some restaurant. A hog. A bandit!"

Irina Mikhailovna thought wearily that, for once, Kondakova was very close to the truth. She removed the warming shawl from the saucepan, took off the cover and stood still, blissfully inhaling the aroma of hot pea soup.

Neither one of them said a word. It was as if Liubka's life story began in the infirmary. Still, Liubka did not look like a person who hid her past.

"You, Rinmikhalna, shouldn't keep your money in the wardrobe between the sheets," she advised once. "You can't be so trusting."

Irina Mikhailovna became confused, blushed, then felt indignant: was Liubka poking around her things?

"I didn't poke around," added Liubka as if reading her mind. "I noticed when you lent money to Kondakova. A wardrobe and sheets, that's the first place a burglar would look."

"But I don't have any money, Liuba!"

"An even better reason," she replied sternly.

Gradually it became clear that Liubka generally understood life better than Irina Mikhailovna, and was much sharper when it came to money: she knew when and what to spend on, and when to hold on to it. Naturally, it was much more profitable to send Liubka to the market.

Once she arrived home all out of breath and threw a sack of potatoes down in the hall.

"Rinmikhalna! Hand me 80 rubles, quick! A little old woman is selling two chairs! To die for! Belonged to a count! Bentwood, varnished! I bargained for an hour."

"Liuba, we just have a hundred left until pay day..."

"Don't be stingy, we'll come up with something!"

And the chairs were indeed a wonder from pre–Revolutionary life—upholstered in smooth silk, pastel colored flowers curling around a lilac background, a piece of some precious set, who knows by what fate brought to this godforsaken Asian town. Now the chairs stood on both sides of a round table with scuffed elephant legs, their upholstery innocently exuding a lilac fragrance and suggestive of two maids of the court who happened to find themselves by chance at a grimy wayside inn.

It took Liubka one night to make covers for them; every day she polished the elegant bent legs with a special cloth and called the chairs nothing else but "furniture." "What furniture," she exclaimed tenderly." And for nothing, for nothing!"

Relieved, Irina Mikhailovna now handed her pay to Liubka, as she used to do with her mother. She no longer had to sort and calculate, and then to be forced to pull out the last 30 rubles. Now it was Liubka who did the budget. Exhilarated, she would sit at the end of a chair, fanning out Irina Mikhailovna's scant wages in front of her, and, whispering in concentration, would move the bills here and there for a long time, as if in a game of solitaire. And God forbid you distracted her with some innocent question about the soup boiling away on the stove all evening long, for example. She'd bark back:

"Hey, Rinmikhalna! Don't pester me now, for Christ's sake. Can't you see I'm counting! Let it boil, it'll wait, won't it?"

And without fail she'd figure out how to save a dozen or so rubles and would hide them in a fat volume of Gynecology and Midwifery and at the end of the month place them solemnly in front of Irina Mikhailovna, saying, "We're buying curtains."

"Liuba, how about rubber boots instead?"

"Rubber boots next time. Now it's curtains. We've been living like naked, people can see everything."

Once toward evening she went to the store and disappeared for about three hours. Worried, Irina Mikhailovna came out onto the porch with Sonechka in her arms and stood there peering at the end of the side street. Finally, Liubka emerged out of deep shadows at the corner—light, cheerful, terribly pleased about something. In each hand she held an Uzbek galosh with a turned up point.

"Liuba!"

"Check this out! Twenty kopecks a pair!" Swimming out of darkness onto the porch, Liubka pushed a glossy galosh in Irina Mikhailovna's face.

"What's this? Why?"

"What do you mean, why? Here! Twenty kopecks a pair! An old Uzbek was selling them. He was real sneaky. Get this–threw all of them together in a pile; looks like they are all mismatched, rejects of some kind. It was like a huge mountain. If you wanted a pair, you had to crawl around and pick. But it's only twenty kopecks."

"So?"

"So what? I spent three hours up to my neck in all those galoshes. There were also some old women swarming all over them there, but nobody but me could pick a pair," she lined up the soles of the galoshes, knocking them together with glee. "See, almost the same!"

"Liuba, but why do we need galoshes?" Irina Mikhailovna asked in confusion, and something in her face seemed to mute Liubka's bright joy. She became thoughtful for a moment, trying to explain the reasons for her delight, and finally said with conviction:

"Well, Rinmikhalna! Twenty kopecks a pair! I couldn't let it go!"

The coat buying was another notable event. Since Liubka arrived at Irina Mikhailovna almost in her birthday suit and their height and size were similar, many of Irina Mikhailovna's clothes naturally passed on to Liubka. There were now gaps in her wardrobe. Some things they could take turns wearing, but the cold weather was approaching, it was October, and they could not manage without an overcoat; even a light one would do.

Liubka had been inserting their savings in Gynecology and Midwifery for two months and was wearily waiting for Irina Mikhailovna's pay day. Finally, she announced dryly that perhaps the time had come to look for an overcoat. Here Kondakova's nutria fur coat made an appearance. That is not to say that the fur coat had been completely unknown. It had been seen at the post office and around town–a decent coat with reddish streaks. Up until then Kondakova did not seem to want to sell it, but here, suddenly, she did, and not for much money.

Irina Mikhailovna tried it on, looked at herself in the long mirror in Kondakova's armoire; it seemed awkward to think too long about it, and she decided to buy. But when she was ready to count out the money, Liubka burst in, back from her regular visit to the Sunday market.

"Liuba, look, we're buying a fur coat from Ekaterina Fyodorovna," Irina Mikhailovna informed her, "really cheap."

After dumping her bags in the hall, Liubka wiped her hands, and entered Kondakova's room with determination. Wordlessly she pulled the coat off of Irina Mikhailovna's shoulders, spread it in her arms, felt it, and blew on the fur.

"And you, Irina Mikhailovna, always ask your help permission to buy something nowadays?" Kondakova inquired spitefully.

Liubka raised her eyebrows silently, continuing to look over the coat. It's just ridiculous, that's what it is," Kondakova added in a more subdued tone.

Swiftly Liubka pinched a handful of fur, tugged lightly, a patch opened up under her fingers, and long hairs fell sadly on the floor. Another tug and another patch, and yet another.

Kondakova yelped furiously and rushed toward Liubka. But Liubka, nimbly and as if by accident, stuck out her elbow, and Kondakova, having met the steely obstacle, made a whooshing noise and plopped down heavily on her bed.

Lyubka didn't even honor her with a look.

"For God's sake, Rinmikhalna, you're like a child!" Lyubka said with pity, annoyance, and a strange kind of affection in her voice. "You let any scum con you. This fur coat used to be a fur coat, for sure. But now it's good only for some damned wake or for covering a dinner pot to keep the food warm."

She sighed, threw the coat over the head of the deflated Kondakova, and left the room.

"OK now," she said, gently plucking a thin wad of hundred ruble bills out of Irina Mikhailovna's hands. "Dinner is under the shawl. Stuffed cabbage and borscht."

"I'll sue!" Hysterical wailing was coming from Kondakova's room. "According to the law. Destruction of personal property!"

Liubka coolly wrapped her head in a scarf:

"The laundry is soaking. Let it stay until tonight."

She got back late, like a general who's won a brilliant victory, a tired general covered with trophies.

"Here you are," said Liubka with satisfaction, untying a knot on a bundle fashioned from a flowery faded rag. "It's not a fur coat, of course, but it looks good enough," and she pulled out a dark blue woolen coat lined with light blue satin and a glistening buttery collar made of lamb fur on top–a coat of unthinkable elegance. "Brand new. Try it on."

Irina Mikhailovna threw up her hands, draped the coat over her dressing gown, and fastened the buttons with fumbling fingers. The coat fit like something of her own, something from the past, made just for you, worn on your shoulders and warmed by your body. Liubka was crawling around on her knees, straightening the bottom of the coat. Irina Mikhailovna examined the sleeves, the hem. No price tag was visible. Suddenly a terrible idea occurred to her.

"Liuba," she cried, her eyes rounding in horror. "Where is this from?"

Liubka looked up at her rather coolly, and smiled a bitter little smile.

"What do you think, Irina Mikhailovna? That I would bring cops to your house? I'd rather...!" She suddenly stopped and calmed herself. "Don't be afraid, wear it. It's honest goods. An inmate's wife came to see him from Leningrad, she's renting from Auntie Raya. She's here, but he's a goner. So she started getting rid of things. Sold her ring, earrings, now a coat. I didn't bargain with her, gave her everything she asked for, down to the last kopeck." She shook herself. "But it's worth it! Just look at the lamb collar, the color just sparkles!"

The fall passed quietly, imperceptibly. Liubka was still intimidating but fair in her squabbles with Kondakova. During that fall Liubka softened up, ate her fill, straightened her shoulders, now plumped out with a velvety warmth, and it became apparent that her oval face was naturally round, her chin sharp, her lips mocking and that she was actually a very young girl. Perhaps only the gaze of her grey eyes, sober to the point of cruelty, did not allow anyone to suspect Liubka of innocent intentions.

That fall the baby began to walk all of a sudden, prying her fingers from the willow twigs of the carriage, stumbling on her round legs, quietly happy about her discovery. Now she followed Liubka in and out of the kitchen, sometimes plopping down on the floor and working hard and long to get up from her knees. That fall she started talking as well.

"Bi–i–i–tch," she informed her amazed mother, singing out the vowel.

"True, my darling," Liubka responded forcefully, "the bitch Kondakova."

"Shi–i–i–t," added the baby, and in her tenderly lisping, childish transcription this word sounded vaguely Spanish, romantic and sonorous, perhaps suitable for naming a ship.

With surprise Irina Mikhailovna realized suddenly that at night during dinner she would recount her entire day–hour by hour–to Liubka. Liubka would listen glumly, occasionally breaking in with odd little observations.

"...and Moseltsova walks by and says casually, well, she is an elegant woman, that's her main feature, and she says: 'How can you, Irina Mikhailovna, send somebody else's patient to surgery without his physician's approval?' 'Allow me to disagree, Zinaida Nikolaevna,' I say. 'You had a little boy with acute stomach pains waiting for three days... Just ask Perechnikov, I say, during surgery his appendix just disintegrated in our hands."

"You can forget about Perechnikov," Liubka interrupted her suddenly. "She's sleeping with him."

"Who?" Irina Mikhailovna asked taken aback, dropping her spoon in the soup bowl.

"Who else, but that frizzy–haired whore, Moseltsova."

"Oh, Liuba, where did you get that from? On the other hand, it's true there have been rumors."

Medical terms started peppering Liubka's speech, carefully and painstakingly articulated.

"I'm walking today, and they have this cotton fabric for sale, sky blue, to die for! Even my pulse rate was rapid from it–will there be enough or not? With that line crawling along I thought I'd die from tachycardia."

In the fall Sonechka got sick with pneumonia. Liubka blamed herself personally and would jump up at night to make sure the little girl was breathing. When Irina Mikhailovna gave her daughter injections, Liubka rushed around the room, accompanied by Sonechka's ear–splitting howls. And one time she said to Kondakova firmly and politely:

"The child has pneumonia. I respectfully ask you to refrain from smoking. Or I'll beat your face in."

On one of those days, Irina Mikhailovna was delayed at the office and was late for the evening injection. Having opened the door, Liubka calmly noted;

"Why are you so out of breath, Rinmikhalna? I've done it already. "

"What have you done?" Irina Mikhailvona stood motionless with one shoe off.

"What do you mean 'what', the injection! Why are you standing there staring? I did it right: sterilized like you do, twisted the ampoule open with a cotton ball over the top, and did not touch the needle. She didn't even cry." And not without pride she added: "And when you do it, by the way, she always cries."

As usual the work load got heavy in the winter–frostbite, flu epidemic. The infirmary was packed; they were even lying in the hallways.

A harsh, gritty wind scrubbed your face until it turned into red pulp, shook the prickly branches, coniferous from the hoar frost. In the morning the roofs reflected an aluminum tint.

One longed for snow–deep, quiet snow. But January was passing by empty, dry and cold.

In the morning before the rounds, nurse Lena–already past her prime, with pouchy cheeks, elbows and knees, always alert and scared, relentlessly clipping information on foreign policy for their newsletter–asked in a vibrating whisper: "Irina Mikhailovna! Have you read Pravda"?

And right away Irina Mikhailovna got queasy and her stomach

spasmed in sharp fear. She first experienced this gut–twisting kind of fear when she was fifteen, on the night they took her father–the head of the military hospital, a surgeon, a general—simply her daddy.

"They exposed a gang, doctors' conspiracy," Lena whispered, glancing back at the door of the interns' room. You really haven't read Pravda? The article is called 'Murderers in White Coats'...Poisoners..."

"They bring 'Pravda' to the house in the evening," said Irina Mikhailovna white–lipped. Her stomach felt achy and empty; how could this emptiness ache so much? "And the names?"

"Foreign!" Lena informed her animatedly, looked at Irina Mikhailovna and hesitated. "Actually, Perechnikov already called for a general meeting of the entire staff at three."

Such meetings were usually conducted by Perechnikov apathetically, without any civic zeal. But this was a special case. This was a professional, white–coated horror, rustling over the heads of the infirmary's small staff. Medical assistant Kolya Rozhkov was sitting next to Irina Mikhailovna. His wife was about to give birth–she had stayed in the maternity ward for two days already. Her water had broken, and now–this meeting. Kolya was sitting with a stony face and kept hitting his jumping knee in a rapid beat with the rolled up copy of Pravda. Irina Mikhailovna wanted to ask Kolya for the newspaper, but something stopped her. Later they read the article out loud anyway.

The article was read by the head of the local committee, Moseltsova, a pediatrician, a striking bushy blond. It seemed hard to believe that she was having an affair with chief medical officer Perechnikov. Perechnikov was a stooped, boring man with an absurd face that looked like a narrow pant leg—puffy cheeks that came together to form a long chin.

Moseltsova read dramatically and with fire. An intonational exclamation mark punctuated each of the murdering doctors' names, followed by a small but significant pause. And then it seemed to Irina Mikhailovna that everybody looked her way.

In conclusion, Perechnikov mumbled the usual in a dull voice—about the escalating class struggle, about alertness on the part of every aware citizen, about a doctor's professional duty. The moment he finished, Kolya dropped the newspaper on the floor and, pushing everybody out of his way, dashed into the maternity ward.

Irina Mikhailovna waited until the conference room (a small room filled with lacquered chairs bolted together in rows) emptied out, picked up Pravda off the floor, and ran her eyes frantically over the pages. Here it was– "Murderers in White Coats" –her heart thrashed about in the murky depths of fear. "Is there something you don't understand, Irina Mikhailovna?"

Moseltsova was standing in the doorway. She was applying lipstick and admiring herself in a small mirror.

Moseltsova was exquisite–a head of golden hair tilted archly with a spectacular hairdo, a rather full but firm bosom. Exquisite.

She rubbed her lower lip against the upper, puckered her mouth, and her expression became endearing, artless, as a child's. "It seemed t' me–a quick move of the tongue–that my reading was intelligible, right?"

Forcing herself to look silently at the page quivering in her hands for a few moments longer, Irina Mikhailovna finally folded it and stuffed it in the pocket of her coat.

"Yes, she said, you were very convincing."

Moseltsova smiled, almost affably.

"Perhaps a name appeared familiar? I gather, if I am not mistaken, that your family is from Moscow, all physicians?"

Irina Mikhailovna turned her pale attentive face toward Moseltsova. This accursed, inborn remorseful expression of the eyes! How can she make herself inscrutable? Mother could squash people like Moseltsova with one word.

"You are not mistaken," Irina Mikhailovna said quietly. "But for the last twenty years or so my family has been living in Tashkent."

She passed Moseltsova in the doorway, who said to her back in parting: "Too bad you don't use lipstick. It could give you some color."

When Irina Mikhailovna was walking home the wind suddenly died down and it started to snow. The snowflakes were so quiet, sporadic, and aimless as if accidentally released from some heavenly office; one tried in vain to catch another, another a third, but they did not bind together in a flakey swirl, and it seemed that loneliness and wasted life hovered in the frigid air.

The moment she opened the door of the apartment she heard

Kondakova's triumphant voice coming from the kitchen. One second was enough to recognize the text of that article, adorned as it was by wrong stresses and a complete disregard for punctuation marks.

Irina Mikhailovna stood in the darkness of the hall in her coat and rubber boots, listening to Kondakova's victorious voice, excessively loud in their apartment, and imagined a rather horrible scene: how, having made peace on the basis of their patriotic indignation, Kondakova and Liubka study "Pravda" in the kitchen. It would be something like a house meeting–Kondakova would be reading, and Liubka would listen with her chin on her hands, nodding sadly.

She stood in the darkness of the hall, day–dreaming about her mother and at the same time passionately envious of her mother's ignorance and oblivion. She was cursing herself for giving birth to yet another damned, eternally persecuted soul, yet another outcast. This little soul was probably sleeping in its willow cradle, and for her sake it was necessary to make a step, walk down the hall, take off the coat and boots, and–go on living, live for the sake of this little soul until they pinch together your life with their fingers and rub it away to nothing, like a dusty little clump of dead moth.

Liubka was washing the floor in their room, the hem of her dress tucked in its waist–band and her long, sculpted legs gleaming in the twilight.

"Ah, Rinmikhalna," she murmured distractedly, unbending herself. "Watch where you're going in your boots, it's clean in here. Wait." She placed a stool near the door, and Irina Mikhailovna sat down as if shattered. "Did you hear that in the kitchen? The old whore is giving a lecture to herself. This is the second time. She's screeching for me to hear. I'm just waiting for her to start the third round so I can go and dump her on top of her stove."

She wrung out a rag firmly and threw it at Irina Mikhailovna's feet:

"Here, wipe your boots now."

"Liuba," Irina Mikhailovna said in a frozen voice, so inflexible it was painful to speak. "Liuba…it looks like you will probably have to leave Sonechka and me."

Liubka drew herself up, straightened her skirt with her hands and, squinting unpleasantly, said:

"Really? And where should I go? What did I do wrong? Ah?

Rinmikhalna?"

Irina leaned back, felt the coolness of the wall with the back of her head, and closed her eyes.

"You see, Liuba... Perhaps you didn't know...I am of the same nationality as those doctors...poisoners."

"What the hell do you mean poisoners?" Liubka bellowed. "Are you crazy, Rinmikhalna, or what?"

"Shhh, Liuba, not so loud!"

"Don't you give me this shit, I'm not Kondakova, and I've seen plenty of such 'poisoners' inside!"

"But wait, that's not it!" Irina Mikhailovna frowned in pain. "I am saying that it's not safe for you now to stay with us."

Liubka looked at her for a moment, not comprehending, and then laughed giddily, slapping herself on the knees, cheeks, and stomach.

"For me! Dangerous for me! God help me. You really made me laugh, Rinmikhalna." She was truly amused. "Dangerous for me! So it's not you who's unsafe living with my ex–con's mug, but me... Oh, please. What crap." She could not calm down for a long time.

Kondakova's voice thundered from the kitchen. She was going on the third round.

"She's our new loudspeaker. Very convenient, since ours has been out for two weeks. Lemme go and hang her on the wall, so she can reach the outlet with her asshole."

"Liuba, I beg you!"

But Liubka held the door firmly and politely, not letting Irina Mikhailovna out.

"It's not good for you going in there, Rinmikhalna." Gentle movements, an ingratiating voice, stony cheekbones on her harsh face. "Don't worry, I won't kill the bitch."

She left and shut the door tightly behind her. In a minute, the voice in the kitchen stopped abruptly, and quiet descended—resounding and so absolute that you could hear Sonechka's light snoring from her carriage.

Irina Mikhailovna became scared and opened the door a bit. From the kitchen came some pleasant murmuring.

"...your heart'll drip out of you in your snot." Kondakova squeaked and made a shuffling noise, then a chair was moved sharply, something fell down, someone snorted, and again the words flowed on:

“one more time...one mean look...you’ll be crawling around your own asshole. And if you snitch, my people will get you in your grave.”

The entire monologue, like berries among leaves in a basket, was sprinkled with the choicest, superb, and elaborate swearing, so imaginative that it took your breath away. Irina Mikhailovna never suspected that one could assemble such intricate artful constructions from such primitive elements.

The next morning at rounds Kriukov from the third ward, who had been crushed and mangled by a train carriage, had been dragged by Irina Mikhailovna from the dead, Kriukov who called Irina Mikhailovna “girl doctor,” the one who did not forget to add “God bless her,” the carriage coupler Kriukov announced that from this day on he did not wish to be a guinea pig for spying hirelings. He will not allow injections, or IV, just keep that in mind.

Nurse Lena froze in place with an IV stand and a bottle of saline solution in her hands. All of her little pouches began to tremble—cheeks, elbows, knees...

“Whose guinea pig? Irina Mikhailovna inquired, feeling her throbbing face getting hot. “Whose, Sergei Ivanovich? Hirelings’?”

The ward got ominously silent–fifteen beds with critical and stable patients–looking away. Irina Mikhailovna’s blush slowly left her cheeks. She asked quietly and clearly:

“Who else refuses to be treated by a spying hireling?”

Silence. Only the accountant Drynishchin from the construction office, lying on the cot nearest the door, stirred and piped up:

“So should we wait until you poison us all to hell?”

Irina Mikhailovna left the ward and ran to the interns’ room through the hallway filled with hospital beds, hoping that now, during the rounds when it was empty, she could cry her fill at the sink and wash her face with cold water. But about a dozen steps away she heard voices, both muffled and excited:

“...it is a matter of professional ethics!”

“Cut the sentimental claptrap, what professional ethics!” That was Moseltsova’s voice. “Just you wait, the patients will cook up a document, sign it, and send it to the right place, and here you’re talking professional ethics... The entire collective will suffer because of one black sheep. Do you think the simple folk can be fooled? A typical last name and her looks...rather obvious.”

Irina Mikhailovna turned around and left. An old woman called pitifully from her bed: “Little daughter, little daughter…” but she did not turn around. Afterwards this old woman kept calling for her in her dreams, but Irina Mikhailovna kept ignoring her…

Her overcoat remained in the interns’ room. To hell with the coat. It’s just a ten minute dash to the house.

Their deserted side street was suffused in that rare, warm, calm light of an overcast day often found in a spacious room with high windows (a vague memory of childhood—tall windows of the Moscow apartment). A narrow, extended sky over the street seemed like the gray, long unwashed glass of a huge greenhouse.

And then someone cried desperately behind her back:

Ir–r–ra–a–a!!” The tortured cry cut through her, threw her against the wall of the house in an explosive wave of pain. It was her father’s voice. It was her father who cried out so clearly and in such torment: “Ira!”

Her knees trembled slightly; sweat ran down her icy back. Incapable of swallowing air with her paralyzed open mouth, she looked back. Three workers in black quilted jackets were repairing the house on the corner. The one on the ground bellowed once more:

“Hi–i–i–gher!” And those working on the roof grabbed the steel cables in their hands and dragged a bucket up.

Irina Mikhailovna stood, her legs giving way, for another moment, and then finally shuffled home.

Liubka opened the door, saw her, and gasped:

“They pinched the coat!?”

Irina Mikhailovna shook her head and wanted to say something, but all of a sudden Liubka was tilting together with the floor, trembling like jellied meat, and, with her eyes rolling up in her head in a faint, Irina Mikhailovna crashed on top of Liubka with her numb body.

That evening she spent lying down, lovingly arranged under two heavy blankets with her mother’s old coat on top, shivering and listening to the wind outside the window shake the clothesline and make the clothes pins crackle like castanets. Perhaps that’s why she did not immediately discern a knock on the window, quiet and discreet. She jumped up, rushed to the window and saw Perechnikov stomping his feet on the snowy ground and saying something through the glass. She pushed the little window open and heard: "May I have a few words with you? "

Perechnikov had probably been standing there for about ten minutes already, because the fragile layer of dry snow had been trampled to blackness. A long string bag with large holes and a blue bundle inside was hanging from his elbow. Irina Mikhailovna threw her mother's shawl over her shoulders and hurriedly circled the building:

"Fyodor Nikolaevich, what's the matter?"

"Nothing, don't be afraid," he muttered, tossing away a cigarette butt. "Don't be afraid. You left your coat behind today, and I brought it, because it's cold...and...Here, I need to talk to you about something. Damn, don't even know where to begin.

"Why don't you come inside?"

"Oh, no!" He shook himself, raised the collar of his coat. "And, I beg you, my dear, don't mention this conversation to a friend, your in–laws, or a neighbor's chicken."

Under a warm winter hat with flaps his face looked utterly absurd, his puffed out cheeks crimson from the frost, his nose sniffling anxiously. He kept looking at a trash pile near the fence where cats were chasing each other like blue shadows.

"You have such a light coat. Please put it on, for God's sake! I don't want to keep you out in the cold too long, I might as well..." He pulled out his handkerchief and rubbed his nose with it. "You still have a little over a year left to serve on your placement contract, right? So why don't we, Irina Mikhailovna, invent some respectable health condition and quietly and peacefully let you leave this godforsaken place for Tashkent, our capital."

Irina Mikhailovna looked at Perechnikov, saw his red, frozen hand crumpling the handkerchief. He came here in secret, called her to the garbage pile for "a few words." Is he feeling sorry for her?

She put on her wrinkled coat and said:

"You see, Fyodor Nikolaevich, there is no reason for me to go to Tashkent whatsoever. I don't have a soul there besides an aunt who's infirm. And you know perfectly well that nobody will hire me now. You are not naïve, and you must understand that in Tashkent they're really out for blood, much worse than here. And often it's easier to survive in a godforsaken place than in capitals. I am grateful to you for your desire to spare me the scandal. I understand that a person with my last name is extremely inconvenient to you now."

"Irina Mikhailovna, my dear," Perechnikov almost groaned, "I beg you, please don't talk nonsense! No need to insult me. As you see, I came to you…I have always had…great respect…in my opinion, you're an excellent diagnostician, this is God's gift, you know. But what can we do if the times are like these!" He was mumbling, holding on to her arm with his hard, cold hand. "They came, pushed themselves into my office. A collective petition, you see. And I'm obliged to respond…sort it all out. And, perhaps, even inform certain organizations. Moseltsova was mouthing such rubbish. That you have openly expressed your sympathy for the Crimean Tatars. It's nauseating, but I'm obliged to…my position requires…"

"And they said he was having an affair with Moseltsova," Irina Mikhailovna thought idly. "Why Tatars? It seems that the Japanese are more convenient, makes more sense. A Tatar spy–haven't heard anything like this before."

"Do not ignore the danger, Irina Mikhailovna. Do not… you know that I must fire you at the very least!"

"Fire me. I don't have anywhere to run," she said.

Perechnikov kept talking for another five minutes, sounding guilty and persistent at the same time; yet when he realized that she was not listening to him and when he looked into her eyes, which astonished him suddenly with their universal, infinite anguish, he waved his hand and moved to leave. But then, after walking just a few steps, he was back suddenly, asking softly:

"Will you clean for Ismailov at their construction office? I will try to put it together."

"I will," she said indifferently.

Perechnikov dragged his left leg a bit as if pulling a heavy cannon ball made of a dark shadow. Irina Mikhailovna watched him drag his reduced shadow across the snow and could not understand what it was that she found so ludicrous in this man before.

After returning to the house, she was silent for a long time, listening to the now familiar lullaby, half–sung, half–murmured by Liubka. Then she said thoughtfully:

"If something happens to me, Liuba, take Sonechka to Tashkent, to my aunt. I will write down an address for you."

A stranger pro–o–o–mised
Cloth for my mo–ommy

"Forget it, I won't cart the baby devil knows where," Liubka mumbled to herself. "I'll manage somehow… am not a cripple."

He's a ch–ea–ea–t, your mommy'll weeeep,
Now sleep, my baby, sleeeep.

That night, from her bed thrown together in the corner, Liubka whispered, in bits and pieces, the details of her life. The final barrier between them, created by their upbringing, education and life, fell apart. One pariah opened up to another.

Liubka remembered her real parents only vaguely, dimly, like in an old amateur photo; she knew only that her family was penalized as kulaks and exiled to Siberia, that on the way, two of her older brothers died from starvation and that her desperate mother gave the two–year old Liubka away to a couple of professional thieves at a Semipalatinsk train station. The childless Kat'ka was attracted to the blue–eyed little girl with translucent skin, and, in exchange for her, they bestowed upon the exiles a loaf of bread, three herrings, a head of garlic, and a large piece of soap.

Liubka was saved and at the same time doomed.

Just six months later she could expertly climb into small narrow windows, scurry around train stations ("Auntie, I'm lost, I need to go to the bathroom," while the compassionate woman's bags and suitcases changed hands behind her back), beg on trains, pretending to be an orphan, etc. In all fairness, both the aging Kat'ka and the virtuoso burglar Spike loved the little girl in their own way, did not abuse her (didn't lay a finger on her, Liubka clarified with pride) and at times, having realized that something was amiss, would even send her to school. But Liubka was growing up to be fierce; nobody could order her around or lord it over her, and, at fifteen, she could yell at the kind alcoholic Spike, or tell Kat'ka to go shove it.

So, when, after a long binge, Spike had a stroke and, sprawled out and mumbling, was left on Kat'ka's hands to soil himself and die, Liubka, calmly and with authority, took on the "business." And all of them–Ditch, Swig, Kitty Cat and Dusty–obeyed her.

"Because I have the smarts," explained Liubka in a passionate whisper. "I have the entire job planned out in my head, so it's done proper and clean, and what can they do? Rob, push, get stinking drunk and get seven in the slammer. They nabbed me because of these mangy suckers."

When she finally fell silent, Irina Mikhailovna raised herself on her elbow and said into the gathering darkness of the corner where the leader of the gang, Liubka, was lying:

"You're gifted, Liuba, and strong. God willing, we survive this nightmare, we'll go to Tashkent, and I'll set you up in night school. And then–in a nursing program. A girl I went to school with works there. I will make, "she almost blurted out "an honest person," stumbled, blushed in the dark, and said firmly: "a nurse out of you."

Ismailov hired a cleaning lady. Not Irina Mikhailovna, however, but Liubka. When she found out what Irina Mikhailovna planned to do after being fired, she created a real storm at home.

"Push a mop around! "She yelled thunderously in front of the stunned Irina Mikhailovna. "Spread out rags under that frizzy–haired whore's feet!"

"Liuba, it has nothing to do with Moseltsova, it's a construction office, a completely different building."

"I'd rather die than even once let somebody anywhere see you with a bucket!"

Liubka was terrifying, did not listen to any objections and her eyes flashed. The next day she went to Ismailov, got everything settled right away, and joined the staff of the construction firm.

Now it was Irina Mikhailovna who sat at home, fried potatoes and with an orphan–like impatience waited for Liubka. Stirring the porridge, she sometimes thought with a bitter smile that, overall, it was all very funny and in good company she could, tastefully and with humor, tell a story of how she became Liubka's housekeeper, and a clumsy and useless housekeeper at that. Should she demand a day off from Liubka, some vacation time? Her father knew how to tell such stories, without inventing anything even, just picking certain isolated incidents and bringing them into ridiculously absurd proximity. In a word, the only thing missing was good company.

Twice during these weeks Perechnikov crept out of the darkness in front of the window and silently, skillfully, tossed in crumpled 30–ruble bills, like a ball into a basket. Irina Mikhailovna tried to return them the same way, but Perechnikov, staring goggle–eyed and comically waving her away with his palms, escaped hurriedly, dragging his shrunken black shadow in the snow.

Toward March the thin snow melted, but the cold wind continued to shake the clothes pins outside, bending and breaking the twigs of poplars on the vacant lot. The spring days were bare and drafty–uninviting.

Liubka would come at night exhausted, rush to devour overdone or underdone potatoes, and report in a hushed voice:

"They haven't turned off the radio in two days. The moment they start on a health bulletin, everybody freezes, and it's so quiet, you can hear an eraser rubbing on a piece of paper."

Irina Mikhailovna listened, nervously interlacing her thin, doctor's fingers with short, round nails, and her gaze slid away beyond the window to the vacant lot with the garbage dump.

In one such moment Liubka suddenly stopped chewing and said, looking into her eyes:

"Rinmikhalna! You're always quiet, so quiet. You're a doctor, after all. Tell me, do you think there really is a chance the Boss'll survive? "

Irina Mikhailovna twitched, cast a haunted look at Kondakova's door and, also gazing into Liubka's eyes, whispered distinctly:

"Stop blabbering, Liubov' Nikitichna!"

That day Irina Mikhailovna put Sonechka down for a nap and sat down to mend stockings. Abruptly the door banged open, somebody was running down the hall...Liubka burst into the room. Irina Mikhailovna raised her suddenly dry, sunken, terrified eyes at her. She was silent.

And Liubka was silent too; her fists were clenched, and she was looking straight ahead with an odd expression of inspired hatred, the way a blood avenger probably looks after having murdered the family's worst enemy.

"My God," Irina Mikhailovna whispered.

"Croaked!" Liubka exhaled in a short burst of air.

Irina Mikhailovna tossed the stockings away and started to cry.

Liubka rushed toward her and hugged her fiercely.

"Liuba, be quiet, you really shouldn't say that" Irina Mikhailovna whispered, sobbing. "You mustn't...talk... that way."

"We can, we can!" Liubka repeated, triumphant and ominous. "He croaked, he croaked. The pock–marked dog's kicked the bucket!"

All night long drawn–out sobbing was heard from Kondakova's room. She emerged in the kitchen for a minute to boil water for tea–bloated, old, with smudged eyebrows. Howled a couple of times over the boiling kettle.

"Look at this," said Liubka with some respect, "look how she's taking it. Rinmikhalna, you know what I think? A lot of people all over the country are probably bawling today, just like her.

"A lot," Irina Mikhailovna answered solemnly.

Toward the end of April a warmth pushed in from the desert, the sand dried out from the rain and, spinning around in funnels, the wind plucked quivering, scarlet leaves of poppies off the roofs of little adobe huts. Tiny grey lizards basked in the sun.

Irina Mikhailovna was reinstated at the infirmary, Liubka–in her kitchen.

Toward the end of April Liubka became restless.

On the eve of the 1st of May holiday she was sitting silently by the window, glancing occasionally at the police attaching a flag to the building. Sonechka kept calling for a potty in vain, then peed in her pants in desperation. Liubka changed her distractedly and did not get up from the stool in front of the window until it got dark, staring gloomily at a black sky of fake–diamond stars. In the morning, having combed her hair to the accompaniment of resounding march music, she said:

"Rinmikhalna, give me some cash. I'm going out."

It was said in that familiar tone which left no room for questions or clarifications.

Irina Mikhailovna shrugged her shoulders: where in this little town can Liubka "go out"? But she gave her almost all of the money she had. Have fun, Liubov Nikitichna.

Liubka went out and–disappeared.

A day went by–no Liubka, another day, and another. Irina Mikhailovna could not sit still from worry, but something kept her from going to the police. Liubka would not have approved of that move.

Late at night on the third day (Irina Mikhailovna was already in bed and was even restlessly dozing off) somebody knocked on the door lightly. Recognizing this knocking in her sleep, Irina Mikhailovna jumped up, ran barefoot down the hall, opened the door, and gasped.

Liubka stood in the doorway with a face luminous in the moonlight and haggard from drink in an unbelievably elegant spangled gown that looked like it had just been ripped off the shoulders of a star in a musical comedy. Her low–cut neckline swooped down, coming together in a wedge on her stomach. Her breasts, pushed from the sides, jutted out in the center of her chest like two half moons made of steel.

The Milky Way rose over Liubka's crazy head and collided with eternity. The dark Asian sky, swaying and swirling, was big with innumerable worlds of stars.

Hovering over all of this in her imagination were dramatic modulations of a mezzo–soprano, something out of "Rigoletto." The whole picture seemed an extension of a dream. And in this moon–lit, wavering, cold dream Liubka solemnly bowed low before the stunned Irina Mikhailovna and said in a sonorous and sober voice:

"Irina Mikhailovna! Many thanks for everything. You took care of me, made me warm, didn't lock your cupboards, and addressed me with respect. I will not forget you until I die. But now give me my passport, I'm leaving," and she waved her hand in her special way, as if to say that words were not necessary.

With a heavy heart and feeling that Liubka was lost, Irina Mikhailovna, still moving like a sleep walker, took Liubka's passport from the wardrobe and handed it to her. Liubka kissed the sleeping Sonechka and went outside. On the lower rung of the porch steps she gripped Irina Mikhailovna's shoulders and looked at her for a long time without saying anything, taking her leave. Suddenly they moved toward each other and embraced. Irina Mikhailovna started to cry. Liubka turned around and started off.

"Liuba!" Called Irina Mikhailovna in a tremulous voice. She was shivering violently. "Liubov' Nikitichna!"

Liubka turned around, the spangles of her dress gleaming theatrically in the dark:

"Now you don't have to lock the house at all. My people are keeping an eye on it. And, for Christ's sake, don't go looking for me. Don't dirty yourself with such shitty company."

The dark Asian, swaying and swirling, was big with innumerable worlds of stars. Life went on, not stopping for an instant. The mezzo–soprano who came out of nowhere sadly lamented this life, this darkness, and this town–a bizarre growth on the edge of the desert–and the people who lived here for some reason or other.

Liubka disappeared into the darkness of a warm night. That year she turned twenty three. Her employer was a little younger.

What happened was that Liubka got jailed. The kind major Stepan Semenych somewhat reproachfully told Irina Mikhailovna, who had been completely overwhelmed by the entire affair, that Liubka and her accomplices robbed the Tashkent opera house (there's the reason for a sparkly dress and prophetic mezzo–soprano trills). On top of that they took the restaurant's daily take and made a mess of the props room. They knocked out the guard and, as a parting gesture, dressed the unconscious man as the Sleeping Beauty, then put him in a crystal coffin where he rocked suspended on chains until the arrival of the cops. In other words–a nightmare. "It goes to show you how much you have risked, Irina Mikhailovna. It's horrible to think what danger you put yourself and your child in."

Sonechka had to go to daycare. But Irina Mikhailovna did not stay too long in the little town anyway. She worked for a year and some months according to her contract and then left for Tashkent. Her aunt, who was still alive, took her in and obtained a residency permit for her.

Then Sonechka's father turned up unexpectedly, still bound by obligations to his other family, deeply guilty about his children, but burning with the desire to help everybody, love everybody, and to ease their lives somehow. That very summer he got tickets to Sochi, and Irina Mikhailovna pocketed her pride for the sake of her child, resigned herself to the situation, and took Sonechka to the seashore. They came back tanned, both freckled, both big nosed, happy, and wearing sun–dresses. Irina Mikhailovna acquired a beige Chinese raincoat gathered at the waist, lipstick, a powder–case, and "Red Moscow" perfume. Life gradually took on flavor, meaning, and colors.

Perechnikov, who came to Tashkent for professional development courses, found her about seven years later. By that time Irina Mikhailovna was the head of the department of internal medicine in a large hospital for infectious diseases.

Perechnikov had not changed and once again seemed to her a bit ludicrous, especially when he coughed into his fist: then his cheeks puffed out, and his face resembled a pant leg even more. He talked at length and in great detail about the little town which had grown (you wouldn't recognize it!), about the extended infirmary, their acquaintances. He talked, and it all seemed to Irina Mikhailovna so distant, provincial and alien, as if she did not spend the hardest three years of her life there.

"And you don't even appreciate what role you played in my life," Perechnikov suddenly said, smiling shyly. "You remember Moseltsova, of course? We were ready to sign the marriage papers, and then your affair came up in 1952. How a person can show her true self–I mean Moseltsova. I couldn't look at her after that, she became so disgusting to me. That was it!" He laughed. "After that I didn't dare risk changing my bachelor's lot."

As he was putting on his new Chinese shoes in the entrance hall, Perechnikov suddenly thought of something and pulled out a folded postcard frayed at the edges.

"I almost forgot! Have been carrying this around for almost four years, just so that I'd have an excuse to see you. Here, it came to the infirmary. It's nothing special, just congratulations."

Irina Mikhailovna took the crumpled postcard into her hand and all of a sudden her past moved closer, then flew toward her, and overtook her with the creaking of the willow carriage, the castanet clicking of the clothes pins outside the window, cold winds and:

A stranger pro–o–o–mised
Cloth for my mo–om–my...

"Dear Irina Mikhailovna and Sonechka!" was written in a large and bold hand and surprisingly without any mistakes in grammar. "Our sincere congratulations on Women's Day, we wish you...," and the rest the way it is usually done–health, happiness, everything that a person needs. And then a signature: Liuba and Valentin.

No address, no hint of where to look for her. What a character! All evening long Irina Mikhailovna hung around the house, feeling out of sorts. Finally she started ironing a big pile of laundry that had waited to be done for about two weeks. She moved the heavy iron over the smooth surface of a duvet cover and remembered–the creaking of the willow cradle woven by the Japanese Taketori, two almost identical Uzbek galoshes (twenty kopecks a pair), Kondakova's balding fur coat. She thought about going to visit her mother's grave when Sonechka was out of school. Sonya twice asked her from under the blanket:

"What's wrong, mom?"

"Nothing."

The creaking of the carriage, the black Asian sky stretching over two young girls hugging one another forlornly at the edge of the night on the bottom step of the porch, and—

A stranger pro–o–o–mised
Cloth for my mo–om–my.

What a character! No address, no hint of where to find her.

He's a ch–ea–ea–t, your mommy'l 'll weeeep,
Now sleep, my baby, sleeeep.
Sleep, my baby, sleep...

Translated by Nadya L. Peterson

The Brother's Keeper

Vladimir Makanin

My brother ran away from me at Kursky. The depot then was an ordinary railroad station, not the modern monstrosity of cement and colored tile that it is today. It housed a crowd of people in its lobby and had all the warmth of a truly human space. Benches filled the middle, with people sitting shoulder to shoulder. That's where they slept, yawned, ate–and kept a hand on their suitcases and eyes on the Gypsies. The Gypsies themselves were actually headed somewhere by train, just like everybody else.

Ticket counters stretched out on both sides. My brother and I didn't know which window sold tickets to our hometown, whether we should step to the right or to the left, around all the benches of people sleeping.

The same moment we came to the same conclusion. "You go that way and I'll go the other," my brother said.

"If our window turns out to be on that side, don't wait for me. Get in line right away. Know what I mean?" I said.

"Gotcha," my brother said. "Will do."

We split up. Our window turned out to be on his side, but he himself didn't turn up.

A no show. Just vanished. For a while I kept waiting, thinking he was making his way through the crowd. A few minutes ago I had given him twenty–five rubles.

The money was for his ticket and something to eat, for a twenty–four–hour trip. After he disappeared I tried to guess how many days he could hold out on such a small amount. I decided that if he really tried–three days. Okay, five. Then he'd come back to my apartment. There was no place else.

At home my wife said I was an idiot.

"You shouldn't have left him for one minute." She added, "You needn't have put that money into his hands."

I kept quiet.

"You yourself had to buy him the ticket."

I thought it might happen that the very same day he would realize how wrong he had been. He would come back to us to sleep. But he didn't come.

Next, I went to the dorm at the university where he had taken entrance exams. The truth be told–where he tried but failed to pass the entrance exams. He had missed the cutoff by two points. Then he hooked up with a cute girl, who did get admitted. A real knockout, as he said. She got a passing total score. Even more points than she needed.

Her name was Vika. To me and others the name sounded affected. But, all in all, she was a girl like any other.

"So where's my brother?" I said as I walked into her room, without so much as a "hi." "I don't know."

"You mean you know but you're not telling?"

"I don't know."

She had sky–blue eyes that looked deceitful through and through.

"So you don't know that he ran away from me at Kursky station?"

I took a look inside her closet. My brother wasn't there. Once, between two of the exam sessions when he should have been cramming like mad, I had found him in that same closet. There he had been–standing inside, straight as an arrow with his head slightly bent down.

"So you know, but you're not telling?"

"I don't know."

I didn't have anything against Vika herself and nothing against her blue eyes. It was something else, simple and ordinary.

It was just this. She got admitted and he didn't. Then, naturally, he had to leave Moscow and go back home. Where our mother lived. Where he was supposed to live. He had to leave and get a job there. Or do something. He couldn't just hang out a whole year till the next entrance exams.

But he didn't leave. He was living somewhere in the dorm. Twiddling his thumbs and saying he was in love.

I was his tutor in all the entrance exam subjects. I was his keeper. While he was taking the exams, he lived at my place. Now I had to do the next thing–send him home.

Essentially during this period I was expected to be both mother and father for my young brother. Even more. Mother and father and conscience and brains and whatever else you like. And guard and keeper.

He was even the first to pick up on this game. He could have said no to it. He could have, let's say, put up some resistance. But he agreed.

He agreed on the very day that he arrived–I saw that in his eyes. He got off the train already as someone protected. Then on the very spot and without choice, I became the keeper. Cool! One more pair of guys bound together and tossed out into the world.

That's the way it went. The porters on the platform were clamoring. He had arrived in Moscow to take the exams, and here he was: getting off the train, looking at me–the brother who had come to meet him–and with each of his little steps down from the train, I was being made more and more into his keeper. And I didn't want that at all. It's not my role.

At this point it's time to take stock. The kid didn't get accepted by the university: number one! He ran away from me: number two! Now he was hanging out in this huge city with his Vika. Or maybe alone. And I myself had put into his hands the money that made it possible.

Deep down I felt rotten about all this. That's what you get for taking on a role that's not yours. That's what you've got coming. I walked back and forth in the apartment and tried to remember. How many people in my life had watched over me? Many and various ones came to mind–the good and the bad. The total came to about forty, if I started with kindergarten.

Right then I decided that from that time on I wouldn't stand guard over my brother.

"Not even go look for him?" my wife asked. "After all he's roaming around alone. It's a big city. Anything can happen."

I hesitated but said firmly, "I won't go look for him."

"And what are you going to do?"

"Nothing. Count the days."

I actually did count days. I was perfectly convinced that he wouldn't survive on that money for more than five days. Five days. Even if Vika's parents were to send her some money.

My wife got anxious. "How can you sleep, eat, walk around? You sleep while your very own brother is in trouble!"

"Where do you get that he's in trouble?" I answered, trying not to prolong a quarrel.

"You really think everything's fine?"

"Maybe so, maybe fine. After all it's his honeymoon."

"Lout!"

I was immovable, but she was still worried. Me, I had sworn not to play the guard. Now I swore to eat, sleep and live. Not–come what may–to sound the alarm.

My cousin and her husband came over. Just dropped by. They were family, elderly, and, therefore, possibly wise people. Of course my wife let everything slip. Of course we spent the whole evening talking only about my missing brother.

The relatives' opinions were divided.

My cousin said that I should run around and look for him and at the very least, one more time take a look inside Vika's closet. Well, if not in the closet, then under the bed. My cousin, as I knew, was a good woman.

Her husband smiled with a broad and open grin. He said, in the way only blockbuster movie heroes do, "What's the point of chasing after him? Let the boy experience some freedom." Then he added: "See, you gotta live. He came to Moscow and started spinning in a whirlwind. If he's strong, it won't destroy his life."

He stressed that youth belongs to youth. He himself was close to fifty. To keep him from being sent to the front in '42, his relatives got him a deferment. Actually they got him transferred to a factory where such deferments were possible. Relatives are relatives. For them, even at age twenty, he had been and still remained a boy. In advance they saw the moist clay of a freshly dug grave crumbling over him, over his soon–to–be close–cropped soldier's head.

Here he was–he had survived. Near fifty and he had become a children's author. Even a good one. That's no paradox, it's a fact, simply so.

Since he understood the psychology of children and adolescents well, he advised me. "Let him be. Let him have a good time. Let him taste some freedom. Youth…is like young wine."

What's more, he said, I shouldn't do anything to interfere in his behavior. But be observant emotionally, try to look at things from his point of view, think about him and if anything happens, then immediately and unconditionally stretch out a hand to him. This was very close to the truth. The bitter taste in my mouth even told me that. But mainly, I wanted to be just such a keeper–invisible to anyone.

Then they left, my cousin and her writer husband. Late that night my cousin called. "Do you think maybe he'll be thrifty . . .?" she asked in a whisper.

"What do you mean by thrifty?"

"He's only eighteen years old, you know."

But I sketched out for her how twenty–five rubles would vanish in two days. And after that? Then hunger will set in. One day of hunger. Two days of hunger. On the third, or at the very most on the fifth day, he'll ring my doorbell.

"Oh, I don't know," said my cousin.

She started crying. Tears were her only recourse. Her husband, the expert on child psychology, wouldn't give it a second thought, but she couldn't possibly fail to worry.

My brother came on the fourteenth day. That was a long time, heroically long.

He was barely able to stand.

"Sit down."

He glanced around.

"Sit down."

My wife was still asleep. I gave him some bread and sausage. A roll of soft cheese also turned up in the fridge. I don't remember another time when I saw somebody eat so fast. While he ate, we both stayed silent.

Then he just sat nodding off.

"Wanna sleep?"

"Uh–huh," he said. It didn't even occur to him to tell me something about these two weeks.

I put him to bed. While fixing the covers, I asked, "Well, now at last you'll go home?"

"I'll go."

"And where's your suitcase?"

"At the baggage check."

"It's been there all this time?"

"Yep."

"You didn't lose the check number?"

"No, what do you think!"

I tried to start a conversation. I said it this way: "Well...or just stay a while longer. Don't rush. Moscow's an interesting place."

But he didn't answer, missed the irony–he was already asleep.

I told my wife that, well, it was all over. The finale. He came back.

"Was that him in the kitchen? Oh, geez! I was wondering what that noise was."

"He had an appetite."

"You brought him to it. Your own brother chomping food down like a wolf. Aren't you ashamed?"

She still hadn't forgiven me for not running around and searching, for not sounding the alarm, not making a fuss.

I remember one summer especially well. A summer when my brother was still a little boy and I was a student. I came home on holidays, and he was at a Pioneer camp, where I went to visit him. When I arrived I saw a big Ping–Pong match underway. A little girl was playing against a boy, and a crowd was standing around. Everybody was rooting for one or the other and cheering wildly. Only occasionally, during quiet moments when the crowd was catching its breath, the little celluloid bounces resounded. Pong. Pong. Pong. Pong.

I tapped some boys on the shoulder and asked where my brother was. They all looked at me like I was crazy. How could someone just then ask a question like that? The crowd roared. At that moment you could ask only what the score was and who was leading. An old cook told me where my brother was. She was carrying some bones out to the dogs.

"He ran into the woods. In that direction."

I found him at the edge of the forest, where the trees ended and a meadow began.

The field was knee high in grass. My brother also saw me from a distance and froze. It was sunset and the grass was streaked by its rays. My brother stood relaxed, one knee slightly bent, in a white shirt and a red tie with a metal clasp–as if frozen for all time in that moment of his boyhood.

Cutting across the meadow toward him, I smiled from a distance–brother to brother. Who would have pictured him in a few years, when he would shoot up like a pine sapling? And that I would once find him in the closet of a woman's dormitory room!

Squinting against the sun, I walked over and asked him what he was doing there, on the meadow. He answered, "I'm catching bumblebees."

If at eighteen he hadn't run away from me in Kursky station but instead had become a genius, say, somebody like Galileo, I would have forever remembered that moment with the bumblebees. I would have told everyone about it, that such a genius can be foreseen. That already in childhood he was searching for his own path. He had his own view of things. He was far removed from the noisy crowd. And on and on.

At the moment when I left the dorm my brother naturally didn't climb out of the closet–he hadn't been there, that much I verified. But suppose . . . he crawled out from under the bed, wiped the sweat off his face and went over to Vika.

"You're alive?" she grinned.

"Whew!"

Standing side by side they looked out the window. Below, I was slowly, slowly making my way across the square, with the regal stride of a jackass. I walked toward my bus under their gaze. Several times I imagined that to myself.

I imagined how right then he kisses her from joy that he had made me look like such a fool, and she–him. He–her, etcetera. But I remembered about the money and somehow stopped the scene. First, my brother would want to buy some wine before the store closed, and only later would come the "etcetera." He said to her: "I'll run buy it." And she: "But what about the money? Let the shit go." "It'll be okay." "Maybe you don't need it." "I need it. I'll make it quick." And he dashed off, spent his last rubles, and very soon they were in bed together, and he was telling her how he had run away from me at Kursky station.

He told her about the Gypsies and how people watched them out of the corners of their eyes. Those people had suitcases, but the Gypsies had just bundles. He got around to the other side, because even as I watched for him, I got distracted by the Gypsies and by all those who sat with one eye on their suitcases and the other on the

Gypsies' movements.

Then he took off and became his own free man in Moscow. He brought it off, didn't get lost.

If probing deeper into the situation, Vika would ask, "Aren't you scared?" he answered, "What of?" And laughed. "If something happens, I have a brother here. My keeper."

Maybe he told her how sensibly and discreetly I watched over him. Lightly. Quietly. He took off but I didn't start a fuss, just once dropped in, just to ask.

I don't run around making a stir, don't stand guard, don't peek into windows. But that way he feels even stronger that he's not alone and that I'm somewhere close by. Not far away, here in the city. His brother.

Their money problem especially nagged me. Two possibilities existed. My brother and Vika are living on one little budget, trying to make it last as long as possible. That would be tolerable. That's reasonable. Man and wife, essentially . . . . But they would be too green for that, for them money was a romantic question. For them, in fact, the question wouldn't even arise. Each will be on his own. My brother's knees and hands will shake from never having enough to eat. So he will spend as long with Vika as he can make it.

When on the fourteenth day he came, I fully expected his account of it all. How it really went. And what he thought about me, his keeper. But he didn't initiate the conversation, not a word. He didn't even make up some story.

Me and my brother went to the train station in the morning. We bought him his ticket. That's when again I pulled out twenty–five rubles, handed the money over to him, and he took it.

He didn't smile, didn't make any remark about this second occasion. He wanted to sleep, that was all.

His train wasn't due to leave for four more hours. There was no sense in going back to the apartment just to sit for an hour. No choice but to hang out there near the station. We would have to hover somewhere in midair for four hours.

"Wanna go to a movie?"

"No."

"What then?"

"Better to grab something in the cafeteria."

He wanted to eat again. And we had just had a big breakfast.

He picked at his food in the cafeteria. He wanted to sleep.

"Did you get enough?"

"Seems like I'm full."

Then we sat for a while on a garden bench in front of a building. It was the usual tiny Moscow resting spot with four benches, one on each side, forming a square. We sat on one of the benches. In the middle stood a kind of cement cup, inside it something resembling a fountain. Out of order, of course.

My brother kept yawning. I asked him some questions. I wanted badly to find out something, so I asked him, but as if I didn't much care.

"So how's it going with you two?"

"Say what?"

"I mean about Vika."

"Uh . . . ."

"What did you decide?"

"Nothing much . . . ."

I nodded, of course. Yeah, I understand, yeah, fine.

If I had been a dumb and pedantic keeper, like thousands, he, like it or not, would have said that with Vika it was like this . . . she had finished a technical school and now was in the university. Her parents are such–and–such people. And they agreed, like, to write letters to each other. Or, say, to meet on school breaks . . . But I didn't want to be one of those thousands. And I didn't find out a thing. Zero.

The sun was beating down. The little rest spot was getting sultry. Suddenly I too needed a nap. I shut my eyes slightly.

When I woke up my brother wasn't beside me any more. But I saw him nearby.

Three girls were sitting on the opposite bench, all three eating ice cream and laughing. They wore the uniforms of cashiers from a large store in the neighborhood.

My brother was telling them something and they were laughing. Not a trace of his fatigue was left. Something inside me flipped over: what if he should run off with one of them? It was an absurd thought but enough to wake me up for sure.

The girls just then stood up–they were leaving because their lunch break was over. My brother was leaving with them.

I didn't call out to him. I restrained myself and went on sitting there the while, my eyes closed as if sleeping. As they left the bench area my brother put his arms around the shoulders of two of the girls. They laughed again. At the very exit of the resting spot, a short post stuck up, probably the remainder of a turnstile, and my brother, still clinging to the girls, didn't know which way to go around, to the right or to the left? In the end he banged straight into the post. All three of them got stuck. Passersby, mainly grannies pushing baby buggies raised a ruckus. They couldn't get through to the park benches. My brother and the girls went on laughing.

"You took a little nap?" he asked when he came back.

"Yeah, a catnap."

"Still an hour to go before the train. I got the girls' addresses."

"From those same girls?"

"Yep."

"You'll write them?"

"Not for sure. Maybe even I will."

He gave a grin, as if confidentially. "One of them is not very pretty. So–so. But I got her address too."

We were silent.

Later he put his arm around my shoulder and said that it was only an hour till the train. It was about time to say good–bye.

"You're still a kid," I said to him. "You're only eighteen. How come you weren't timid? These past days."

"What's there to be timid about?"

"Lots of stuff. Your first time in Moscow, alone in the big city."

Then he said something more or less like this. In this huge city he had had a keeper. Someone who didn't intrude, didn't meddle or tell him what to do, but at the same time remained a keeper.

"OK, man. That'll do," I said.

"Honest," he said, in a surge of feeling. "Honest, that's the way it was!"

I felt warm all over. I even had the impression that I was blushing. Quickly I changed the subject. Only some five years later, in quite a different conversation with him, it came out–plain and simple–that then, talking to me on that day in Moscow, he had had in mind blue–eyed Vika. Not me.

But at the moment I sat beside my brother as a person who had honorably fulfilled his duty. As an older brother. As a keeper, in the best and most humane sense of the word. A whole forty minutes were left till the train. I just sat there relaxed and happy.

Translated by Byron Lindsey

The Three "Loves" of Masha Peredreeva

Galina Shcherbakova

When Masha Peredreeva found out how much IT cost in Moscow, she couldn't sleep all night. She lay there thinking. It's just as well I read it with my own eyes. Seriously if anyone had tried to tell her that people paid 100 rubles for it, she would have laughed in their face. A hundred rubles! After she finished at the teacher training college she'd be paid less than that for a whole month's work–a whole month! And people were being paid that much money for just a few minutes. It wasn't as if they were being made to hump steel girders or look after pigs. Take her mother, for example. She was a cultural official with the local council and earned 150 rubles a month, including traveling expenses. All that traveling gave her chronic cystitis. The conditions she had to put up with when she made the rounds of the villages! Her doctor had said to her, "Olga Sergeyevna, it's no laughing matter for someone in your condition to be taking your knickers off in freezing cold outhouses or cabins. You must make up your mind. What's more important–your health or your status?" She settled for status. She was known throughout the region–without her there would be no movies, no culture–nothing! "I don't work for money. If we followed the capitalist path, who knows where it would lead."

"As if we know where this path is leading us," Masha would say.

It was clear to her that her mother's opinions were often motivated by grievance and poverty. She had reached the ceiling of her life's potential, and no amount of battering would break through that ceiling. She could go no further with her secondary education (she was trained as a projectionist). True enough, she had been a party member for twenty–five of her forty–three years, but she wasn't sharp enough to use this to her advantage. She was like a fire extinguisher–producing huge amounts of foam and noise, but never achieving anything. Masha would look at her mother and think. God save me from a life like that. No husband. No money. Ill health.

What she did have was an apartment. Yes, a good apartment–one bedroom, all the modern conveniences, on the second floor, even with a telephone. Her mother worshiped the apartment. She used to take Masha to see the wooden tenement where she had grown up. The people in the tenement still remembered her. Unlike Masha they thought she'd really made something of herself. "I haven't gotten anywhere!" She would say, waving a hand self–deprecatingly. But her eyes sparkled. She desperately needed to be reassured, to have her successes enumerated in detail And the simple people from the tenement would bend over backward to please her. "Just think about it, Olga," they would say. "For a start you've got your own apartment. Two whole rooms for the two of you, and that's not counting the kitchen–you could easily just live in the kitchen if you had to. It's big enough. Look at us. –Never mind the bathroom! You could live in there too–you've got running water in the kitchen as well, haven't you?" Her mother would laugh, delighted by the conversation. Then the good–natured people from the tenement would heap more praise on her because she had a white–collar job, and didn't have to go out to work with rakes and pitchforks.

"I don't despise any kind of work," Masha's mother would say to them. Ultimately they mentioned the district council. They did not disguise their attitude toward the council–no description was too bad for it, but they tactfully avoided mentioning Masha's mother in connection with it. "You're such a saint, Olga. You don't realize what kind of bribery and corruption goes on in there." Olga would rebuke them. "You ought to be ashamed of yourselves, saying things like that!" But Masha agreed with them entirely. She secretly believed that her mother must share their opinion, she wasn't a complete fool after all! But her mother didn't go to the tenement in search of such primitive harmonizing. She went there when she felt as if she was festering inside, when her boss had given her a tongue–lashing, or when her quarrels with Masha almost reached the point of violence. These were the moments when her mother would put on her best dress, sling a bag over her shoulder, and return to her roots. She would always be warmly welcomed. "You're our girl, Olga! And you're such a pet–you never forget us, even though you've risen so high." And her mother would swallow spoonfuls of praise, soothing away the insults in her life. She heard the same things repeated a million times, the remarks about her apartment and her clothes ("Is that an imported dress you're wearing, Olga? You'd never be able to make that yourself. The cloth is garbage, true, you'd find better cloth here, but the design ... and what pretty straps. Look how they fit together!"). And about the power of the council. "We know you don't take bribes, Olga. But the way the rest of them carry on, it would put the fear of God in you! They're not afraid of anyone."

Masha pitied her mother and despised her. Sometimes the former dominated her feelings, but more often the latter. When she felt pity she dreamed about taking her mother to a Central Asian spa she had heard about so they could cure her mother's cystitis. She would spare no expense to send her mother to a dry climate and put an end to all her business trips. When she was overcome by feelings of scorn, she thought, you're so keen on going back to your tenement, you stupid cow. Why don't you go back there for good? They've got fancy rooms there too. The ones at the end of the corridors have two windows, and even a little entrance hall. Why don't you go and live there! When I get married and have children, what man will tolerate living under the same roof with you? You're nothing but an old windbag–always saying that all men ought to be shot. What are you going to do once you've shot them all? I suppose you like living alone with your cystitis? Or do you?

Her mother was slightly paranoid on the subject of voting. She was in favor of open voting, as a matter of principle, considering it more honest. A long time ago she had been up for election to some kind of committee. They had all heaped praise on her, and then almost everyone crossed her name off the list on the ballot paper. Masha couldn't remember exactly what they were voting for, but her mother was utterly shattered by the experience. Masha couldn't understand either. Why had they praised her so highly if they were then going to cross her name off the list? She tried to imagine herself in a similar situation, but found herself giggling helplessly. Nobody had ever nominated her for anything. Whenever she was at any kind of meeting, ever since she was a small child, she had been prone to collapsing in fits of laughter.

"Comrades! I declare this meeting open."

That was enough to set her off. They would have to take her out of the room. Her mother dragged her to a doctor, who diagnosed nervousness and instructed her to chew gum during the meetings. We have Soviet–made gum now, but at that time it took some looking to find it. Masha's mother used to go to the district center to get it. By now Masha had grown out of her giggling fits, but the memory of them lived on, with the result that she was left alone at meetings. She would sit at the very back, sucking a lollipop or chewing gum, and copy song lyrics. She had a more extensive song book than anyone else at college. It included Pugacheva, Kuzmin, Minayev, Aguzarova–everyone!

Masha thought Soviet culture was a lot more interesting now than it had been in her mother's time, when they used to line up on stage like a load of imbeciles and stand stock–still with their hands on their hips. They didn't move an inch, never mind tap dancing. Nowadays things had changed–it took your breath away, the way some of them could sing and dance. You couldn't deny that the arts were improving in spite of people like her mother trying to stand in the way of change. What bugged her more than anything was that her mother couldn't stand the folk choirs either, but she still organized them, cultivated them, encouraged them. But as soon as a choir showed up on the TV she'd switch to another program, quick as a flash. She tried to justify herself on the basis of Pavlov's dogs, saying people needed variety.

"Those dogs would have croaked if they'd been forced to listen to your choirs," said Masha.

Her mother would scream at her until she was blue in the face. It was just as well they had two rooms. You could always shut the door and turn up the radio. There was no way her mother could out scream Soviet radio.

What brains she had! They'd chew up anything. She jumped out of bed. She'd started out shocked by that article in the paper and ended up thinking about her mother and the tenement. Masha had once said to her mother, "You take up too much space in my life."

"What's that supposed to mean?" Her mother bawled. It didn't take much to get her going.

Masha, barefoot and naked, went to the kitchen for a drink of water. As she passed her mother's room she could hear her moaning in her sleep. The nighttime moaning had frightened Masha as a small child. She used to fling herself on the bed, crying, "Mommy,

Mommy!" And then she'd get a smack for waking her up. Her mother always said that she hadn't been dreaming about anything that could possibly make her groan. In that case why did she sob, grind her teeth, and toss from side to side in her sleep? She herself admitted that her husband, Masha's father, even used to hit her because of her sleeping habits. Masha could understand the way he felt. When they had lived in the club she hated her mother at night, too. All that u–u–u–u–h, a–a–a–h, o–o–o–h made it impossible to sleep. Masha kicked an armchair in the darkness. The chair creaked. Her mother gave a sob, fell silent for a moment, then began moaning again.

An old mirror hung in the kitchen. They had bought a new pier glass, then didn't know where to put the old one. They tried it all over the place and ended up hanging it above the kitchen table. It looked quite good

There Masha stood by the stove. From there she could see herself clearly in the mirror. Her figure was not ideal by today's standards. She had a big bust and bottom and a fine waist. Her legs were on the heavy side, but straight–you wouldn't have been able to slide a knife between her knees. Her skin was good–not silk, but white velvet with a pinkish tinge. And when tanned, it became a delicate golden color. She had a lovely stomach–oval shaped and with a deep belly button. She'd never had a single blemish or pimple in her life. Her face wasn't as good as her body. A big mouth with fleshy lips, which some people found attractive. For color, she only had to bite her lips from time to time, and she never bothered with lipstick. Admittedly her eyes were rather small. But with a bit of blue on the eyelids and a pencil line to lengthen the corners, they weren't such a bad shape, she looked almost Egyptian–quite stylish. Masha often wondered. Where would we be without makeup? How did they manage in the old days? Her mother said that they had managed well enough with lipstick and powder. But that probably meant that some people managed all right and some people didn't. She didn't believe everything her mother told her. Now of course there was much more to choose from: shadow and shiny stuff to put on your eyes and imported colors of lipstick. If you took a bit of trouble with yourself you couldn't go wrong. Her best feature was her hair. Thick and unstyled, like a fur hat. She didn't have to do anything special with her hair, just leave it alone. Even its chestnut color was natural–they called it "hellbraun."

Masha turned her back to the mirror. She had a nice way of turning–quite sexy. There was no question but that she was worth that much money, so she'd better go out and earn it. She'd be a real fool if she didn't make use of her knowledge, now that she knew 100 rubles a time was just waiting to be collected.

Her mother came into the kitchen half asleep. She'd been unable to find the switch in the bathroom.

"What are you doing standing there with no clothes on?"

"None of your business!" snapped Masha.

"Go to hell!" Her mother slammed the door and rattled the toilet seat. Masha dreamed of the time when she would have saved up enough money so that she would never have to live with her mother again. What else would she do? She'd take herself off to the Baltics. Of course Russians weren't very popular up there, but she was better looking than their women, there was no doubt about that. She'd buy herself an apartment by the seaside, and then she'd see. 'Maybe she'd get married, or maybe she wouldn't. When she was rich. ...

Her mother finished in the bathroom and came into the kitchen. She looked at Masha. "Haven't you stood there long enough? You haven't even shut the curtains."

"They're welcome to have a look–if they're not asleep," said Masha. "Anyone who's not asleep deserves a bit of pleasure."

"I had a better figure than you when I was your age," said her mother.

"You couldn't have!" Masha was indignant.

Her mother took the bait. She took off her nightdress and stood naked beside Masha. Masha moved away fastidiously. She couldn't bear to be close to another person's naked body.

"I'm slimmer than you, for a start," said her mother, examining herself in the mirror. "Anyone would think you were the one that had a child, not me."

"You're flabby," countered Masha.

"Flabby!" her mother cried. She stuck out her elbow and started jabbing at Masha. Then suddenly her expression turned sour and her face drooped. "I don't know how you have the heart to say things like that to your own mother. You're my own flesh. You've taken all my strength, my vitality. You wait till you have a baby. You'll be flabby yourself, and then your daughter will say mean things to you."

"For a start I'm not going to have a baby," said Masha. "Only a fool would give birth to a child that was going to grow up poor. And if I do have a baby, I'll make sure I look after myself. I won't let myself go."

"To hell with you." Her mother sounded indifferent as she walked away, dragging her nightdress along the floor, and Masha–who was fair minded–noticed that her mother had a beautiful cleft running down the center of her back, and a small, neat bottom. Her legs were slimmer than Masha's, too. From behind she looked like a young girl, if you ignored the chemical bush on her head. Her hair was a real mess. Dyed, poisoned, sparse, and tortured into shape. Masha even began to feel sorry for her.

"You'll do! Still fit for service." Masha tried to sound encouraging.

Her mother froze in her steps, then turned around. "You fucking bitch!" she hissed, clearly but under her breath.

Occasionally her mother's humble origins would come out in the form of foul language. Masha was shocked when she did this. She herself might call someone a fool, or a pain, or if she was really driven to it, a cow. But that was as far as she would go. It wasn't that she deliberately stopped herself from saying anything stronger. The words just didn't find their way into her mouth. In this respect Masha considered herself superior to her mother. In fact she considered herself a cultured person in general. She ate with a knife and fork. She always greeted old ladies before they greeted her, but never greeted men first. Her speech was regularly punctuated with "please" and "thank you." She did not point, nor did she swear. The other girls in her group used to say, "If you're really trying to give someone a piece of your mind, it doesn't mean much if you don't swear."

"You're only lowering yourself," replied Masha.

Her mother was foul–mouthed. A tenement is a tenement–it will always leave its mark. Masha couldn't even walk past it without feeling disgust. Even when the lilac was in bloom–and the tenement was completely surrounded by lilac bushes–a stale smell seemed to hang in the air: a mixture of cabbage, soap, old mattresses, boiled laundry, cats, mice, stale alcohol, gas stoves repeatedly doused with water, and stronger than anything else, a smell that hung stubbornly in spite of the fiercest frost or burning summer heat–the smell of the Tenement Itself. Everyone has their own smell–miners, black people, nurses. So did the tenement. It was a smell that concentrated many things, and it was a fertile environment for bad language, as natural as a fish in water, dust in the air, or a worm in a pile of dung. But the fact that her mother still occasionally came out with tenement–style language, despite the fact that she had long ago stopped living there, simply proved what an uncultured person she was. Masha invariably pointed this out to her.

"You may be a cultural official, Mom, but you're not exactly cultured yourself. You ought to watch your language."

"And you're too cultured for your own good," her mother would snap. Masha's plan of action was as follows: on the weekend she would go to the district center. There were hotels and even a particular hotel for foreigners there. She would try her luck. In any case, she would have to be a total, complete, utter fool not to seize this opportunity.

Toward morning Masha fell asleep. She did not hear her mother leave for work. Nor did she know that as her mother stood in front of the mirror in the kitchen, gulping down hot tea, she had tried to understand why her daughter had been roaming around the apartment naked in the middle of the night. She felt slightly disturbed. As a woman, and a local council official, she was upset by modern youth. They drank and smoked and took drugs. They believed in neither God nor the devil. They had babies and then abandoned them. Sex did not frighten them in the least. She had recently been shown some classified statistics on this subject at the council. Dreadful. Of course she had total confidence in her Masha. She was a proud girl with a mind other own. But still, she ought to keep an eye on her. After all, she was fully grown now, and there were certain urges. Masha's mother choked on her tea. She was filled with a malicious fury, rising up from her stomach like bile.

"I'll show her urges! I'll show her what happens if she feels like doing something!" she said to her reflection. "I'll sew up her privates with a needle and thread, if that's what it takes."

After those words she calmed down. For God's sake, whom could she possibly be getting it on with and where? She studied at the teacher training institution–and there wasn't a single boy in the place. There was only one male teacher–the man who took them for PE. And he was due to retire soon, and he had a harelip. He was the kind of man you'd only go for if you'd spent a hundred years on a desert island. Victor Korshunov, one of Masha's schoolmates, used to date her. He was a nice enough boy, polite and well–mannered. But he'd gone off to do his army service two months ago. They'd sent him straight to Afghanistan. God forbid anything should happen to him. His mother Nyusya worked in the shoe shop. She walked around looking completely gray with grief and fear. You could understand it. He and Masha didn't write to each other–she would have known if they did. She was sure nothing had happened between them. They just hung around together, sometimes went to the movies.

Masha's mother felt calmer as she set off for work. The sight of potato peelings on the stairs did not improve her mood. Their neighbor always spilled something out of the bucket when she was taking her garbage down. She'd already had words with her.

"You ought to know better than to throw your garbage everywhere, Mrs. Chebrikova. It's not your own house. It belongs to the state, and you live here rent–free. So please be so good as to keep the place clean and decent." Please be so good–she remembered saying that.

"I'm so sorry," replied the neighbor, slamming her door loudly. What could you do with people like that? She'd apologized, but the potato peelings were still lying there.

Masha arrived in the town at noon. She'd have to while away the time until evening. When the other girls went to look around the shops, Masha realized she had to get her thoughts sorted out, no matter what bargains she might be missing in the shops. She had an aunt living in the town, her father's sister. They hardly kept in touch, but Masha decided to go and see her. She knew her mother wouldn't thank her for it, but nobody was asking her opinion today. Masha bought some asters–a bunch of five, freshly cut and bound together–and headed out. Her aunt lived on the seventh floor of a nice apartment building, with an elevator and a garbage chute. Admittedly running water only reached as far as the fourth floor, but there were plans to install a pump to raise the water higher. So far nothing had been done. At night her aunt collected as much water as she could in bathtubs, buckets, and 50–liter tanks. Wherever you looked there was some kind of container of water. Even mayonnaise jars were filled with water. Of course this made the apartment damp. Wallpaper had started peeling off after a month, and the edges hung down. But apart from that it was a nice apartment. Folding glass doors, a covered balcony, all three rooms separate. Her aunt was a doctor.

"Hello, Auntie Shura!" said Masha, trying to sound as friendly as possible. Auntie Shura stood looking at Masha, apparently failing to recognize her. Then Masha thrust forward her bouquet of asters.

"Good heavens!" said her aunt. "I didn't recognize you. Where did you come from? Come in. I'm just getting ready to go on duty." Very good, thought Masha. I'll manage without you.

"Where's Uncle Kolya?" she asked sweetly, taking off her shoes and putting on a pair of men's slippers.

"Uncle Kolya's out fishing. He's been gone since last night."

"What a pity," said Masha, secretly trembling with delight. "And what about the boys?"

"They're fishing too. I let them take the day off from school. Get a bit of fresh air in their lungs while the weather's still nice. And if there are children around, the men will have to watch how they behave. It might make them drink a bottle or two less."

"We're supposed to be on a college trip," said Masha. "And I decided I'd already seen everything they were going to show us. If I've visited those battlegrounds once, I've visited them a hundred times ... so I thought I'd come and visit you."

"It was a very good idea." Her aunt sounded uncertain. "Only I have to go to work. You should have written or phoned to let us know. It's better to warn people nowadays."

"I'll wait for you," Masha suggested.

"I'll be gone for twenty–four hours," said her aunt. Then suddenly an idea occurred to her. "Could you mind the water tonight? You could fill the canister. Only you'd have to do it after midnight."

Masha had no idea where she would be after midnight. But she said firmly, "No problem."

"Then you're welcome to stay." Her aunt went into the kitchen, and began taking the lids off cooking pots and frying pans.

"I'm afraid there's only leftovers," she sighed. "I don't really cook when the boys aren't around. You'd go mad, cooking for the three of them every day. But you can help yourself to what there is."

"Don't worry," said Masha. "A cup of tea will do for me."

As she handed the keys to Masha, her aunt asked, "Does your father ever write?"

Masha shook her head.

"I don't hear from him either. I suppose he's stopped paying the alimony too?"

"Last month."

"Oh yes, I forgot you're eighteen already. How's your mother?"

"She's all right."

"Why didn't they stay together?" Her aunt sighed, looked at Masha, and decided that this was the right moment to kiss her–for everything. For the asters, for turning eighteen, for remembering her aunt, for having a scoundrel for a father who had run off God knows where.

Masha began to get ready. She mustn't waste the water. So she poured a little water into a basin and sprinkled in a few drops from each of her aunt's flasks and bottles. She washed herself slowly and meticulously. As she washed she planned what she was going to do with her first 100 rubles. She decided to put it in a savings bank. The best thing would be to save up carefully and then buy something expensive, like a real fur coat or some gold jewelry. Of course her mother would be amazed. "Where did you get the money?"

But once she had the money, that kind of conversation with her mother would be easy. She'd be operating from a position of strength.

"Your party loyalty really got you a long way, didn't it?" Masha would ask her sarcastically.

Her mother's face would flush, and she would yell–a sure sign that she had nothing to say. Good! It would be crucial to mention the Party at the right moment. Masha hated the Party even more than she hated the Komsomol. They were nothing but a bunch of windbags who didn't even believe what they themselves said. They just kept playing the same tunes to get ahead in the world. As Masha saw it, the Communist Party was like a high–rise building. Her mother was doomed to stay on the ground floor until the day she died, whereas other people could get themselves up to the top.

Masha laughed, dabbing at her toes with cotton balls. You could be sure that the people up there got regular water supplies. Her mother would rant and rave. ... She was already over forty, and the ceiling over her head was reinforced with steel beams. There was no chance of her moving any higher. First, if you were honest, you were a fool; second, she didn't have enough qualifications, even officially; third, if she'd had any sense she'd have gotten a job in retail, where it's impossible not to do well. But she chose culture. Broken musical instruments and costumes made of old sacking. When Masha became rich, her mother could scream to her heart's content. Scream away! You can have a fit if you like. Masha would tell them all to go you–know–where. And as for Victor Korshunov–she'd send him to hell in a basket. When he came back from Afghanistan she'd walk right past him and ignore him. ... No, she wouldn't ignore him ... she'd stop and talk to him, but in such a way as to put him in his place once and for all.

Of course he'd earned a few words of thanks. "Thank you, Victor, for your service to the Soviet Union!" Now Masha wasn't afraid of anything. In fact, to be honest, she'd never been afraid of this. She remembered how, just before he left, when he already had his army haircut, Victor had flung himself at her feet. She never would have expected him to behave like this. Quiet, gentle Victor had never said "boo" to a goose, and then suddenly there he was, grabbing her legs and wheezing passionately.

"Be my guest!" said Masha. "Do you think I'd grudge you a little thing like that!"

She had felt a combination of shame, disgust, and pain, but all these feelings were somehow vague and shallow. The strongest sensation was that of Victor's shaved, prickly head rubbing against her cheeks. Victor had talked about marriage before that. "We could get married tomorrow if you felt like it. Would you like to?" Afterward he stopped mentioning it. At least he stopped suggesting they might get married the next day. He put marriage on a more distant time scale. Masha noticed the change immediately, and thought, "You swine!" But she didn't say anything, because she never imagined she might become his wife, not even in her wildest nightmares. It was the kind of idea that went with war and the end of the world. But she still noticed that Victor had recanted his former position. After he left, he faded away rapidly. He said he would write. "Just you wait and see! And make sure you answer." "Uh–huh," she replied. "Why don't you come to the station tomorrow?" he suggested. "Okay," she agreed. As it happened, she did go. Her girlfriends had said, "Let's go down to the station. There's a brass band."

They arrived. The station was swarming with people. Victor was surrounded by a lot of shop assistants and his mother, who worked in the shoe shop, kept walking around him. The way Victor called Masha over to stand beside him was typical of his character. Masha almost burst out laughing. His mother stopped her frenzied dance and looked at Masha. She took a long time appraising her, but when she had absorbed the information that her son had a young lady standing beside him, she called out in a thin, nasty voice, "Well, here comes the bride! The turtle dove has flown in to honor us with her presence!"

The final curtain fell on the performance of "The Send–off." They all went their separate ways, and that was the end of it. Victor never wrote, and when they were selling imported boots in the shoe shop, and Masha tried to make signs at Victor's mother from the end of the line, she pretended she hadn't seen her.

She bought the boots anyway. One of the other girls got a pair that didn't fit, so she sold them to Masha. She only paid an extra ten rubles.

The local Intourist hotel was located in Pioneer Park. The name of the park was given credence by the plaster figures of girls and boys and classic Marxist–Leninist slogans plastered all over the place. You couldn't move without bumping into one of them. Either a boy reading a book, or a little girl frozen in an eternal salute, or a huge human head. Whoever designed the park obviously thought that Young Pioneers only needed to see the heads of great men–they weren't of an age to benefit from the rest of the body.

Rumor had it that at night in this park, decked out as it was in exemplary fashion with such plaster ideology, things far removed from the ideas represented by those plaster heads were going on. But that's what parks are for–even Young Pioneer parks. Masha sat down on a bench near a fountain. The water came jetting out of the mouths of fishes and poured straight over a pioneer, who stood in the center playing a bugle. Masha deliberately posed in a way that would make it obvious she was alone, but that would also allow her, in the event of an unforeseen occurrence, to run around the fountain and rush down one of the paths, where every third person was a public–order volunteer wearing a red armband. Not that you could rely on them. The worst kind of racketeers wore armbands. Their armbands were nothing but red herrings.

It was already getting dark, but the park was not yet lit up. The local authorities had launched a campaign to save electricity. A special duty officer was responsible for giving the order to switch on the street lights. The duty officer stood at his window and watched the streets getting darker, and the Pioneer Park turning from bottle green to dark blue, then grayish, and finally plunging into total blackness.

The first man broke away from the crowd and walked across to Masha firmly and confidently. He was quite a handsome fellow, but definitely a Russian, not even a Georgian.

"Feeling a little bored, are we?" he asked, plunking himself down on the bench beside Masha.

"I'm just sitting here." Masha was nothing if not truthful.

"How about if I suggested something a little more interesting?" asked the Russian.

At this point there was a gap in Masha's well–planned scheme. She didn't know whether it was expected for her to name her price up front, or wait to mention money after everything was over.

Masha was afraid of making a tactical error. She had been concentrating so hard on doing and saying the right thing, that for a moment she forgot where she was, why she had come, and who was waiting for her answer. She sat as if turned to stone, like the plaster girl who sat nearby reading a copy of The Young Guard. She didn't even notice when the man–he was surely a Russian, not even a Georgian–suddenly jumped up shouting, "Nellia! Nellia!" and disappeared.

"That's great!" thought Masha. As soon as anything happens I lose my head.

Then she sighed with relief. After all, she needed a little while to get used to sitting on the bench.

Luck was with her. Another man came up to her. He was a Soviet too, but this time not a Russian, he was very dark. He could have been a Moldavian, or perhaps an Armenian. Who else could be that dark? Anyway, he certainly wasn't from the Baltics.

"How about it?"

Scum, thought Masha. He's some kind of country bumpkin. What a fool.

"Get the hell away from me!" she said quietly.

"Watch it!" said the dark man, but he kept his distance as he sat down on the bench. Two people could have sat between them.

"Where do you come from?" asked the dark man.

How can he tell I'm not local? Masha was alarmed and began eyeing the passers–by nervously. The girls looked classy, dressed to the nines. Masha made a quick assessment, comparing herself to them. She couldn't see that she was any worse–looking than them, nor was she any more attractive. Why had he asked where she came from? "From here, of course! I come from the seventh floor, where there's no running water," she countered wittily, just to show him what kind of person he was dealing with.

"You can't fool me," said the dark man. "You can't have left the village more than two hours ago. You still smell of cow sheds."

Are you mad?" cried Masha. "I've never been near a cowshed in my life!"

She leaped from her seat just at the moment when the duty officer, with a heavy sigh, decided that it was not within his power to save the council any more on its electricity bill.

Masha, furious at the dark man's unkind words, was bathed in yellow light, which made her look rather attractive. Anyway, one of a group of boys who were amusing themselves by throwing their cigarette butts into the mouths of the spitting fishes came over to her. He was a strong, well built boy, Russian of course, but he looked quite like an American. That was how Masha described him to herself–an American type. If you can't get the genuine, pedigreed article, you might as well get something along the right lines.

He took Masha's hand firmly but not roughly and turned her around to face him.

"Hey, where are you going in such a hurry?" he asked.

"Some guy is bothering me," Masha replied.

"Not your type, eh?" asked the "American."

"A piece of scum," said Masha.

The young man looked Masha up and down, he even walked around her, in order to examine her from all angles. He made approving clicking sounds with his tongue.

"Will I do?" he asked politely.

"We'll have to discuss it first," Masha spoke precisely. The conversation was moving along in a satisfactory, businesslike way. It was a relief to discover that some people could get on the right track immediately. "What would you like to know?"

"A hundred rubles," said Masha. She mentally congratulated herself and gave herself credit for the calm way she had said it. Everything was going very nicely indeed!

The young man rounded his lips and let out a bird–like, whistling sound, but he didn't let go of Masha's hand. He whistled a strange tune, using his lips skillfully like a musical instrument, then asked, "Is that a contract for the whole family?"

"What do you mean?" Masha didn't understand.

"Boyfriend? Husband? Father? Mother? Who's on the payroll?"

"What are you talking about?" Masha exclaimed. She realized now he was joking, but he'd thrown her off balance for a moment.

"Okay," said the young man. "I agree."

As Masha had expected, there were no lights in the seventh–floor window. But she looked up just in case. She didn't want to take any chances. As they went into the apartment the young man immediately turned on the light, which meant, thank God, that they avoided tripping over any buckets of water.

He made himself at home. Masha didn't know whether to be pleased about this or not. He was strolling around as if he owned the place. Well ... it was someone else's house, after all. He quickly figured out everything about the family. There were two teenagers living in the apartment–both of them boys. And their father was a fisherman.

"None of your things are here," he said. "How are you related to them?"

"She's my aunt," Masha replied.

"Ah!" he said. "So you're on tour ..."

"What?" She didn't understand. She didn't know what he meant by the word tour. She knew the word of course, but she couldn't figure out what he meant by it.

Later, while it was going on, Masha wondered where he was going to get the money. He was lightly dressed, and there was no sign of a bulging wallet anywhere on him. It couldn't be in that little pocket closed with a zipper. If it was, then it had to be just one, high–denomination banknote, because the pocket wasn't bulging. Masha began to feel a little anxious about the question of money, even though everything was going according to plan. When she had undressed and lain down on her aunt's double bed, he had looked at her cheerfully, and said, "Not such a bad hundred rubles'–worth, for a country girl! What a lovely, strong little calf you are!"

She didn't like that. It reminded her too much of the cow sheds. Making sure not to mention her first name or surname, she pointed out that she came from an educated family, and he had no call to talk like that. They'd never kept cows or even goats. And they didn't know anything about such things.

Once again he rounded his lips and whistled his birdsong in her ear. It tickled, but she managed to say that she wasn't some kind of cowherd. He jumped lightly from the bed, lightly slipped on his trousers and rattled the bracelet of his watch. Masha watched with satisfaction. There was definitely something American about him.

"Hey!" said Masha, as he headed toward the door.

"Oh, I'm sorry!" The "American" tapped his forehead, and, as Masha had guessed, he fumbled in the zippered pocket.

He stood over her, strong and handsome, and tossed a ruble coin in the air.

"Here!" he laughed. "Catch it!" Well, Masha wasn't the kind of girl who would put up with that kind of treatment.

She grabbed hold of him. For a moment he was taken aback, confused, which gave her the advantage long enough to rip his shirt. "Pay up, you snake!"

His shirt parted down the middle from the collar to the belly button. He came to his senses and sent Masha sprawling across the bed. Lying down is not a strong position from which to fight, and unfortunately the principle that you should never hit someone when they're down has been consigned to history. The young man had no qualms about hitting Masha. He hit her proudly and confidently, from a position of strength and justice. Masha did not want to cry out and breathed hoarsely. The bastard realized that there was no danger of her making a noise, and he hit her for a last time, particularly painfully. She couldn't help screaming but he was clever enough to cover her face with a pillow.

Masha heard him close the bedroom door. For a while she howled into the pillow, but, typically for her, it was more from humiliation than from pain. She could stand pain, but what she couldn't bear was any kind of insult or humiliation. Everything had gone wrong! He had twisted her around his little finger as if she were a small child. She'd fallen for it like complete fool. She should have questioned how a young guy like that would have a spare hundred rubles. That had been her mistake. Of course the article she had read didn't mention age. Mainly it talked about foreigners. But where was she supposed to find a foreigner? Never mind, thought Masha, let this be a lesson to me. In a minute she would get up and start over. As her mother would say, you get two new plates every time you smash one. That's the law of life. Masha switched on the light and looked at herself in the mirror. Her face was all red, but apart from hat she looked all right. It could be worse. Now she would use some more of her aunt's water–a bit more than she should. She'd have to bathe her eyes, and anyway ... almost swaying, Masha went into the bathroom, and what she saw nearly made her cry out loud.

All the water had been poured out. The buckets and jars had been neatly turned upside down, and on top of one of the jars lay the bouquet of asters she had given to her aunt. Even the teapot lay on its side. So that's how he'd tried to get even. Even the mayonnaise jars had been emptied right down to the last drop. Masha rushed to the tap which was making a rustling sound, then a promising gurgling noise, then a furious howling of pipes, followed by a silence broken only by the sound of Masha's beating heart. The only water left was in the toilet. Masha drank a little, washed herself and bathed her eyes. Then spitefully, she flushed away the remaining water and walked out of the apartment.

She dropped the jingling keys into the mailbox. In another burst of spite, Masha thumped the box with her fist and headed for the station. She'd gotten nowhere this time. Never mind! She was glad she was the only one who'd had a bad day–her aunt hadn't been too lucky either. If everything had gone well for Masha, she would certainly have taken care of the water and filled the canisters. But as it was, all she'd gotten was a slap in the face, and if they still expected her to do the decent thing, well they'd picked the wrong girl. She didn't care what her aunt said or thought. The next time Masha wouldn't use her apartment. She'd learned her lesson. It was amazing how that guy had figured it all out: "There are none of your things here," he'd said. Meaning, I can cheat you, you fool. You haven't even got the right to live here. Next time she'd plan everything out, right down to the last detail. She'd know better next time.

For now she had to go home. She could catch the night train mother always rode when she'd been to town. Masha bought a ticket and sat down to wait. The places where he had hit her began to ache, and she could feel her eye swelling up as people looked at her. Masha covered her hair with a handkerchief. "Those hooligans in town," she would say to her mother, who would start shouting. "Young people nowadays have no discipline! They deserve what's coming to them! We go on fussing over them, dancing to their tune. They ought to be shot as an example to the others, the bastards."

Masha's mother was strongly in favor of execution by firing squad, on principle. She believed this to be the only way of restoring order to the country. She had even worked out a precise, arithmetical system for the process. "If you shot one in ten, the other nine would behave themselves properly. Now you can't say that people in general wouldn't benefit. One sacrificed for the good of nine!"

Masha was convinced by the one–in–ten formula. Admittedly, when she proposed the system in class one of the girls had said, "And what if you turn out to be the one?"

"What for?" Masha was indignant. "What have I ever done? I'm not a thief or bandit, am I?"

But, to be honest, she did start to feel a bit uncomfortable about it. There were thirty of them in her class. Which three should be shot? Masha was no better or worse than twenty–five others in the class. There were five who always got top marks for everything, and it was sickening to see them working desperately to get their excellent exam results so they could get into college. To be fair, they should be the ones to be shot. But you could look at it in a different way. For this reason, Masha became rather more wary about repeating her mother's words in public.

Her eye had swollen completely shut by the time she got home. As soon as her mother saw her standing in the doorway, she said, "You can tell people you've been stung by a bee. There are some really poisonous ones around these days. It's something to do with the chemicals they spray on the fields."

Her mother did not believe the story about hooligans, but for some strange reason she did not shout or throw herself at Masha. She just became quiet, then she thought up the idea of the bees, and finally she blurted out, "You know Masha, if you're thinking of getting married, you needn't think I'm going to let you live in this apartment. There's no room for two families in here. So just bear that in mind. You haven't got anything."

"No," Masha agreed. "I haven't got anything."

Then, somewhat illogically, her mother began to enumerate indignantly all the things that Masha did have–two pairs of high boots, a coat with a mink collar, and another light one made in the GDR, a Polish raincoat, and a fox fur hat, and a pair of jeans, and about five jumpers, an anodized watch, and the gold pendant she'd been given for her eighteenth birthday, and the turquoise earrings. Is that nothing? Is it? What have you ever done in your life? You've never earned a single kopeck. How dare you say you haven't got anything. What you haven't got, my dear girl, is the apartment–and you can put that in your pipe and smoke it. Masha calmly told her mother where she could stick her rotten apartment.

So that would have been that. Except that bees can't make you pregnant. Not even with the chemicals they spray on the fields nowadays. And that's what happened to Masha, even though she refused to believe the doctor at first.

"What do you mean?" she said.

The way that old cow looked at her made Masha itch all over. She could hardly keep from scratching herself.

"You're already heavily pregnant," the doctor said nastily. "Four months gone, young lady."

The whole thing didn't add up. That meant she'd gotten pregnant a month too late for the father to be Victor, and a month too early for it to be the "American." So Masha could meet the doctor's contempt with her own scorn. So much for science!

But there was no denying it was a major nuisance. Of course, if Masha had been prepared to behave differently, burst into tears or act frightened, she could have gotten herself out of the situation one way or another. But Masha was proud. She decided, for the time being, to treat the diagnosis with skepticism, since there was confusion about how long she'd been pregnant. It couldn't have happened to her. She wasn't such a fool. She always kept track of her safe days. True, it had been a spontaneous thing with Victor, but it couldn't possibly be him.

Masha's mother was preparing to go off to a big regional conference of cultural officials. Masha had long believed that her mother had some kind of personal interest in these meetings. She gave herself such a thorough cleaning in preparation, you'd think she was being paid for it. She wasn't being paid. She was the one who was paying. She always came back from the meetings having run up debts of about 200 rubles. And she never had anything to show for it. Which must mean she was paying her own way, the old fool. But Masha was indulgent toward her mother. Let her carry on like that, if that's what she wanted! How much longer did she have to go? Obviously, when she was near home she had to keep herself on a short rein. But everyone has to let their hair down sometime.

Her mother came back from the hairdresser with so much hairspray on that when they sat down for a cup of tea and the draft from the window blew toward Masha past her mother's head, Masha felt so nauseous she only just made it to the toilet in time.

Her mother launched into a diatribe against modern food. God knows what they put in it nowadays! Nitrates, chlorates, radiation. To say nothing of the water ...

But Masha knew that the only reason she felt sick was because of the smell of her mother's hair.

"Are you going to go and see Auntie Shura?" asked Masha, apparently out of the blue, as she lay on the sofa with a damp towel on her forehead.

"What have I got to talk to her about?"

That was exactly what Masha needed to know.

Then Masha threw up again, and again, and she said to her mother, "Just stay away from me, okay! It's your hairspray that's making me puke."

Her mother moved farther away and said, "If it was anyone else but you, I would say they had a bun in the oven ... it was just the same with me when I was expecting you."

Masha said nothing. Her mother also fell silent. She walked to the door, and stood looking at Masha from a distance.

"You go off to your conference!" Masha waved a hand. Her mother left without another word, and Masha started thinking. She thought hard. Abortions, she believed, were bad for one's health. Once you've had one you're a sick person for the rest of your life. On the other hand, having a baby is a nasty business too. Not always, but in her situation. You'd be stuck with the label forever. Masha had an irreproachable reputation. No one could find a bad word to say about her–but if she had a baby, she could forget her good reputation. She was in a real mess.

Toward evening, the day after her mother had left, Masha knew for certain what she needed to do. She dressed herself smartly in a light coat and a crepe de chine dress with shoulder pads, a bright scarf tied to one side around her neck. She even wore a pair of sheer stockings and she sprayed on some on her mother's "Sardonix No. 3" perfume.

Masha walked along the street, delighted with herself. What a gorgeous young girl, she thought. It's a lucky boy who gets her as a wife. She's sure to have beautiful children too.

The Korshunovs lived in the part of town where the private houses were. They had a brick house with a verandah, a big garden, a garage, a shower in the yard, and a huge water tank painted orange.

Masha took it all in at a glance. It would be a good place to bring up a child. Better than living in a concrete box. Victor's mother was standing on a stool under an apple tree, pulling branches toward her with a stick and picking the autumn apples. Masha noticed how carefully the shop assistant worked. She had only to shake the tree a little, and all the apples would have fallen off. But she took great care. She laid the apples in her apron, which she held up with one hand.

"Good evening. Auntie Nyusya!" said Masha, opening the gate.

Nyusya stood on the stool and looked at Masha, her face completely expressionless.

"I've come to see you. Auntie Nyusya," Masha continued, even though she knew it sounded stupid. Who else could she have possibly come to see?

"What do you want?" asked Nyusya. She didn't sound hostile, just completely uninterested. Masha sighed secretly, regretting that she could not find exactly the right words, tried and tested, to say to Nyusya.

"Please come down from your stool!" Masha suggested in positively angelic tones. "Come down!"

"Victor, my darling son, what's happened to him?" cried Nyusya in anguish. She flew, rather than climbed down from the stool, scattering her harvest of apples as she went.

"Nothing's happened to Victor! Calm down!" said Masha. "What a state you're in ... now be careful."

Nyusya, terrified and panicked, was fidgeting, her mouth half open, her apron aslant, and the stick in her hand dragging on the ground. She looked completely idiotic.

"I've come to tell you some good news," said Masha. "Some very good news."

"Well then?" At last Nyusya began to breathe freely. "First she terrifies me, then she says she's got good news. What are you trying to tell me?"

"I didn't mean to frighten you." Masha spoke clearly.

"Just tell me why you've come!" shouted Nyusya. "You've made me drop my apples all over the place. What kind of news can you possibly have for me?"

Masha gave a merry laugh. She thought to herself, I'm doing well here.

Any other girl would have come in tears, but I come bringing joy. "I have joyful news for you." Those were Masha's exact words. "I'm expecting Victor's baby. Congratulations on becoming a grandmother, Auntie Nyusya!"

Nyusya collapsed onto her stool and sat frozen to the spot, her eyes gaping. Masha picked up an apple from the ground, went over to the tap that stood nearby, washed the apple carefully, and took a big bite.

At this Nyusya came to her senses. "Oh yes, my Victor! Oh yes, as if he wouldn't have told his own mother! Oh yes, if every tart from off the street came in here! Oh yes, pointing the finger at my son, who's never done a thing wrong!" She ranted on in this fashion, placing enormous emphasis on the words Oh yes, in a way that began to annoy Masha.

"Stop saying 'Oh yes' like that! You sound as if you're on parade!

Victor promised to marry me. You can ask him yourself if you want, but I'm not insisting on getting married. I just came to do the honorable thing and tell you. Your blood is already flowing in my body."

Masha had struck upon this phrase the day before, after her mother had left. It seemed to her the most crucial of all the things she could have said. She mustn't play for pity or sympathy, but on the idea that the blood was already living, pulsing within her, just waiting for the right moment to come into the world, that there was no looking back.

She threw the apple core over the fence into the neighbors' garden and walked out of the yard, as proud and beautiful as could be, and Nyusya ran after her, shouting, "Prove it! How can you prove it? Anyone could say that. You could pin anything on any honest boy! Prove it! Just you prove it!"

"Just wait till you see the baby!" said Masha. "Then you'll see for yourself!"

As usual, Masha's mother returned from her business trip with new debts. She seemed somehow old and exhausted, but the first thing she said, even before she said hello, was, "Have you been feeling sick again?"

"Only if I smell gasoline or hairspray," replied Masha.

"So who's the father?" Her mother's voice sounded dull and weary.

Masha had been expecting a fight, and this took her by surprise.

"It's Victor Korshunov," she answered.

"Try telling that to other people, not me." Her mother made a strange laughing sound, as if she was being strangled and tickled simultaneously. Masha was silent. She'd said all she had to say.

"Victor's got nothing to do with it," her mother sighed. "It was that time you came home with the bee sting."

Masha turned on her. "Why do you keep talking about bees?"

"It was those bees," her mother repeated. "Have you been to see the doctor?"

"Yes," said Masha. "And I've been to see the Korshunovs. I've told them."

Her mother looked at Masha like a mother looking at a newborn baby, amazed and fascinated by the creature that has issued from her body.

"And what did the Korshunovs say?"

"Nyusya started screaming at me. She didn't believe it."

"She's no fool. But we'll bring her around. They've got their own house, haven't they? Quite a big one. I wonder how she's going to get out of it?"

"She can't get out of it," Masha said calmly.

Again her mother looked at her as though seeing her for the first time.

"You should go to your grandma's in the country to have the baby, and then we'll bring it back here and show it to them."

Masha was impressed. It was a clever plan for confusing the dates. Her mother had reached check and checkmate in one move.

Then her mother made another important move. She went to see the Korshunovs herself. The whole family ganged up to drive her away. Nyhsya had enlisted her husband, Victor's stepfather–a great bull–like man who worked as a driver, the bull's daughter–a sharp–tongued little twelve–year–old, and Victor's Grandma Sanya, who had spent her entire life selling sunflower seeds outside the movie theater. At first she had sold them for 10 kopecks a glass, then they went up to 15, and now the resourceful old woman had increased the price to 20 kopecks, at the same time reducing the size of the glass by almost half.

They called Masha's mother every name they could draw from their knowledge of plain Russian speech, attracting quite a crowd in the process. But she might as well have been covered in armor plating. She spoke to them clearly and precisely. "Stop your shouting. You can't change the facts. If you're determined to take such an inhumane attitude to a future Soviet citizen, you will find yourself in big trouble. It's possible that the police will decide to investigate your whole family. As for you, Nyusya–a shop assistant! Your husband's a driver and your grandma's a profiteer. I could have all of you brought up on more than one count. And we wouldn't hear another peep out of you."

They all continued yelling, but Masha's mother walked away proudly.

"They've got a nice place there," she said to Masha later. "Did you notice? They're building an extra floor onto the house."

"Really?" Masha was surprised. "I never noticed. Who'd have

thought it!"

In short, the visit to the Korshunovs cleared the whole thing up. Masha registered at the prenatal clinic, making sure all the evidence pointed to Victor, and went around in a state of great tranquility, which was most important in her condition. She had the following conversation with her mother.

"So who's the real father?"

"Victor," said Masha. "What are you talking about?"

"Oh, tell me." Her mother waved a hand. "I only want to make sure he wasn't a drunk or something. It can affect the baby you know!"

"He wasn't a drunk," Masha replied.

"And he wasn't sick?" Her mother wouldn't give up.

Masha remembered the well–fleshed body of the "American"–smooth, gleaming, strong. A hot, dizzy sensation boiled somewhere down in her stomach and rose up to her head, fogging her brain, and her heart cried out, her lips were moist, and her teeth chattered.

Masha shook her head drunkenly. "As healthy as they come," she said hoarsely.

But her mother couldn't leave her alone. "And what was he like to look at?"

Masha tried to remember what he looked like, but she couldn't. She could see the torn shirt, the hairy chest, the chain around his neck, the white strip from the watchband on his suntanned wrist. But that was all. She couldn't remember anything else. He was handsome, not like Victor.

"Victor isn't so bad looking either," her mother said. "If the army doesn't ruin him. You could do worse. And he always did well at school, didn't he?"

"He wasn't bad," answered Masha.

"Maybe this will give me a chance to get my own life sorted out at last," her mother sighed. "Once you've gone I'll have a bit of space of my own. There is someone, but he's got nowhere to live. He's stuck sharing an apartment with his ex–wife. And there's no way he'd come here. He doesn't want to cope with you. Where he is now may be a dump, he says, but at least he's with his own ex–wife and his own daughter. You can understand him. As soon as you started acting up, what could he do? Go back to his ex–wife? She would have already notified the authorities that he'd officially moved out."

"You ought to go ahead and get your life sorted out," Masha agreed. "If you wait much longer it'll be too late. I'm not planning to sit around here much longer. I don't want to rot in this hole till the end of my days."

"What's wrong with it, if you've got a nice place to live? I don't understand you."

"Nobody has a nice place to live here." Masha spoke emphatically. "It would be a lie to say they did. What about Auntie Shura–she's got an apartment on the seventh floor. There's an elevator, but no running water. Is that what you call a nice place?"

"What do you want?" her mother was amazed. "There's a shortage of water everywhere. They even turn the water off in Moscow sometimes."

"Moscow isn't the only other place in the world," Masha said mysteriously. "Take the Baltics for example. That's where you find real culture."

"What have the Baltics got to do with anything?"

"Oh they've got something to do with it," said Masha, even more mysteriously.

"What are you scheming?"

"Oh nothing," said Masha. "I'm just thinking out loud."

After some time Nyusya came to call. She came in but wouldn't sit down. She stood by the coat hooks and said, "Victor doesn't agree with your story. I'm telling you once and for all. You'd better find yourself another fool."

All of which was very amusing, particularly because Masha had received a letter from Victor that very morning.

"Dear Masha!" he wrote. "My parents have just told me the news. As an honorable man, of course I am not going to deny what happened between us. I admit what happened. But I still have my doubts. I hope you're not trying to take me for a ride, Masha! First you say no, then you say yes. It doesn't quite add up. If it's my child, then all well and good. If it's someone else's–thanks but no thanks! I'm telling you straight. I could get killed out here any day. War is a matter of life and death, so I don't want to risk my life for no reason. You must write to me and explain everything. And I don't want you trying to make a fool of me. Although, I repeat, I admit what happened, another man could have denied everything in my place. But you know me, Masha, I'm not like that. I believe in certain standards, but you must believe in them too. So write and tell me the truth. All the best–Victor."

"So he doesn't agree with my story?" Masha laughed, producing the letter. "That's very strange. In his letter to me he admits everything."

And she read out the phrase "I admit what happened."

Nyusya stretched out her hand toward the letter, but Masha's mother shielded it.

"This is an important document," she said. "If you don't want to settle everything pleasantly ..."

At this Nyusya burst into tears and said to Masha's mother, "You're just taking advantage of the fact that you work for the council. You think that just because you've got some power, poor people like us have no rights."

"Poor! Don't make me laugh!" Masha exclaimed.

"Why can't we sort this out pleasantly, Nyusya?" Her mother's tone was irreproachable. But Nyusya gave a sob, called them a few unprintable names, and left, slamming the door.

"There's nothing they can do now," said Masha's mother. "Give me the letter, and I'll get a copy of it made tomorrow. And you'd better get yourself off to the village. To hell with the lot of them. You're better off as far away from the scene of the crime as possible."

Life in the village was intolerable. Two tiny, low–ceilinged cells steamed up in winter. Masha's room was separated from her grandparents' by a spotted calico curtain. The old woman came in carrying a bucket. "You can use this for your business."

At first Masha was revolted by the idea, but after she'd tried running outside through the muck once or twice and squatting over a stinking hole, she accepted the bucket. She even got used to the idea of them carrying it out for her after she'd used it.

"Don't you worry," her grandmother would say. "I'll take it, it doesn't weigh anything."

One thing tormented her. The old couple woke up very early and began talking in loud voices, noisily eating last night's borscht, carrying on loud discussions about what they should feed "her with the big belly." These long, noisy mornings filled Masha with such revulsion that she found herself thinking quite seriously. What possible reason can there be for people like this to live? Why? What earthly purpose do they serve? From the cow to the vegetable garden, from the vegetable garden back to the cow. Is that really a life? No interests, no pleasure.

"Have you washed out the jars for the tomatoes?"

"Of course I have!"

"Last year you didn't do it properly and they went bad."

"Stop fussing."

"You listen to me. You only made that borscht yesterday, and it's already going off. Why's that, then? It's the tomatoes, isn't it!"

"You're going off yourself. There's nothing wrong with the borscht. It's supposed to taste sour. It's not just any old soup."

"Shall we kill a chicken?"

"Well, I'm not sure. We can't feed her nothing but chicken."

"Well, what the hell are we supposed to feed her? She won't eat the same as us."

"So sorry, madam! We haven't got any fancy–schmancy sausages."

Masha pulled the quilt over her head. Here, under the blanket, her feelings of hatred melted away. She remembered how her mother had brought her here as a child, and how deeply and peacefully she had slept under this same quilt, after having had to sleep on boxes with brass instruments stored in them. She remembered when her mother had left her father. "There were lots of reasons, but the main reason was his jealousy. I wasn't even allowed to smile at another man, or shake his hand. He was suspicious of everyone." Perhaps he had reason to be suspicious, mused Masha, when she was a little older. But her mother's behavior never gave any real cause for suspicion. Anyway, she always felt her mother had the right to relax a bit. But she never got involved in anything. There was some man on the scene now, but in the past ...

After she'd left Masha's father she'd gone to the council looking for work as a projectionist. They said to her, "We don't want to hide you away in a box! A lovely lady like you ought to be put on display."

So they appointed her director of a club and gave her a room in the tenement. Once she had had a good snoop around, she found the room in the club building where all the musical instruments were stored, lined up in rows. Adjacent to the room was an indoor toilet (which had never worked) with some mops in it, and there was even a little storeroom with a window and a couple of electric sockets, which could be used as a kitchen. Masha's mother had dragged in a couple of display boards showing milk yields and livestock weight increases and fenced off a little passage of private territory in the public foyer. Here they moved in, having secured a water supply to the bathroom. Her mother calculated correctly that they stood a better chance of being allotted a decent apartment if they were living in the clubhouse than if they were living in the tenement. After the stifling, stinking tenement, the club seemed like paradise. They could watch the movies for free, it was quiet during the day. The only inconvenience was having to sleep on boxes– and even that only seemed uncomfortable after Masha came back from the village, where her grandmother had put her to sleep in a soft feather bed, covered with a quilt. She used to sleep until noon, unable to wake up until her grandmother came in and started dragging the quilt off of her.

"You'll get a headache," she would say. "The sun's already high in the sky. It's time you woke up. You'll sleep through the day of judgment."

Sleepy and sluggish she would go out into the sunshine, onto the warm, wooden porch, sit down, screw up her eyes in the bright light, stroke the cat. There was a smell of earth, grass, apples, and milk. Her whole body felt relaxed, heavy and light at the same time. It was a feeling she would remember all her life.

Her mother used to say, "I hate that village."

And Masha would reply, just to spite her, "Well, I like it."

Now she realized that she hated it too. She hated everything: the people, the houses, the animals, the plants. What was it all for? What was the use of it?

But when she was under the blanket something incomprehensible happened. The hatred disappeared, dissolving in the stuffy warmth and giving way to a kind of sweet, pervasive weakness, even tenderness toward those two old fools who had never seen or experienced anything good in their entire lives. And it was in this state that Masha found them a little niche in the wealthy, independent, radiant future she had created for herself on the shores of the Gulf of Riga. Why shouldn't they come too!

They could live with her, water the flowers, and feed her chickens. Of course, she would divide the house up so they had a separate entrance, but there was no reason why they shouldn't come and live there. Only she'd have to get them to dress like human beings, decent clothes and shoes. Masha poked her head out from under the blanket to get some air, and caught sight of her grandma's calloused heels, and her shuffling toes, which seemed to have become welded into a solid mass, the nails so thick that no scissors could have cut them. All her life the old woman had walked barefoot, all year round, except when it was cold enough for felt boots. Her grandfather, on the other hand, wore rubber boots winter and summer alike–squelch, squelch, squelch.

"Have you got your eyes open then?" asked the old woman. "Will you have a drop of borscht?"

Dear God, why are they alive?

"Is there any tea?" asked Masha.

"Well, the water's boiling. ..."

"I'm talking about tea, not water!" Masha retorted.

"I know I made some yesterday. Now where's it gone? We never really drink it ourselves."

"You have to make fresh tea," Masha explained patiently for the umpteenth time.

"Whoever told you that?" Her grandmother sounded angry. "That's nothing but a pointless waste of money."

"Have you always been poor?" asked Masha. She made some strong, fresh tea just to spite them and drank it with cherry jam and biscuits.

"What do you mean, poor?" The old woman didn't understand. "We're no worse off than anyone else. You've never seen real poverty. We've never gone hungry since 1933. We've always had bread and potatoes."

She became pensive. "Things were bad after the war. There's going to be famine again, I thought to myself. But your granddad knew what to do. He went off to work in one of the little mines they were digging out around here. He earned good money–well, even though the money wasn't worth anything, we weren't going to die of hunger. We kept rabbits. And when he had an accident, when the mine caved in, it was already Khrushchev's times."

"No it wasn't," said Masha's grandfather, squelching around in his rubber boots. "The mine collapsed in '52, at Whitsun. ..."

"You don't know what you're talking about," the old woman interrupted. "Whitsun was the time you cut your arm because you were drunk. The pit caved in two years after that. Your arm was all crooked. And I said you ought to stop going down the pit ... but you always were a stubborn, Ukrainian so–and–so. And then they started closing down the smaller pits and driving prospecting shafts. It was dreadful work. But you couldn't say anyone was poor. No, we've always lived very well."

Masha was beginning to perk up. "What do you mean by 'very well'?"

"I mean we've always lived very well," the old woman said proudly.

"We've always had our own house and our own vegetable patch. We've never had to go running to the neighbors. I couldn't abide that. We've always managed to feed ourselves and keep ourselves in clothes and shoes."

"You're nothing but paupers!" Masha screamed at the top of her voice.

"Just take a look around you!" She jabbed her finger at the iron bedstead, the chest of drawers with no handles, which the old woman had inherited from her own grandmother. How old was it, for God's sake? She pointed at the smoke–blackened iron stove, the green cooking pots, the tapestry with swans worn away in the years since the war. How many times had the edges been turned under to hide the holes worn by the nails on which it hung from the wall? It was nothing but a bunch of old junk! Nothing that a normal person wouldn't have felt ashamed of.

"Listen to her!" shouted the old woman. "We're not good enough for her! Well you were glad enough to come here to have your baby. Why hasn't anyone invited you to stay in their luxury apartment?"

"The only possible reason for coming to a place like this is to give birth or die," Masha laughed.

"How can you say those two words in the same breath?" Her grandmother was outraged.

"That just about sums it up!" Masha shouted cheerfully. "You're born and then you die. And if you want to live, you'd better avoid this place like the plague."

As winter approached and the old woman had already taken to wearing her felt boots, a letter arrived from Masha's mother. "Nyusya refuses to say hello if she sees me in the streets, and she's doing her best to blacken your name right, left, and center," she wrote. "I'm afraid you're not going to get anywhere with her." Enclosed was a letter from Victor.

"I'm not admitting that it's my baby yet." The word yet was underlined. "A blood test will prove it one way or the other, and that way no one's going to be taken for a ride."

Masha wasn't even slightly upset. There's nothing Victor can do to get out of it, she thought. She tore out a yellowing page from the notebook where her grandmother wrote down the dates of religious festivals according to the new calendar, and wrote Victor a brief, unambiguous note. "You're a fool, Vie! It makes me wish you weren't the father of my child. No one could say fate dealt him a good hand as far as his dad's concerned. We can do as many blood tests as you like. Send them through the post."

After she had written the letter she walked around in the first fall of winter snow, unable to stop laughing.

One day her mother showed up, she'd caught a lift in a van. She could hardly bring herself to look at Masha, and when she did, her eyes were dull, as though covered by a film. Masha was surprised. What's gotten into her, looking at me like that? To be honest, she could have arranged an abortion if it came down to it. Of course, Masha didn't want to, but her mother hadn't suggested it. If her mother did raise the subject of an abortion, she was going to say: "Childbirth is a healthy process. It's good for the system, whereas an abortion is like an explosion. It can cause so much damage that you can spend the rest of your life putting yourself to rights. And I've only got one life."

The last words were not her own. She'd met a beautiful young woman on a train once who had said this to her. She made sure she had a good look at the woman, checked out her tights, her outfit, her earrings.

Watched how she combed her hair and rubbed cream into her skin with her fingertips before she went to sleep. And it was this woman, a single mother, incidentally, who said these wonderful words to Masha: "I've only got one life."

Her words cut Masha to the quick. Masha couldn't resist asking a question about the child, and the woman answered, "Every woman ought to give birth, for the good of her own health, otherwise you don't get rid of bad blood. No one knows what happens to it. It might turn into cancer. That's why you've got to live as nature intended. I've got a gorgeous little boy. I love him so much–he's a real joy. And I'm in perfect health. You can see for yourself!"

With that, she pulled down her pants to reveal her suntan. For the first time in her life, Masha experienced a sense of rapture at the sight of someone else's well–groomed body. Her stomach was so beautiful. And the band where her suntan stopped was well below her belly button, just above where the pubic hair started. You had to hand it to her! She must have been over thirty, and she was so perfectly formed and groomed–you almost wanted to sink your teeth into her! That was the right way to live!

Her mother said, "You're going into the Dawn of Communism maternity home. I've talked to them already, and they've got an experienced midwife. And I've persuaded the foreman to take you there in his car. He'll drop you off."

"God help you!" said the old woman. "He can promise anything you like, but he won't take his car out in winter. He saves it up. I'll talk to the gypsy for you. He's got a good horse. If you leave the money to pay him."

"How much?" Masha's mother asked.

"Maybe 10 rubles." The old woman seemed unsure.

"A taxi would cost less than that!" Masha's mother squealed. "You think we've got enough money to start paying out 10 rubles for some dirty old horse!"

Her mother left 5 rubles.

Masha went to see the foreman herself. He made a lot of clucking noises with his tongue and looked Masha up and down at length, "Well you have grown up into a fine girl!"

Masha accepted the praise and allowed him to touch her here and there–it was for a good cause. She found it quite interesting to see how a man reacted to a situation like this, and to discover how easy it was to manipulate him.

"Of course I'll take you to the hospital!" he promised. He spoke ardently, squeezing Masha's breasts at the same time. "It wouldn't be right not to help out, would it?"

Masha went and had a look at the gypsy's horse, just in case. It wasn't such a bad little horse–smooth and well–built, which was more than could be said of the gypsy. "How much would you charge to take me to the 'Dawn of Communism'?" asked Masha bluntly.

"As much as I feel like!" answered the gypsy. "We're not a taxi, you know. We're living creatures. We'd have to see."

But in the end it didn't happen like that at all. One morning before she had given birth, having just sat down on the bucket, she overheard her grandparents talking. They were under the impression they were talking quietly, but in fact–bu–bu–bu, bu–bu–bu–she could hear every word.

"It would have been a disgrace in the old days, for a girl to get herself pregnant without a husband–the kind of disgrace you'd never live down," said the old woman, as she ate her morning borscht. "But nowadays they spit in your eye, and you don't give a damn."

"What do you mean, she hasn't got a husband?" Masha's grandfather didn't understand. "He's off at the front, fighting the Afghans."

"You don't believe that story do you?" The old woman laughed. "Are you really daft, or are you just pretending? They just picked him out of a hat ... they don't know who the real father is ... there's no doubt about that."

"That can't be right." The old man was outraged. "Her mother would never allow that kind of thing. She's a party member."

"For heaven's sake!" The old woman went on gulping down her soup. "The party members are the first ones to get up to those kind of tricks. Who's always out on the tiles around here then? That Komsomol secretary! That's the way they all carry on. And Maria's no different. She knows how to handle men. But you're such an old dolt, you don't even see what's in front of your eyes. If you ask me, the best thing would be if that baby was to die."

Masha's grandfather spat three times, indignantly, to keep the devil away.

"There's no two ways about it. That's the best thing that could happen!"

Masha was amazed at her grandmother's grasp of the situation.

Who would have thought she was so sharp? She may have been stuck in a village all her life, but that didn't stop her sniffing out what was going on. Obviously Masha took after her. Her mother didn't, she wasn't particularly bright. Otherwise she would have made sure she had a better life. True, the kind of life her grandmother put up with didn't exactly suggest a great intellect either. But Masha explained this to herself on the grounds that in her grandmother's day no one had any idea about decent living conditions. They just thanked God if they didn't starve to death. You had to take things like that into account. But if the old woman was young again today! She'd make something of herself, Masha was sure of that.

And the very next day it happened. It was all over in a flash. The old woman only just managed to grab the baby as it came out. For a moment Masha thought she was going to drop it. And there was a moment when Masha's grandmother looked at the baby as she was cutting the umbilical cord, and thought, a lovely, healthy little great–granddaughter–what a waste. But all these were only passing thoughts. They were too busy to think–cleaning the baby with a cloth, wrapping her up, helping Masha expel the placenta, giving her something to drink, changing the sheets on her bed–tiny, insignificant acts to do with preserving life.

"Just look at her!" the old woman said happily. "She's a little darling!"

On a page from her grandmother's notebook Masha drew a chart, showing when the baby had supposedly been born. It was for the benefit of those misbegotten Korshunovs. Just as well she was a big baby. There would be no problem moving her birthday forward a bit.

Masha's mother asked, "What date shall we put down?"

"Here," said Masha, holding out the sheet of paper.

Her mother looked at the baby for a long time. Masha watched her and saw in her eyes none of the murky confusion that clouded them when she turned her face toward her own daughter. The old fool! thought Masha. Well, there's no point getting angry with her.

Giving birth had done Masha's looks no harm at all–quite the reverse. She had become ripe and voluptuous. She tried out her new appearance on the foreman. When he saw her he swayed slightly and stretched out a hand toward her. But her situation had changed now.

Masha said to him sternly, "You watch where you're putting your hands!"

And she went proudly on her way.

The gypsy too, made approving clicking noises when he saw her. "D'you need the horse then, gorgeous?"

"Leave me alone!"

Everything was going very well. She was too attractive for her own good. Masha gazed at herself in the mirror, and thought. Yes, I'm too attractive for my own good. If only it would last.

When spring came she went back to live with her mother.

"Let's make this clear from the start–this is only a temporary arrangement," her mother said. "You get yourself fixed up at the Korshunovs. They've already got the attic ready." And then she screeched, "I've done my bit! You got yourself into this mess, you can sort it out yourself. I'm in no state to carry your burdens for you."

In the same breath, she began cooing sweetly at her little granddaughter, "You're my little doll, aren't you! My little chicken! Who's Grandma's precious flower?"

Masha didn't resent her mother's attitude. She knew herself that they couldn't go on living in the same apartment. They would end up poisoning one another. So Masha dressed the doll up in her best finery, put her in the carriage and set off for the Korshunovs' house. Since her last letter, in which she had wittily suggested that Victor send a blood sample through the post, Masha had heard nothing. Masha considered the problem at length and finally decided to send him another letter.

"Hi, Vic! How are you enjoying army life, soldier boy? Made any good friends? You're making a big mistake not writing to me. It doesn't look good. You'll have to come back here sooner or later, and the whole town knows you're the father of my child. Everyone's congratulating us on our gorgeous daughter–she's a real stunner and well–behaved too. It's no trouble putting her to sleep. You should also bear in mind that I've registered you as the father on her birth certificate. Things will only be worse if you make a fuss. When it comes down to it, you and I are both Komsomol members, and the Komsomol never turns its back on one of its own. Just try getting around it when you apply for a job or a place in college. They gave me a layette at college. We couldn't use it because our baby's a big, healthy girl, and the diapers and jackets they supplied were made for some poor, skinny little thing. A big thank you to your parents, who haven't given me anything for the baby. All I want to know is, what are you planning to do? There's no point burying your head in the sand– you're a father now, with family responsibilities, and that's the long and short of it. See if you can't find me a sheepskin coat–I hear there are tons of them in Afghanistan. I'm a size 48, medium height, or a size 50 would do if it's not too wide across the shoulders. Make sure you get something for yourself too. You'll have to have shoes and clothes to wear when you get back, and the shops here are totally empty. You certainly won't find any real good stuff. Your parents have built an attic onto their house. They've done quite well for themselves. Could share a bit. If you think about it, I'm sure you will agree that you'd prefer your child to grow up in a brick house, not a concrete box, breathing air scented with trees rather than gasoline fumes. Don't disgrace yourself by turning your back on a helpless woman and your own child, Vic.

"Your own Masha."

Masha was pleased with this letter. She had always been good at writing essays, avoiding clichés, and managing to find the right, human touch. If it weren't for the commas, she would have been a top student in literature, but she was never too hot on grammar. Commas, and especially dashes were the death of her, and for that reason she never liked literature. The better you manage to express something in words, the greater the danger of missing out on some punctuation marks. But she had a good style. That's what her teacher used to say to her. "You've got a good style, Masha."

Masha pushed the carriage, aware of the admiring glances of passers by. People kept coming up to her, wide–eyed, saying, "You look great, Masha–like a film star!" She knew they were telling the truth. She was imbued with a film star's beauty. And her little doll was all pink and lacy. The two of them together were a real picture.

The Korshunovs wouldn't even let them into the yard. Masha tugged and rattled at the locked gate. On the other side of the gate a huge dog leapt at the end of a chain, barking so diligently that eventually he barked himself hoarse. The house stood as if abandoned– not even a curtain twitched. It was a Sunday, and Masha couldn't believe there was no one home.

Masha crossed to the other side of the road, only for the sake of the baby who was upset by the dog's barking and was beginning to thrash about in her lacy nest. Masha sat down on a bench to wait. Sooner or later someone had to come out of the house to go to the bathroom.

But the Korshunovs proved to have great stamina. Nobody emerged. Masha had time to give the baby a bottle, change her diaper, and still the house was silent. There was a net curtain hanging at one of the attic windows, but not at the other. Masha imagined Nyusya, her nose pressed to the curtain, waiting for Masha to go away. But Masha sat and sat, and if Nyusya was frozen forever in that absurd position by the window, then it would serve her right for treating other people, that is to say, Masha and her doll, so badly. They ought to take her into their house–it was the least they could do, if only to do the right thing by their soldier son, Victor.

That day Masha waited in vain, although she certainly was winning the public over to her side. Apparently everyone turned on Nyusya afterward, saying they didn't know how she could be so hard–hearted. What do you expect, Nyusya? They all do things the wrong way around nowadays–first they have the baby, then they get married. What are you being so stubborn about, Nyusya? What do we live for at all, if not for our children and our grandchildren? And you've been presented with a granddaughter ready–made.

In short, everyone started crying shame on the Korshunovs. And when Nyusya tried to say that no one could prove it was Victor's baby, they answered reasonably that, indeed, no one could prove that sort of thing. Maybe in the old days it was one boy and one girl, but now they all had two or three boyfriends, if not seven or eight. Everything was going to the dogs, but you could be sure of a girl like Masha. She'd grown up into a fine girl. And everyone knew her mother–that dragon down at the city council. She never would have stood any nonsense from Masha, she'd given her a strict, old–fashioned upbringing. So it's more than likely that baby is your granddaughter, Nyusya. And she's such a little doll–just like a baby out of a fairy tale. The spitting image of Victor. Same eyes, same nose, same eyebrows. Anyone can see she's a Korshunov. You don't need blood tests.

"She'll come around," said Masha to herself, thinking about Nyusya. She was still waiting for a letter from Victor. She was sure it would bring good news. After all, he wasn't such a bad guy. Not too much of a wild fly–by–night. He will do for the time being. Masha had him pretty well pegged. And he was bound to love the baby. Masha even considered the possibility that when she was very rich she might keep him at home. He could busy himself around the house. She would have a large house by then, and there would always be plenty that needed doing. Masha tossed her head, and from her throat issued a strange sound–neither singing, nor the shriek of a bird–it was impossible to describe, and quite involuntary. It was the kind of sound a bud might make, if a bud could speak as it burst into leaf; or like the jubilant shout of a flower, if a flower could shout, as its petals opened in the morning.

"What's the matter?" Her mother was frightened.

"Nothing." Masha covered her mouth with her hand.

"You were making a funny noise. Maybe you've got polyps?"

"What are you going to think of next?" Masha shuddered fastidiously. Polyps? The very idea!

Since the baby was born, Masha had been in a state of exuberant good health. She experienced a sense of delight, for example, at the wonderful ability of her own legs to walk, to climb, to run. How well her fingers moved! She couldn't get over her legs! Every cell in her body seemed to be bubbling and singing, and Masha thought, I've come through childbirth so well. It must mean everything else will go well too. I'm going to get my house on the Gulf of Riga! I'm really going to start living!

The Korshunovs were not prepared to give in. On one occasion Masha pushed the carriage to the shoe shop and stood outside the glass window just opposite where Nyusya was working. As soon as she caught sight of Masha, the old fool stormed off to the other end of the counter, forcing the entire line of customers to turn around and face the other direction. Masha was left looking at a sea of backs.

Masha also liked sitting by the fountain on the square outside the council building. Here, more than anywhere else, she found herself filled with confidence in a wonderful future. The dark blue fir trees, yellow sand, the fountain lined with colored tiles. The council building was cleaned up to a spotless shine out of fear and fawning respect. Masha thought and thought and at last remembered the word she was looking for–oasis. It was an oasis. It was true that few people gathered or spent time sitting there. Mostly they hurried across the square. What could an oasis like this offer to an ordinary person? People just came and went, with only one purpose driving them: food and clothes. Masha had different goals, for the moment she was a nursing mother. Her only aim was to breathe the air, and of course to attract the attention of passers–by. But this was so simple, so superficial it could hardly be called a goal. A goal was something different, something you struggled to achieve. Masha was content simply to sit on the bench–with obvious consequences: Who is that charming young mother? Which family is she from? And so on and so forth.

Before they heard the news that Victor had been killed, something happened.

It was a fine day, and Masha had taken her doll for a long walk. When she came home she found her mother reading the same old newspaper with the article giving details of the rates they paid in Moscow for IT. In all her life Masha had never seen such an idiotic expression on her mother's face. She was sitting there like a half–witted servant girl with her mouth hanging open, flabbergasted. She might have turned to stone.

"Have you read this?" she asked Masha.

"Ummmh," Masha replied.

"Who would've believed it!" Her mother's voice was almost inaudible.

"So much money just for one time. And here we are, running ourselves ragged."

Masha grinned to herself. She couldn't believe the stupid old fool was considering a change of career. She really had lost her marbles this time! Masha's mother went into the bathroom and started crashing around with basins and splashing water. Masha knew what was going on. Her mother sometimes did this to hide the fact that she was crying. If she'd had a quarrel with her boss, she would come home and make a huge racket in the bathroom. Eventually she would emerge, flushed and red–eyed. It was as well to be careful with her on these occasions. Masha prepared herself mentally for any attack that might be coming her way. She was expecting a tirade to the effect that her mother was sick of having Masha around the place, that her life was her own, and there was no reason for the two of them to be constantly in each other's hair. They must each take responsibility for themselves. So take your precious baby and get yourselves off to where you belong. They've already put net curtains up in the attic. Expensive, German net curtains, what's more. Those shop assistants are nothing but a pack of thieves. They always seem to have the best of everything–and you can try every trick in the book, but you'll never find anything decent to buy. At first it looked very much as if things would go as Masha expected. Her mother came out of the bathroom, red and puffy, but the speech she made followed very different lines.

"Is that what we're building communism for? So they can live in the lap of luxury, in private apartments? What kind of system is this? The whole nation sweats blood, and what do they spend their time doing? How much does a miner earn compared to what those hookers are getting? This kind of thing didn't go on when Stalin was in charge. He would have packed all of them off to the camps, and they would have had to tie up their privates for good. What we need is another Stalin! I can't believe we've sunk so low. Those brave young women who fought with the partisans in the war–you wouldn't have caught them carrying on like this! And now they're all at it! They deserve to be shot or hanged. Immediately–without trial. Where did you get this paper?"

Masha was shocked. It was all so primitive. She had never thought of her mother as an intelligent woman, but she hadn't believed she was quite such an imbecile.

"All work is worthy in this country," she said. "You know that."

"You call that work?" cried her mother.

"What do you call it? Relaxation?!" cried Masha.

They stood facing one another, breathing heavily. Masha's mother was considering the possibility of grabbing her daughter's luxuriant hair, while Masha prepared to seize hold of her mother's arm and shake her until her stuffing came out.

At that moment the doorbell rang, and they both twitched violently, forcing their faces back into normal expressions. And there's nothing so surprising about a bit of breathlessness these days: They could have been washing clothes, cleaning the floor, ironing ... there are thousands of things a woman might have been doing to make her breathless.

A young girl was standing at the door.

They didn't recognize her at first, but she didn't keep them in suspense for long. "Our Victor's been killed in Afghanistan. Mom's yelling for you to come over."

Masha's heart pounded as it had never pounded before. Everything's working out perfectly! she thought. This is absolutely perfect!

"Dear Lord!" her mother sobbed. "Our darling boy!"

Masha was horrified. What was she carrying on about? Then she realized. Her mother wasn't so stupid after all! Why hadn't she realized herself that she should start weeping?

Masha turned away. She didn't want them to see her bewilderment. She decided that she should neither howl nor weep. She would opt for a state of stony–faced shock.

And that was how they arrived at the Korshunovs' house. Masha's mother, sobbing with all her might, so you never would have guessed she was both a party member and a council employee. Masha, frowning and silent, her lips compressed. And the baby playing with the lace on her clothes and blowing bubbles with great delight, entirely oblivious to the historic moment she was living through.

After that everything went so smoothly that Masha found herself repeating, "May he rest in peace!" It could scarcely be better than what was happening here on earth!

Nyusya swept up the baby out of the carriage and hugged her close, calling her "my own flesh and blood." And that was only the start ... It turned out that the news of Victor s death had arrived at the same time as a letter. Victor had written,

"My dear family. Mom, Uncle Volodya, Grandma, and Vera! I am writing to tell you that I am still here in one of the most dangerous places in the world. Somebody has to do the shooting. The men here are all determined to do their best to make sure the forces of progressive Afghanistan are victorious. To put it bluntly, I'm fighting. And so I spend even more time thinking about the peaceful life at home. Especially about the baby–which might be mine. Of course we can only get definite proof when I come home and they do blood tests. But as it is, I can't deny she might be my daughter, and I want to do what I can to help her. I see a lot of children here, and I feel so sorry for them. How can I let a little child grow up an orphan, even if I'm not a hundred percent sure she's my daughter? Please, Mom, don't say anything horrible to Masha–you'll feel so ashamed if we eventually get married. I'm coming around more and more to the idea of marrying Masha. She's a serious girl, and I know she wouldn't be a millstone around my neck. So you do your bit, and I'll write and reassure the young mother. She's asked me to get her a sheepskin coat, but I haven't seen any here. Maybe you could ask at the shop and see if you can buy one. Mom? You'll have to give her some kind of present anyway. I want to see you all. I'd love to taste some home cooking. It's not that the food is no good here, but I'd just like to taste some of my favorite food. Pickled eggplants maybe, and roast pork with potatoes. It's strange, the things I miss most out here. My love to you all.

"Your son, brother, and grandson."

They had prepared huge amounts of food–eggplants, and roast pork and potatoes, and wine and vodka to drink, because they had decided to celebrate everything all at once: Victor's funeral, a housewarming for the attic, and a christening for the baby. They were amazed to discover that Nyusya had personally, of her own free will, written out a will, turning over the attic to the baby, and she'd deposited some money in a savings bank for her. And she said to Masha, "You finish your schooling. We'll take care of the baby. After all, she's our own flesh and blood."

She also presented Masha with a sheepskin coat–only a Mongolian one, but none the worse for that. It was a bit on the stiff side, but what could you expect from the Mongolians?

"Not bad, as leather goes," said Masha's mother, but Masha could see she was envious. She'd never had a leather coat, nor was she ever likely to on the money she earned.

The Korshunovs said to Masha's mother, "Well, we're practically related now. Don't you worry, we'll leave you to live your own life, but you won't be too proud to help us put in an order for some corrugated iron to build our garage. It's nothing to you after all."

You mustn't think that Nyusya was a hard–hearted woman, more preoccupied with the thought of getting hold of some corrugated iron than with her grief. But her sorrow was eating her away. In the past month she had lost almost thirty pounds and had taken to wearing her daughter's clothes, which looked rather strange on her–all bows and frills and baubles. But Nyusya was the kind of woman who took everything to extremes. If she decided to hate someone, she did the job properly; if she lost weight, she practically starved herself to death; and if she loved someone...

When she came home from work she would kneel down beside the baby's crib and stay there for hours and hours. She would kneel there, talking to the baby. "You've got our Vic's nose ... I can tell already. When you're older it will get a bit broader, then everyone will see. And your little eyebrows ... thick until the middle, then nothing at all. Never mind, my darling ... we'll buy you a French eyebrow pencil, and you'll pencil them in, won't you?" And without pausing, she would start speaking to Masha. "And don't you even think about buying makeup off those gypsies. You'll poison yourself. They ought to be shot, those gypsies–nothing better to do with themselves than wiggling their bottoms at men and spreading their lice around."

Masha went back to college. Her life was calm and orderly. But Masha had not forgotten her dream. She would have to make another trip into town. The only thing that held her back was the thought of facing her aunt She didn't think she should poke her nose in there again. Or perhaps she should ... her aunt had bumped into her mother in town some time that spring–her mother was on one of her conferences for promoting culture and was running along the street. Masha's aunt stopped her and started crying.

"Why did Masha have to take it out on me, playing that dirty trick with the water? It wasn't my fault you split up with my stupid brother. What have I got to do with it? I've always got on well with you and treated Masha as if she was one of my own, and then she goes and does that to me."

"Why did you pour all her water out?" Masha's mother was mystified. "What's she ever done to you? She always tried to smooth things over between your father and me. She's a good woman."

Masha almost burst out laughing, but she managed to contain herself.

She contained herself to such an extent that she said nothing at all.

Nyusya was summoned to the local army recruiting office and told that she was to go to Moscow to receive some kind of posthumous medal for Victor and meet some of the men from his regiment.

They were meeting to unveil a memorial, or something of the sort.

"I haven't got the time to be going up to Moscow," said Nyusya, waving a hand "You ought to go, Masha, you're his wife. And I haven't got anything to wear. Everything's too big for me. Look!" Nyusya put on her new leather coat and practically disappeared inside it. She looked terrible.

The coat fit Masha perfectly. The expensive garment looked dazzling on her.

The recruiting office didn't care one way or the other. They wrote down Masha's name on the invitation and issued her a third–class train ticket.

Masha was stunned, not to say deafened, by Moscow. She took to cleaning her ears out in the evening, wondering whether perhaps they had been blocked up by the dust. Or maybe they were producing more wax than usual because of the change in the climate? There were soldiers, songs, demonstrations. They drove around Moscow in a stuffy mini–bus–the kind of dirty, dusty vehicle you traveled in when you were hired to help with the harvest. The hotel was, as Masha discovered, uncomfortable and far from the center of town.

From the window Masha could see a gray, depressing station platform. Looking at the scene, you'd never think that Moscow was a capital city, and not some little provincial town. Even the people waiting on the platform were the same–loaded down with shopping bags. Masha had not expected any of this. She watched the people crowded into the foyer of the hotel, all of them in Moscow on business; and they were just the same–weary and exhausted. Masha began to entertain doubts about the veracity of that newspaper article. There wasn't even a whiff of the wonderful life Masha was seeking. Where was she supposed to find people playing for real stakes in this pit of human perspiration where happiness was measured in terms of grabbing a seat in the bus, tracking down a piece of sausage in the shops, and sleeping on a cot in a hotel? It occurred to Masha that there were simply too many people.

They once had a meeting at school to discuss national food supplies. Everyone had to propose a solution to the problem. Some people came up with ideas for vegetable gardens, rabbits, or simply eating less. Then Zina got up. She was the kind of girl who didn't care what she said. And she said, quite bluntly, "Some people shouldn't be allowed to live."

"What do you mean by that?" they asked her. Zina began to count on her fingers. "We don't need cripples. We don't need loonies. The same goes for people with terminal illnesses."

They argued themselves hoarse. It turned out to be the most interesting meeting they'd ever had. Even their teacher joined in the fray, shouting and screaming with the rest of them. She was in favor of getting rid of loonies, but insisted that the cripples should be left alone–someone might love them, after all. Then the principal showed up–he had always been a little weird–and started shouting at their teacher. "Do you realize what you're saying? Have you any idea what this means? It's practically tantamount to fascism." The teacher burst into tears, saying she had joined the party before he was even born. Anyway, they started ranting and raving between themselves and never gave the rest of the group a chance to finish the discussion.

But here, in Moscow, Masha remembered the meeting, and started thinking about Zina's idea. Zina was the kind of girl who took everything to extremes, but this time she had really gotten to the root of the problem. Somehow, the number of people had to be regulated. Take old people for example. There were more old people than ... it would be quite fair to make a decision on how long people should be allowed to live. Say, sixty–five years ... and then that would be it. ... A cutoff point ... make way for someone else. Of course there would be exceptions made for really great people. It could be put to the vote, and if there was a majority saying you were truly great, then you'd be allowed to go on living. Someone like the comedian Arkady Raikin. Obviously everyone would vote to keep him alive. Masha mentally removed all the old people from the Moscow crowd. Immediately the scene improved. Why had the government never hit upon such a simple idea? There was nothing heartless about Masha's scheme. In fact she was being very humane in setting the cutoff point at sixty–five, which was, if anything, too generous. Eventually Masha came to the conclusion that the newspaper article had been nothing but a pack of lies. None of the things it claimed actually went on in Moscow. At least Masha hadn't seen them, and she couldn't imagine where to begin looking.

The days passed quickly and pointlessly. Masha did not join the crowds of mourning women at the meetings and demonstrations. Of course she was sorry about Victor. He hadn't been concentrating, the stupid fool. He'd done a great job, leading a whole group of soldiers out of an ambush, and then once they were well out of it he'd jumped out of the undergrowth and shown his face. Who would have expected Vic to do something so stupid? One of the men spoke very nicely about him and was polite and respectful toward Masha.

"Don't forget, Masha, wherever I am, if you ever need anything for yourself or your little girl, I'm always ready to help. Igor Kostin, at your service!"

Masha looked at this Igor, and didn't know whether to laugh or cry. He was a puny, weedy little fellow with a skinny neck and bluish pimples on his face. He had a patchy beard, which he was stupid enough to allow to grow. He was so small and scraggly. It was embarrassing the way he kept coming up to her. Masha began to avoid him. Fortunately he was so thick–skinned he didn't even notice.

Her mother had given her some money. For some reason she had decided that they would be taken to special shops in Moscow. This was not the case. The people who knew the city went under their own steam, but Masha was in Moscow for the first time. Once she followed the crowd into some department store or other and then allowed herself to be swept out again. That's not to say that she was some kind of wimp with no idea how to get herself a place in line. But Masha had other things in mind. If none of what she had read in the newspaper article was true, she must clear her head of the ideas the article had planted there and find an alternative route to wealth and a life beside the Gulf of Riga. Perhaps she should consider going into trade? Nyusya had already said to her, "Where's your high school education going to get you? Of course you must finish your studies–people respect a few qualifications. But then you ought to come and work at the shop. I can get you a job on the haberdashery counter."

Masha grimaced. You scratch my back, I'll scratch yours. What kind of a life was that? Shop girls never stopped being shop girls. She wanted to do something where she'd be her own boss. That was the main thing–to depend on no one but herself. Taking no favors, and giving none either. She wanted independence.

Shop work would be a last resort. She hadn't come to that yet.

There must be other ways to get on in life!

Masha was faced with the problem of finding out exactly what they were.

Masha was sharing a room in the hotel with a woman from the western Ukraine whose son had been killed. Masha, who was nothing if not objective, thought to herself. If I looked like that, all the wealth in the world would come running to me if I so much as whistled. This was despite the fact that the Ukrainian woman was, by Masha's standards, already quite old, namely thirty–seven. But she looked like a queen, even though her clothes were nothing special and her face was expressionless with grief. It wasn't that she didn't see Masha, but somehow she failed to take her in. On the second night, as they were going to bed, she said, "You'll find another one..." and she waved her hand. Masha wasn't sure how to take it. She decided the woman was right, and she wasn't about to try and prove her wrong. They're not crazy, those Ukrainian women. She had come across them from time to time and noticed that they had a way of always getting right to the heart of the matter. If the two of them had met in happier circumstances, Masha would have asked Sophia's advicc about many things. She had a good head on her shoulders. But now it was a bit tricky to know how to start. Eventually Masha got her chance.

Sophia came back from church in the evening. There were some Georgian men, or maybe they were Armenians, who had already started pestering her in the hotel. Anyway, they were from the Caucasus and they were rich. Sophia was so pale that Masha gasped. She looked like death but so handsome, Masha couldn't take her eyes off her. And then these Georgians or Armenians came knocking at the door. At first they knocked gently, then harder, and then they started kicking it loutishly.

Sophia cracked her knuckles, whispered something to herself and opened the door. They stood there in the doorway, a crowd of dark–skinned, lustful men with lecherous eyes, big noses and jaws. Sophia covered her face with her hand, and said one word. She said it twice: "Git! Git!"

Masha could not see Sophia's face, but she had a good look at the way the men fell back, their impudent energy drained away. She was impressed! Afterward Sophia went into the bathroom for a long time. When she did emerge she was as silent as ever, her eyes downcast. Evidently she had no desire to discuss what had happened, but Masha wanted to.

"These Moscow girls," she said. "You wouldn't believe how much they charge. That's why the men try it with anyone from out of town. They earn a hundred rubles a time! I read it in the paper."

"They're not human beings, they're animals," replied Sophia and lay down on the bed, turning her face to the wall.

Why aren't they human beings? Masha wondered. Everyone's a human being. What about models who walk about on stage in swimming costumes? Probably Sophia considered them to be depraved creatures too. Masha felt angry with herself. You've picked a great person to pour your heart out to, you fool! What can you expect a woman who's already thirty–seven years old to understand about modern life? It's true that Pushkin died at that age. Masha felt sorry for Pushkin. There was no denying he was an ugly–looking man, and he didn't have much money either, but he had married a beautiful woman. You make your bed, you have to lie in it. Of course poetry's all very well, but to be honest, you can't really call it work. She pitied him–a good man in his own way, but irresponsible. A superfluous man, to put it bluntly. And superfluous men get shot. Masha was rather proud of these ideas–they were entirely original, not taken from anything she had read. But she deliberately said nothing out loud. Nobody ever tells anyone else their innermost thoughts. But that doesn't mean they don't think. Masha looked at Sophia, lying on the bed with her face to the wall, and wondered what the main thought in her head could be as she hurried to church. Perhaps she cursed the Soviet government, which had taken away her son first to battle and then to his grave? Would she ever say such a thing out loud? Not likely! But you can always think. You can turn your face to the wall and think. And that was how Masha was going to follow her thoughts. She had no particular feelings about Soviet power–in fact she was perfectly satisfied with it. If she'd lived in a capitalist system she might have been a servant, but as it was ... all roads were open to her. All she had to find out was whether the newspapers told the truth. There was no time to lose.

Masha had noticed the major a long time ago. She had noticed the way he kept looking at her during the first meeting she went to.

Amid the crush of bodies, the tears, the embraces, there was this major, who had never fought at the front himself. He was ginger–haired, strong–looking with glinting, steely eyes, small but well–built. Anyway, there was this major, who had never fought at the front, and he looked her up and down from head to toe. Then he looked at her again, this time walking around her. Masha sneered to show her irritation and suspicion. After that, whenever he saw her he would fix his gaze upon her, and stare, like a cat staring at a baby chick. There is no denying that Masha was pleased by the attention. Of course this was a sad occasion, but there was no reason for everything to be gloomy. It was important to her to know she was attractive enough for a man to look at her in that way. She wasn't forcing the major to stare at her after all. On their last day in Moscow they were taken to Red Square. Masha gasped–it was so beautiful. Far better than any of the pictures. She stood there gaping, and the major hunted her down and attached himself to her. He started pointing out different buildings, showing her what was where.

"That's an exhibition hall. Have you heard of the artist Glazunov? The line waiting to see his exhibition went right around the building. That brick building is the Lenin museum. And over there is the university. The main part of the university is out on the Lenin Hills now. But this is the original building. Can you see the Intourist? It's a first class hotel."

"And they stuck us out in the back of beyond!" Masha felt insulted. "We never got a chance to see Moscow at all."

"You can only stay there for foreign currency," replied the major. "Foreign currency is worth more than ordinary money. What the government is trying to do..."

Masha let down her guard at the point where he started talking about foreign currency and the government's plans. Two forces seemed to have collided within her. The powerful force of the beauty surrounding her, which had momentarily knocked her sideways, and the secret force burning within her. The beauty of Red Square had paralyzed her, but her secret, inner force attached itself to the major. This might be it! Why not? And it had all happened so suddenly!

He led Masha around, holding her by the arm. They didn't seem to be going in any particular direction, but all the time they were moving farther and farther away from the group. His hand was burning hot. What did it mean? He looked around and hustled her into the minibus. Inside, it was empty, dusty, and grimy.

As Masha yielded to him, she managed to say that nothing in life was free–she wasn't an idiot, and she'd read ... but either the major didn't understand her, or he didn't hear, or he didn't take any notice. He muttered something to her about the advantage of being dead–because then you don't know anything. Masha wondered what he meant and who he could possibly be talking about. Then she realized he must be referring to Victor. The major was slightly inhibited about the idea of taking a dead soldier's girlfriend–but not so inhibited as to stop himself from doing it!

Afterward he shot out of the minibus like a bullet from a gun, without so much as a backward glance at Masha. And then he disappeared, as if into a crack in the ground!

She was filled with hatred. Is that it? she thought. Is that the way it is? Just because she came from the country, they could treat her like that? She wasn't going to stand for it! She could have that major reduced to a pulp on two counts.

She would go straight to the Central Committee and tell them what had happened. He wouldn't get away with it! But in her heart she knew there was no one she could turn to. She'd been a fool. What she needed was experience, and that was exactly what she didn't have. She'd have to get her brain into gear. She wanted big things, and not just a little sex! Sex as such left her cold.

When Masha climbed down out of the minibus, she realized that the whole thing had only taken a couple of minutes–just enough time for the traffic lights to change once. The sun was setting. Masha wiped her flushed face with the hem of her slip. "Damn the lot of you, I don't care if you look at me. Parasites, bastards, vermin!"

She took a deep breath and walked away, following her nose. Her nose led her toward the Intourist hotel.

They can just wait, she thought. When I'm rich, when I'm very rich, I'll strangle all of them. All of them! One by one...

Translated by Rachel Osorio

Teardrops on the Flowers

Evgeny Kharitonov

Only yesterday and where is it now? Old crowds have mutated into new crowds, a mood has passed, and lovers are ex–lovers.

Life assumes new forms I can't adapt to: Vocational Training Institutes, pop groups, Swedish love communes. Encircled by a world which has no place for me. I hear the young say. "You are no longer of interest to us, but you are admirably qualified to understand us, so we shall show you our genius. Understand it." I know, though, that when it is at last my cue they will run off, except for some who will stay out of politeness. And those who run off will be the ones I fancied, and those who stay will be the ones I don't.

I am an old man now and new things bother me, the ever–changing fads designed to make us obsolete.

I planted the flowers facing me, but they have turned away to face the sun, and now I am in the row behind.

Once upon a time I went out to my grave to sit a while, and eat an egg to my health. I sat and I sat, and what did I see? I saw nothing. I couldn't see, only hear. And smell. So there I sat, smelling, and a little flower came flying up to me, flapping its little arms and legs. "Hello, little flower," said I. "What do you want of me?" "Give all of your life to me," said the little flower. "Here you are, little flower," I said. "Take all of my life, and give me in return all of my death." Then I died, and he grew where I had been.

I had not the strength for living, and couldn't find the pulse anyway. I wanted fixity, motionlessness. All I ever asked for was a corner where I could rest, bide a while, have a smoke, be still, stretch out my legs, or maybe just turn up my toes. I always pretended, of course, that I only had to fall in love truly to find hope. I would catch fire, burst into life, my real, exotic temperament would blaze forth. How could it be expected to blaze forth until it had something to feed on? Of course, nothing much did come its way. For that I would have had to fight, and know how to provoke interest, and I was no good at that. I spent all my time concentrating things in writing. I got into writing because I wouldn't have been any good at standing up straight: and I was no good at sports.

Mostly I made friends with girls, away from the roughness and fighting. Playtime scared me. Hordes of crude, truculent, heartless, unfeeling, spiritually stunted adolescents rushing out to punch each other up. I would press up against a wall with my eyes shut, or stay in the classroom.

(Shall we start now on disentangling of causes and effects, or shall we recognize that the cause was not what caused it?) Your author, at all events, became ever more isolated, and scurried ever deeper into his dead end. Goodbye. May you too find your dead end in life.

Is everything in my life by now really so settled and obvious, with no nook left out of which something unexpected might turn up? Perhaps that's a prerogative of fresh young things, and it's time now for me to join the grumblers.

"Do you enjoy grumbling?"

"Very much so. A most accomplished grumbler, I am. Hey! Where do you think you're going? Can't you see I haven't finished grumbling to you yet?"

Today I was hit by my hundredth birthday. Everything there is to say I have already said and thought in my life.

A poet hasn't, after all, got that much he can say. He just repeats himself again and again. It's a trial to read his collected works and see how a person can go over the same ground again and again.

For all that, the aim remains constant: to break through to truthful utterance, which is bliss. To give voice to truth uncontestable.

Despite which, the germ of untruthfulness is lodged within each of us, and all because prudence bids us stay on good terms with each other.

I brushed against her. Heaven forbid she should think to sway back against me. Nevertheless, brush against her I did out of a humane sense of obligation, because from the way she was looking at me I could tell how much she wanted that. She probably thought

I just didn't approve of all that common cuddling. Actually, it was not a sense of obligation that made me do it, but more that I did not want her to stop liking me. I did not want to see active dislike in her eyes, and coldness because I hadn't touched her.

It does get to you rather when some girl who has been pursuing and doting on you, and thinking it an honor that you deign to be escorted by her or let her invite herself round, suddenly drops you. Even if she has been beginning to get on your nerves, it makes you want to continue the cruel game you have been playing with her; cruel because you were deliberately being polite and solicitous when that was the last thing she wanted. Your friendliness was a ruse to keep her from being forward and coming on too strong when, wittingly or unwittingly, she had been wanting it for ages. Why weren't you getting on with it? Poor girl. Until now she had known where she was in her dealings with men, or lads, and the male of the species in general. You had pout and flounce. Certain things they mustn't be allowed to get away with. You must be haughty, raise their hopes sometimes but then, once you had them horny, become unapproachable again. Suddenly all these tactics she had been assimilating since childhood, from her mother perhaps and her girl friends, these feminine wiles which were supposed to enable her to outsmart any man, were something he was better at than she was.

It was she who had to keep phoning, to try to engineer an invitation to come round, to work out ways of sitting next to him; and it was she who was reduced to a frazzle. She was on the receiving end of smiles of amity when that was not at all what was wanted, and which were quite the wrong sorts of smiles anyway. She had been invited to stay the night, although as yet she had no inkling of this, because she would not be coming alone, but bringing a girl friend who would be bringing a boy from the club, and because afterwards the boys and girls would be sleeping in separate rooms. She may still have hoped that this was all just her well brought–up host being respectable. Everything was wholly inexplicable, until somebody at last explained what was going on, and she was left with a wound in her heart which would never heal. To allow at least a scab to form she has resolved to stop going to the club. If by mischance she should meet you in the Underground she will be civil, asking how things are, but terminate the exchange just a little curtly. You aren't exactly stung, but you want the game to continue. You suddenly rather wickedly wish her in love with you again. Not that you are upset, altogether, but you do feel just slightly miffed by the idea that somebody can fall out of love with you. You even sometimes think it might be a good idea to ring her up on some suitably practical pretext, just to set her little heart a–flutter and make her want to devise a reason to ring you up, when needless to say you would again talk to her in the old way, within the bounds of your humane sense of obligation, even though there is cruelty in your humaneness. You like her being unable to catch you out as to where the cruelly lies, even though she knows it is there, but at the same time can't imagine what you can be guilty of, when all there is on the surface is civility.

At least this game still amuses me, so I can't completely have lost interest in people, or in life for that matter.

In the ordinary course of events, the woman at your side ought really to be in love with you. She should be someone who has heard all about you from your own lips, and with whom meaningful glances can be exchanged over some silly, good–looking young post office clerk; or tender golden–tongued songster with a voice bigger than his throat (but a chicken for all that); or a boy going by in the street, or one who's come to repair the fridge. You can't exchange that sort of glance with your straight peers, who only share such looks with their friends a apropos of mare–like women trotting by. It is nonetheless important (as well as being agreeable) that this confidante who understands you and your every mood so well should be (platonically) in love with you. Try, even so, not to be left alone with her. When you and she are together in public she can read your glances at other people and interpret all your moods. You are talking to a young man who has come to the club to see you. It is clear from certain amusing inconsequentialities in the conversation how much you fancy him, and how little he understands where you are at. Who will provide an audience for your dark smile, who can pick up the nuance in an apposite remark, a solitary word deftly slipped in but rich with all your very special experience? He understands nothing; she sees it all. Who could you find better able to savor your sad maxims?

What kind of woman should she be? Not intellectual, that's for sure: not the sort of woman friend who's as up on everything as you are yourself. How are you to make something of a person every bit as intelligent as yourself? No intellect, if you are to have any prospect of success. Then you can goad her, order her around, swear at her, even, possibly, knock her about a bit. And love her for it. She doesn't want to be physically large or, heaven forbid, liberated, and of course she should be young: and stupid, so you have no qualms about telling her she is a silly cow. She should keep asking you how things should be done, and sing while she is doing them, or rather, hum quietly so as not to disturb you.

Any respect for her as a person and you're dead. How can you imagine someone naked and looking up at you from below if you are on terms of understanding courtesy with you? You would be making a mockery of her dignity as a human being.

S. noticed I was enervated as long ago as 1961, so what can you expect nowadays. It showed in Physical Education lessons at school, and in my coordination. I am hopeless at jiving. Good jivers bounce; the music pulsates through them and they devise a succession of rhythmic figures as they respond and react to it. God grant arrhythmic me just to remain on an even keel.

In my compositions I try to collect as much as I can, droplet by droplet, in order to produce a tight, saturated, compressed lump, a vision of life, concentrated and condensed. I do it for my soul, and I do it to pretend to others that in my own life I am no less dazzlingly intense and resilient.

Art can be a thing composed from fragments, lots of itty little bits and pieces glued together to form a whole. The pieces are assembled and something extra inserted. Or art can be a gasp! A song! A bull's eye scored! A javelin hurled and soaring home! If there is talent. The first kind of art can have sophistication, and entirely merit your putting on your spectacles to scrutinize it, or listening intently to what is in there for the hearing. But talent takes your breath away, catches you up and carries you off into the empyrean.

The first kind of art can sweep you off your feet and call you to join forces with it to do battle or to love. It is a song which teases you to sing along. But with the second there's no question of your joining in. Your part is to listen with delicacy and succumb to enchantment, to catch a soft, far distant music. The first blares at you until you practically have to block your ears or give up and say, "Earth, take me!" The second demands that you pick up the libretto and read it carefully, while the words of the first you have no trouble remembering as you pound the rhythm out on yourself. "Hey, that really says it all!" and all pile in together.

There is something strange about the second kind of art, something as weird and hypnotic as the life of fish in an aquarium, another mode of being you look at or listen to as something apart from yourself: while the first infectiously draws you into the dance, brings the tears to your eyes, and makes you want to sing and dance at the same time. The first calls to people, while the second is apart from people, absorbed in its sacral, secret patterns, capable of enchanting even through glass. The first sweeps people off their feet and makes their hearts beat faster. The second you have to penetrate, and there is pleasure in the very reading of it and the penetrating. While the first itself does the penetrating, and seizes, pierces, and drags you along; and may afterwards seem to have been vacuous.

I really should get into pop culture. How many times I've longed to. What sophistication can rival its vulgarity? Alla Pugacheva finishes belting out her latest hit in my flat, only to start up again ten windows along.

Where is love, sweet, swooning, ineffable love, for hard–to–please old me. I've got the flat, the evening, some remnant of youth, and it's summertime, but I haven't got the friend I need. So I'll go on remembering those four months, less and less veraciously, gradually forgetting that even that time things were not really right. No! I take it back. Everything was great. At least let me keep my ability only to have to think something was great for it to have been so. Only it got in the way of my writing, and was no help at all in integrating the different parts of my life (because nothing which prevents you from living alone is compatible with my kind of writing). The only solution is to get a cat and magic it into a seventeen–year–old schoolboy who looks like me, only prettier.

I would put a saucer out in the kitchen for him, and take him for a walk every morning. He would scratch at the door if he wanted in, and be at home to greet me. He would be lying curled up at my feet as I wrote these words. And I would perform experiments on his body and register the readings with my heart.

I need a younger brother who needs an older brother.

The door was heard to open. I came in and over to me. We embraced with dry, careful bodies, not wishing to seem too ardent or to crowd each other, very close; knowing all there was to know about ourselves, real lovers. We have a shared childhood behind us. Only we couldn't have children.

I once fell out of one world and into another, and now I live in the gap between two worlds. A world of family and loyalty where I was looked after, and a world without families, of infidelity, where you look after yourself.

Here comes old age, where old men look much like old women, and little old ladies look much like little old gentlemen. How awful!

Something (and I Know What) holds me back from doing something they would say was really good and successful. You should have nothing in your life: no successes, no familiar faces, and then! And then!

Only then would your soul have its desire, and your face the necessary pallor (the red blotch on your nose notwithstanding).

If only everything were like that, life would take a different course: but "if onlies" don't come to pass, because I am at home in yearning.

I shall never find happiness: of course not. I am incapable of feeling it. For some reason I can always see its down side, an insight I could do without. It irritates me that I know that I could do without it. I know you can know too much; but still I know it.

Yesterday I seemed to be within an ace of what I long for, and I blew it by being too clever by half.

Oh, my demon. Will I ever be free of this knowing?

It's all just shapes, and correlations between objects. Which objects exactly is immaterial to this knowingness. Everything is functions and circuits. Perhaps spirit is in there somewhere, but not soul: or heart. A heart needs something to grow up against. More specifically, it needs to cling to who you are; what you like; what makes you cry; what makes you close your eyes with joy; what you were taught as a child; how you were spoiled when you were little.

A person needs an anchor and a faith to share. Not just any anchor and not just any faith, but his own particular Anchor and his particular Faith. If you share our Faith, be one with us; but if all you are looking for is a faith, then you might as well go to hell. God is on our side. And no, it's not that you might as well go to hell, but you really will Go to Hell. God is on our side. Not just any god, the Real One. Don't take me for a mathematician!

Preserve the nation. Preserve our people. What for? Why not encourage an influx of new blood? Isn't the alternative degeneration and stultification? Why is every species and every individual so desperate to preserve itself from outside interference? Because there's a law of self–preservation? At all events, if there is a higher law which requires that a body should be open for the successful functioning of its metabolism, we have no plans to rise to that level. Our instinct is identical with the law of self–preservation and it is, not to allow our present selves to be destroyed. That is what our intellect, and indeed our heart dictates! (How wise of God to endow us with anti–Semitism.)

I should have been a soldier: new soldiers drafted in every year; you're doing your bit for the Motherland; and you're bound by regulations which haven't been dubiously devised by you for yourself.

Nothing is such a turn–on as the agile movements of the young as they run, jump, charge about, soar on the horizontal bar, somersaulting, their vests working up and their trousers working down to the coccyx, records of all that hot, youthful energy. Where there is health and youth, there too there is war!

MY IDEA OF HAPPINESS

Going into a bathhouse and simply, effortlessly scoring. Unfortunately I can't do it. I'm hopeless at chatting up. You need low cunning. It's no good just going over, as I once did on a railway station at the age of nineteen, and naively propositioning an agreeable deity sitting on a suitcase. He reacted as if I were diseased. You need cunning and you need the knack, all of which grates on the Soul of the Poet. Well, all right then, so what do you have to do? Don't pose, for a start. Keep your cool. Don't get too involved with him, and when he starts wondering why you're talking to him anyway, don't start being afraid he's going to bawl you out or laugh at you. Don't be afraid of getting your fingers burnt. Do remember nobility of spirit has no place in courtship rituals and the making of conquests, which demand both agility and a readiness to crawl, and possibly a familiarity with and willingness to resort to the language of the gutter. You need an up–to–date grasp of contemporary values, and the ability to sustain a conversation if you are not to get precisely nowhere. B. is amazing the way he can touch them up on an overcrowded bus. He puts his hand straight on their flies, the targeted fifteen–year–old quite often gets a hard on, and presses right back at him. If he pulls away and swears at him, it just runs off Boris. He even turns nasty himself, demanding to know what is going on. Or so he says.

Anyway, to return to bathhouses. You really do need to know what you are doing. It's no good being embarrassed. Slide up the bench to him and get chatting. If he says something rude, just move on without feeling you've been humiliated or lost your dignity. In this life happiness is turning your own trick, won with your own fair hands, not one somebody else has found, and you managed to grab a bit because they did you a favor. Get out there and do your own cruising. Don't be a Chekhov character in a shitty closet. You need strong nerves. Don't lapse into mute, hopeless melancholy. Go for it. Stalk them, feel your way, spy out the land like a Jack London hero. Lie, if you need to, make promises, get them interested, and then go for it! Don't settle for exquisite sorrow. Right now there's no one around to admire it anyway. Heaven knows. I used to rely on fellow feeling. I thought you could score by being understanding.

You end up getting so understanding you decide to back off because he doesn't really seem to want it, out of fairness. Who's doing who a favor?

Let us turn now to the hunt and the mug's morality of waiting to be asked. We kid ourselves there is something attractive about that tragic pose in Death in Venice, when all there is behind it is cowardice and a lack of initiative. Remember, you don't even have an audience to admire your tragic indecision and hopeless gazing at the object of your love. Phaedra paralyzed in her hopeless passion is all very well in the theatre, although she would still look good if she were getting somewhere. Even so, audiences in Moscow went away or dozed off over that Italian film Portrait of a Family in an Interior. Who wants to look at some admirable old gentleman who may be wanting who knows what? If there's something he wants, why doesn't he come out with it? The truth of the matter is he's scared of getting his old bones broken or being called a rude name, although of course he tells himself it's just that he doesn't want to upset a young man needlessly, and that he's very tactful and aware that his quarry has quite different interests. Well he may, but the fact is that old men doing nothing and getting nowhere is a dismal spectacle which just makes everybody feel miserable and worried they'll end up like that themselves. Another point to remember: if you spend an age working out how to make a move and wondering what to say, you're in for a long wait. You hang around hoping he'll notice you and start propositioning you himself. No chance. He needs nothing. You've just got to get in there and get on with it. The longer you put if off the more inexorable the paralysis. Oh dear, you're going to start thinking, it really would seem strange if I were to start trying to talk to him now. He's seen me looking at him: he might think I've got designs on him!

And then, of course, you need to know where to look for it. For instance, there was that girl who came round to say hello from Alex. She got a temporary residence permit for Moscow working for a domestic services firm called "Zarya". It's just the same as in the old days when country girls came to the city to find work as maids, only now the maids come through "Zarya" and do home visits, and tend to be embarrassed about writing home about their new job. So there all these young single girls are, living in their hostel, or rather in an ordinary flat the firm gives them, with a kitchen, bathroom and three rooms with two girls crammed into each. "And do you," I enquired, "by any chance also have young men coming to work for you in "Zarya" in return for a temporary residence permit?" No. They didn't have boys; it was purely girls' work. There were, however, boys who polish floors and clean windows, but they were Muscovites, not boys from the country.

There you have it! All you need to know about scoring in Moscow. You phone for a floor polisher. He arrives, takes his shirt off and gets down to his floor polishing. You put on some music (better get Sasha to copy some of the latest groups), offer him a shot of vodka or three. The pictures on the walls speak for themselves, and start him asking questions. So much easier to be interesting in your own home. There are always attractive young men working for the post office, of course, but they fix the telephone in no time at all. Floor polishing takes time: time for me to spread my net. Pity they aren't country boys, though. Now where would you find country boys? Of course! In Rural Vocational Training Institutes. How to establish contact, though? Tricky, until you remember that in the vicinity of student hostels are canteens where students eat. In the canteens are toilets. Leave your phone number there, appending a false name just in case. I was once telephoned by a youthful voice of a kind to raise your hopes which asked for Victor. "Victor? There's nobody of that name here. You must have the wrong number," I said despondently. He rang again. "Is Victor there?" "What number are you dialing?" "Such and such." "Well that's the right number, but there's nobody called Victor here." A week later somebody else phoned, also for Victor. Oh my goodness, what had I done! Victor was the name I had scribbled beneath my telephone number in the summer. I'd forgotten all about it. In the summer the students had gone home to their mommies, and now here they all were back for the beginning of the academic year.

Perhaps I ought to seek out a military unit and spy on their routine to see what time they get out on leave. There might be a suitable nearby spot there too where I could leave an open invitation and my telephone number. Or in the Suvorov Military Academy. I remember once on the train from Kaluga cruising a whole succession of empty carriages until suddenly, a carriage with lovely military cadets! I sat down on a vacant bench. Along came another man up to the same game, saw the cadets, and decided to sit beside them. "Is this seat free?" he asked. Naturally, he immediately aroused their suspicions; they gave him a dirty look, and told him to push off. Nice try, all the same. Quick reaction, not a moment's hesitation before initiating the conversation. The longer you think about it, the harder it is to get started, and don't be afraid of getting the brush off. "Oh, well," you could see him think. He did push off, and went on his way, but then started to cry.

THEM

Beneath that hard shell of masculinity, then, every man is hiding a soft heart of melted butter. You know you are going to have to do a lot of flattering, indulging, and coaxing before he opens up for you like a flower. The probability is that all men would all love to open up, and don't for fear of being taken advantage of. That solid shell of invulnerability is defensive.

You know, there is an age of man when he wants to cuddle but somehow there are no girls around yet, so he and his friend sit with their arms wrapped round each other, or one stretches out on the other's lap. It's not what you think, though. Not naughty homosexuality. It's just that he had nowhere to put the warmth inside him, so he leans on his friend for the time being. The crux of the matter is that I never wanted to move on from that temporary state. In fact, I had a passionate desire to stay in that delicious state forever.

But what about THEM: the red Indians and seafarers who love to explore? How am I to do justice to their inner world, when they (our worlds) are so different? Their love of adventures and sailing ships is alien to us and makes us turn up our noses. We do not read the same books, about caves, and Indians, and pirates, and kindred nonsense.

For all their youthfulness and rosy cheeks, you sense they have within them the soul of a redneck. I, on the other hand, even having lived among them and assumed the aspect of a hard man, have the soul of a soft, frightened, shivering little boy, though I keep it well hidden behind a facade of stern eyes firmly in their eye sockets. While they, for all their youthful, vulnerable, lightweight appearance, bear within them the germ of a redneck. If we were the same age, they would hoot with laughter at me. We could never get on together if I were young. I would never be able to abide their crassness and spiritual immaturity, their tales of how they got drunk and talk of cars. I would have no place among them. They have no conception of meekness, dissimulation, or guile, of what it feels like to be afraid of being the odd one out, or to wonder what another boy may think about you, or be afraid he might not like you. All right, all those things are present in them too, and yet they are not same things, and they are not present to the same degree. As for the things they find amusing: getting drunk in the countryside and chasing a duck out of a pond on to the bank and wringing its neck. (Heartless butchers, one of their girls lovingly called them.) They had no feeling for the duck, or for the peasant woman who owned it.

Undoubtedly there was something that needed to be overcome at a particular age; a need to leap for the parallel bars, without being afraid you would fall off. Lord love us, though, what's a boy to do later on when he finds those who have overcome and conquered nothing so utterly delightful, those who have had the courage to tarry in that earlier state! What heroic resolve to stay weak! Reading made me a dreamer. Or perhaps it was the other way round, and my disinclination for energetic games set me among the readers and dreamers. At all events, it was soon a closed circle. I began to live in daydreams, and, as if that weren't enough, as I grew older, my aspirations grew less, before finally vanishing completely.

Goodness, how I am drawn to that pillow, to lie down and rest on it.

"Good day to you, Divan Divanovich!" "Good day to you, Slobodan Sleepitov."

I hit on the idea of connecting the front door bell to a bell push by my pillow, so that when I was lying there in the dark going to sleep, hoping someone might be just about to come to see me, I could surreptitiously press the button and the harsh ringing of the bell would fill the entire flat. It was a game for playing with your heart and, sure enough, my heart stood still.

You ought always to be ready for the worst, and then it will be easier to bear. Just to be on the safe side when I was little, I always thought as I was pushing my feet into my gym shoes that a mouse might have crept into them. If there had been one, at least I wouldn't have a sudden fright; and if there was not, and of course there never was, you could think, "Wow, thank goodness for that." It's a pity though that nowadays you are always ready in your heart for the mouse, and can't just take things as they come. Even now when I pick up the telephone receiver, I am ready for it to be the investigating magistrate, and when it isn't, I still think. "Thank goodness for that." Having an investigating magistrate in your heart doesn't make for easy living. That's just what Christian morality wants too: everyone feeling they are in the dock the whole of their life, and not having a good time.

Two books are being written: the one that we are writing, and the one that is being written about us. We are the kitchen writers who write in the living room, and read in the kitchen to our visitors. But a graver volume is being written about the kitchen writers by Them, and it is locked behind seven seals, and read to no one.

In those two books there are two main questions: "Who is answerable?" and "What are we going to do about it?" To this the answers are: "Nobody is answerable," and, most importantly. "We do not need to do anything about it."

A writer must have a pretty fair idea of the disposition of forces in a city for the KGB to want to recruit him.

You've already done them a favor by their having got to hear about you. Everybody the KGB takes an interest in is already complicit with them, since if they call you in they have at least managed to find out about you.

But we can't suppose that anything they can do we can do. Let's face it (face what?) Let's face it anyway, what are we (they) to them (us)? What we? What us? Shit!

That character (Tyurmov) is bound to phone again tomorrow. They may not bother putting me inside, just as long as they can keep me shit scared.

I gave Gulya a guitar to take my manuscripts to the West, and have been thrice, nay, a tenfold punished for the fault of giving away a guitar someone had given me as a present, and for not making an open–hearted gift of it but for giving it in return for a favor. My nemesis is that none now shall learn the burden of my lay. Having given the guitar away I was unable to learn to play it, and now I never will, because you can't buy them any more for love or money. For the rest of time all that remains for me is to write delicately wrought prose of no interest to the simple–hearted young, while my songs everybody would have loved. How justly God has punished me.

Now none shall learn
the burden of
my lay.
(Caw! Caw!)

No, talent is not some young man amazing us by the ease with which he can compose a song or put together a stack of poems in next to no time. Talent is doggedness. When nothing is coming out right, but still you are damned if you will do anything else, even if nothing ever comes out right for the whole of your life.

Please, all I want is to fill up just this one little sheet. You have made up your mind, and what preoccupies you now is not what you are going to fill it up with, but just the task of filling it up with something. Three–fifths of a page left. I'll never get it filled, unless by writing that I'll never get it filled. That's true weakness (fit for heroes). Nobody will ever know how heroic I was. Will anyone ever critically analyze my work? No chance. What's at stake is more important than whether they will or not. There's a curious occupation (they thought, seeing me intermittently jotting things down on a scrap of paper. Hey, you, up in the Circle, behind the pansies,...). Perhaps I should try thinking something about them. Whew! Thank heavens. Not, not thank heavens just yet, two more lines to go before it will be thank heavens. Only one more now. Now only half of one. Now I don't know how much more. Right! That's it.

For the first five years or so I would write one poem every couple of months or so. One time I took six months over a poem, working flat out: no going out, no breaks, just half a year spent composing it until I got it more or less right. I would never have admitted to anyone how hard I found producing it. I'm deeply impressed now when I look back at the extraordinary potential for diligence I once demonstrated.

So what was going on, and what is it that continues to be going on? I spend my time constantly mulling over one and the same thing, just one thing, constantly. Only when I stop thinking about that one thing all the time do I copy it down and put it in my collection. That's the long and the short of it. Only things which are new and fresh really work.

I am a little mouse. Hither and thither I scurry, looking for a crust of bread.

How many extraneous strata have been laid down in the course of my life, burdening me, when what I need is a light structure, unencumbered (if somewhat convoluted).

And I need children too.

Right then:

He married a woman. He was happy with her. They had children. The children did well. They had useful, interesting jobs, and more than once achieved official recognition for their work. They helped each other; they loved each other; and God loved them. They had friends, and they got together with them on official holidays. But their flat was falling down. It had seemed all right when they moved in.

Dear, oh dear. Isn't everything unstable? Isn't it sad how nothing seems to last forever?

Without a good job and contacts how can you fix up a proper future for your son? We wouldn't want him ending up in the Vocational Training Institute. He's not too keen on book learning. Bit of a loser, really. The wife and I did our best to make sure he would grow up along the right lines, get a good schooling, grow up a respectable man with a higher education, in a good profession, but he got in with the wrong crowd. What can you do? Perhaps the army will knock some sense into him. After he's out he can go to college and get some professional qualifications. Just so long as he doesn't turn into a self–employed artist, or a poet. That's all we need. Or a genius. Lead a normal life, that's the best thing to do. Get a hobby he quite enjoys, within reason. And give us some grandchildren, too. Then we'll be happy.

Of course, I haven't produced any children to make my parents happy (yet), so perhaps he'd better not take me as a role model.

I started daydreaming that I was not a genius, but just a chap who was good at his job. A utilitarian age calls for specialists. Right: I would be a children's writer, proud of having my work officially recognized. In any case, what a splendid vocation: using language to inculcate the attitudes I delight in those who will grow into young men. After all, your childhood impressions determine the kind of adult you become. How important Yevgeny Shvarts's children's plays were to me. Damn him for being a Jew (God bless him). How gentle and humorous and warmhearted they were. (Only we weren't allowed any Emperors with No Clothes, or Dragons Doing Battle with Authority.) And other children's writers like Arkady Gaidar, and Samuil Marshak. There's really no reason to be ashamed of doing something useful: the children would be in my hands, and would speak using my words.

Weak boys (and girls), please pass it round that I am a tyrant. And I will love you.

Right, then:

His mother is a lonely woman who smokes and rates love above everything else. You do meet ageing women like this, and some even have an only son, and want to show how liberal their views are, and think they are not the same as everybody else, and that this is something to be proud of. Oh, I am not like all those other mothers. I am very understanding. I don't mind if he isn't like the other boys, either. The main thing is to be free and to love, isn't it? What does it mailer whom. Who cares if it is another man: after all, I am a woman who smokes, and is very understanding, and never goes lo bed before three o'clock in the morning. (How completely ridiculous! Mothers arc there to keep you on the straight and narrow.) So, where were we: she has a young, effeminate son, and let's say I come home with him and stay the night. The mother and I have a tacit understanding. She is glad her son has such an agreeable gentleman friend. We put our heads together to decide what to do with him to make sure he doesn't go off the rails, and everything turns out for the best for him. I am direct with her, like a son–in–law, and she and her son have their own girlish discussions, which they don't let me in on, on how lo handle a man. She gives him positively gynecological advice, and gets him the best quality Vaseline. No. Witch Hazel, antiseptic and sphincter–relaxant. They are more like girl friends than mother and son. Oh, one other thing. Mother–in–law and I decided at one of our family meetings that it was time for the boy to make The Decision. I spared no pains, and took him to see a proper surgeon, in Hungary. His mother and I were worried to death, but everything went well. Now I wear the dried amputated member in a rather large locket as a memento of our sacrifice.

1. "He beat me and taught me everything there is to know, and He passed me on to a Georgian who did with me whatever he wanted. With men it's important to know how to behave, of course, I had no rivals. After they'd been with me they lost the notion of going with girls, I was that devastating. I knew every nerve in a man's body, and how to play on it until he was groaning in ecstasy and oblivious of everything. I could get anything I wanted off them: the star from the Kremlin tower, if I wanted.

"He fucked me until I bled, until I passed out, and he taught me everything there is to know. I am grateful to him for that now, because afterwards there was no one to rival me at my art. How he taught me? He would beat me if I did not come at the same time as he did. Even if I did, he would beat me all the same, but once and for all I learned to come at the same time as a man is coming in me. How he would beat me up, just using my stretched dick. He'd stretch it (when I had a hard–on) and strike it, or slap it, or punch it on the nose. I just screwed up my eyes like a kitten. He taught me only to answer to a woman's name, and to be that woman in body and soul. He never asked me whether I wanted it or not. He would just masterfully seize my head and thrust me down to his dick. And afterwards he would beat me again. The men I serviced later might go wild, and kiss and bite my little hole they so loved to get their lousy sausages up; but he was a real man, only beating and teaching me. He would even make me bring the belt, and obediently take down my trousers, and lie down in front of him with my butt up. That was my training in the university of life, and after that I did the work my degree qualified me for. But you know all about that."

(Pants Off: a Novel)

2. A man fell head over heels in love with a certain young man, but he (the young man) decided he had had enough after one time with him. The man kept phoning and wanting to come round, but the young man did not really need it any more. All the same it was quite fun simply to let the man have his way, without love, like a slut. The young man enjoyed being screwed, admittedly, but when it was over, that was it. There was nothing more he wanted from the man, except to be rid of him. But he kept ringing every day, desperate to come round. So then the young man decided to tell him he had made up his mind to live with a certain woman who had supposedly been his girlfriend years ago, and who he had started seeing again. Sorry about that. When the man rang up he would keep saying. "Sorry, I can't. She's at home; I can't talk now. Sorry." Then one time he gave in, and when the man rang again, he told him to come round, because she was out today. So there he was waiting and waiting for the man to arrive, and in the meantime psyching himself up with fantasies (about the Georgian), until he couldn't stand it any longer and decided to jerk off while the other was on his way. As soon as he'd come he thought, "What use is he to me now? I'll only have him lying beside me all night trying to kiss me and stopping me sleeping. Fuck him!" (The other man was on his way on the bus by this time; now he could hear him coming up the stairs to the flat.) The young man quickly put out all the lights and pinned a note to the front door saying he was sorry, he couldn't sec him, he'd had to go away on urgent business. The man rang the doorbell. The young man was standing inside the flat on the other side of the door, not breathing. He bent down to the floor, and started meowing to kid on that he and the imaginary woman he'd been going on to the other about had got themselves a family cat, and had gone out and left the

cat mewing on its own.

Thus that night did he keep himself pure and free from abomination; perhaps the cross helped too, which he slipped on as the doorbell rang, admittedly with the intention of looking prettier.

Well now, is all this ME or NOT ME? (as I said one day when I had been looking through these patterns I make). It certainly seems to be me; but then again, it also seems not to. If I were in a literary magazine surrounded by other writers, then it would be me; but being here alone on a desert island, just me on my own, it can't be, but anyway...

Why, oh why can't I just fly right away into the lovely world of wonder–conjuring words, unshadowed of distress, gay columbine, saved–soul–stirring, blond–brow hazel–eyed, kiss–curled, seventeen–autumnal, navy–red starring...

For heaven's sake, stop worrying. Everything you write will be fine. And even more so everything you don't.

Translated by Arch Tait

An Individualist's Notebook

Yury Mamleev

This old, battered notebook was found beside a garbage pile by one Ivan Ilyich Puzankov, a night watchman. He would've used it to wrap fish in, but in his drunken state he began to read it. By the time he'd read a few pages, he was gasping, convinced the DTs were upon him. Actually, what alarmed him most was the fact that he wouldn't be able to drink any more vodka, though he was still 200 grams short of his regular liter. However, fiercely adjudging that us proletarians had never yet been beaten, Ivan Ilyich crawled off regardless to the nearest pub. There he sold this improbable notebook for a half–pint of beer and some sprats to a shifty–eyed, sick–looking intellectual, who preserved it in spider–webs and incomprehensibility.

An Individualists Notebook

All right, so I'm a nasty piece of work. Yes, and I'm all the nastier for writing about this so lovingly; I'm cursing myself–useless bugger, demented halfwit, you want a good thump–but I'm in love just the same! And how! In seventh heaven.

Still, it's a bit off, loving yourself that way . . . Especially after all that's happened . . . oh, yes, that was quite something! Actually it all started from the fact that it wasn't myself I loved, but her. That's truly amazing–loving another human being. Deep down in your benighted soul, unburdened by gravity and the terrors of egoism, to feel so light, just so light, and somehow ennobled. Yes, I'd confer that on anyone in love–a title of nobility.

She was an extremely high–class girl; infernal to a degree, poetical and given to sleepwalking. I loved her passionately, but in a sad sort of way. I would hug her to myself, gaze into those soft eyes of hers with a kind of piercing madman's stare, and she would cry. She cried because the expression in my eyes was decidedly not of this world. And anything that wasn't of this world would call forth streams of tears. She didn't cry like other people, either, but in some unearthly fashion; it wasn't tears she wept, but thoughts; she would start thinking, she'd drift off somewhere, and tears would flow at the mere touch of her despairing thoughts.

She was a very nervous person. Which of course was just what I needed. At nights I would kiss her lonely, cold feet, and whisper nightmares to her. I would stroke her translucent skin, in its softness also not of this world, pierce her flesh . . . and murmur, murmur ... of my terrors, of my profound despair at living among people, of death. I spent the entire honeymoon telling her about death. I spoke metaphysically, with little yawning abysses, with awesome, sinister pauses, when everything would come to a stand– still; and prostrating myself before her beautiful, naked, inaccessibly mystical feet, I would howl in a shrill voice, begging her to save me from my fears, from life, from death . . . Poor little creature, how could she endure all this!

All the pus, all the paranoid ulcers of my miserable soul I spilled out before her eyes, in ecstasy, squealing, riven with anguish. And this I called true love. Yes, that's how we loved one another, whole days on end wandering our locked rooms, alone with our nightmare, and the dark, taciturn sky, watching us through the windows.

Zina was quite often silent, becoming ever more wrapped up in. herself. For my part, I would whimper, and look at her, and construct entire worlds. She was frightened of my worlds, and appeared to weep for them. Actually, in her own way she was quite abnormally schizoid, and could take the simplest, most trivial phrase and play around with it, construct a whole 'world', then go off into it and hide. But she'd have had to fly some to keep up with me, oh yes, sir! Anyway, that's how we looked at one another, lonely, disheveled, each from our own worlds, singing our secret stories. We lived on our nerves, on our nerves, yes, the whole time!

You think we didn't sign up at the Registry Office, go through the formalities, get our names down . . .? I'm supposed to be a mystic, so there was none of that? Oh, there was, there was, all of it. The Registry Office, the idiotic wedding, with the idiotic relatives and the potato salad, and even 'Let's have a kiss, then!' . . . Actually, the way I felt, it was as if somebody else had been married off, not me . . . That lot had nothing to do with me . . . And my bride seemed to me like a fairy–tale creature, descended from her celestial abode, while all around us were nothing but swine and mongrels . . . That's why the impression I'm left with of our wedding is of one long grunt. I took an instant dislike to her parents, hated them with a fierce animosity, for the very reason that through Zina, these creatures had had the audacity to become my equals.

I must say that if there's one thing I can't stand it's ordinary people, who make up 90 percent of the world. I'm ready to bet that any murderer, pervert or alcoholic is better and more noble than your average man ... At least there might be some repentance and fear in a criminal's miserable soul, and a drop of sweat on his brow, from some sort of feeling, but your ordinary person doesn't even have that much–he's a speaking machine, anti–spiritual, pathologically stupid, and regarded as possessing sound good sense. But in comparison with him, any cretin with so much as a smidgen of originality is a veritable philosopher. Just take a look at the eyes of your average man, see what's there: a cycle of ideas, fixed forever, locked up in their own bestial stupidity, and a total absence of the higher emotions. As far as your average man is concerned, first place in the hierarchy of values is occupied by the thing, the material object, the money, but not the idea, not the feeling, and never a nasty whiff of repentance . . .

And why is that? It's because the ordinary person is too stupid to apprehend the spiritual and in order to bolster himself, he's forced to cling to externals, and set a higher value on material evidence of whatever kind, or worse still–to some sort of intellectual folly, assuming our ordinary person should suddenly latch on to an idea.

Her family conformed exactly to that familiar plan. Even in terms of his personality, her brother was pathological with it. An extremely uptight, niggardly young man, he denied... himself all pleasure except hoarding money. I remember one evening, after he'd munched his way through a crust of black bread and an onion, he delved into his suitcase and drew out a huge wad of notes, and began stroking them ecstatically, drooling, pressing them to his heart and mumbling, "This is the only thing that makes me feel like an intellectual."

He needed money not in order to spend it, but to feel like a human being, to give him self–esteem, and he placed money above everything else in life. He actually had an attack of nerves once, seriously, when he heard somewhere that Churchill used to read

Shakespeare.

"How can a great man be bothered with rubbish like that?" he declared, baffled. Yes, that came as a real blow to him, psychologically.

He had absolutely no faith in poetry, or painting, or religion, all of which he considered mere fancy. He was sincerely convinced that people not only don't believe in God, but never have done, and that the sort of person who might believe in God, in idealism, in poetry, simply didn't exist, and anything that had been written in books about such a person was mere propaganda.

"How can you prefer the invisible to the visible?" he would say.

His parents, well–off engineers, were just as stupid, but not quite so pathological.

In the beginning, when I was still at the courtship stage with Zina, I was very quiet and withdrawn, so that they took me for just an excessively shy and tongue–tied young man, but in general pleasant enough. Anyway, they made no objection to the marriage. However, two days after the wedding, I showed my true colors. We were staying at her place to begin with, so everything was out in the open. My guiding principle was to go my own way, but not to object verbally; on the contrary, to agree with everybody and appear, at least superficially, to be going their way. That was essential: physically, I couldn't bring myself to talk with them, let alone argue. I felt crushed and humiliated as it was, on a par with some sort of idiotic, useless, material substance, sitting with them at the same table, compelled to listen to them. My nerves were in a terrible state.

"Sasha (that's what they call me)–Sasha says he's really house–proud, and he's going to help us look after the dacha," Zina's mother shouted to the whole kitchen.

But every Saturday I ducked out of socializing with them, preferring to go off into my own world. I mean, my own little worlds I practically worshipped, feasted my eyes on them, and they were as close and as dear to me as my own body . . . And I stewed in their juice, as if in my own blood, and didn't like people touching them.. .

However, her parents soon saw through me. I remember lonely evenings drinking tea, when the whole family was assembled. The dead lamp with its dark–blue shade had a certain wisdom and individuality, compared with these commonplace persons seated around the table, who were in no way worse than anyone else.

While I said nothing to them about anything, I could feel an inexpressible delicacy and tenderness in my heart. My thoughts were sentimental, otherworldly, and able, it would seem, to raise the dead.

"Sasha, why don't you go down to the dacha, why don't you buy cutlets, why don't you learn some poems?" Zina's mother asks me, tentatively.

"I'll definitely do all that on Saturday," I reply, calmly and imperturbably.

But inside I'm beginning to feel sick because they're looking at me as at another human being, their equal.

"Why can't they sense my singularity?" I'm thinking, "Can I be ordinary!? Actually, when I answer them, I become ordinary. It's terrible."

"But it's the same every time, you always promise to do everything on Saturday," says Zina's mother, impassively. "That's four months gone by already, and you haven't done a thing."

Her eyes are watering with malice. Zina's father looks as if he's dreaming he's at an official reception. I say nothing. They're struck by my otherworldliness. They can't define it in words, they're lost in conjecture, but they can sense a vague something. And they find that so scary that Zina's brother drops a slice of bread on the floor.

"Maybe you think you're cleverer than us?" her mother asks me, coldly.

Again I respond with some nonsense or other, which makes the whole situation even more sepulchral.

"Maybe you'd like to speak to him?" they ask my Zina.

Defensive tears, however, well up in her eyes . . .

Yes, there were quite a few jolly evenings of that sort.

Poor Zina–she loved her parents unthinkingly–had to flap around between me and them. I found it difficult to control her during the day (they kept confusing her with their common sense), but at nights, and whenever we were left alone tête–à–tête, I was her lord and master. At that point my worlds went into action. In the end, in order to shut myself off from her parents, I decided to answer all their questions with my own made–up words, so that they could understand nothing and were horrified. "With a ring of other–speech, I shall auto–partition myself from external cretins." I would giggle then in my mind.

So now if they tried to elicit from me whether I loved Zina, I would answer, "Yip–yap–yoof–woof." And if, for instance, they were to ask me why I didn't think much of some fashionable actor, I would say, "Ribble–fribble–cribble." And if they got all angry and neurotic, reflecting on my assertion that the moon was hollow, I would respond monosyllabically, "Moo." To each question, I would have a different reaction.

The funniest thing was that they thought I was just acting the goat. Anyway, that couldn't go on, and I started whining to Zina at nights, that we should move out to my place. She knew perfectly well what I was up to, and reckoned I was still treating her parents fairly decently. She couldn't stand the idea of moving into my filthy, solitary rooms, crammed with prehistoric furniture, like something out of touch with this life. But she knew she would find tenderness there. Tenderness, which fogs the mind, and which can perhaps even be transformed into torment, into torture; tenderness which hung poised over our unfathomable fear . . . We moved into my flat...

And I was absolutely fine there, at peace, out of touch . . . And I opened up before my darling wife genuinely, truthfully, the whole way . . . "Isolation, separation," I used to squeal in her ear hole at nights. But she started having nightmares, and I loved to watch her having them. My nose for such things was quite extraordinary; the minute a nightmare presented itself to her in her sleep, I would ease myself awake, jump up on the bed, without waking her, light a little candle (stored for the purpose in my bedside table) and sit calmly and pleasurably gazing at her face. Her face was extremely expressive; white and tender, quivering slightly, as if there were snakes crawling underneath the skin. She was obviously frightened . . . Later, when it was all over, I would waken Zina and begin whispering transitions, mysterious dreams to her, inflaming in her a pathological pity for myself, and then violently take her.

In the agony, the drama of the sexual act, I sought a release and a refuge from those Higher Powers, which created us against our will. During all those minutes, my thoughts and words, directed at Zina, were the creations of the Spirit in its most mysterious, and stark–naked intimacy.

"Complication, copulation," I now squealed in her ear. In the mounting squall of the sexual act I could force her to see the entire life of man, fragile and doomed, like sperm itself, vile, decaying, in its rising, its clinging passionately to delicious pleasure, and its fall into nothingness. I made her imagine that the sweat of voluptuousness was the sweat of death, and that the exhausted end of the sexual act was also the symbolic end of our human life, a life just as ill–begotten and as doomed to speedy extinction, as an eruption of semen.

Finally, she would get into such a state that she would kiss the residual splashes of my sperm, tenderly, achingly, murmuring that they were the tears of a broken life. "I'll drink deep, deep," she would moan ecstatically.

And all these little acts I made her carry out in profound secrecy, by candle–light, under the blanket, like something deeply vile, yet intensely intimate and personal.

And when we weren't shuddering in physical tremor, but lying serenely contented, in spiritual vein, do you imagine that we were any less wrecked?! Absolutely not. It was just how we saw it. After all, our condition was one of peace, a state of the mind, as if we had no bodies.

Indeed, we had no bodies, but we did have eyes . . . And naturally, she cried a lot. She used to rush around my solitary, schizophrenic rooms, where every stain frightened her, and seemed like an entire world. Moreover, I used to starve her. Hunger, of course, tends to enhance the body's otherworldliness and fragility; it calls forth torrents of whimsical sublimations, wonderful desires. I mean, no thinking person will ever admit to being hungry; instead they think, I'm missing something, something obscure and mysterious. That's how I was able to awaken her higher faculties. Spirituality, spirituality–I wanted as much spirituality as possible.

My other method consisted of arousing her fear of death; for my own part, I have a pathological dread of death, to the point of convulsions, and I reckon that the Creator still owes me an answer, on bended knees, as to why I'm so festeringly mortal, and like unto die–albeit theoretically–at any minute.

Well, sir, at that point we had various trifling illnesses, she and I, so that we had abundant grounds for our fears, sure enough.

Murmuring sweet nothings to her in the troubled half–light of our room, I would kiss her exquisitely swelling left breast, with its affecting little mole–a place on herself which she too loved, and couldn't look at in the mirror without weeping–and I would say, "This will die," clinging with my lips to her blissful throat, I would whisper, "This too will die," and achingly, mystically gazing into her eyes, into those pure, unfathomable eyes of hers, I would pronounce, "And even that which lies behind these lovely eyes, will also die . . ." And she would understand that her soul would perish, her poor, gentle, lost soul, like a little boat on some remote forest pond. Through this constant emphasis on the reality, and at the same time the horror, the absurdity of death, as the ultimate end of the "I", in tandem with the calculated arousal of unrestrained love for this doomed "I" of mine–I brought her to a bizarre state of being, like that of a dream, in which someone is holding your hand, but you can't wake up, and never will wake up. Just before the end, her mind on death, as if whipped up by fear, she would start throwing plates, moaning, trying to climb the walls, especially when in my solitude, worn out by the horror of death, seeking an answer to nothing, I hid myself in that dark, cobwebby corner and tearfully kissed my own hands and feet.

Poor little thing, she kept on forgiving me. Out of kindness, I have already said, out of affection. I mean, you must realize that over all the gloom, the pathological terror, the hotchpotch of ideas, lay an unearthly, sickly cast of tenderness. Such tenderness, as unites two people in the death cell. The tenderness in the glance of a man being led through the streets to the guillotine, and who sees amidst the crowd Her–the one who might have been his Only One, and who does not know, and never will know it. And finally that tenderness with which a mother gives her own child poison, in order to save his soul from mortal sin, and to grant him the Kingdom of Heaven.

That's how our days passed, but of course not everyone measures out their life in days–for me, this was one long spiritual outburst, an endless wind, rushing into the Unknown.

Did she understand me? What was in her eyes, enfeebled by the touch of madness? For me, she was what I thought of her, but what did she think of me?

Yet with every drop of my sweat, with every suppurating wound of my neurotic soul, my soiled idealism, I loved and pitied her, seeing in her the living tiny scrap of my 'I', tugged this way and that, arrayed in female garb.

As I stroked the sovereign white skin of her thigh (all the while quietly running to seed), it was as if I was caressing my own heart. I so enjoyed seeing myself outside of me, and at the same time wanted to devour that little blob of my 'I', to absorb it into myself.

However–and here begins the final act of the drama of our relationship–the more I wanted to absorb her, to make her my own, the more I found myself bumping into something hard and impenetrable, as far as I was concerned, some little alien kernel of the spirit. It was something inimical, resilient, some kind of "not I", from which I was repulsed, and retreated into myself.

Gradually, at first only on certain days, as if I was coming to my senses out of the creative vortex of love, I began to look on her with horror, through other eyes. In her peculiar inclination to domestic comfort, and her yearning for security, I suddenly caught a glimpse of materialism. Not that I myself rejected that, but it began to dawn on me that she attached more than minimal significance to externals. It also became clear that there was a very great deal I could not express to her, and that many, many of my secret wild fantasies sounded much more cosmic in the pristine Solitude of my own soul.

Zina subtly detected my cooling–off, and at first felt a sense of relief: I was no longer tormenting her. She became childishly joyful, like a butterfly, fluttering out of the gloom. And she attached herself even more strongly to me, in gratitude for the peace. There was something strange and wildly unreal in the fact that amid the sepulchral atmosphere of our rooms, the dereliction of our cupboards and armchairs, stored with the tears of my dreams and falls, her animated, idiot voice kept on delightedly twittering, as if she had just been rescued from the abyss within herself and in her beloved.

Yes, at first it was as if my silence–the terrible specter of the end of love–had resurrected her . . . Poor little creature . . . She so longed for basic human happiness, and animal warmth . . . Why then had she fallen in love with me?

More and more the chief token of our relationship came to be our undimmed scrutiny of one another, over a pot–bellied teacup, and despite the fact that in an environment like ours, the cheery, cozy little teapot looked ever so slightly tinged with madness; Zina was content even with that. Alas, her moment of happiness did not long endure. She began to realize, horror–stricken, that along with the departure of the nightmares and visions, I had also left her–I, whom she loved so much–and that the price of a healthy mind was the end of love. She then became dreadfully, hysterically distressed. I can remember lonely days, inexplicably torn out of the encircling world, when the two of us would be sitting in our apartment in the pure afternoon light, which now divided us more than the most profound darkness; she would rush around the room, wailing: "Sasha, Sasha, where are you?" And from the lonely sanctuary of my armchair, sitting by her side at the window, I would answer: "I've gone to my own world."

And tears of pain, as if they had been wrenched out of her, would burst into her eyes, while I kept coldly and eerily silent: within the forbidden charmed circle of my Solitude, my little world became even more profoundly secret, and dear to me, even sweeter than when I had first discovered it.

With every passing day I withdrew farther and farther from her, and from the surface of life; it could be compared to an invisible flight, a journey into unknown depths; in the beginning, the faint and smoky lineaments of reality were still visible; later, as the motion accelerated, they were glimpsed more and more intermittently, until finally they merged into one far–off, indistinct and hazy outline . . . Where is the world, where is Zina?! She began to strike me as quite commonplace, simple, easily grasped; I caught myself thinking I could see no difference between her, and that tree looking in at us through the window.

Along with the loss of spiritual interest in her, I also lost interest in her flesh; her body began to frighten me: it was–as I recall–very close, and dear to me, and at the same time was becoming remote. At nights, in the confused little world of our apartment, when my night vigils were in full swing, continued out of sheer inertia, tapping my fingers on her naked, transparently white back, I would often find myself wondering if it wasn't the wall I was tapping. Her body was leaving me, going off into the shadowy far reaches of a world not mine.

I tried physically to stimulate myself, yelling: "Mysteriousness, mysteriousness, let's have more mysteriousness," and I would place her body, prior to taking it, in various crazy, absurd positions; mystery–yes, that's what was still lacking.

Zina realized it was no longer possible to establish spiritual contact with me, and lapsed into a kind of weak–minded decisiveness; occasionally in a despairing mock–frenzy of kissing, she would suddenly begin biting me, with an insane urgency, as if she wanted to bite through my outer casing, and peer into my soul. Biting, while her eyes cloud over with rapid, fleeing tears. Yes, she understands everything.

Either that, or she would suddenly begin muttering poetry to herself, all jumbled up with her own crazy thoughts, and start to hallucinate, even, as if the entire abyss lay open before her enfeebled eyes.

In this way, pathetically doomed and alone, wholly focused on herself, on her own torments, she would again arouse me, in a disturbing, delicious surge; it seemed as if the spirituality in her had reawakened, and I plunged joyfully into her gentle, evanescent shoulder.

But these were mere hysterical outbursts, scarcely hinting at the full horror of the truth.

I was already aware that I looked on her as upon an object, a teacup, which one can smash, without any movement of the heart.

There was a blank, chilling void in my soul.

In the end I grew intolerably rude to her; communications between us were brutally and crudely severed; I did nothing but yell at her, and only just refrained from beating her; she was quite numb from suffering, and simply went with the flow. Without making either a clean break, or any attempt at rapprochement with her, I became even more obdurate in my selfishness, and did absolutely nothing for her.

But the more roughly I used her, the more tenderly I used myself . . . and that tenderness reached such a pitch that I strove to detach myself wholly from my surroundings, feeling an inexpressible self–pity.

Often, convulsively secluded in my own room, I would sit by the heavy drawn curtains, and with my eyes half–closed, write stories. But in my hand–my snow–white, slender fingers–there was no pen; these wonderful, mysterious, half–created works were composed for myself, in the dumbstruck, the forbidden temple of my soul, half–dreaming, no attempt to pin down my thoughts for a rough draft, since I could understand myself from the merest hint. I loathed all paper, readers, pens, letters, my friends and my enemies both–and on that account I made no notes, preserving everything in the solitary coils of my pure "I" ... I savored voluptuously the very fact that no one, apart from myself, could hear my stories.

Meanwhile, these fragmented, schizophrenic scenes played on. My beloved Zina kept whining, crying because it meant she was a fool, if I didn't want to talk to her. Her parents slammed the doors, and sent for the police. Meanwhile I kept building my worlds. A soft light played over our rooms, various people's stupid ugly mugs came and went, and my poor little heart composed unheard–of feelings. I felt so much better, so inexplicably, strangely better. And my world grew apace, as they left me in peace.

Zina quite often left me to go back home, but on the other hand, much to my surprise, a strange new visitor started calling on me at nights. I called him Yury Arkadievich. And He would come so quietly, so enigmatically.

I would be lying at nights, under my sweaty, thought–drenched blanket, feeling only the sweetness of existence–the oneness of my body. Then at precisely two a.m., there would be footsteps in the hall–so soft, and mystical, like the movement of a pendulum. And in my wretched soul–in response–a desperate, aching feeling, as if my beloved comes to me from afar ... I was terribly afraid I would scare Him off. He was so quiet, and not of this world. He would dust off the chair, place a cushion on it for comfort, and sit down. I would say nothing. And there would be such a blinding light in my brain, that it was as if neither England, nor the moon, nor Zina existed, and only Yury Arkadievich and I existed. A total absence of any kind of external reality. Nothing but the reality within, the genuine reality. As in the world beyond.

Yury Arkadievich would be silent at first, metaphysically silent and aloof. His face was remote and distant, like that of an Eastern sage, and He would gaze silently at his hands–so soft and gentle, so white–in mystical contemplation, lightly stroking them, in perfect bliss, in a manner inaccessible to mortals. Undoubtedly, He was very much in love with himself. Then we would sit and talk. He would do most of the talking, while I listened, awestruck.

"Your work's no good, my dear Sasha, no good at all," He would reproach me. "Not enough maniacal frenzy. Not cut off enough. No, my dear sir, you're still only en route towards God."

"Which God, Yury Arkadievich?" I timidly enquired.

"Your inner God. The solipsistic one. The one that lurks in our 'I', and in no other place. Because there is nothing, except that superior 'I'." Yury Arkadievich would smile blissfully. "And we must discover that God, my dear Sasha, and gradually become Him."

"And you must urge me on, Yury Arkadievich," I listened agog. "Drive me towards that God, please."

"A little more 'I', more 'I–ness'," He would sternly answer me.

"You have yet to discover your immortal essence, you are neither the Creator, nor the master of your own world, you simply take refuge in it ... That's why it's so flawed and unstable. It's still not a world, but only a beginning, a mere drop . . . And you must spit in humanity's ugly mug, yes. Spit in all seriousness, conscientiously."

And then Yury Arkadievich would be gone. He totally overwhelmed me with his own emanation and solipsism. I could feel they had already crossed all boundaries.

And indeed I well understood that there was much, in both quantity and quality, I had still not achieved, and that Yury Arkadievich was right to urge me on to new horizons. I was still weak, and very young, nervous, and too dependent on external circumstances.

Occasionally, by way of distraction from the solipsistically blinding truth of Yury Arkadievich, I would pose myself a really stupid question: "Who is He?" Not in essence, of course–I knew that perfectly well–but to outward appearance? Did He exist on the "hallucination–delirium" plane, or the so–called "real" one? If on the "hallucination–delirium", well, then, I would do Him honor, and when He appeared again, fall down and bow at his feet, sir, yes. Because that would mean He had come from the world beyond.

However, He might've been on the 'real' plane, just as in a drug–induced euphoric state I quite often forget everything, talk to passers–by on the street, and sometimes make them a present of my keys. Then I remember nothing about it. So even He could turn out to be one of them.

Anyway, one day I saw Yury Arkadievich in a shop, standing in line for galoshes. He was standing there quietly and patiently, like everybody else, as if He was hiding. And He was showing the solipsistic radiance around his head to no one, the crafty devil.

But that too could have been a "hallucination". And in the long run I concluded that the "hallucination–delirium" plane, and the so–called "real" one were effectively the same, and it was foolish to try and distinguish them.

Zina has walked out on me for good, I think. Yury Arkadievich scared her stiff. During one of his visits, she spent the night in an adjoining room, heard everything, and screamed wildly a couple of times.

I was left with a certain sadness myself, after a visitation by Yury Arkadievich: I felt downcast, because I was still only en route to my internal God, that I was still a weak, sniveling wretch, with too much faith in the reality of my surroundings; I felt that the genuine, solid growth still lay ahead of me, but for the present there were only buds.

Yury Arkadievich could also see this perfectly well, and not wishing to hurry the pace of events, began visiting me less and less often.

Meanwhile life tormented me as before; already I could scarcely appear on the street; I only rarely went out into the kitchen, or the hall; I felt painfully humiliated that I was forced to speak to people, to be with them in the underground, even to stand near them. The very sight of the city, the buses, traffic lights, humiliated me. "The whole world must dance to my tune, and have no existence in its own right," I would wail hysterically to myself, caressing my soul.

"Why doesn't anyone notice how great I am?" I howled bitterly into my pillow on one occasion. Yury Arkadievich–I remember it well–appeared in an instant.

"You're praying for recognition from the world, young man," He said angrily, "Well, how can you beg recognition from something which itself needs your recognition? It's not you that needs to beg the world, but the world that must beg you, for its fight to exist."

In my mind I already understood Him, but these magnificent ideas had yet to reach my skin, tender and cut to pieces as it was by the people who encircled me.

And I would run around collecting things, building castles in the air, making threats, but it was hard for me all the same.

However, I soon found consolation. I can't imagine why I hadn't thought of it before. I have in mind a grave matter, apropos the dear departed. I shall begin with the fact that death entered my soul along with my mother's first kiss–a cruel death, moreover, "atheistic", a precipice overhanging nothingness.

In my childish dreams and terrors, in the distorted outlines of objects in the darkness–I could already see that unimaginable, all–negating nothingness.

In my sweat–soaked, trembling little body, and pathetic, pulsating little veins–in my own consciousness of myself–I could feel that nothingness spilling out over the whole world, from the vanishing stars, to the squashed flies, that cold, inexorable nothingness, lying in wait, biding its time.

And it seemed that if after death, supposing once in a million years, for only a minute, even, we might look out again on some kind of world, and feel our 'I'–then by that act we annihilate this unbounded horror, a chill eternity of utter negation. After all, I will never again exist, never.

Later on there were many theories, books, dissertations, triumphantly and for all time purporting to free us from that blank nightmare, but–never forget! . . . that first intimation of death was allowed entry into our soul, along with our mother's first kiss, along with the first light of day, from childhood on. And because of that it lived in the depths of my soul, lurking within me like some terrible monster.

However, that's only one side of the question. After all, death may have been atheistic, but it was a mystery none the less. And they couldn't kill a mystery. And that's why, ever since childhood, I've kept alive a prayerful reverence and trepidation in my heart, before the frozen features of the dead.

I needed no fairy tales, no songs of any kind, as long as I could gaze upon the departed dead.

And that profound horror of nothingness left me, moved somewhere off–center, and by contrast, the consciousness of extinction aroused in me only a sense of mystery. That was made easier, obviously, insofar as I couldn't see myself dead, but only other people, while that horror of nothingness sprang up always in darkness, in solitude.

And now this side of death has taken a serious grip of me, even unto my very bowels.

Life was so bleak, with its utter hopelessness and materialism, its bestial stupidity and clarity, that Death–uniquely seen and felt by everyone, the Great Mystery, but a mystery that smacks you in the teeth–appeared as a genuine oasis amid a torrent of decrees, of porridge, televisions and impenetrable "logic".

There was something profoundly intimate and mystical about the observation of death, which I could make my own, belonging only to me ... In a word, a great many complexes were woven into one at this point: the estranged, and the voluptuous, the wild and the repressed.

Autumn was already drawing on. I picked out for myself a grimy, mud–spattered cemetery on the outskirts of Moscow. Nearby, touching the heart with its own mystical ordinariness, stood a sort of half–canteen, half–pub. I used to arrive there while it was still morning–always the same old stuff: would the deceased be there now? To make certain, before dropping into the pub, I would phone the cemetery boss. The boss, a sour–faced, half–drunk old geezer, invariably recognized my voice and answered me at tedious great length, about who was being buried, what age they were, what they had died of, and where they had found a spot for the grave. He was convinced that my interest in all this was some sort of official business, beyond the reach of his dull wits. Because of that he was really quite frightened of me.

When I got a favorable answer, I would first of all lose myself in a filthy, darkening corner of the canteen, by a low–level window, out of which I could see the ramshackle gates of the graveyard, just about ready to fall apart. I would order up a glass of beer, and two or three sprats. Then I would close my eyes, and go off into a trance.

My worlds stealthily entered me, along with the sharp–tasting drops of alcohol, their warm, spontaneous thoughts, and the soft, distant footfalls of the approaching funeral party. The first phase of my spiritual voyage of discovery passed entirely in that pub, in grimy warmth, in expectation, waiting amid the flies, the stolidly chewing faces, and the cats, half–crazed with repletion.

My entire being quivered, and I foreknew the knock of the approaching corpse; an incomprehensible, doomed feeling of joy, wholly self–contained, entered my soul. I began stupidly giggling, yes, I'm here alive, and he's dead.

That thought had an extraordinary effect on me, raising my self–esteem, the intimacy and blessedness of my life to unbearable heights. I would ever so gently stroke my knees, luxuriating in the fact of my existence, and everything around me: the ceiling, the cats, the chairs, the fat women, all seemed dead and motionless, encircling with their mindless, hostile wall, the delicious, solitary tremor of my "I" and my flesh.

At the peak of ecstasy, I was so immersed in the purity of this thought, that I felt quite feeble–minded, and this was extremely pleasant.

I was giggling, pouring beer over myself, pulling the cats' tails.

Then the next phase began. Deeply affected, staggering a little from my thoughts, I went out to meet the funeral procession. My earlier joy had evaporated, and I now gave myself up completely to a transport of otherworldly mystery. Bobbing up and down slightly, I tottered along behind the coffin, and I kept thinking that they were burying some part of me: half of my leg, a precious drop of my soul, or simply a finger.

Thus I felt as if the coffin's inimitably mysterious path to the grave was my own bitter–sweet journey somewhere within that space between our world, and the world beyond the grave, when our spirit is leaving us, but hasn't yet gone. The soul still can't cut loose from the dreams, the weeping and wailing, and the visions of this world, which now takes on, at the moment of separation, some kind of other, unreal sense; and I would look with a fresh eye at the tall trees lining the cemetery paths, in which the sound of the wind was now transformed for me into the parting songs, never before heard, of this earthly world, revealing its hidden face only at the point of death; but from far off, a dark mysterious rhythm was already entering this same soul–the rhythm of the abyss beyond the grave.

This phase came to an end at the graveside itself. And when the corpse was placed alongside the pit, the first thing I did was to try and look into his face. Now and again, as a counterpoise to the grand and the dramatic in my make–up, the forces of idiotic hilarity spill out and take over. I would have a sudden urge to spit in the deceased's face, and occasionally an absurd feeling of anticipation would grow, that the deceased would suddenly awake, and spring up; I'd close my eyes tight, and open them: what if he made a run for it?

However, the basic content of this phase was death itself, and contemplating the face of the dead man.

I was intoxicated with the coldly rigid features of the corpse; and it seemed to me that if I were to stare into that face, stare long and hard to the point of madness, then I would strip away that frozen, nightmarish death–mask, and beyond it glimpse the riddle of life, the riddle of my own self. My heart missed a beat, surrounding nature assumed a subtle, fantastically morbid aspect; every little bush became either an imp, or a Faust. Even the fat, ridiculous relatives at the graveside seemed significant. I was being borne beyond imagining to the Altar of the Great Mystery, and in the turns and twists of the road that led there, I came to love my doomed self, with even more heart–rending intensity. And after the burial, wandering the silent alleyways of the cemetery, I would prostrate myself, shrilly praying for pity, before the green trees, the dogs and the sturdy beggars who happened to cross my path.

We take pity on people because there's something they lack: money, intelligence or a woman. But I was howling about another kind of pity: a warm, crazy, sexually deranged pity for one's own pristine, doomed 'I', for one's trembling, perishable existence, so precious, and so casually abandoned before this incomprehensible world–that was the kind of fierce, pathological pity I asked for; but the trees in their solitude made no answer, the dogs barked and ran away, and the beggars crossed themselves and cleared off . . . And I realized that that kind of pity, I could get only from myself, and that out of that pity, something truly great must arise . . .

So that's how I live now, in empty solitude. I go to my beloved cemetery almost every other day. I eat right here, beside the mystery. Everyone knows me now. The relatives of the deceased, the next in line, are forewarned about me. Some of them are extremely friendly, and will stand me a vodka after the burial; others give me a wide berth; still others think I'm some kind of government agent, and refuse to go on with the funeral.

I've had fits of ecstasy several times, when I've been in some sort of witless stupor, or in delirium, beyond the frontiers of my worlds, and climbed up, elbowing them all out of the way, to kiss the departed dead. One old geezer hurled his galoshes at me at one point. . .

A couple of times my beloved Zina has come running up to me in my cemetery pub. She just looks at me, looks at me wide–eyed, then sighs and hurries away . . . I've nothing to say to her any more...

However, Yury Arkadievich–thank God!–has begun to visit me again, albeit in the mornings now.

The last time He winked at me, and fixing me with His eye that way, said: "Well, Sasha, wouldn't you say your youth's at an end? Isn't it time you were setting off on that decisive, mystical journey?"

... At which point, the individualist's notebook breaks off.

Translated by Stephen Mulrine

The Dead Hour

Nina Sadur

No one will ever find out about the two of us. Even my wife. I need only her, this delicious woman, her slender smoldering body. I love to caress her delicate head, like the head of a bird of prey. Sharply surveying the summer steppe. Her long neck. Narrow shoulders. Her skinny hands, not at all weak. All of her, with her tiny breasts, her flat stomach, and long teenage–boy legs. I never thought I'd ever have such a woman. My type is well–developed forms, not really forms but something boundless, big, that you let yourself sink into. My type is domineering housewives in comfy robes. Women with the settled–in smell of a deeply recessed, sleepy, darkish life. This boy–woman, thin to translucent with the cold light of morning, who knows nothing of heavy home–cooked meals and the irretrievable depths of decaying couches; who knows nothing of time standing still–she has never before aroused me. Anxiety not only set off her contours, but also showed through between her legs. She could provoke neither passion nor even fleeting desire. There was no stopping her, she flew by, shifting, like a landscape in the window of a tram, like dry twigs in the dusty wind, like another man's woman whom, though beautiful, one doesn't bother to look at. One doesn't dare. But I dared. And now we are together. Lyuda is my wife. Lyudmila Stepanovna. She has an exceptional talent for business. A "business woman." In the years of the crash she ran cheap goods, while I quietly, angrily drank. Later, she opened a store, then another one, now she has a chain of some sort of trading posts and warehouses. "Who needs you, with your doctor of fucking history?" That's what she used to shout in a congested voice, storming into our tiny apartment with her checkered bags, shaking the snow off her cracked sneakers. Now she doesn't shout. Only once in a while she'll say:

"Lyosha, you could work at a school. You could be a history teacher. There are prestigious ones, too." It's not the money she needs it for. Now that she's a rich, well–groomed lady, she pities me–a failure. I disgust her. When she comes home I catch her frightened look. Dirty jeans and torn slippers, a stretched–out sweater and wide red eyes–that's me. I say:

"Hello, Lyudochka." In fact what I'm saying is "Idiot." Then I say: "What kind of teacher? What kind of history? You idiot, history is no more." She doesn't understand that time has stopped, that it's fallen through the cracks, disappeared. Because she's always in motion. And this inconsequential bodily motion is what gives her the strength to live. She, the idiot, doesn't understand that life is no more. That dangerous black–market time taught her something, something that she forgot to share with me, her own husband. She left me alone, the cow, and hit the road for bread and milk. She's got what you call an instinct for life, and this instinct, you see, has won. She thinks she knows something. And she thinks I'm the idiot. But now everything's changed. In the evenings, when my wife is making supper (strangely, she hasn't given up this activity), I can shuffle by in my slippers, approach her from behind and, in a friendly manner, grab her ass or slip my hand in between her tits and hastily feel around for the familiar butter–rich flesh. She freezes over her pot and concentrates on my hand. But at that moment it's over. I step away from her, putting my hand behind my back. I say: "Honey, are the goodies coming soon?" I don't belong to her, I belong to another woman. "Freak," my wife mutters under her breath, moving her satin fragrant body (fullness becomes her, especially now that she busies herself with her looks), "freak... stinking drunk." "Soon, bunny," she replies sweetly. And we both know that we hate each other's guts. At night. And it's at night that everything happens. In that deadest hour when the house, the street and the neighborhood, all Moscow sleeps heavily, knocked out by the day's work. And so, kicking off my torn slippers, I creep up oh so quietly to fondle her, to touch her shapely body. "Where were you when you were black–marketeering, my dark–eyed one?" I whisper. "What happened to you on those shifty paths of street peddling?" Her skin is surprisingly smooth and warm. She slips and slides under the palm of my hand. The idiot girl snorts in pleasure, and having waited for when she's come to the very edge of sleep on the brink of waking, quivering all over, when her face quivers in expectation, I carefully move away, get up and without switching on the light, go down the long hallway to my study. There's no need to consider the study, as the idiot–girl considers it her study. Just because she makes all that fat, stinking money. A study is a study, and its boss is a man. At the very least, it's my Lives of Remarkable People on the shelf, and my vodka, "Privet," in the bar. And the swivel chair on wheels–also mine. I go down the dark hallway of our endless apartment to my study, thinking about how happy I am, how happy! I run my hand over the wall as I go–my fingers will never get used to the silky wallpaper, they search for the uneven relief of the oil paint from our previous life, when the history of the USSR was a science, when time only flowed forward, when I was a Doctor of History, and the idiot–girl was the young, dark–eyed Lyuda, the rector's secretary. But I shuffle along in my torn–up slippers and I am happy in the dark! The idiot–girl is asleep, replenishing her strength before the work day, and I am awaited by my beloved. I enter my study and only now do I switch on the lights. Yes, she is already waiting for me. No one will ever, ever catch us! We've worked out an ingeniously simple scheme for our meetings. And even if it happens that my wife, snoring hard in a distant bedroom, wakes up and drags herself into my study, I can make it look like I wanted to have a drink to ease my insomnia and flip through The Life of Giordano Bruno. And she won't be able to find fault with me whatsoever! And I will pour her a glass of the Italian wine that my woman and I have grown to adore. Wine that makes your lips start burning and leaves a faint taste of silver in your mouth. Let my wife also taste the pressings of Tuscan vineyards. I'd even–why not?–push her roughly, as if with passion, right onto the floor, right onto the rug, take her brutally, without caresses, thrusting right into her so that her round legs would flail behind my back and so that her head would beat against the corner of the desk. So that she'd groan in gratitude and delight. I'd do that so that my woman could watch us with her bird–like head bent toward her narrow shoulder and pensively biting her sharp nail. But... these are empty fantasies! My wife will not come to the study. She's an idiot. Every night I slip some sedative into her tea. And by the way, that's why she's started snoring. Disgusting! And now I enter the study and turn on the light. We need a lot of light, pitiless light, like on a photo shoot. For a minute we stand stunned. We just stare at each other. Every time it's like the first. Then, coming to our senses, we strip feverishly. And if she's wearing her little black dress–my favorite–she waits for me to pull my shirt off over my head and throw it aside and, taking a step toward her, stand completely still. Only then does she pull the strap lazily from one shoulder with cat–like movements, then the other one, and the black silk slides down to her feet. This dress calls for no bra, and she's left standing in her narrow little black panties. She turns her back to me and arches her back, thrusting out her round little rear. She shimmies her buttocks–the stripe of her panties is pinched between the cheeks. I unzip my fly and take out my hardened cock which I clench and stroke anticipating the pleasure of it resting against that strip of fabric between her buttocks, of tearing though it and starting to search blindly for that longed for little hole. And in the meantime my hands will feel around the desk for the jar of Vaseline and, chasing away the persistent cock, my finger will lubricate the anal aperture, enter it and massage it tenderly a while, and only after that, hard as a knife, my cock with its bulging head will break into the anus and she, letting out a scream of delightful pain, will tremble and shake in my arms. I will pull her onto me, squeeze her buttocks, pluck at her nipples, knead her stomach, massaging her swollen womb, let her suck on my finger, and I will pound her sweet behind restraining and restraining myself and then, pulling out of her abruptly, I'll quickly turn her around to face me and cram my throbbing cock into her mouth, press her face against my stomach and fill her throat with my boiling sperm. But we're not there yet. She knows that she'll have to yield to me, that she will stand on her knees before me, that I'll bend her cute head down to the ground and she will lick my toes, that she'll have to tie my hands behind my back so that I can investigate her body with just my cock, timidly touching her from earlobes and armpits to the hollow of her bellybutton and her protruding clitoris, which she's always happy to present to me. And here, without the use of my hands I must take possession of her or else she will spring on my face and I'll have to suck her clit until I suffocate. Because she's insatiable. And every single time, she and I come up with new games. But now we are standing half–undressed and I'm forbidden to touch her. Once, lost in admiration of her, I simply got plastered. Too much "Privet". And when, staggering, naked, with the empty bottle in my hand, I came toward her, her pupils twitched with enmity. I did not heed the signal; I wanted at least to nestle up to her. I let the bottle fall from my hand and opened my arms to embrace her. I stepped toward her in order to feel with all my skin her coolness and warmth and deep pumping blood. But I felt only icy cold. It seemed as though I had leaned with my whole burning body against a winter window pane. That's how she punished me. After that I would never get drunk in her presence and especially never pushed intimacy on her if she didn't want it. That time I woke up alone on the floor, on the vomit–covered rug. And she would not come to me for seven days. She is proud and vulnerable. She does not forgive easily. She demands total obedience. How did we meet? I can't recall anymore. Now it seems to me that she has always been there. I call her Vita. She likes to hear me say her name. I always say it silently, with just my lips. "Vita." It means life. We finish our wine and if–only if–she wants it, she will let me touch her. She is rather capricious and nervous. And I must submit to her. I must catch her every word until I've grasped her with both arms and only after I've drawn her close to me I know that she is here, with me, mine. The boy–woman, she is at the mercy of unstoppable motion, resembling the motion of the landscape in the window of your tram. Completely unobliging, attached to nothing, she responds to your caresses like an animal, but only while you haven't scared her off. One time, after a long exhausting period of her eluding me, I grasped her so tight that I nearly broke her ribs. She let out a scream and tried to break free. In her eyes I noticed the same fear that I had seen before, when I stupidly got wasted. This time I thought she was even more unattainable than before, that we were separated by the dark void of night; that she, my Vita, her pink narrow body glowing in the darkness, was laughing at me and, while presenting her warm little body for the most refined, torturous caresses, she remained somewhere there, beyond the glass of the window, to watch me indifferently (without emotion), beyond the high wind of my seventeenth story, in the empty basement of the winter night. It was so frightening that I almost broke her ribs. I started bawling like a child, splattering her face with tears and saliva, while she, paying no mind to the pain of my embraces, only slightly opened her mouth and bent over, pulling me down after her into the thick nap of the rug. Now we've finished our wine, she has let fall the hand that was holding the wine glass and, lifting a now empty hand, stroked herself, first her face, then her breast and her stomach. At her mons, her hand hesitated and she looked at me questioningly. I understood that I should take off my jeans (it is rather stupid to stand there with my warlike cock sticking out of my jeans). Gratefully, I undressed. Now naked I felt a greater freedom. With a fingernail, she caught hold of her narrow panties and pulled them off, first one leg and then the other. I took a step toward her.

I've gone completely bonkers. Bonkers! For good. And it's got nothing to do with Vitali, not at all, though he's got everything–a body, a face, a brain. It's about the goat, that is, my husband, the idiot. Why do gals get married anyway? It's a long time now since I was that Lyudochka, the rector's secretary, who you could soften up with a chocolate. It's a completely different life now! Anyway, now I have Vitali. My driver. I could see pretty well how he was eyeing me. But I've got a rule: no hanky–panky on the job. Especially with the driver. No more will men get power over me. You've got enough from me, my dear goats! That little girl Lyudochka, she's dead and gone. I brought Vitali with me to Turkey instead of the idiot. But nothing happened between us there. Vitali worked for me as my driver, my bodyguard, and my maid. But this time I got really fucking fed up. It's been a long time since you could pull the wool over my eyes. Big time scholars, historians, please! I don't give a shit! I see before me an honest–to–goodness goat, bald, unbathed, in foul–smelling jeans and torn slippers. "With rabbit eyes," as Pushkin or somebody said. And Pushkin wouldn't lie. Not only do drunks cook their brains, but their eyes fill up with blood, too. But this time I got really fucking fed up with it all. And after a full day of yelling yourself hoarse, talking with all sorts of riffraff, and having had it up to here with those blockheads from the Caucasus, and setting up the street sellers in some rooms, and looking after the goods...anyway, this idiot, living in a warm apartment and on my money, goes and does this! Anyway, after what he's pulled off, I said to Vitali: "Now look here, my little boy, just because you've crawled into my bed don't think you're the boss here. In the end, you have to do as I say." First Vitali nearly peed in his pants he was so scared. He just looks tall, reddish, with a nice face, but in his soul he's just a girl. But now... So, Vitali comes to me late at night, actually at daybreak, after four A.M.–in winter it's the darkest time of night in that dead hour, everyone's sleeping like corpses, even insomniac drunks fall into their inflamed dreaming. Vitali carefully shuffles the key into the lock, the lock clicks, and Vitali creeps down the dark hallway to me, he comes into the bedroom and lies down in my bed still warm after the idiot. It's so dark, you could poke your eyes out (heavy curtains hang over the windows, and at this hour the lights are out in the neighboring building. We can't see each other, and we do such things that though we're adults and not the most bashful ones, we try to forget them in the morning. At night we're like wild animals. I started dragging Vitali home to spite the idiot. But gradually we lost our vigilance. That's how much the surrounding darkness had absorbed us. One time, having frolicked to exhaustion, we even fell asleep. At dawn I woke to the sound of snoring. It was Vitali. I managed to push him out of bed and send him on his way. A minute later, the idiot stumbled in smelling of sour wine (which gives me heartburn, some side–effect of the bad diet of my business trips). He tumbled right into the warm depression left in the bed by Vitali. I was scared that he might notice the wet sheets or the smell of a stranger. I was also worried that they might have run into each other in the dark hallway of our apartment. But, of course, the idiot didn't notice a thing. Falling face–first onto the pillow, he crushed me with his heavy arm and started to snore. (He's got this thing about checking on me–in his sleep, in the middle of the night, he puts his arm on me to make sure I'm still there. And where would I be, I wonder? Would I fly off? Melt away?) I couldn't get to sleep after that. That near collision really got me so worked up that I tossed and turned and even rolled into my idiot who lay like a log, drunk and snoring. After that time I started keep Vitali till the very last minute, till I couldn't keep him any longer, till it was already getting light and I could see his shock of wavy red hair atop my husband's pillow. Then I would let Vitali go, and he'd get dressed nervously and nearly ram heads with the idiot in the hallway. Vitali's always asking me: "Lyudmila Stepanovna, why the hell do we take the risk? Why do we go to your place? Why don't we go to mine?" "Vitali," I say, "do you like your job? And my body? So do as you're told, and keep in mind, I won't stand for any of your bright ideas." "But I," says he, "nearly bumped noses with your spouse today in the hallway. I jumped back into the bathroom..." "He's impotent," I say, "that's the problem, Vitali. Look after your equipment, my boy." And sometimes I like to come home like a good housewife, put on my house dress and go straight to the kitchen. Cook up some borscht, roll out some cutlets with mashed potatoes. I really love doing it. The idiot hangs around behind me, waiting for a cutlet. And I'm shouting at him not to get in my way. Or I'll give him a ten and send him to the supermarket for some mayonnaise. But I wouldn't have known a thing. And there wouldn't have been any Vitali, if it hadn't been for that cup of tea! When I was almost finished drinking it, I realized something wasn't right. The next morning, waking up with a heavy head, I realized that the idiot had sprinkled in some sedative. At first I got scared–there was no telling what madness a drunk could come to, especially with a successful wife. On the next day I pretended to drink the sedative and turned in. We lay in bed so long that I almost fell asleep. When he got up and snuck out of the bedroom, I looked at the clock: it was past four. After waiting a little, I walked out into the dark hallway. (When I got my hands on a good chunk of money I bought two apartments on the top floor of a seventeen–story apartment building–I love being up high–and remodeled them into one.) Somewhere at the end of the hallway a strip of light glimmered. I realized–it was my study. That's what I call that room. During the day, the idiot hangs out in there from morning to night, smoking sweet cigarillos and guzzling his foul–smelling "Privet." I forbid him to go into my study, but he does it to spite me. I knew it: "Gonna have a drink." And I decided to chase him out. But, approaching the door, I thought hard on it: "Then what's the point of slipping me a sedative? If he needs a drink, and in my study to top it, why does he want to put me to sleep? I wouldn't get up at night because of it. I'd chew him out in the morning." I leaned against the door and listened. That's right, he was talking to someone. Someone was in there! And then I heard a drawn–out moan and a wave of heat surged over me. The idiot had a woman in there! And they were making love! For a week I walked around like I was sick. I was so confused; I had no idea what I was to do. I even started drinking that crappy tea with the sedative, I didn't know what to do anyway. And a week later I said to Vitali: "Vitali, do you want to see what kind of panties I've got on?" Until an idea came to me. An idea about the darkness. It came to me yesterday at sunrise. Yesterday was a day of innocent cooking. But this idea woke me up around sunrise and it sat me up in my bed: "And why haven't I seen his woman? Why don't I go in and take a look at her? Why do I do it with Vitali in the dark? For me, that woman is in the dark. And the man who I sleep with is in the dark. I see only the stupid mug of the idiot with his red eyes and drooping lips. And where's that young little Ph.D. of vanished history, with his blue eyes and slender neck? The one that was afraid of the rector's capricious dark–eyed secretary? And the one who wasn't afraid to take her away from that same rector, a fat boar. Oh god, where has my life gone! So I got up and went down our hallway to where, at the end of it, the strip of light shined yellow under the door. I'll see his woman and say, "Get out of here, you stinking goat, out of my life. And take your bitch with you. Ge–et o–o–out!" Quietly I opened the door a sliver. In the room filled with moonlight, with his back to me and right against the window stood my absolutely naked husband. He held a glass of wine in his hand and clinked it against the black windowpane. He finished the wine and with a strange, slow–motion gesture, put the glass down on the windowsill. And just as slowly, as if asleep, he opened his arms wide. As though he wanted to embrace someone. But, embracing the air, he pressed his arms against his skinny body and began to caress himself. He whimpered softly and licked the windowpane. After the licking, he started to masturbate in a frenzy. Gazing at this, I had barged into the room, so weird and wild and improbable was my husband's behavior. I had already forgotten what I had come for, and I wanted to leave. But I came out into the middle of the room and finally I saw what I had come to see, what I couldn't see from the doorway. The one whose signs I had looked for every day in the study and never found–not a single cigarette butt, nor a hair, nor even a scent. That special scent of a woman who is loved. The woman. I saw my husband's woman. In the apartment house opposite, window to window, in the brightly lit casement, stood a naked woman. This naked woman also drank wine, embraced herself, and gazed from the glowing window at my naked husband. Their movements were so practiced, that it seemed to me as if they were not divided by the black abyss of the courtyard, the howling winter wind, the mean bitch of night. They were going at it full steam. In the morning I dialed Vitali. Now this is how we live. Our nerves are frayed to the maximum. We've all lost weight. We move as if in a trance, as if someone forgot to turn on "morning calisthenics" in our brains and went to work leaving the cheery radio on in an empty apartment. Our empty minds are filled with an unreal, sickly light, but we wait for one thing only–that dark hour before dawn. I wait for the dark hour before dawn when the blind–eyed idiot carefully gets out of bed and starts feeling around the floor with his feet to find his slippers. The idiot's got minus six vision, or maybe minus seven, maybe even eight. Finding his slippers, he trudges the dark hallway and once in the study he turns on the merciless light. He presses himself against the black window pane and he doesn't need his glasses–he can't see worth a damn anyway. He can't see that his naked girl is already waiting at her window. He can't see that his girl is absolutely, utterly naked. There's nothing more naked. Even her head is naked, round, hairless. He can only see the girl's silhouette as it glimmers subtly, faintly across this whole frozen, black expanse of unknowable night. He also becomes a silhouette–a naked, lonely, male silhouette, pressed right against the cruel winter, against the window. And meanwhile, sweating in his fear, Vitali, who miraculously missed bucking heads with the idiot, cowers toward me down the dark hallway. We tear at each other frantically to exhaustion, until we're wrung dry. Vitali starts to snore on my husband's half of the bed, while I lie with my eyes open, holding back my hatred of him, and listen carefully for the sounds of my idiot creeping back from his crooked, sneaky date. I wait for him as I've never waited in my life for anyone. Even the young doctor of the proud history of the USSR. He brings with him that smell. The smell of the abyss.

I don't know what they're thinking over there. Do they see me or no? Their windows are opposite ours. I keep hoping. I have barely any strength. As soon as night comes, in the deadest hour, I raise myself as best as I can. When everyone in the world is sleeping, sleeping like the dead behind all the walls, I come to the window: I grab hold of the chair and push the chair out in front, and so, little by little, I make it there. And I experience such joy–over there, in the building across from ours is a window, and their light is on all night. There's a lonely man there who doesn't sleep. He is like me. He comes to the window, watches me. I wave to him, yell to him. I know: he will not hear me across the yard, across the night. And the wind up at this height. Stick your head out and see for yourself.

I'm left all alone. For food I have half a loaf of black bread and a cucumber. If only some Pioneers would come. But they said there's no more Pioneer organization. That's why my two grandsons–Petya and Pasha–locked my doors. As they were leaving, they said: "Sorry–sorry, granny, but you've lived too long. We're plumbers, we've got our whole lives ahead of us, and we've got to sell this apartment and split it up, because we're young. We'll come back and find you dead on the floor. We'll give you a proper burial." And you, man in the opposite window, why aren't you sleeping? Every night I come up to the window and I think–maybe he's locked in too, that man over there? How can I help him? Is he waving to me, or is it my imagination? Does he see me? I've forgotten now how old I am. I was eighty on the day of the Protection of the Virgin. But when was that Protection ... Back then it was, when we didn't celebrate it, but back then the Pioneers used to come, helped the old folks a great deal. The Pioneers would come all decked in their red kerchiefs, in their little shirts. They'd read the newspaper to me, cook some kasha–what a delight! You can't really guess how they're all doing out there, those people, on the outside. I'm completely bald, no hair left. My dentures, they're broken too now, the plastic ones, they were good dentures. All my clothes have fallen off me. Let it be. One good thing is–the room is warm. Let that man see what I've become in my old age. Let that man figure out that I want to eat. Let him come, read the newspaper, even let him yell at me, scold me, if he likes, but at least he'll go and bring an old granny a little bread and milk.

Translated by Matvei Yankelevich

Mid–game

Victor Pelevin

The stretch of sidewalk alongside the Hotel National, for the last thirty feet of Gorky–Tverskaya Street, was fenced off by wooden posts strung with small crumpled red pennants that fluttered in the cold January wind. Anyone who wanted to go down into the pedestrian underpass to cross the street, had to step off the curb and walk along the line of parked cars, reading the brightly colored foreign–language insults stuck to the inside of their windshields. Lusya found one decal on a huge streamlined bus particularly offensive–"We show you Europe." "We" was obviously the firm that owned the bus, but who was "you"? Somehow she suspected that "you" wasn't some foreigner wanting a trip abroad, but Lusya herself, and the snow–plastered bus itself was Europe–so very close and at the same time quite inaccessible. A soldier stuck his beaming red face out from behind Europe: he grinned in a manner so precisely in tune with Lusya's thoughts that her instant response was to turn on her heel and go back the way she'd come.

Climbing the steps to the open platform in front of the Intourist, she went over to the stall that sold coffee. Usually it would have taken at least five minutes to get to the front of the jostling line, but today was frosty so there was no one around.

Even the plexiglass window was closed. Lusya knocked. The girl who'd been dozing beside the grill stepped up to the counter and glanced with familiar hatred at Lusya's fox–fur coat ("fifteen skins" as her friends called it), the fox–fur hat, and the face with its faint traces of expensive makeup that was looking in at her from the dark, snowy world.

"Coffee, please," said Lusya.

The girl shoved two small metal coffeepots into the layer of sand on the stove, took the money, and asked: "Isn't it cold out there, working the street all evening?"

"What a bitch," thought Lusya, but she didn't answer back; she just took her coffee and went over to one of the tables.

Not a very good day. In fact, it had been a very bad day, no one but drunken Finns lounging about outside the National, and they looked as though they were fishermen. The one brief prospect had been a skinny white–haired Frenchman with rakish ogling eyes, but after making a couple of passes by Lusya, he'd never actually said anything, just dropped his empty pack of Gitanes by the trash can, stuck his hands into the pockets of his sheepskin coat, and disappeared round the corner. Frost. It was so cold that even the drivers who dealt in cigarettes, condoms, and beer had moved their free economic zone off the street into the narrow lobby of the "National," where they were exchanging good–natured abuse with the jolly doorman:

"You used to be big in the KGB, and now you're shit just like everyone else. ... Or maybe you've bought up the entire hall. We've got human rights just like everyone else. . . ."

Lusya went in, bought a pack of Salems from some middle–aged guy with a corroded nose, and went back out into the frost. The foreign clientele were all dozing in their rooms or gazing out their windows at the blinking colored lights of the frozen city, apparently without a moment to spare for Lusya's tender young body.

"Maybe I should go over to the Moskva?" Lusya looked disdainfully over at the grey imperial facade decorated with ten–foot–high blue snowflakes on huge white banners. The fabric rippled in the wind, making the snowflakes look like huge blue lice creeping across the cold wall. "But it's dead over there too ...," she thought.

The entry of the Hotel Moskva was certainly depressing. The howling wind and snow seemed to threaten that at any moment a group of young men with simple open faces would emerge from behind the columns, wearing army greatcoats and holding back Alsatians on broad leashes. Inside, in the broad marble entrance hall, a crowd of Asian drunks was singing some ancient battle hymn, while a different kind of music–bleating restaurant music–was blaring out on the third floor:

"Whoah–oah, you're in the army now. . . ."

Lusya left her fur coat and hat in the cloakroom, straightened her feather–light sweater with the silver spangles and went up to the second floor. This might not be a hot spot, but last autumn Lusya had pulled a German here for three hundred marks and two "Poison" perfume atomizers. He'd been perfect, some kind of aging commercial traveler with a wedding ring mark running round his hairy third finger, a fat little man who had already wound up his business with the Soviet authorities and was on the lookout for a moderately sweet and vaguely dangerous adventure in this wild northern land. A client like that won't hang around on the steps of the Intourist, he goes to some darker corner like the Moskva, or even the Minsk, because he's afraid of having to pay too much. He's sure not to be infectious, and his demands will be touchingly simple. But he's a rarity, and above all, he's unpredictable. It's like angling.

Lusya got two cocktails, sat at the corner table in the bar, clicked her lighter, and puffed the smoke up towards the ceiling. The place was almost empty. Two navy officers in black uniforms were sitting at the table opposite, both bald, with faces as long as the grave. A yellow cocktail waited untouched in its glass in front of each of them, and a bottle of vodka stood on the floor under the table–they were drinking through a long plastic tube, passing it back and forth with calm, precise movements, no doubt just the way they pressed the buttons and threw the switches on the control panel of their nuclear submarine.

"I'll drink this and then go home," thought Lusya.

A cassette player started up, drowning out the music from the third floor, and Lusya felt a slight shudder run down her spine. It was one of Abba's old songs, that one about a trumpeter, the moon, and so on. Back in '84–or was it '85–they'd played that one all summer long on the old reel–to–reel "Mayak" in the office of the students' construction brigade. Where had it been? Astrakhan? Or Saratov? My God, thought Lusya, with a strange feeling, look where life's dumped me now. If anybody had told me back then, I'd have smacked his face. And it had all just happened, all by itself. Or had it?

"Plea–ea–ease may I invite you?"

Lusya raised her head. One of the navy officers in black was standing in front of her, staring expressionlessly into her face, his long extended arms swaying ever so slightly.

"Where to?" Lusya asked in surprise.

"To dance. Dance is a rhythm. Rhythm brings freedom."

Lusya was about to open her mouth to reply when she surprised herself by nodding and getting to her feet.

The black arms came together behind her back like a lock closing a suitcase and the officer began moving around between the tables, taking small steps, drawing Lusya after him, and trying to press his black uniform jacket close up against her–it wasn't even a proper uniform jacket, more like a schoolboy's jacket, only larger and with epaulettes. The officer moved completely out of time with the music. He obviously had his own little orchestra somewhere inside him, playing music that was slow and heartrending. There was a smell of vodka from his mouth, not a sour, stale smell, but cold, pure, and chemical.

"Why are you so bald?" Lusya asked, maneuvering the officer away a little bit. "You're still young."

"Seven years in a coffin of stee–eel," the officer sang in a quiet voice, raising his voice almost to a falsetto on the final word.

"Are you joking?" Lusya asked.

"In a co–offin," the officer crooned, now pressing against her quite openly.

"You were talking about freedom. Have you really got any idea what freedom is?" Lusya asked, pushing him away. "Have you?"

The officer muttered something unintelligible.

The music came to an end and Lusya unceremoniously detached his arms, went back to her table, and sat down. The cocktail tasted disgusting. Lusya pushed it away and just for the sake of something to do she opened the purse on her knees. Leafing through the pages of the copy of The Young Guard beside her compact and her toothbrush (she hid her foreign currency in the magazine because she knew no one would ever bother to open it), she began counting the green five–dollar bills by touch, summoning up in her mind's eye the noble visage of Lincoln and the inscription "legal tender," which she translated into Russian as "legitimate affection." There were only eight bills left, and Lusya decided with a sigh that she'd better try her luck on the third floor, so she wouldn't suffer any pangs of conscience later.

The way upstairs was barred by a thick velvet rope, and a crowd of locals was milling about in front of it, hoping to get into the restaurant. Sitting on a stool in the narrow passage which remained was the headwaiter, dressed in a blue uniform with yellow trim. Lusya nodded to him and, stepping over the rope, went up to the restaurant and turned into the tiled cubbyhole just before the snack bar. There she found a waiter she knew called Seryozha, pouring leftover champagne out of a large number of glasses through a plastic funnel into an empty bottle that was already wrapped in a napkin and standing in an ice bucket.

"Hi, Seryozha," said Lusya, "how's the scene today?"

Seryozha smiled and waved to her. He felt the same disinterested respect and affection for Lusya as a distinguished lathe–operator no doubt feels on Saturday evenings for an acquaintance who is an ace on the milling machine.

"A bunch of crap, Lusya. Two lousy Poles and a Kampuchean. Come in on Friday. The Arab oil sheiks'll be here. I'll sit you next to the sweatiest of the lot."

"I'm afraid of all those Asians," sighed Lusya. "I pulled an Arab once, Seryozha, and you wouldn't believe what it was like. He carried this damask steel saber around in his suitcase, it folds up like, like a . . ."–Lusya demonstrated with her hands.

"A belt," Sergei suggested.

"No, not a belt, it's . . . like a folding ruler. He couldn't get it up without that saber. Didn't let go of it all night long, even sliced a pillow in half. In the morning I was covered in fluff. Good thing they have bathrooms en suite. ..."

Seryozha laughed, picked up the tray with the champagne bucket, and dashed off into the dining hall. Lusya lingered for a moment by the marble railing to take a look at the decorated ceiling–the center was occupied by a huge fresco, which Lusya vaguely suspected showed the creation of the world in which she'd been born and grown up, and which had somehow totally disappeared during the last few years. At the very center ceremonial fireworks blossomed into vast bouquets, and at the corners Titans stood on guard, maybe skiers in track suits or maybe students with notebooks tucked under their armpits. Lusya had never taken a close look at them because her attention was entirely absorbed by the bright trails and stars of the fireworks, painted in colors long forgotten, the same colors with which the morning sometimes paints the walls of the old Kremlin: lilacs, pinks, and pale purples that roused memories of objects that had evaporated with the mists of time past–caramel tins, tooth powder, and ancient calendars that a forgotten grandmother had left behind with her bundle of share certificates.

The sight of this fresco always made Lusya feel sad. The place often induced thoughts of the impermanence of existence, and then she remembered her friend Natasha who had found an elderly Negro to marry her and had almost had her bags packed when suddenly, instead of in warm, well–fed Zimbabwe, she wound up in a chilly Soviet cemetery. Nobody had any idea who had killed her, but it must have been some kind of maniac, because they found a white chess piece in her mouth–a pawn.

Lusya imagined a snowdrift crusted over with ice, and inside it her corpse, her mouth wedged open with a white pawn, and suddenly she felt afraid to stay in this immense, dirty building with its drunken voices roaring and its dishes clattering. She walked quickly out of the hall and down the stairs to the cloakroom. Something must have shown in her face, for the head–waiter glanced at her and immediately turned his astonished gaze away. "Calm down, you fool," Lusya told herself, "how are you going to work with thoughts like that in your head? No one's going to kill you." The music from the restaurant was even clearer downstairs than on the third floor, quieter, but clearer.

The singer howled "who–ah, who–ah" yet again, then the door slammed shut and the wind took up the same song.

A girl was standing by the entrance, wearing a black leather jumpsuit and a green woolly cap. From the copy of The Young Guard protruding from her pocket, Lusya realized that she was a colleague. She could have guessed even without the hint of the journal.

"Got a cigarette?" the girl asked.

Lusya gave her one and the girl lit up.

"Any action in there?" she asked.

"Nothing doing," Lusya answered, "drunken sailors and Sovs. Maybe I'll try the Intourist."

"I was just there," the girl said. "There's a raid on, they've picked up Anya again. Her Cuban general gave her some cocaine and the stupid cow felt so good she decided to tip a waiter twenty dollars, only it turned out the waiter had ideology–he got shell–shocked in El Salvador. He said: If I got my hands on you in the jungle, first I'd give you to the boys to play around with and then I'd stick your stupid bare ass in a termite hill. I spilt my blood, he said, and you're a disgrace to the country I spilt it for."

"It's easy enough to see who's the real disgrace to this country. What's bringing them all out of the woodwork? Have the talks in Vienna run into problems again?"

"The talks have nothing to do with it," said the girl. "There's something new going on. Did you hear about Natasha?"

"Which Natasha? The one who got killed, you mean?" Lusya tried to make the question sound casual.

"Right. The one they dumped in a snowdrift with a pawn in her mouth."

"I heard. What about it?"

"Well, the day before yesterday they found Tanya Polikarpova by the Cosmos Hotel, with a rook."

"Tanya's been taken out?" Lusya felt herself turn cold. "Is it state security? Or the mafia?"

"Don't know, don't know," the girl answered thoughtfully.

"But it doesn't look like it. They didn't take her dollars, or her groceries either. Just stuck this rook in her mouth. Anyway, no point in talking about it now, with the night still ahead. ..."

Lusya reached nervously for a cigarette.

"What's your name?" she asked.

"Nelly," the girl replied, "and you're Lusya, I know. Anya was talking about you today."

Lusya looked at her companion more closely. Those dimples on the cheeks, that slightly turned–up nose, the black mascara–it seemed to Lusya that she'd seen the face before somewhere, seen it many times.

"Where have I met her before?" Lusya wondered, thinking hard. "Maybe KGB?"

"I mostly work the Cosmos," said Nelly, as though reading Lusya's thoughts, "but a week ago they changed all the doormen. You could be an old hag before you get friendly with the new ones. Yesterday they wouldn't let this French guy in because he'd left his hotel card in his room. He kept yelling at them to look in the register, but he might as well have been talking to the wall. . . ."

Lusya thought she remembered now.

"I've seen you in the National," she said uncertainly, "in the bar. You've got a great dress."

"Which one?"

"Brown and black."

"Ah," Nelly smiled. "Yves Saint Laurent."

"Oh, come off it!"

Nelly shrugged her shoulders. There was an awkward pause, and then a young man who'd been prowling round them for several minutes came a step closer and spoke in a fricative voice with a Ukrainian accent, but enunciating very clearly:

"Hey, you broads, got any green stuff you want to shift?"

Lusya glanced derisively at his rabbit–skin hat and cheap leather jacket, and only then at his ruddy face with the small reddish moustache and the watery eyes.

"Whoah, bumpkin," she said, "who's been shipping all of you into Moscow? D'you know what we call green stuff here?"

"What?" the young man asked, blushing through his ruddy complexion.

"Dollars. And we ain't broads, we're girls. Tell your captain his shitty dictionary's ten years out of date."

The young man was about to reply when Nelly interrupted him: "Don't take offence, Vasya. Once upon a time we were all just like you. Here's five dollars, go buy yourself a coffee in the bar."

"You shouldn't have insulted him like that," Nelly said when the young man had disappeared behind one of the square columns. "That's Vasya, the doorman from the Vnesheconombank. They send him over every week to find out the exchange rate."

"Okay," said Lusya, "Anyway I'm hitting the road. See you around."

"Why don't we go for a drink?"

Lusya shook her head and smiled.

"Naah," she said, "see you around."

By the time she had walked as far as the Manege Hall with her arm held out for a taxi, Lusya was seriously cold. Her face and her hands were icy, and as always the freezing weather made her breasts ache. She caught herself wincing with the pain, remembered the wrinkle that was just beginning to trace itself on her forehead, and made an effort to relax her face. A few seconds later the pain passed.

The taxis hurtled by, their small green lamps winking derisively. The taxi drivers mostly dealt in vodka, and only occasionally if the mood was on them would they pick up passengers they liked the look of. Lusya didn't even raise her arm anymore for the yellow Volgas coming towards her, she was waiting for a private car to stop.

She couldn't get the conversation on the steps of the Moskva out of her head. "Tanya's been taken out," she kept repeating senselessly to herself. The meaning of the phrase didn't really penetrate her consciousness. It was getting extremely cold, and her breasts began to hurt again. She could still get to the subway in time, but then she'd have to wander along an ice–covered major road named after some prehistoric monster, alone, in her expensive fur coat, shuddering at the wind's drunken laughter in the huge concrete archways. She'd already made up her mind that that was the way her evening would end, when a small green bus with a double–letter military number pulled up beside her.

The officer at the wheel was her dance partner from the restaurant, but now he was wearing a black greatcoat and a cap with a big tinplate crest, tilted to one side of his head.

"Get in," said the other bald, black figure in the back of the bus. "Don't screw around."

Lusya glanced into the dim back of the bus and was astonished to see Nelly lounging in a relaxed pose on the long side seat, beside the sailor.

"Lusya!" Nelly shouted happily. "Climb in. The sailor boys are cool. They're going to drop me at my place, then where do you want to go?"

"Krylatskoe," said Lusya.

"Krylatskoe too? That means we're neighbors. Come on, get in...

For the second time that day Lusya acted strangely. Instead of telling them all to get lost the way any self–respecting hard–currency girl would, she stooped over and climbed up the steps. The bus immediately shot away, swerved deftly, and went hurtling past the Bolshoi Theatre, the "Children's World" toy shop, the monument to the great artist Dzerzhinsky and his huge workshop, and off into the dark, howling side streets with their half–ruined wooden fences and empty, black, bottomless windows.

"I'm Vadim," said the second bald sailor. "And this (he nodded at the man behind the wheel) is Valera."

"Valer–r–ra," the driver repeated, as though listening to an unfamiliar word.

"Like some vodka?" Vadim asked.

"Okay," said Lusya, "but only through the tube."

"Through what tube?" Nelly asked.

"That's the way they drink it, through a tube," said Lusya, taking the thin, soft end of the tube and holding it to her lips.

It was a difficult and unpleasant way to drink vodka, but even so it was more amusing than swigging from the bottle.

"What a jolly life you do have, girls," Vadim whispered, "and we ...

"Yeah, can't complain," Nelly said, "but I'll take mine in a glass, if that's all right."

"We can fix that."

Lusya suddenly noticed that there was music in the bus too, coming from a cassette player on the engine cover beside Valera. It was the Bad Boys Blue. Lusya liked it, not the music itself, of course, but its effect. Gradually her surroundings felt more relaxed and even natural–the dark interior of the minibus with the two gleaming maritime skulls, Nelly swinging her leg in time to the melody, the houses flashing past the window, the cars and the people. The vodka began to take effect and the mixture of indefinable sadness and distinct fear that Lusya had carried with her out of the Moskva evaporated. An ordinary girlish fantasy filled her heart and mind, a dream, chaste in its very hopelessness, of a suntanned, kind–hearted American, and suddenly she wanted so much to believe the foreign singer when he said we would have no regrets and we would fly away from here in a time machine, although we've been sitting here being jolted about for so long now on this train to nowhere.

"Train to nowhere . . . Train to nowhere ..."

The cassette ended.

The minibus came out on to a wide road flanked by ice–shrouded trees and fell in behind a truck with the word PEOPLE painted in yellow on its tailgate. There was some iron object rattling about in the back of the truck, and the clanging seemed to rouse Lusya from her doze.

"Where the hell are we going?" she asked abruptly, frightened because the scenes flashing by outside were unfamiliar, and not even much like Moscow.

"Ne–e–ver mind that," said Valera loudly, and both of the girls shuddered.

"It's okay, we've just got to fill the tank," Vadim put in rapidly. "We haven't got enough gas to get to Krylatskoe."

"Do we have to go far?" Lusya asked.

"No, no, there's a gas station not far from here that takes the coupons. ..."

The word "coupons" finally laid Lusya's fears to rest.

"We serve in the fleet, girls," said Vadim. "In the atomic submarine Tambov. It's just like a great big underwater armored train with a crew that's one big family. Yeah. . . . Seven years we've been there."

He took off his cap and ran his hand over the dully gleaming curve of his skull. The mini–bus swerved off into a narrow side–street with concrete bunkers along its sides. It looked as though they were already out of the city and in the countryside. From up in the sky the stars ogled them with a cold debauched gleam like the eyes of that day's Frenchman, and the roar of the motor suddenly became strangely quiet, or perhaps it was just that the sound of trucks which had been moving along with them had disappeared.

"The ocean," said Vadim, putting his arm round Nelly's shoulders, "is vast. Wherever you look, an endless grey expanse reaches out on every side as far as the eye can see, and up above the distant starry dome of heaven with clouds drifting by. ... This thick layer of water. . . . The immense space of the underwater heavens, bright green at first, then dark blue, and it goes on and on for thousands of miles. Huge whales, voracious sharks, mysterious creatures of the depths. . . . And just imagine it, hanging there at the center of this pitiless universe is the fragile shell of our submarine, so very, very tiny, if you just stop to think about it ... the yellow gleam of a porthole, and behind it there's a meeting going on, and Valera's giving the report. And all around–just think of it!–the great, ancient ocean. . . ."

"We're here," said Valera.

Lusya raised her head and looked around. The bus was standing on flat snow–covered ground about forty yards from a deserted main road. The engine died, and it became very quiet. Outside the windows the stars were twinkling menacingly and there was a forest in the distance. Lusya suddenly felt surprised at how bright it was, although there wasn't a single streetlight, and then she thought that the snow was reflecting the scattered stars. The vodka was making her feel comfortable and safe, and the fleeting suspicion that something was wrong rapidly evaporated.

"What d'you mean we're here? Are you joking or what?"

Nelly asked roughly.

Vadim took his arm from her shoulders and sat there with his face buried in his hands, giggling quietly. Valera slipped out of the driver's side and a moment later the side door of the bus was whooshed open. Cloud of steams rushed out into the frosty exterior. Valera mounted the steps slowly and solemnly. In the semi–darkness the expression on his face was invisible, but he was holding a "Makarov" pistol, and under his arm he had a large battered chessboard. Without turning around, he shoved the door shut with his left hand, its rubber seal squeaking from the frost.

He waved to Vadim with his pistol.

Lusya slipped down off the seat, sobering up with terrifying speed, and made her way to the back of the bus. Nelly also started backing away, then she slipped on something and almost fell on Lusya, but managed to keep her feet.

Valera stood on the front platform, gripping the pistol trained on the girls as though supporting himself on a handrail. Vadim stood beside him, took out a pistol with one hand, took the chessboard from Valera with the other, and shook the chess– pieces out onto the engine cover. Then he froze, as though he'd forgotten what to do next. Valera stood there without moving either, and a green lamp on the dashboard flashed insistently between the two black cardboard silhouettes, informing the intelligence that created it that everything was in order in the bus's complex mechanism.

"Come on, boys," Nelly said in a low, gentle voice, "we'll do anything you like, just put the chess set away. . . ."

"Chess!" Lusya repeated to herself, and she finally realized what was happening.

Nelly's words seemed to bring the sailors to life.

"That's it," Valera said, and slipped off the catch on his pistol. Vadim glanced at him and did the same.

"Get on with it," said Valera, and Vadim turned away, put down his Makarov on the engine cover and hunched over a package lying beside the heap of chessmen. Lusya couldn't work out what he was doing: Vadim kept striking matches, gazing at a piece of paper, and bending back down to the brown vinyl engine cover, where ordinary mini–bus drivers keep their book of gas coupons, can of small change, and microphone. Valera stood stock–still, and Lusya suddenly had the idea that his outstretched hand was very tired.

Vadim finally finished his preparations and stepped to the side. Four lighted candles arranged in a square transformed the engine cover into a strange altar. At the center of the square the open chessboard glinted in the light, its black and white armies already deeply engaged. Terror had heightened Lusya's feelings to an extreme pitch, and despite her lifelong indifference to the game of chess, she suddenly felt the full drama of the clash between the two absolutely irreconcilable principles represented by the crude wooden figures on the checkered field.

On the home side of the black pieces stood a small metallic figurine: a thin man wearing a jacket, with his cheeks sucked in and a strand of steel hair falling across his forehead–Lusya recognized Karpov's expressionless face. He was about eight inches tall, but somehow he seemed huge, and the flickering candle flames made him seem alive, as if he were making repeated, meaningless small movements.

"The bowl," said Valera, and Vadim took a small enameled bowl out from somewhere in the cab. He set it on the floor, then straightened up and once again they both froze.

"Don't do it, boys," Lusya heard herself say in a strange–sounding voice, and realized she'd made a mistake when the two black figures began moving again.

"You," said Valera, pointing at Nelly.

Nelly pointed her thumb at herself as though asking a question, and the two men in black nodded simultaneously. Nelly walked towards them, clutching the strap of her French hand–bag in her fist and swinging it to and fro pitifully. When she reached the middle of the bus she stopped and glanced at Lusya. Lusya smiled encouragingly, feeling the tears spring to her eyes.

"You," Valera repeated.

Nelly walked on, and stopped when she reached the two figures in black.

"Now, girl," Vadim said in an official tone, "please make a move for white."

"What move?" Nelly asked. She seemed calm and indifferent.

"You decide."

Nelly looked at the board and moved one of the pieces.

"Now kneel down please," Vadim said in the same tone.

Nelly glanced at Lusya again, crossed herself in the wrong direction and slowly sank to her knees, tucking the hem of her skirt to the side. Valera put his pistol away and drew a long awl out of his pocket.

"Lean over the bowl," said Vadim.

"The bow–owl," said Valera.

Nelly drew her head into her shoulders.

"I repeat, lean over the bowl."

Lusya pressed her eyes closed.

"We're here," Valera said suddenly.

Lusya opened her eyes.

"We're here," Valera repeated, lowering the hand holding the awl, "that's not the way a knight moves."

"But that doesn't matter," Vadim said reassuringly, taking Valera by the arm, "it doesn't matter at all. . . ."

"But it does! Do you want him to lose again? Do you? Have they bought you too?" Valera squealed.

"Calm down," said Vadim, "please. Do you want her to move again?"

"He'll lose again," said Valera, "and it'll be because of you again, you stupid bitch."

"Now, my girl," Vadim said in a tense voice, "get up and make a proper move."

Nelly got up off her knees, looked at Valera and saw the awl trembling in his hand. After that everything happened very quickly–Nelly must have finally realized that this was all real. She grabbed up the metal figurine by its head and brought its cubic pedestal down with a scream on Valera's black cap, and Valera slumped into the pit of the steps down to the front door as though it had all been arranged beforehand.

Lusya covered her ears with her hands, expecting Vadim to start firing his pistol, but he squatted down on his haunches instead and put his hands over his head. Nelly swung the metal figure once again and Vadim howled in pain–the blow had caught him on the fingers–but he didn't change his position. Nelly hit him again but he went on sitting there, without moving except to cover his damaged hand with the fingers of his other one, and muttering: "Oh, you bitch!"

Nelly was about to swing at him a third time, when suddenly she noticed the pistol that Vadim had left beside the chessboard. She flung the metal figurine to the floor, grabbed the pistol, and pointed it at Valera, who was hidden from Lusya by a metal partition.

"Drop your gun," she said in a hoarse, manlike voice. "Now!"

A sound of fumbling movements came from behind the partition, and then the pistol came flying out–Valera threw it almost up to the ceiling–and landed on the floor. Nelly quickly picked it up and said:

"Now come on out of there! Hands up!"

Two arms in black sleeves appeared above the partition, followed by a bald head and a pair of attentive eyes. Nelly began slowly backing away down the bus to where Lusya stood frozen in fright. Vadim was still squatting on his haunches, pressing his cap to his head as though a gale–force wind were blowing. Valera glanced at the girls, got down on all fours and began gathering up the chess pieces scattered across the floor. He began singing quietly:

"Seven years in a coffin of stee–eel."

Nelly fired both barrels into the ceiling and Valera jerked to his feet and threw his hands up. Vadim merely pulled his head further down into his greatcoat.

"You lousy bastards," said Lusya, gingerly taking hold of the smoking pistol offered to her, and two black rivulets streamed down her cheeks.

"Now you listen to me," Nelly hissed at the two officers in black. "You, don't move, and you," she turned the barrel of her gun on Valera, "get behind the wheel. And if you so much as brake in the wrong place, I'll plug hot lead into your bald patch with this rod, and you'd better believe I mean it. ..."

The law–enforcement slang had an instant effect on the sailors. Hardly a trace of Vadim's forehead and cap showed above his shoulders, the rest had all retreated under his great–coat, and Valera actually sat down on the chessboard, knocking over the burning candles, and swung his leg rapidly into the cab. The motor rattled into life and the bus crept out onto the highway.

"Nelly," Lusya said suddenly, "tell him to put on the Bad Boys Blue."

Nelly didn't say anything, but Valera had obviously heard, and the music began to play. Vadim swayed on his haunches. At first he sobbed a few times, then he began howling from deep in his belly and shaking all over, shifting from one row of seats to the next. At one crossroads Valera turned and said to him:

"Stop that whining, you carrion. . . . You're a disgrace to the entire fleet. ..."

But Vadim carried on sobbing: it wasn't as though he was crying over what had happened, but more as though he was mourning something else, as though he'd just remembered a stamp album he lost in his childhood. Lusya's felt how her woman's heart was moved by him, and then her hand came across the bottle with the tube stuck into it, still lying on the seat.

"That's the house," said Nelly, pointing to a tall sixteen–storey building along the road ahead of them. "Drive to the entrance, Baldy. . . Open the door."

The door hissed open.

"Are you handing us over to the Commandant's office?" Valera asked. "Or what?"

"You scum–just get lost," said Nelly, "and if I ever. . . . I've never worked for the pigs."

"That's what I meant," Valera reasoned calmly, "the best thing is a civil settlement. What about the pistols?"

Nelly thought for a moment.

"See that snowdrift?" She pointed to a heap of snow about five yards from the bus. "We'll throw them down to you from the window. We don't need any extras on our rap sheet, do we Lusya?"

Lusya nodded in agreement. She was quite calm now; she felt like a heroic little machine gunner.

"Stay in the bus for five minutes, you scum, got it?" Nelly said, when Lusya was already outside. As she got out, Nelly picked up the metal figurine from the floor and tucked it under her arm, and Lusya saw Valera clench his fists tight beside his distorted face as he gave out a quiet groan. Vadim just carried on sitting there with his hands over his head.

They walked backwards all the way to the entrance. The bus's engine was growling softly and through its windows they could see the two motionless black figures.

"Into the elevator, quick," Nelly muttered. Lusya ran after her to the landing in front of the elevators, but then Nelly suddenly dashed back to her mailbox, opened it, took out a fresh copy of The Young Guard, then ran back again. The elevator arrived just at that moment, and when its doors closed behind them Lusya relaxed completely for the first time.

"What a day!" she thought, squinting at the small head protruding from behind Nelly's arm.

"Were you really scared?" Nelly asked.

"Just a bit," Lusya answered. "They're a pair of maniacs, they'd have done us in and dumped us in a snowdrift till spring.

With pawns in our mouths. Hey, they're the ones who killed Natasha and Tanya. . . . What'd we let them go for?"

"Just look here," said Nelly, opening her new journal at the last page and holding it up in front of Lusya's nose. "See the size of the print run?"

"Well, so?"

"So. Every forest has its own garbage men. They keep the numbers in balance."

"That very cynical of you," Lusya muttered.

"Life's a cynical business," answered Nelly.

The lift stopped at one of the upper floors, Lusya didn't notice precisely which. The door of the apartment was the only one on the landing not covered in artificial leather, just plain wood.

The lock clicked as it opened.

"Come in."

Nelly's apartment was in an extreme state of disorder. The door into the single room was ajar and the light was on–Nelly must have left it on when she went out. There were clothes thrown about everywhere. Bottles of expensive perfume lay around on the floor like vodka bottles in the flat of an alcoholic. Standing on the carpet among the haphazardly scattered magazines (mostly Vogue, but there were a couple of Newsweeks) there were several ashtrays bristling with butts. On the floor by the wall stood a small Japanese television, with a huge black twin–cassette deck beside it. By the window was a small bookshelf, with at least ten swollen copies of The Young Guard standing on it–even in her best times Lusya had never accumulated more than five, and for a moment she felt jealous. There was a sour scent in the air and Lusya immediately recognized it as the smell produced when spilled champagne is left to evaporate for a few days and turns into something like a blob of glue.

Pride of place in the room went to a double bed so huge that at first it could easily be overlooked altogether. On it lay a blue duvet and several flannel sheets in various colors, a gift from fraternal Vietnam.

"She brings them home as well," thought Lusya, looking carefully at the metal figurine, "so there can't be anything to be afraid of in that. I'm not the only one. . . ."

"Grossmeister Karpov," she read from the small grey piece of paper glued to the cubic pedestal.

Nelly was left wearing a green woolen dress with a thin black belt which went very well with her black hair and green enamel earrings.

"Take your coat off," she said, "I'll be back in a moment."

Lusya took off her fur coat and hat and hung them on the deer antlers that served as a coat rack. She raked in two different slippers, slipped her feet into them, and went into the bathroom, where the first thing she did was to wash away the black cosmetic rivulets on her cheeks. Then she joined Nelly in the kitchen, which was just as untidy and had the same sour smell of stale champagne. Nelly was gathering various bits of food into a plastic bag: two boxes of chocolate marshmallows, a stick of cervelat sausage, a loaf of bread, and several cans of beer.

"For the sailors," she said to Lusya, "to cheer them up a bit.

That one that was sobbing on the floor. ..."

"Vadim," said Lusya.

"That's right, Vadim. There was something, something really touching about him."

Lusya shrugged.

Nelly put both pistols in the plastic bag, then weighed the heavy figurine of the great chess player in her hand and finally set it on the fridge.

"It can be a souvenir," she said, opening the window.

Thick clouds of steam burst out of the kitchen just as they had out of the bus half an hour before. Down below the bus looked like a green Christmas–tree ornament and two long shadows swayed across the ground beside it. Nelly tossed out the bag, which shrank as it flew through the air and then thumped down on the snow–covered rectangle of the lawn. The two black figures immediately made a dash for it.

Nelly hastily closed the window and shuddered.

"I'd have thrown a brick at them," said Lusya.

"Never mind," said Nelly. "They'll find this harder to take.

Want some tea?"

"A drink would be better," said Lusya.

"Then let's go back in there, and take this guy along with us.

. . . I've got half a bottle of Johnny Walker."

Lusya remembered that Johnny Walker had reputedly been the favorite tipple of the deceased comrade Andropov. My God, she thought suddenly, how recent all that was–the snowstorm on Kalininsky Prospect, the struggle for discipline, the gentle face of the young American pioneer girl on the television screen, the slanting blue signature, "Androp," under the typed text of the reply. . . . And what was his harsh soul now whispering to the tender young spirit of Samantha Smith, who outlived him by such a short margin? How fleeting is life, how frail is man. . . .

Nelly was hastily clearing away the overflowing ashtrays, the tights hanging inside–out on the back of the armchair, the grapefruit skins and biscuit crushed into the carpet, and soon the only things left on the floor were a pile of magazines and the iron grandmaster.

"There, that's a bit more civilized. ..."

Lusya sat down on the edge of the bed and took a gulp from her wide glass. After the vodka from the plastic tube, she didn't even notice the taste, only a slight burning in her throat.

Nelly sat down beside her and fixed her gaze on the small figurine in the center of the carpet.

"You know," she said, "I read this fairy tale in some book or other. Two armies are fighting a battle on a plain, with this huge mountain towering up above them. And up on the summit two wizards are playing chess. When one of them makes a move, one of the armies down below starts moving as well. If he takes a piece, soldiers die down on the plain, and if one wins, then the other's army is wiped out."

"I've seen something like that . . . ," said Lusya. "That's right, it was in Star Wars, the third film, when Darth Vader's fighting that other one on his starship, and it's like the same things happen down on the planet. Are you talking about those two head–cases?"

"I was just thinking," Nelly went on, ignoring Lusya's question, "maybe it's all the other way round?"

"How d'you mean?"

"The other way round. When one of the armies advances or retreats, one of the wizards has to make a move. And when the other wizard's soldiers are killed, he takes one of his pieces."

"I can't see any difference," said Lusya. "It just depends what side you look at it from."

Nelly reached out a hand holding the thin black slab of the remote control towards the television, and multicolored ice–hockey players began flitting silently across the screen.

"So what are the two armies?" Lusya asked. "Good and evil?"

"Progress and reaction," said Nelly, in a tone that made Lusya laugh. "I don't know. Let's watch this, shall we?"

The ice–hockey rink disappeared and a plump man in glasses appeared, standing beside a large wall–mounted chess board.

"Events have taken an unexpected turn in the final stage of the match for the world chess championship," he said, louder and louder–Nelly kept clicking the button on the remote control.

"When the game was adjourned Black clearly had the advantage, but a paradoxical move by one of the White rooks has produced an intriguing situation. ..."

The figures on the board moved with loud thumping sounds from one square to another.

"One of the two officers, I beg your pardon, bishops, that form the foundation of the Black position came under attack, and the threat was actually produced by the challenger himself, who had failed during his time away from the board to analyze all the consequences of an apparently ill–considered move by a White knight."

The screen switched to a close–up of the commentator's fingers and the profile of a white knight.

"Black's white–square bishop has been forced to withdraw. . . ," the figures thumped around the board again, "...and the position of the black–square bishop is almost hopeless."

The commentator poked a finger at the white squares on the board and then at the black squares, twirled his hand in the air and smiled sadly. "I hope we shall know how the game ends in time for the evening news bulletin."

The screen was filled with a large field, hemmed in on both sides by long fences running as far as the forest which bounded the field in the distance. At the bottom of the shot there was a stretch of a main road, with the figures of the weather forecast crawling slowly along it–most of them beginning with a heavy minus sign that looked like a brick.

"I could just take one of those bricks and smack Valera's bald head with it ...," thought Lusya.

"D'you know what that music is?" Nelly asked, moving closer to Lusya.

"No," answered Lusya, moving away, and feeling her breasts beginning to ache again. "They used to play it all the time at the end of the news program, but now they don't use it very often."

"It's a French song called Manchester–Liverpool."

"But those are English cities," said Lusya.

"So what? The song's French. You know–all my life, we've been traveling in this train, I don't remember Manchester and I'll probably never get to Liverpool."

Lusya felt Nelly move closer again, until she could feel the warmth of her body through the fine green wool. Then Nelly put her arm on her shoulder, another indefinite gesture that could have been taken for a simple expression of liking, but Lusya already knew what was coming next.

"Nelly, what are you. . . ."

"Ah France," Nelly sighed in a barely audible voice, and her arm slipped from Lusya's shoulder to her waist.

The news program finished. Then the screen was occupied once again by the announcer, and then by some run–down work–shop with a gloomy–looking crowd of workers in caps standing in the center. A correspondent with a microphone popped up, and a table appeared with portly gentlemen in jackets sitting behind it. One of them looked Lusya straight in the eye, hid his indecently hairy hands under the table, and began speaking.

"Paris . . . ," Nelly whispered in Lusya's ear.

"We shouldn't do this," Lusya whispered, mechanically repeating the words of the talking head on the screen, "the workers will not understand and they will not approve. . . ."

"Then we shan't tell them," Nelly murmured in reply, and her movements became even more shameless. She breathed the bewitching fragrance of "Anais Anais," with perhaps a lingering, slightly bitter note of "Fiji."

"All right then," Lusya thought, with an unexpected sense of relief, "this will be my final examination."

Lusya lay on her back and looked up at the ceiling. Nelly was gazing thoughtfully at her profile, with its delicate covering of powder.

"You know something?" she said after a long silence. "You're my first."

"And you're mine," Lusya replied.

"Really?"

"Yes."

"Does it feel good with me?"

Lusya closed her eyes and nodded ever so gently.

"Listen," whispered Nelly, "will you promise me one thing?"

"Yes," Lusya whispered back.

"Promise me that you won't get up and leave, no matter what I tell you. Promise."

"Of course I promise. You don't have to ask."

"Did you notice anything unusual about me at all?"

"No. You know a lot of militia slang, that's all. But if you work for them, what business is that of mine?"

"Apart from that. Nothing else?"

"No, nothing at all."

"Okay then. . . . No, I can't. Kiss me. ... That's it. Do you know who I used to be?"

"God almighty, what difference does it make?"

"No, that's not what I meant. Have you never heard about transsexuals? About sex–change operations?"

Lusya was suddenly overwhelmed by a fear even worse than she had felt in the bus, and her breasts began aching terribly again. She moved away from Nelly.

"Yes, what about them?"

"Okay, then just let me finish," Nelly whispered hurriedly, as if she were afraid she wouldn't be given enough time. "I used to be a guy. My name was Vassily, Vassily Tsyruk, Secretary of the Regional Committee of the Young Communist League. I used to go around in a suit with a waistcoat and a tie, holding all sorts of meetings. . . . Personal cases. ... All those agendas and minutes. . . . And then on the way home, I'd pass this hard–currency restaurant, the fancy wheels, the babes like you, and all of them laughing, and there I was in that shitty suit, with my badge and my moustache, carrying my briefcase, and they're all laughing and going off in their cars, driving off somewhere to enjoy themselves. . . . Never mind, I think. . . . I'll serve my time in the Party, then I'll be an instructor in the City Committee–I had everything going for me. And then, I thought, I'll live it up in restaurants much better than that, I'll go all round the world. . . . And then, out of the blue, I went to this Palestinian friendship evening . . . and this drunken Arab, Avada Ali, threw his glass of tea in my face. . . . And so the Regional Committee started asking me: why are people throwing glasses of tea in your face, Tsyruk? Why do they throw them in your face and not in ours? I got an official reprimand entered in my file. I nearly went insane at the time, and then I saw in the Literary Gazette that this guy, a Professor Vyshnevsky, did operations–for homos, you know, but don't think I was like that, too. ... I wasn't deviant. I just read that he injected various hormones and changed your psychological makeup, and I was having a real hard time living with my old psychological makeup. So, to cut it short, I sold my old 'Moskvich' and went into the clinic. I had six operations in a row, and they were injecting me with hormones all the time.

Then a year ago I left the clinic, my hair had grown already, and everything had changed, I walked along the street and the snow–drifts looked like the cotton wool used to look under the Christmas tree. . . . Then I seemed to get used to it. But just recently I've begun feeling as though everybody's watching me and they all know all about me. So then I met you and I thought I could check to make sure whether I really am a woman or. ... Lusya, what's wrong?"

Lusya had drawn away, and now she was sitting by the wall,

squeezing her knees against her breasts with her arms. For a while neither of them spoke.

"Do I disgust you?" Nelly whispered. "Do I?"

"So you used to have a moustache," said Lusya, pushing aside a lock of hair that had fallen over her face. "Maybe you remember you had an organizational deputy? Andron Pavlov? You used to call him the louse?"

"Yes, I remember," Nelly said, astonished.

"He used to go and fetch your beer, too. And then you opened a personal file on him because of the propaganda display? That time they drew Lenin in gloves and Dzerzhinsky without a shadow?"

"How could you. . . . Louse, is it you?"

"And it was you that made up that name for me–what for? Because I hung on every word you said, and sat up every evening till eleven signing minutes? My God, how different everything could have been. . . . D'you know what I've been dreaming of for the last two years? Driving past your Regional Committee in a Mercedes 500 dressed to the nines and seeing Tsyruk, I mean you, walking along with his little Tartar moustache and his briefcase full of minutes from meetings, just to look at you from my place on the back seat, to glance in your eyes and then look straight through you, at the wall. . . . Not to notice you. D'you understand me?"

"But Andron, it wasn't me. ... In the Party Bureau Shertenevich said that the deputy for organization had to bear responsibility. ... It was such a scandal, the oldest party member in the region went crazy, the old fart, when he saw your stand. He was just buying some kefir. ... No, Andron, honestly–is it really you?"

Lusya wiped her lips with a sheet.

"You got any vodka?"

"I've got some neat alcohol," said Nelly, getting up from the bed, "just a moment."

Covering herself with the crumpled sheet, she ran into the kitchen, and Lusya heard a rattle of plates. Something made of glass fell on the floor and shattered. Lusya coughed and dribbled on the carpet, and then she wiped her lips hard again with the sheet.

A minute later Nelly came back with two cheap glasses half– full of liquid.

"Take that. . . . Regional Committee glasses. ... I don't even know what to call you. ...”

“What you used to call me. Louse,” said Lusya, and there were tears in her eyes.

“Oh, forget it. You’re just like some stupid woman. . . . Here’s to our meeting.”

They drank.

“D’you ever see any of the old gang?” Nelly asked, after a pause.

“No. I hear rumors, though. Remember Vasya Prokudin from the international section?”

“Yes.”

“He’s been married to a Swedish guy for more than two years now.”

“What? You mean he had the operation too?”

“No. In Sweden you can marry a giraffe if you want to.”

“Ughu. I was just thinking. He had terrible pockmarks, and a squint.”

“There’s no way to understand these foreigners,” Lusya said wearily. “They’re so spoilt for choice, they just go crazy. Just recently I saw one guy in the metro, about forty years old, face like a brick, hardly any forehead at all, and he had a copy of The Young Guard in his bag. So there must be some demand even for that. .

. . Hey, listen, do you remember Astrakhan, the building brigade?”

Nelly looked at Lusya tenderly.

“Of course.”

“Remember they kept playing the same song over and over again? About the trumpeter? And about dancing under the moon? They were playing it today in the Moskva.”

“I remember. I’ve got it here. Shall I put it on?”

Lusya nodded, got off the bed, threw a sheet over her bare shoulders and went over to the small table. Behind her the music began to play.

“Where did you get the operation done?” Nelly asked.

“In a cooperative,” Lusya said, surveying the boxes of French tampons strewn across the table. “Seems they pulled a fast one. Instead of American silicone, they put in some rubbishy Soviet rubber. I used to work the Finns on the railway platform near Leningrad, and I thought I would shatter in the frost. And they hurt a lot of the time, too."

"That's not the rubber. Mine often hurt as well. They say it passes after a while."

Nelly sighed and fell silent.

"What are you thinking about?" Lusya asked after a minute or so.

"Oh, nothing. . . . It's just that sometimes, you know, I still feel as though I'm following the party line. Throwing sausage out of window to sailors. D'you understand? It's just that times have changed."

"Aren't you afraid they might change back again?" Lusya asked. "Honestly, now?"

"Not really," said Nelly. "If they do, we'll just have to cope. We've got plenty of experience to rely on, haven't we?"

The pale dawn of winter spread across the wide open field. A small green bus was driving along the deserted highway. Every now and then the bright red name of a collective farm leapt forward to meet it on a sign by the road, and then a few ugly, crooked little houses would go hurtling by, followed by another sign with the same name, only this time with a thick red line running through it.

There were two naval officers in black inside the bus. One, who was driving, had a bandaged head, on which his cap was balanced with difficulty. The other one, sitting on the seat closest to the driver's cab, had bandages on his hands. His face was puffy from crying and smeared with chocolate. He was leafing through the pages of a thick white copy of The Young Guard and grimacing in pain as he read in a loud voice.

"A taste for discipline. Discipline and nobility. Discipline and honor. Discipline as an expression of the creative will. The conscious love of discipline. Discipline is order. Order creates rhythm, and rhythm gives rise to freedom. Without discipline there is no freedom. Disorder is chaos. Chaos is decay. Disorder is slavery. The army is discipline. The important thing, as in the tempering of steel, is not to overheat the metal, and to avoid this it is sometimes allowed to cool off a little. . . ."

The bus swerved sharply, and the officer in the back dropped his magazine.

"What d'you think you're doing?" he asked his colleague.

"You losing your grip?"

"How could we let them go ... ," his colleague groaned.

"Now he'll lose. He'll lose to that ... to that. . . ."

"They let us go," the other sailor replied acidly, hunching over the magazine. "Well, shall I carry on reading?"

"Haven't you recovered yet?"

"No. I'm not even close to recovering."

"Then read about the greatcoat."

"Where's that bit?" the first sailor asked, fumbling with the dirt–stained pages.

"Have you already forgotten, you bitch?" said the second sailor with a twisted smile. "You've got a very short memory."

The first sailor said nothing, and just gave him a glazed and wounded look.

"Start from the word 'Lermontov'," said the second sailor.

"Lermontov," the first sailor began, "once called the long–waisted Chechen coat the finest costume in the world for men. In terms of symbolic significance, the Russian officer's coat may now without hesitation be ranked alongside the Chechen coat. Its form, silhouette, and cut are perfect, and most important of all–a very rare occurrence in history–it became a national symbol following the battles of Borodino and Stalingrad. The artist can trace its silhouette in ancient frescoes. Even if all the designers in the world were set to work, they could not create a more perfect or more noble costume than the Russian greatcoat. As Colonel Taras Bulba would have said, 'Their mousy natures would not be up to the job. . .'."

"It doesn't say 'colonel'," the second sailor interrupted.

"No," said the first sailor, running his eyes over the page, "that word's in a different place: 'A father's behest is a report on how you are living your life. Let us recall Colonel Taras Bulba. Manhood is primarily a moral category. In this. . . .'"

"That's enough," said the second sailor. His face seemed to have lit up from inside at those final words, and the black dots of his pupils shifted confidently from the highway to the moon where it hung, gradually growing paler, over the snowy wall of the forest.

The first sailor put down the magazine on the vinyl surface spattered with blobs of candle wax, pulled over a box of chocolate marshmallows, and began to eat. Suddenly he started to sob.

"I always listen to what you say," he said, grimacing with the effort to control his face as he wept, "I always have, ever since we were children. I copy everything you do. But you went mad ages ago, Varvara. I can see that now. . . . Just look at us–bald, wearing sailor's vests, drifting around in a sardine–can and always drinking, drinking. . . . And this chess business. . . ."

"But this is a battle," said the second sailor: "a battle, no quarter given. It's hard on me, too, Tamara."

The first officer covered his face with his hands, unable to speak for a few seconds. Gradually he grew calmer, took a marshmallow out of the box, and shoved it whole into his mouth. "How proud I used to be of you! I even felt sorry for my girlfriends who didn't have any older sisters. . . . And I followed you everywhere you went, everywhere, and I did everything you did. . . . And you always act as though you know what we're living for and how we should live our lives. . . . But now I've had enough.

Scared to death before every checkup, and then the nights, with that awl. . . . No, I'm quitting. I've had it."

"And what about our cause?" asked the second sailor.

"What about it? If you really want to know, I don't give a shit about chess."

The bus swerved again, and almost ran into a snowdrift at the roadside. The second officer grabbed hold of a handrail with his bandaged hands and howled in pain.

"No more! I've had it!" shouted the first one. "From now on I'm thinking for myself. You can go back to your Tambov. D'you hear me? Stop the bus!"

Collapsing back into bitter sobbing, he took several IDs of various colors out of his pocket and threw them down on the brown vinyl. The pistol followed them.

"Stop, you pig!" he shouted. "Stop, or I'll jump while we're moving!"

The bus braked and the front door opened. The officer leapt out on to the road with a wail, clutched to his chest the bag with the cervelat sausage and ran off diagonally across the immense square of virgin snow enclosed by the highway, the forest, and the fences, running towards the forest and the moon, which was already completely white. His movements were awkward, almost elephantine, but he moved quite quickly.

The second sailor silently watched the black figure gradually become a smaller and smaller mark on the smooth white field. Sometimes the figure stumbled and fell, then it got up and ran on. Eventually it disappeared completely, and a small, bright tear rolled down the cheek of the sailor sitting at the steering wheel.

The bus started moving. The officer's face gradually recovered its calm expression. The teardrop trembling on his chin dropped on to his uniform jacket and the track it had left on his face dried out.

"Seven years in a coffin of stee–eel," he sang quietly in greeting to the new day and the open road, as wide as life itself.

Translated by Andrew Bromfield

Prime Passed

Galina Shcherbakova

Your prime is a flowering. It's when you're overflowing with the bounty of God, of nature, mother, father... I don't know what else. It's when you're at the top and, if you flap your arms, you don't have to be afraid of hitting the ground and breaking into pieces because you'll surely fly, fly like a bird. This happens to a woman when she's around thirty. And it doesn't come twice. If you missed it, let it go, then too bad, it's your own business. This was explained to me by a certain expert on women who, with his cultivated sense of smell, could discern the fragrance of this blooming and, be assured, was precisely there where the table was full of goodies.

But once I witnessed with my own eyes how someone in her prime ended up badly, even though she bloomed to such a degree that other, less radiant women went crazy from humiliation. When lilacs bloom, daisies and buttercups hide and wilt. Even a fool knows that. As they say, the energy is not the same.

Fanya worked as a typist in a newspaper's editorial office and was so pretty that at times, if the photographer happened to be walking by with pictures at press time, this beauty of hers could hold up the newspaper's deadline. In a word, God forbid someone passed her, carrying cartridges–the machine gun would go freaking dead. Of course, she was photographed by everybody–this way and that.

At the time it wouldn't enter your head that you could be paid for the photos, that a face was merchandise, and so on. The pride of being on the first page of a newspaper, standing under a banner, of your face pictured on a cake box or on the cover of the women's magazine "Krestianka"–that was enough. When Fanya got married and gave birth to Ksiusha, naturally a photographer showed up right away and took a picture of the happy mother. Ksiusha's bald little head turned out badly, like a small cantaloupe. But does it really matter what kind of head we're born with? While pushing its way into the world, the head can crumple for sure. And then we straighten out. And, as you know, even if there are some people around with cantaloupe heads and smashed crowns, then, perhaps, it's only one hundredth of a percent. No more. Anyway, for a girl there's absolutely no problem: the hair will grow, we'll curl it, and then where is it, the little cantaloupe?

Ksiuha's father was a local writer. Well, let's clap our hands and stamp our feet! Already in Khrushchev's time he told stories about the horrors of collectivization and intimated that he had a novel written on the subject. But who could even think about publishing it then? He did not live to see glasnost, though, due to his Russian weakness for vodka which he put away in great quantities, so there wouldn't be any left for the young ones.

When it became possible to publish anything, the beautiful Fanya was asked to bring the late Grisha's novel. "Let's look it over. His time has come," they said. She brought the dirty, stained manuscript to the editorial board, and, already from the second page, the face of the old drunken hack began to grin at them: he who could neither tell a story, nor notice a detail or a word–in short, nothing. They had to return it all to Fanya and say something. People were much more timid about it than necessary. "My God, she laughed, I always knew he was as much of a writer as a bullet made of turd. You were the ones who were running around him clucking like hens. He was a complete asshole. See, Ksiusha is also slow, gets F's in all her subjects. And this is in the third grade. But I will not send her to a school for retards. I'd kill everybody first."

But, what if Fanya really thought the novel was a masterpiece? You see this among wives and widows all the time.

Fanya bought a bottle of wine, and everybody in the typing pool drank with her to the repose of Grisha's soul and the repose of his novel. "I'll use it for kindling," she said.

Fanya lived in a small house nestled among big ones. When he was still alive, Grisha was afraid of big houses, heights, elevators, curving staircases, and thieves hiding in the attic. The authorities respected Grisha, as well as his frailties regarding city life. Let the man live with a chimney, if this makes him write better for the people.

The house didn't bother anyone and threatened to remain there for a long time. Those, who occupied houses with modern conveniences, were even charmed when the smoke wafted from the chimney in the middle of the yard, since nothing is valued with us more than smoke and nostalgia. And so, while stroking the ribs of their radiators, the inhabitants could observe the writer Grisha Shchukin going up in smoke for the second time. Yet how can you identify smoke? Its substance is ephemeral and transient. One minute you see the smoke pushing mightily out of the chimney and the next–where is it? Just try finding it in the sky! In short, when we describe irrevocable failure as "going up in smoke," we are right on target.

Many became close to Fanya on the basis of this affair with the novel. It was as if they saw her sharp mind and perspicacity, not just her beauty.

After burning the manuscript, Fanya put on her shortest skirt and her tallest boots and went to the maintenance section of the regional committee, which was getting ready to certify a new nine–story building. She told the manager that she was scared to be alone in the house, and that Grisha kept moaning and making the floorboards creak. All of the apartments in the building had been already spoken for, but, as we realized later, Fanya arranged herself in front of the manager in precisely the same way Sharon Stone did in the movie Basic Instinct. Of course, she didn't demean herself by coming to the regional committee with no underpants at all. And here lies the most profound and fundamental difference between Fanya and Sharon. Fanya had certain notions about things. The distributor of the apartments had not seen the American movie, but he did see Fanya's charms and understood they were the best in the world. Therefore he intrepidly crossed out the ophthalmologist who fitted contact lenses for the wife of the secretary of the regional committee. The lenses had already been fitted, while the white flesh had been given only in its visual form, and what a flesh it was! A whole bunch of reasons was heaped together: a large archive of a national writer, a possible museum in the apartment, and so on. A woman had a hard time heating the place, since this had been the writer's hobby. The manager didn't know about the novel going up in smoke, and Fanya kept crossing and uncrossing her legs slowly. This was how she ended up in the ophthalmologist's ninth floor two–bedroom apartment where she generously and tirelessly showed her gratitude to the comrade manager. And, when she learned about the ophthalmologist, she made an appointment with him as well. Why deny happiness to a man?

Everybody courted her. The male population just could not restrain itself. Sometimes she hid in the photo lab with one of the more fortunate admirers. She would walk there shoeless, on tiptoe, so as not to clack her heels, but would return carrying herself proudly, not just clacking but banging victoriously. Such a public display remained a mystery to all. Naturally, and even quite easily, scandals and fistfights broke out. Once the trade union committee was shaken up when the director's husband, who worked as a driver, emerged from the photo lab covered in Fanya's perfume and lipstick. Regrettably, his wife was standing in the hall just then, holding a step–ladder while someone screwed in a light bulb. She could have let go and killed the man, but Vera Karpovna waited until the light was back on, folded the ladder, put it in the corner, and only then followed her husband into the men's room. He, instead of destroying the evidence, was blissfully examining it in the mirror–who would have thought that a men's room didn't guarantee protection against invasion by women? Vera Karpovna entered, waving the pissing men away (who needs you), turned her husband's face toward her, and smashed it so hard that she knocked out a tooth and broke his nose, since she was hitting him with a bunch of keys and a plastic eyeglass case. Fortunately, she didn't have any other weapons. Then she convened the trade union board and raised the question of Fanya's moral probity and her consequent firing. The situation was quite thought provoking. First, there weren't enough typists in the editorial office; they needed three, but only two were working. And one of them was still an apprentice. Second, Vera's husband walked around with a face fit for plastic surgery. Fanya, on the other hand, was saying she was not even near the photo lab–did anybody see her? Did they? Nobody saw her.

Vera was summoned to the editor together with all of the members of the trade union board and, "instead of dealing with this whore," Vera screamed later, "he called us a hot bed of hooliganism and, on top of it, brought up the money for office supplies that he himself let us spend on the space heater. We used to freeze to death here from October to March, you know."

After this incident Fanya became watchful and pensive. It's one thing when you're a beauty with a husband, no matter how bad, but a different thing altogether when you're a widow with a child. Fanya's charms were not paid for–this was the time of free love, exclusively out of desire and without material incentive. Whatever else you might say, socialism had its pluses.

Now she had a good "writer's" apartment, partly furnished on the proceeds from Grisha's Tales of my Barefoot Childhood. The book, three printers' sheets long, the assistance from the literary fund, plus Fanya's inventiveness, with her brilliant "will take whatever you don't need." The apartment had style, and under Fanya's knitted covers people's old things began to appear almost modern.

She decided she'd rent out one room–what would have been Grisha's office–to a single man who, with his rent money, would restore the overall financial balance. How much did the alcoholic husband use to bring anyway?

Her call was answered by a young designer of great potential, who was lured from another town precisely with a promise of an apartment, but, as is often the case, had to wait just a bit longer: look, the last floor of the building is already complete, we'll pay for your hotel. And just then Fanya turned up. Is it necessary to mention that he followed her without asking about the rent or the location of the apartment? He walked alongside her and was so happy with this degree of closeness that he actually did not notice that the building in question was in the very center of town, that it was "prestigious," that there was an elevator woman who was knitting something long that stretched all the way down to the ground, or that they took off to the top, the ninth floor. Zhora Markin never in his life had seen the likes of this apartment. He was young and uncomplicated. The light current of air created by their entry into the room made the long gray stem of feather–grass in a thin vase bow its head from side to side as if to say, "Hello." Below, on a carved, wooden plate cracked stones twinkled with their rather expensive innards. Chalcedonies of various kinds...Oh, Zhora, Zhora! He who has not seen Fanya will not understand you. She stood behind him and her breath was hot on the back of his head. Then a girl with a silly smile came in and, when asked her name, announced she was Ksiusha, went to third grade, wasn't a good student, but that it didn't matter.

"What does?" asked Zhora.

"You have to be a good person, and I am that."

"Really?" Zhora was surprised at the depth of her answer to such a simple question.

Another time he would surely have calculated this phrase mathematically, would have turned it this way and that, and even inside out; he liked playing with words. But Fanya was standing right next to him. She asked the girl: "Did you say everything you wanted to say? Go to your room!"

"A good little girl," said Zhora.

"She already told you that."

Zhora agreed to all of the conditions: 70 rubles a month, no broads, tea and coffee in the morning are included. Bed linen is changed regularly, but it's the Laundromat for his personal stuff.

When Zhora was returning to work he became anxious about having forgotten something very important. He was straining to remember, but he couldn't recall what it was. Back in his hotel room, while packing to leave, he happened upon a frame with a picture of Natka. He looked at his fiancée and understood that everything had been taken out of "that house." The house by the name of Natka stood empty, drafty, and he saw curly wood shavings, long hidden in some crack when the house was still alive, scatter all over the floor, playing in the freedom of the now abandoned dwelling. Zhora was a thoughtful man. He realized these were not absurd fantasies caused by a strange enchantment, but a dislodging of a lesser power by a greater one. "This is how it happens evidently. Not gradually, but right away: I fell out of love." But the enunciated word did not stir up the attached notions of pity, compassion, or guilt. Not at all, in fact quite the opposite: rejoicing, rapture, and desire were pulsing and shouting in him so powerfully that he took Natka's picture and shoved it into a hole created by a swollen floor board which the chamber maid tapped in with her foot every morning. Today she was in a hurry since the maid on the seventh floor didn't show for work, and she was told that, if she cleaned the seventh floor, she would get overtime plus a day off. The game was worth the hurry. The hole was barely covered, the girl Natka lay there, and it was Zhorik who tapped in the board. Anybody would have seen an analogy to a funeral here, but Zhorik did not see it at all. He was just hiding from sight something that had become meaningless and so needed to be covered up and totally blotted out. If somebody told Zhora yesterday that this was in his nature, he would have laughed loudly, even raucously, because he considered himself to be faithful and decent.

But a transition occurred. Dying is probably similar to this. You still hear the potatoes hissing on the stove, and it smells so good, but suddenly there's nothing, simply nothing. No hiss, no smell, no you. Though you don't wish to believe this, you still desire, after dying for everybody else, to remain in some form, and finish watching the movie about who will eat the potatoes and who will wash the dishes. Zhorik, however, patted down the floor boards and already that very evening was sitting in Fanya's kitchen and having tea with a rather cheap sausage, since Fanya decided right away that for the tenant she was a poor widow, otherwise why rent in the first place?

On the following day Fanya confessed to her fellow typist that this one made a pass on the very first day, despite the presence of a child, and she had to "hit him in the mug" and to explain that rent plus getting laid is called marriage, and that she plans to marry, because it's normal, while for an occasional fuck he will have to go someplace else.

"Then we'll get married!" said Zhorik

"What do you think?" she asked her co–worker who wrote on moral and ethical issues, which meant she knew everything.

The fact that the co–worker herself was divorced, lived in a communal apartment, and that nobody ever stood in line for her heart, didn't mean a thing. She was the one who gave advice. And Fanya, who knew about relationships with men of all kinds and qualities, came to her. Her friend liked this a lot–the inept one got a kick out of instructing skilled and experienced women. She never took pity on anyone. Other people's divorces–and in an editorial office they know about those more than anywhere else–created in her a light cheerful repulsion mixed with excitement. She did not like women, and did not hold out hope to any of them. She advised Fanya to stand firm until the very last. The last day was the fifth one. This turned out to be a long deadline. Fanya decided there was no use waiting for a secretary of the regional committee or an academician of medicine. You never know what overhead expenses might accrue in the form of previous wives, children and reprimands from the Party. A promising, energetic and unattached designer was a decent enough option.

Definitely not worse than a writer. She looked at his passport–no marriage stamp. She questioned him in detail about his parents and their position. Zhorik's mother was scheduled for breast surgery, but after fifty you can do pretty well without a breast. Moreover, according to Zhorik, her husband adored his mother all his life like a madman. Fanya liked this, because it indicated Zhorik's own good genetic foundation. It was on that day, when Fanya succumbed to Zhorik's passion and to his oath to marry her here and now, that he took her picture. She brought the portrait to the editorial office, and everybody came running to look at it. She was standing with her back to the window, and the window frame created a frame for her. Her arms were crossed and lay on her shoulders. Eternally beautiful arms against the background of a black slip, also forming a frame for her neck and head. Whether it happened accidentally, or whether Zhorik was a master at composition, but the picture could be magnified from the arms up, and then it was a completely different portrait. The self–hug was very expressive and somehow the essence of everything. The thin neck was turned a bit to the left and down and made Fanya's face a touch more asymmetrical than in real life. The corner of the mouth was lowered a little, making the right nostril look sharper and emphasizing the slender and refined nose. But the most important thing was the eyes. They were slightly different. The left one was veiled by the eyelashes a bit and did not see anything much, while the right one saw very well, fairly glittering through the eye lashes. Fanya was very beautiful in this picture. She was exquisitely beautiful, which, naturally unnerved the photo editors, those same ones who had taken pictures of the girl this way and that, but not like this! They slandered the non–professional for the light not being set up correctly, for the left side of Fanya being darker than the right, and the wrists on the shoulders done any old way, with no "sculpting." But it was the criticism of the envious. Fanya was perfect. True, there was something disturbing in this picture, something diabolic. The picture was printed in the newspaper as a study, and the editorial poet wrote four heartfelt lines for it. This newspaper lay on everyone's desk, opened to the page with Fanya. And they kept glancing at it furtively, sensing that the force living in it (in Fanya or in the picture?) was demonic and was undoubtedly about to reveal its hidden essence. The large right eye appeared as if alive and was full of such hatred and power that it gave you goose bumps up and down your spine. Or the nostril began to suck the air so hard that people ran to open the window. Those who worked in the editorial office came from all walks of life and did not indulge in mysticism, but they started to hide the newspaper. The head of the propaganda section just burnt it in her waste basket while at work— just to be on the safe side. To her misfortune, she was reading The Portrait of Dorian Gray at the time and became fearful of potential bloody knives.

Things were moving along toward the marriage license bureau. Fanya ordered a dress of blue satin. Everybody was surprised, since blue was not her color; she had brown hair, and red, white, and green suited her, while blue made her look older and less sophisticated. But, after that picture, Fanya's faith in her omnipotence became unshakeable. Just stand half naked in front of a window and, voila–half a column in the newspaper. She said she'd made blue work for her.

It seemed that only two weeks went by after Zhorik's arrival but how many events have occurred and how many emotions experienced! People were interested to find out whether his mother would be discharged from the hospital in time, and Fanya said: "No, it's not just having an appendix out, this is much tougher."

While settling down in the new place, Zhorik occasionally recalled the empty apartment he had buried in the parquet floor. But the more time went by, the more he thought about N. with irritation and anger because, in a typical honest, male way he blamed her for his feelings about the empty nest. She was the one who removed all of the belongings from the inner dwelling of his life, who else? Bitch! When this word appeared in front of his eyes, he went berserk–inside of course, not in front of others–and at one point in his anger he understood suddenly that something was wrong with him. A sickness of some kind. He recalled Natka, so good and close to him, and, most important, sitting now with little Nikolasha, because grandma was in the hospital and grandpa was with her. Zhorik realized that in all this time he never thought about his son. Not once. Here one should mention that this was not at all surprising. The son was brought up by his parents since the age of six months, when his young wife died in the first year of college. She had leukemia, nobody knew about it, she even gave birth to a boy, and then suddenly–she was gone. This was a terrible first year of college–death and birth together. The parents were afraid for their son and, without thinking twice, took the grandson. But, of course, there was nobody else to do it anyway. Nikolasha didn't have other grandparents. In fact, he became their child, and the young Zhorik looked at the little boy with surprise and bewilderment. When he saw Ksiusha, he was about to say that he also had a son, but somehow his thoughts and impressions got all mixed up, and he did not say anything. And in the next days he did not have a good moment to do so.

When his mother was sent for surgery, and he had to leave, Natka said that she would take the little boy: she lives next to his school, they get along splendidly, and... Zhorik and Natka were going to get married right after his mother was discharged from the hospital.

The phenomenon of Fanya had not been programmed. It was truly a phenomenon.

On that day, after Zhorik experienced his recurrent spiritual fever, having remembered his son, he decided to tell Fanya everything. It would be easy. Fanya would understand this whirlwind of feelings that eliminated everything in its path. And now, when the blue satin dress was already being made, it was their sacred duty to take the boy. He was so smart and would help out Ksiusha when she felt stupid. Fanya talked about it openly anyway.

Fanya came home from the fitting with a headache. The color wouldn't work, and there was no time left to find another.

"A boy? What boy? I can't stand boys! He's living with an acquaintance? Well, that's very good. Grandma will come back, and he'll be her pride and joy in old age."

"He is not a boy. He is my son," said Zhorik. "And I adore him, like I adore you."

"Can you imagine?" Fanya told everybody afterwards. "Do I need this? I could give birth to his boy myself, if he asked me. But this way, out of nowhere, already a grown child on my head, you have to feed him, wash for him, and he'll pee on the bathroom floor."

"But why would he pee like that?" They did not understand her

"Like a man. Even you, who live with them, don't know that they always do this–lose the last drop. I was simply waiting for the formalities to be over to rub Zhorik's nose in it. Grisha was the same...

To be honest, I don't know about others. And a child is a child. He may not even flush. And I will have to teach him? My God, what a mess. Really, is this my last chance? And now, just think of another angle. The cancer ridden mom will die anyway, if not now, then later. And he'll bring the grandpa here as well? As it is, it's crowded with Ksiusha, she's not tidy and occupies a lot of room... I said this to him: it's too crowded with a boy. Looks like he got offended. Turned around and left. He'll come back, where else would he go. They don't just leave me like that. He'll come back and accept my conditions. I was honest with him. If he had told me right away... The way he sees it I bewitched him, so he lost his memory..."

"But what if he doesn't come back?"

"Wanna bet?"

They bet a bottle of vodka. What else can they bet in an editorial office? It's so sweet to drain it, even though each would get only a drop at the bottom. There is no better moment in the middle of a work day. For feeling as if something lifts you. And for ten free minutes of limitless soaring.

Zhorik did not return. Fanya had to bring the vodka. Barefoot, she dashed to the photo lab beforehand, and it was obvious she had been treated and cheered up. They drank to the hope of not being cheated by life. Someone said that maybe Zhorik would come back, but Fanya told them the important news: while she was away, Zhorik took all of his belongings, using his own keys which he then left with the neighbor. Fanya said that he did not take her gift, an expensive coffee cup she had given him for the house warming.

"That's how he is. He has enough decency in him for one cup. But he wants me to take his boy and live with him."

"You didn't love him," said a young typist who worked part time.

"And do you know what that is?" Fanya asked. "Explain it to me."

"Well, said the girl, it's when you have a sinking feeling right here..." and she pointed to her sweater.

"This is for children," explained Fanya, "my Ksiusha feels this way when the pimply Kostya pushes her on the swing. Later it will feel like this in another place. And they made up a word for it–an orgasm. A good word, correct, really gets the meaning across."

They didn't suspect that Fanya had so many words in her, and so they decided she was disheartened about what had happened. But no. Her face didn't show any disheartenment. It was calm. Only it had become–if you looked at it from the side–like a sharp axe.

Zhorik did not reappear. He got an apartment and brought his son and Natka to stay with him.

Still, it's easier for men to handle such things. Fanya, however, faded in the meantime and began to look more and more like the woman people feared in the picture. What's there to be afraid of? Just a woman like any other, one who has everything she needs. But still not the same! As if someone just went and shifted something in her face. And everybody understood it was not just someone but that damned Zhorik who clicked his camera. Clicked and disappeared. They felt sorry for Fanya. Not even her but her vanished beauty. Strangely enough, nobody gloated over her misfortune. We are idiots, you know, and still believe in the absolute falsehood of beauty saving the world. It's not love that saves, but kindness, but we're not smart enough to see this. So we grab on to beauty. And babble on about it... What salvation! And, most important, why should they save us fools?

Fanya married a widowed lieutenant–colonel whose son studied at the Suvorov military academy. The colonel was proud of his beautiful wife and was scared to death of her. In the evenings they liked to walk along the local Broadway, but nobody turned around to look at Fanya anymore. Sometimes they met Zhorik and Natka who were also out. Zhorik and Fanya never looked at each other, but an arc of hatred was clearly visible over their heads. It stayed in the air for a long time, and it was better not to walk under it.

Translated by Nadya L. Peterson

Babel in Paris

Evgeny Shklovsky

Babel loved plump women.

Where there's lots of flesh there's lots of sweetness. Lots of warmth, heat, tenderness, a caress of sunshine and a velvety splash of the sea. In the damp, spongy folds of skin and in the large soft breasts, whether at rest or swaying gently in motion, there is the comfort of a gently rocking cradle.

French women–take your pick–were thin and wiry, coquettish and agile like monkeys.

Hard to keep your eye on them. They slip out of sight. They were the incarnation of sin, a sharp, sudden dream that flashes by, leaving you disappointed and dissatisfied. With a serious demeanor they constantly rushed somewhere (to a lover's rendezvous?) or with similar deliberation chatted furiously at sidewalk cafés, paying attention to no one else. Or sat silently, either mysteriously staring straight ahead or scanning the sides. Each one had male friends, but they, too, seemed detached. They would appear exactly at that moment when Babel had singled out a woman that he might approach and strike up a conversation with.

French women resembled Martians.

They drove Babel crazy. There was no enveloping softness and tenderness in them. They made your head spin, like a whiff of their perfume–that enduring Gallic glory. They aroused you, summoned you somewhere, electricity charged the air around their strong, sinewy, musky bodies (Babel's caught the smell), and the only upshot of all this were itches and scratches, the same as from those insatiable insects that feasted on Red Army soldiers during the Russian civil war.

Ah, Place de la Concorde and Place Pigalle, the poetry of Paris under its yellow lamplight!

But salt–the salt in French women–clung to your lips, just as if you had taken a dip in the sea. Babel didn't like swimming. He preferred to stand on the beach and watch the waves lap indolently on the shore. During a storm, when they reared up into a great swell, they were like the female passion–a passion that he loved more than his own delight. The spectacle excited him more than the pleasure: it pried open something limitless, insuperable, larger than woman alone. The great riddle of being that had bedeviled him since adolescence, which was impossible to express in words, try as he might.

However, besides the pale, nimble, elusive French women, there were also African women. He sensed a hot tenderness in their great legs and the smooth vibration of their whole bodies, moving as if to a drum beat in the blood. When they walked past, ample breasts swaying, Babel froze, his gaze fixed to the figures: there was so much rhythm and African passion in their dancing, rocking gait. African women smelled of roasted chestnuts and vodka distilled from maize, the hot sweat of a kitchen and coals of a hearth.

The one complemented the other: they had a different rhythm of life, different pace and different amplitude.

In African women a black sun kindled its own dark, bewitching fire.

In French women a setting, European sun smoldered low.

Two suns burned over Paris. From hotels of the night came faint wafts of perfume, wine and the sweat of love–making. From the dark windows slightly ajar you could hear heated whispers, little cries and sighs, laughter and moans. It seemed that all of Paris at this late hour was immersed in the sweet labor of love, and those who cooed on lighted terraces or at café tables were awaiting in secret anticipation their own hour.

Babel was going out of his mind. Images of intertwining bodies gave him no peace as he strolled alone through the darkened, mysterious little streets and listened keenly to the call of night and peered into dim, beckoning interiors of bistros where black silhouettes lolled around the bars. Faces paled over by the fatigue of night like autumn leaves by a first frost returned his curious, avid glances. The languor of these bored yet inquiring looks excited Babel, but he stifled it, in embarrassment straightened the glasses on his nose, hunched his shoulders and quickly slipped on by–a short, stocky little guy with a big forehead who had accidentally been cast into this inscrutable, entrancing, rich, poor, free–spirited, zesty city, liberated from prejudice and hardened in languid pursuit of its own pleasure with a sure knowledge of the art.

Any random Jacques who had sat through the day in his office but had 100 francs in his pocket was a king here. Babel didn't have so many francs, in fact quite few, and he needed to live a while longer in this city that caused his head to spin, and he mentally calculated again and again his meager resources, tallying them up by the day. Even when he didn't do that, he deprived himself of essentials, almost going hungry. He wrote the editors of distant Moscow magazines and tried to squeeze out at least a little money as an advance on some future story. But when the money came (oh, a miracle!), it vanished without notice, and in distraction Babel would think that he had stuck it in some unlikely spot, and in the garret he rented on a top floor he spent time ransacking his pockets. If even anything turned up, it was some small coin–a centime that had accidentally slipped through a hole into a jacket lining, and being near–sighted he would study it thoughtfully through the thick lens of his round glasses.

Unfortunately he was estranged from this holiday. But still it was a paradise, a blessing of fate (especially after the Russian slaughter house), and life for the sake of life and not in the name of some undefined shining future. Not blood, not the constant fear of an accidental or an intentional bullet, not the wails of victims of rape and murder, not the groans of the injured, not the nauseating sweetish stench of rotting human corpses and horse flesh hanging over the Galician steppes, not the bitter taste of wormwood lingering in the mouth and not the wind–burned, calloused, cracked skin.

Ah, Paris, the grey islands of palaces that seem to emerge from a fog, the hull of a civilization sinking into oblivion, blazing, limousines in clouds of exhaust, romantic sighs in the shady alleys of Bois de Boulogne and the cows munching on spindly grass in outlying workers' districts–ordinary, fantastic, captivating life, the secret of which pursued him remorselessly. In contrast to Russia–dismembered, hemorrhaging, oozing pus–this place seemed so far from that non–existence and so peaceful that its very calm, the measured pace itself and the engagement of people in the routine matters of daily life were so striking to him that he tried to find in it all at least something that reminded him a bit of life's tragic nature.

To be without money is uncomfortable but hardly a tragedy.

Tragedy remained in Russia, where there was no pity and everyone moved along the razor's edge, along the edge of an abyss. Babel loved sharp feelings.

He wanted to go back to Russia. To Russia, which was contorted in labor pains, trying to produce in the world something unprecedented, some unimaginable and extraordinary beauty. Babel needed to constantly feel this spike, this sting ready at any moment to pierce you–the sting of uncommon beauty.

In the worst case what's left for a Russian writer to do?

Only to wander dismally, shuffling the worn soles of his shoes along clean washed streets under the trees spread out along the River Seine, stare at the skinny streetwalkers sipping absinthe in sidewalk cafés hospitable to all, and agonize about the inability to understand and describe this plump–figured honey of a girl with slim French legs–Parisian life.

Translated by Byron Lindsey

Two Days in the Life of Zhenia D.

Elena Muliarova

Introduction

Zhenia D., a young but experienced journalist, is listening to her favorite Classic Rock station where Olya Z. is the deejay. Olya Z. also happens to be an editor at a women's magazine L. for which Zhenia writes everything. Zhenia D. is multitasking: dancing to Classic Rock, jogging over to the computer and quickly, in synch with the music, typing articles about: seborrhea, kidney stones, psychological hang–ups, and having sex with a man in tights. Zhenia D. is in a rush. She wants to spend her Sunday with a friend, not worried, being happy, not thinking about seborrhea, or sex with a man in tights. She wants sex with a man without tights.

Chronicle

Sunday

5:15 p.m. Zhenia D. meets her friend Peter O. at the Kuzminki subway station, planning to go over to his place and have a good time. On the way they buy a watermelon.

5:45 p.m. In Peter O.'s kitchen Zhenia D. and Peter O. eat: shrimp cocktail, lobster tail, shrimp rolls, and the watermelon on the side. They drink Riesling.

6:25 p.m. Taking the Riesling and the lobster tail with them, they move to the living room. They smoke their first joint to the music of Eric C. Zhenia D. asks Peter O. to imagine a civilization where people cannot defecate on their own and, precisely because of this, have to find a partner in life ASAP. Thus, the very act of defecation becomes highly tabooed and poeticized to the utmost degree. Peter

O. tells Zhenia D. approvingly that the controversial writer Vladimir Sorokin is no match for her.

7:15 p.m. After Eric C. they move on to the music of Boris G. and continue to drink Riesling.

7:40 p.m. They smoke their second joint. Zhenia D. puts on her glasses to see Peter O. better and then lies down on the floor. Peter O. says that, in his opinion, this is exactly the way to have a good time.

8:15 p.m. Zhenia D.'s conversational abilities are fading; she begins to read an issue of Bear, a men's magazine devoted to the business of porn. The article about oral sex draws her attention.

8:30 p.m. With Peter O.'s help Zhenia D. learns how to pronounce the word "cunnilingus." Afterward they discuss the chemical composition of sperm as described in Bear. Zhenia D. expresses her desire to ingest the substance for its vitamin C content. Peter O. promises Zhenia D. to buy her some vitamins at the pharmacy. Zhenia D. agrees on the condition that the vitamins he buys are expensive. Riesling.

9:10 p.m. Clumsy movements. Close contact. The music of D. D. which inspires Zhenia to imagine a star role in D.D.'s video clip. Discussion of hitch–hiking in America. Conversations about holiday expectations, fears of dying, and preparing for eventual old age. Peter O. informs Zhenia D. that he is ready. Zhenia D. expresses her envy. Riesling.

9:40 p.m. The third joint. Zhenia D. loses her voice.

10:00 p.m. Separate showers. Together in bed. Energetic if brief sex, which does not prevent Zhenia D. from experiencing L. in all of its astonishing power. Peter O., with characteristic incisiveness, observes that at the moment, which the writer Snegova (for whom Zhenia D. had worked for two years) calls "the sweet convulsion," Zhenia D.'s heartbeat accelerates five times its normal rate.

11:00 p.m. Conversations that later lead to feelings of inferiority. Preparations for sleep.

11:20 p.m. Zhenia D. jumps up and announces that she cannot spend the night at Peter O.'s. Peter O. is somewhat surprised. Zhenia D. asks Peter O. to remain in bed and not see her off. Feverish packing. Peter O. gets up only to hear Zhenia D. say that all that he has taught her in their time together is how to destroy affection. Zhenia D. then informs Peter O. that in fact he could have taught her something better.

11:40 p.m. Parting at the door. Out of the blue Zhenia D. blurts out that she loves Peter O. very much.

11:45 p.m. Zhenia D. decides to call Peter O. from the street and tell him that in fact she does not love him that much. Zhenia D. discovers that she left behind both her cell phone and the diskette with the article about psychological hang–ups, where in a veiled form she expresses everything she does not dare tell Peter O. in person. Zhenia D. does not go back for her things and, feeling virtuous, heads toward the subway.

Monday

12:40 a.m. Zhenia D. gets off at the Kaluzhskaia subway station, gets into a cab and argues with the driver who tells her that Zhenia D. herself does not know where she lives.

1:40 a.m. Zhenia D. drinks tea in her own kitchen and works on the crossword puzzle in Olya Z.'s L. magazine.

1:30 a.m. Falls into a troubled but dreamless sleep.

10:40 a.m. Awakens to a vicious hangover, regrets about her aimless life, terror and surprise at the thought of yesterday's confession to Peter O., as well as anxiety about the loss of her cell phone. For an hour tries unsuccessfully to call her own cell phone or reach Peter O.

11:40 a.m. Takes a shower, goes back to bed, listens to Liapis T.'s song "In a White Dress," agreeing woefully that "it's love next to her, the angel is near, he's stretching his wings, it's love, don't hide your heart, the angel will hear."

12:10 a.m. A phone call from her teenage neighbor with a request to lend her 3 rubles.

12:20 p.m. A phone call from Lyosha B., the editor of the TV program About IT, asking Zhenia D.'s permission to use the excerpt from Snegova's book, in which she writes about "It," on his program. Zhenia D. agrees and complains that the devil made her say the L. word to Peter O. yesterday. Lyosha B. expresses his sympathy and invites Zhenia D. to the taping of the episode "IT on the Radio" on his program About IT. In addition, he coyly expresses a wish that the devil would make her say the L. word to him. Zhenia D. replies that she doesn't want to say it to him but promises to come to the taping if she feels really shitty.

12:40 p.m. Zhenia D. finally reaches Peter O.'s office where she is told that he went home sick. With her customary impulsiveness, Zhenia D. thinks that Peter O. got sick because of her talk about L. which, upon reflection, Zhenia D. decides is not L. at all but rather H., or perhaps S. Attraction, or maybe just a desire to have an optimistic check mark in the "personal life" column.

1:00 p.m. Zhenia D. is cold and takes another shower. While in the shower she hears the phone ring and, thinking that it's Peter O., runs to pick it up. It's not Peter O. but the Classic Rock deejay Olya Z. who is also an editor at L. magazine. Zhenia D. tells Olya Z. that she is cold, naked and wet, and Olya Z. replies vehemently that she will not let Zhenia D. abandon her, that she needs Zhenia D, and that she cannot do without her. Zhenia D. realizes that she is hearing the words she wanted to hear but not from the right person. This, however, does not daunt Zhenia D. and, shedding tears of joy, she returns to the shower.

1:30 p.m. Zhenia D. reaches Peter O. at home and tries to weasel out of the confession she made to him yesterday. Peter O. tells her to stop talking nonsense and informs her that he got sick from the sea food they ate the night before. Zhenia D. is slightly disappointed about the reasons for Peter O's indisposition and tells him she will stop by for her phone.

2:00 p.m. Zhenia D. writes several articles for L. magazine which she sends by fax and then, after consuming a plate of spaghetti, goes to the magazine offices herself.

5 p.m. Zhenia D. greets Olya Z. with the words: "I am bringing you the piece, will you kiss me dear, please." Olya Z. gives Zhenia D. a happy smile and makes a gesture indicating that Zhenia D. is not all there. Zhenia D. perches on the chair next to Olya Z. and tells her that she is even more stupid about men than Olya Z. Olya Z. asks for details.

5:15 p.m. Zhenia D. recounts the story of her weekend. Olya Z. particularly wants to know about the sea food. All of a sudden, Zhenia D. blanks on the name of the food. Olya Z. suggests that it was shark tail, which leads to an extended exchange of silly jokes and sexual innuendoes about sea food. Zhenia D. laughs so hard that she falls off the chair. The copy editor sitting nearby asks them to be quiet because Zhenia D. and Olya Z. are preventing her from correcting mistakes in their own articles.

5:45 p.m. Olya Z. and Zhenia D. move on to the discussion of the best way to ingest sperm. Inna V., the editor of the section "The Music of the Human Soul," regards the two obliviously chatting "ladies" with disdain.

6:00 p.m. Olya Z. teaches Zhenia D. to tone up her body with simple exercises and nearly falls off her chair. Saying good–bye, Olya Z. comments enviously, that Zhenia D.'s life is really full. Zhenia D. happily agrees.

6:10 p.m. Zhenia D. discusses work related issues with the editors at L. magazine.

7:00 p.m. Zhenia D. gets off at the Kuzminki subway station and heads for Peter O.'s place.

7:10 p.m. Peter O. opens the door shakily and asks Zhenia D. if she by any chance has any Pepto–Bismol. Zhenia D. replies that she does not and expresses her willingness to go to the pharmacy right away. Peter O. declines and hints that it would be better if Zhenia D. left. Zhenia D. leaves.

7:50 p.m. Standing in the rain by Peter O.'s pharmacy for forty minutes, Zhenia D. ponders whether or not to buy Pepto–Bismol and take it to Peter O. Then and there Zhenia D. realizes that the feeling of L. she experienced recently actually was, still is, and quite possibly would remain L. and nothing else.

8:00 p.m. Comforted by this understanding, Zhenia D. decides that she has earned a treat. She goes to the Kuzminki market and buys vegetables, fruit, and, for dessert, her favorite item–a cup full of dirty, toasted sunflower seeds for two rubles.

8:20 p.m. Zhenia D. boards the train, sits down and opens L. magazine. She reads her own article about "It" and discovers that Olya Z. used O. Mandelshtam's lines in the epigraph. Zhenia laughs, looks at the lovely faces of her fellow passengers and experiences, completely inappropriately but powerfully, both L. and H.

Conclusion

Zhenia D.–young but experienced.
Education–some college.
Nerves–sensitive.
Psyche–unstable.
Adaptation capabilities–advanced.
Social life–yes (as of now)!
Favorite cities–St. Petersburg, Jerusalem.
Favorite color–bright blue.

Favorite man's name–Andrei.
Favorite woman's name–Nina.
Favorite writer–Gazdanov.

Ideally would want to die a dramatic and noble death, involving perhaps a generous blood donation. Envisions her life as a theatrical production punctuated by catharses.

Thinks that it happens to her more often than she deserves.

Translated by Nadya L. Peterson

Contributors

Nadya Peterson is an Associate Professor of Russian at Hunter College of the City University of New York who also teaches in the doctoral program of the Department of Comparative Literature at the CUNY Graduate Center. She is a specialist on contemporary Russian prose and women's literature. Peterson is the author of Subversive Imaginations: Fantastic Prose and the End of Soviet Literature, 1970s–1990s and of a number of articles on various aspects of Russian studies, including "Witches and Victims: Folklore in the Writings of Nina Sadur"; The Private 'I' in the Works of Nina Berberova"; "Dirty Women: Cultural Connotations of Cleanliness in Stalinist Russia"; and "The Games Women Play: the Erotic Prose of Valeriia Narbikova." She is a published translator and the author of a Russian language textbook.

Writers (in alphabetical order):

Evgeny Kharitonov (1941–1981) A professional actor, choreographer and psychologist, Kharitonov, who earned a doctorate in Cinematography from the All–Union State Institute of Cinematography in Moscow, was also a controversial and innovative writer whose deeply emotional and nuanced writing made its mark on contemporary Russian literature. Because he wrote of gay love and the Moscow gay underground, he could not be published during the Soviet period. Some twelve years after his death of a heart attack at forty, Kharitonov achieved instant notoriety and wide acclaim when his principal output, a volume of verse and prose, Under House Arrest, written between 1969 and 1981, appeared in Russia in the early 1990s. 1993 saw the publication of a two–volume edition of his works that served as a source for numerous translations into many European languages.

Boris Khazanov (1928–) While studying Classical Philology at Moscow State University in the late 1940s Khazanov was arrested for anti–Soviet propaganda and sentenced to a corrective labor camp. Upon his release in 1955, Khazanov attended medical school in Kalinin, received a Doctorate of Medicine in Moscow, and worked there as a doctor in various clinics. In 1974, he became science editor of Chemistry and Life, the popular science journal of the Academy of Sciences. A prominent member of the underground publishing venue samizdat, who translated banned texts of Western theologians and philosophers, Khazanov was forced to emigrate to West Germany in 1982. After 1989, his novels and stories have been published in Russia and appeared in translation in Germany, Italy, and France. Among his literary awards are the 1995 Heidelberg Literature in Exile Award and the 1998 prize from the Russian journal October. In his fiction Khazanov focuses on the fate of the individual in the twentieth century and on such issues as homeland vs. exile, love and sexuality, Christianity and Judaism.

Vladimir Makanin (1937–) A major Russian writer who even under heavy Soviet censorship managed to write uncompromising, philosophically unconventional fiction. Born in the Urals, Makanin was trained as a mathematician at Moscow State University and later as a film–maker. In the 1960s his original and thought–provoking stories won him wide acclaim among the Russian intelligentsia. Makanin became particularly well known with the publication of his 1982 novel The Forebear which relates a story of a Russian faith healer. Makanin's novels have been translated into many European languages. His novel Manhole was short listed for the Booker Russian Novel Prize in 1992 and published by Ardis in English translation. Makanin's Baize–covered Table with Decanter won the Russian Booker Prize in 1993 and published in English by Readers International in 1995. In 1998 Makanin was the recipient of the Pushkin Prize, followed in 1999 by the Russian state prize for literature. In 2001 Makanin received the Italian Premio Penne.

Yurii Mamleev (1931–) One of the best–known underground writers of the 1960s in Russia, Mamleev was born in Moscow and educated at the Moscow Technical Institute for Forestry. In 1974 Mamleev emigrated to the United States, in 1983 moved to France, and now divides his time between Russia and France. He is the author of the novel The Vagrants (written 1966–68), a number of short stories and essays, as well as several volumes on philosophy.

Mamleev's works were first published in his native country in1989. Mamleev's libertarian pessimism, his interest in the shadowy margins of his characters' psychology, and his focus on the body are shared by other writers of the late Soviet period. Mamleev offers the reader a deliberately apolitical narrative, emphatically unanchored in the contemporary social debates about the future of his society. Yet the pointed focus on the absence of moral foundations and the primary emphasis of Mamleev's work on the issue of survival are indicative of a shared mood of a society on the brink of a drastic transformation. Mamleev strips his narrative of the familiar logic of a realistic representation, offering instead a loosely plotted contemplation on the realities of life and death.

Elena Muliarova (1964–) The youngest writer among the contributors to the volume, Muliarova is a professional journalist with a degree in geology from the Moscow Geological Institute who received her literary training at the Gorky Literary Institute. Muliarova's articles on various topics have appeared both in online and offline publications. In the late 1990s Muliarova published several Romance novels under the pen name of Yulia Snegova. Her first work of fiction under her own name appeared in 2000 in an anthology Very Short Texts.

Viktor Pelevin (1962–) One of the most acclaimed and successful writers to emerge in the post–Soviet period, whose exuberantly satiric novels and short stories capture the essence of his fast changing society. After high school Pelevin received a degree in electromechanical engineering from the Moscow Power Engineering Institute, followed by training in creative writing at the prestigious Gor'ky Institute of World Literature in Moscow. Pelevin's first story was published in 1989, and for the next three years his short stories appeared in various magazines and compilations, making him a prominent figure among the SF fans and garnering several awards. His works are couched in the trendy language of Western postmodernism, science fiction, as well as pop–Buddhism, Eastern mysticism, and ironic–nostalgic Socialist Realist parody, but are also evocative of the writings of Nikolai Gogol and the 1920s avant–garde. In 1992 a book of Pelevin's collected stories The Blue Lantern received the first annual Russian Little Booker Prize, and next year his first novel, Omon Ra–a surreal satire of the nature of reality in the Soviet state–propelled him from relative obscurity to instant fame. In 2003 Pelevin won the National Bestseller Prize. Pelevin permitted all of his texts in Russian predating the year 2000 to be published on the Internet for non–commercial use. New Directions publishes English translations of Victor Pelevin's work including Omon Ra, A Werewolf Problem in Central Russia, Yellow Arrow, and Blue Lantern and Other Stories.

Dina Rubina (1953–) A prominent Russian writer who is fast gaining popularity in Israel where she now lives, in the former Soviet Union, and among Russian émigrés in the United States. Born in Tashkent, Uzbekistan into a family of Ukrainian Jews, Rubina was trained as a musician at the Tashkent Conservatory, then taught at the Tashkent Institute of Culture and translated Uzbek authors into Russian. Her first story, "Unsettled," was published in the literary journal Yunost' when Rubina was sixteen. In the 1980s she moved to Moscow where she continued to write and publish, even though full recognition of her talent by prominent journals had to wait until after her emigration to Israel in 1990. Since then Rubina has produced a number of novels, stories and essays that made her one of the most widely read and admired Russian writers today. Rubina's prose is deeply psychological and moving and her concern is with her characters' humanity and ability to survive under the most trying circumstances. Her An Intellectual Sat Down in the Road received the 1990 Arie Dulchin Prize for Literature. Her novel Here Comes Messiah was short–listed for the Russian Booker Prize and awarded the 1995 Israel Writers' Union Prize for Literature. In 2006 yet another of Rubina's novels, On the Sunny Side of the Street, was short–listed for the Russian Booker Prize.

Nina Sadur (1950–) A highly regarded, innovative and often controversial writer, Sadur established herself in the 1980s as a leading playwright of the "new wave" of Soviet dramatists who broke free from the constraints of psychological realism typical of the Soviet theater. Her significant works in prose, appearing in print only in the 1990s, consist largely of short fiction, which displays well her technique of shifting narrative stances and her preoccupation with the theme of escape–in particular from dull, everyday realty into the world of folk beliefs and the supernatural. Born in Novosibirsk and educated at the Gorky Institute of World Literature in Moscow, Sadur endured years of official neglect and had to support herself by working as a cleaning lady at the Pushkin Theater. Her break as a writer came in 1987 when the student theater of Moscow State University staged her play The Weird One. Productions by more established theaters followed, and her reputation as a brilliant playwright was firmly in place. Her main protagonists are predominantly female, whose refusal to conform to societal norms make them both vulnerable and empowered. Her most ambitious work from the 1990's is the novel The Garden which uses modernist, destabilizing devices to describe post–Soviet reality. In 2001, several of her stories were published in The Russian Playboy. Sadur's plays and fiction have been translated into many European languages. In 1997, she received the journal Znamia's literary award.

Evgeny Shklovsky (1954–) A journalist and literary critic of note, Shklovsky was born in Moscow and educated at the University of Moscow's School of Journalism. Shklovsky's career as a writer of fiction began in the 1970s; his works have enjoyed popularity in his native land and have been translated into several European languages. Shklovsky's prose is both lyrical and psychological: his larger works are characterized by elaborate plots and a focus on different aspects of human behavior.

Galina Shcherbakova (1932–) One of the most popular and widely published contemporary Russian writers, Shcherbakova concerns herself with urgent social problems of her time, such as the disintegration of the traditional family, violence, and lack of spirituality found in contemporary Russian society. Born in the Ukrainian city of Dzerzhinsk, Shcherbakova was trained as a teacher in Cheliabinsk where she briefly taught Russian language and literature. She then worked as a journalist for several newspapers and journals in Rostov–on–the–Don, Cheliabinsk, Volgograd, and Moscow. Her literary debut came in 1979, with the publication of a collection of novellas The Town Remained on the

Right, when Shcherbakova was in her late forties. Broad acclaim and unprecedented popularity followed with the publication of the novel You Wouldn't Believe It in 1983. She is the recipient of the 1995 fiction prize from the journal Novyi mir. In 2006, Sherbakova's novel The Mark of Lilith was nominated for the Russian National Literary Award "Bol'shaia kniga."

Liudmila Ulitskaya (1943–) The first woman writer to be awarded the prestigious Russian Booker Prize in 2001 and a recipient of a number of other important literary awards, Ulitskaya is one of the most prominent and popular representatives of contemporary Russian realist prose. Her works combine traditional plot and narrative techniques with an unusually candid treatment of conventionally taboo subjects, as well as previously censored topics in Russian history and religion. Born in Bashkiria of Jewish parents, Ulitskaya spent her childhood in Moscow. A graduate of Moscow State University with a degree in genetics, Ulitskaya briefly worked at a genetics lab and then, after the lab was closed down, as a researcher for the Moscow Jewish Theater. Work on film scripts led to writing. Ulitskaya's characters come from all walks of life, but her protagonists are mostly female, Jewish, Central Asian or Crimean Russians of Greek descent. The theme of the family in twentieth–century Russia is prevalent in her works.

Middlebury Studies in Russian Language and Literature

Middlebury Studies in Russian Language and Literature seeks to expand our knowledge of the latest developments in linguistics, literary and pedagogical scholarship devoted to Russian language and literature. The series includes analyses of texts and authors, translations of significant literary and scholarly works, and writing on theoretical and applied linguistics with special attention to new methods for the teaching of Russian language and literature.

For additional information about this series or for the submission of manuscripts, please contact:

Thomas R. Beyer, Jr.
c/o Peter Lang Publishing, Inc.
Acquisitions Department
P.O. Box 1246
Bel Air, MD 21014-1246

To order other books in this series, please contact our Customer Service Department:

(800) 770-LANG (within the U.S.)
(212) 647-7706 (outside the U.S.)
(212) 647-7707 FAX

Or browse online by series:

www.peterlang.com